The Bells of Bournville Green

ANNIE MURRAY was born in Berkshire and read English at St John's College, Oxford. Her first 'Birmingham' novel, *Birmingham Rose*, hit *The Times* bestseller list when it was published in 1995. She has subsequently written fourteen other successful novels, including, most recently, *All the Days of Our Lives*. Annie Murray has four children and lives in Reading.

ALSO BY ANNIE MURRAY

Birmingham Rose
Birmingham Friends
Birmingham Blitz
Orphan of Angel Street
Poppy Day
The Narrowboat Girl
Chocolate Girls
Water Gypsies
Miss Purdy's Class
Family of Women
Where Earth Meets Sky
A Hopscotch Summer
Soldier Girl
All the Days of Our Lives

ANNIE MURRAY

The Bells of Bournville Green

PAN BOOKS

First published in Great Britain 2008 by Macmillan

This edition published 2012 by Pan Books
an imprint of Pan Macmillan, a division of Macmillan Publishers Limited
Pan Macmillan, 20 New Wharf Road, London N1 9RR
Basingstoke and Oxford
Associated companies throughout the world
www.panmacmillan.com

ISBN 978-1-4472-0647-7

1 3 5 7 9 8 6 4 2

A CIP catalogue record for this book is available from
the British Library.

Typeset by SetSystems Ltd, Saffron Walden, Essex
Printed and bound by CPI Group (UK) Ltd, Croydon, CR0 4YY

Visit www.panmacmillan.com to read more about all our books
and to buy them. You will also find features, author interviews and
news of any author events, and you can sign up for e-newsletters
so that you're always first to hear about our new releases.

Acknowledgements

I would like to express my gratitude to the following for their help in my research for this book: Sarah Foden and her colleagues at the Cadbury archive and especially to Cadbury girls Marjorie Hill, Valerie Fletcher and her husband Brian and Pat Harrison, all of whom were so generous with their time and conversation.

For those who would like to find out more about my books and writing, you are warmly welcome to visit my website, at: www.anniemurray.co.uk

Part One

Birmingham, 1962–3

Chapter One

December 1962

'What the flippin 'eck's the matter with you two today? It's Christmas isn't it, not a wet weekend in Bognor?'

They were in the Girls' Dining Room at Cadbury's, which was decked out festively with streamers and tinsel. The young woman who had spoken, one of their group of pals, had plonked her soup down on the table and pulled up a chair beside Greta and Pat and the rest of them.

Greta looked up, managing to pull her round, pretty face into its infectious smile.

'That's better – yer enough to put me off my dinner – faces as long as Livery Street! Nothing up, is there?'

Greta didn't want to say what was wrong. Quiet, steady Pat was her best pal from when she started at the Cadbury works three years ago, and she kept some things even from her. She didn't feel like pouring out what had happened this morning in front of the rest of them: the row with Mom, the angry, bitter words.

'Oh, I'm all right,' she grinned. She always tried to be the life and soul. 'It's Pat here who's down in the mouth.'

Pat never had it easy, and today her gentle face looked pale and strained.

'It's Josie – she was took bad last night. We didn't get much sleep.'

Pat's older sister Josie was severely handicapped and it was all Pat's Mom could do to look after her. Pat carried a heavy burden of care as well. She was a quiet, sweet-natured girl with thick brown hair, always tidily fastened back for work, and a lovely dimple which appeared when she smiled.

'What's wrong with her?' Greta asked carefully. Josie, a woman of twenty-one, could neither speak nor walk.

Pat shrugged. 'Dunno really. You know what she's like – she can't say. She was running a fever but she was ever so restless all night.'

'Poor thing,' Greta said, her blue eyes full of sorrow for her friend.

'Never mind, worse things happen at sea, eh?' Pat rallied herself. She never liked to dwell on difficult things. 'I'll get this cuppa tea down me and I'll feel better. I'm just a bit whacked, that's all.'

'I bet you are,' one of the others said sympathetically. 'You coming to the hop after? Do yer good!'

Every Monday there was a lunchtime dance in the Girls' Gym, where they jived and bounced during the dinner hour.

'Oh, not today,' Greta said. 'I'm not in the mood.'

'Ooh dear – you have got it bad, Gret!'

'Eh—' Pat nodded across the room. 'There's your Mom. Ooh, look at her hair!'

Greta glanced round to see her mother, Ruby Gilpin, advancing across the dining room, like a ship in full sail. She worked at Cadbury's three days a week, in the Filled Blocks section where there were a lot of part-timers. Buxom, pink-faced and smiling, she had given her hair a peroxide bleach yesterday and it crouched in startlingly bright, lacquered layers on top of her head. She was calling to one of her friends over by the long windows which looked out over the winter grey of Bournville Lane. She completely ignored Greta, as if she was invisible.

'Can't get away from the old lady, can I?' Greta rolled her eyes comically. As usual she acted as if she had not a care in the world, though inside she boiled with hurt and anger. She could still hear the shuddering slam of the front door when she stormed out that morning. The rows had got worse lately, but there had never been one this bad before.

But Pat was watching her. 'Is everything all right?' she asked softly.

'Oh yeah – course.' She brushed it off, nudging Pat in the ribs. 'Why wouldn't it be?'

Pat's life wasn't easy, but she didn't have a mother who had already got through three husbands and several other blokes since, so that you never knew who'd be there when you got home or what might be going on. Greta avoided taking anyone back to the house. God knows, if her employer had any idea how Ruby carried on she'd surely be out on her ear! Cadbury's, who expected virtuous conduct from their employees based on their own Quaker principles, were very strict about drinking and moral behaviour, but so far Ruby had got away with it. And Greta was ashamed even to tell Pat all of it. Pat's family had their problems, but Pat had grown up in Bournville, with an apple tree in

5

the garden and piano lessons and a Mom and Dad with a couple of children. And Pat's Mom looked after Josie beautifully.

Pat looked doubtfully at her but she wouldn't push it, not in front of the others. She turned to look out of the long dining-room windows.

'Looks as if it's coming on to snow,' Pat said.

'A white Christmas,' someone else said. 'So they say.'

They ate up their soup and cobs and chatted about this and that. Greta and Pat were in the Moulding Block, on the wrapping machines for sixpenny bars of Cadbury's Dairy Milk. One of their friends was on Chocolate Buttons, which had only been launched a couple of years earlier. Wherever they were working, though, they always tried to make sure they met for the dinner break.

They quickly cleared up their plates and headed off to put their overalls on again to start work, Greta trying to crack jokes and look cheerful. But Pat stopped her, a hand on her arm, pulling her out of the way of the stream of Cadbury women leaving the dining room.

'You and your Mom had a bit of a ding-dong?'

Greta nodded, shaking her head fiercely because to her annoyance she felt her eyes filling. It all seemed to well up lately, all these angry, desperate feelings.

'What – over *him*?' Pat winked. 'Surely she can't have anything against Dennis – he's squeakier clean than a freshly washed window.'

Dennis, who worked at Cadbury's maintaining the machines, was very sweet on Greta, as were several of the other lads, drawn by her curvaceous figure, her sunny golden-haired looks and lively personality.

Of all the girls, she had the most attention from the Trolley Boys, who came by at the end of the production lines to take away the packed boxes of chocolate. Most of them were in their late teens and pestered the girls determinedly. Greta had had to learn ways to brush them off with a verbal put-down, as she got pestered more than most, though she enjoyed the spark of flirting with them as well.

Greta couldn't keep it in any more. She needed to relieve her feelings. 'Not Dennis! *Him* – Mom's flaming latest – Herbie Small-Balls!'

She saw Pat crease up with giggles at this and couldn't help joining in. Greta's Mom's boyfriends were always a source of mirth, but of all of them fat, balding Herbert Smail, who fancied himself as a big noise down at the Leyland works in Longbridge, had to be the worst of the lot.

'Getting serious is it?' Pat said, trying to contain her laughter and be sympathetic.

'Yes – and it's not *funny*,' Greta said, giggling unstoppably as well. She wiped her eyes, careful not to smudge her eye-liner.

'Come on you two – quit yer tittering and get back to work,' one of the older women said.

'I'll tell you later,' Greta said gratefully as they headed back over to their block under the ominously grey sky, amid the drifting smell of liquid chocolate which they were so used to they barely noticed it any more. 'But ta, Pat – you've cheered me up already.'

'Glad to be of service,' Pat said with a wink.

They went back to the belt by the wrapping machine, with its endless river of little bars of chocolate. Greta looked across at Pat, feeling a bit ashamed. Here she was, making heavy weather of her life when she sensed that Pat had more weighing on her than she ever let on either. She caught Pat's eye and winked at her.

Where would I ever be without my pals? she thought.

Chapter Two

What had done it that morning was finding Herbert Smail sitting there large as life and twice as ugly at the kitchen table.

'Morning, Greta,' he said unctuously as she appeared, fortunately already dressed, instead of wandering down in her nylon nightie as she sometimes did for an early-morning cuppa.

Greta jumped, heart pounding. Refusing to look at him she went to the teapot, to find it had the dregs in it, still warm. She had no idea he was there! And now he'd very obviously spent the night in the house. The only blessing was she hadn't heard anything – God what a thought!

'You stricken with premature deafness by any chance?' Herbert said, rather less pleasantly. He pronounced it 'prema-tewa', rolling his r's in an affected way. He was one of those know-it-all types, thought he'd swallowed the dictionary. 'I believe I was speaking to you – or was that just a figment of my imagination?'

Greta scowled.

'Yeah, and this is my house and if I don't feel like speaking to you first thing in the morning, I won't – and I don't, all right?'

She stumped off back upstairs with her cup. Lukewarm tea was better than spending another minute in the kitchen and having to see his pink neck, his fat belly bulging under that sludge-green cardi and his greasy comb-over. Mom must have truly lost her mind to go anywhere near a revolting slob like that!

Greta dressed furiously, trying not to think about the sadness of her mother's life so that she would have to feel less resentful towards her. But of course it all welled up anyway, the thoughts and memories. Her elder sister Marleen's Dad, Ruby's first husband, Frank Gilpin, had been in Bomber Command and was killed flying a raid in 1943. Then Greta's own father, a GI called Wally Sorenson, had been a 'D1' – killed on the first day of the D-Day landings on Omaha Beach. Wally's kindly parents Ed and Louisa Sorenson had made Ruby and her two daughters warmly welcome in their home in Minnesota after the war. Greta had adored her grandparents, who were kind and loving and made her feel as if she had a proper family, and it had looked as if they could have a good life over there. She still used their name, Sorenson, her father's name.

But then of course Mom had to go and pick some walking disaster of a bloke to marry. Ruby's marriage to Carl Christie had lasted barely a year, and it was the most frightening time Greta could remember in her life. Christie had turned out to be a damaged and violent man who had terrorized Ruby and reduced her to a frightened, unkempt woman with no confidence left, before she had finally managed to rouse herself and get away from him. And it hadn't been just Mom who had messed everything up. Greta pulled her stockings on with furious resentment. Marleen had gone off the rails as well, causing all sorts of trouble, running wild until Ed and Louisa Sorenson had had enough and washed their hands of the family.

'We're always your grandparents,' Louisa had told

Greta, tears running down her gentle face. They were God-fearing Christian people and were at their wits' end with Ruby and Marleen. 'We love you, Greta. You remind us so much of our beloved Wally and we'll write you, dear. We do so want to have you in our lives. But we just can't tolerate this whole *situation* any more.'

Although Ruby and Greta had kissed the Sorensons goodbye, turned their backs on the dream of America and returned to England, Marleen had flatly refused to come. She had taken off, aged only seventeen, with some man who she said was about to marry her. Ruby had seemed unable to stop her, and they had heard from her only twice since, once to say she was married and then, last year, to report the birth of a baby girl called Mary Lou. She was still living somewhere in Minnesota.

And she'd better bloody well stay there, Greta thought, rage swelling in her over the loss of her grandparents. Marleen always did spoil everything.

Leaning close to the tilted mirror over her chest of drawers, she applied a thin line of eye-liner, as much as she could get away with at work. She combed her thick, shoulder-length hair, curling it under at the ends. It would have to be tied back and tucked under a cap all day at work so she wanted to make the most of it now. Even in the cheerless morning her hair looked vividly blonde. Angry and churned up as she was, she produced a smile, seeing her expression echoed in the little white-edged picture she had of Wally Sorenson, tucked into the edge of the mirror. She could easily see from where she had inherited her big, square teeth and broad, healthy-looking face.

'Hello, Dad.' Her eyes filled as she hungered for this

man she had never even met, for the idea of a father who would have been kind and all-embracing, who would have swung her up in his big strong GI's arms and cuddled her and given her love of a kind she had never had from a man.

Wally Sorenson, she could tell by the way her Mom talked about him, had been the one man Ruby had ever truly loved and the one really decent one she had ever had in her life. The war had robbed them of him, and Mom and Marleen, between them, had robbed her of her grandparents as well. Yet Mom was forever on about Marleen, worrying to her friends, especially Edie when she was round here. Marleen this, Marleen that.

Greta fastened the top button of her blouse, which kept slipping undone, and as she did so she heard the front door slam shut. So he'd gone, had he? Bloody Herbert Small-Balls, the sweaty old sod – good riddance!

Downstairs smelt of frying and Ruby was by the gas stove. Her navy work skirt hugged her broad hips very tightly and the sleeves of her cream blouse were rolled up her plump arms. The overall effect was of buxom largeness, and even more so with her new ash-blonde hairdo piled on her head, little wisps of fringe hanging stiffly down her forehead. She rounded on Greta, her face pink from the hot stove, and slammed a plate on the table with a slice of fried bread and an egg on it.

''Ere, get that down you.' Her hands went to her hips and she stood over the table where Greta had sat down sulkily. 'And what the 'ell d'you think you're playing at, speaking to Herbert like that? He said you were bloody rude to him!'

Greta felt her temper flare immediately.

'No I wasn't.'

''E said you were.' Ruby wasn't budging. ''E was quite put out. You've got a nerve, wench, going on like that.'

Greta stabbed her knife into the egg yolk, which trickled stickily across the white plate.

'It's me who lives here, not him. I came down in my nightie – it was embarrassing.'

'This is my house!' Ruby erupted. 'It's my business who stays here and who doesn't, and I don't need a little bint like you thinking you can insult my ... my ...'

'What?' Boiling over, Greta stood up so abruptly that the chair fell over and crashed on to the linoleum. 'Your boyfriend? The latest in a long line, eh Mom? Have you taken a *look* at him? I'd've thought you could do better than that!'

Ruby's face turned even redder. 'He may not be in the first flush of youth but neither am I. And he's all right to me – he's got a good job at the Leyland – prospects. I s'pose I'm not meant to have any life apart from working and cooking and scrubbing for you, eh? I want a bit of life for myself as well as all that drudgery ...'

'Drudgery! Oh don't come the martyr with me, Mom – you hardly lift a finger! It's me left doing all the cooking and cleaning when you're gadding off with your latest seedy bloke in tow. How many is it now? Albert, Emlyn, Sid ...'

'Well you're a fine one to talk, my girl. You've had more blokes buzzing round you than I'd had hot dinners at your age!'

They were yelling now, across the table.

'Well where d'you think I get it from? My glowing example of a Mom!'

'Don't you talk to me like that, my girl!' Ruby folded her arms and pitched her voice lower suddenly, so that it was intense and threatening. 'I've had enough on my plate, bringing you and Marleen up with no help from anyone . . .'

'What d'you mean?' Greta could feel herself saying worse things than she ever intended, as if they were gushing out of her. 'You're always spinning that sob story of yours, but I seem to remember being brought up by Mrs Hatton back then, not by you – you were always off chasing summat in uniform . . .'

Frances Hatton, a kind Quaker lady, had helped both Ruby and Edie a great deal during the hardest days of the war. A retired midwife, she had even delivered Greta when she was born one winter night in her house in Bournville. Frances had died after the war but Greta remembered her with great affection.

Ruby's eyes narrowed. 'I don't know what's got into you lately, my girl. You were always the quiet one, not like Marleen with all her carry-on. But now you're getting just as bad and she's constantly a worry – I don't hear from her for months on end and . . .'

'Marleen this, Marleen that – it's always her isn't it? All I ever hear about is your precious Marleen! It's all right for her over there in America! All you ever think about is her when she's the one who's nothing but bloody trouble. She ruined everything for me. She took my grandparents away from me and she wrecked *everything* . . .'

Sobs were rising from deep inside her. Until now she had not realized quite how angry and hurt she was about what had happened during their brief 'new life'

14

in the USA, how much she resented both Marleen and her mother because of that madman Carl Christie, because things had not turned out how they might have done.

'She stole America from me! I should have stayed over there with Ed and Louisa – at least they loved me. And all you can think about is Marleen and your *vile* string of men. You're both as bad as each other ... You disgust me, both of you ...'

Afraid she might break down and cry Greta pushed the sticky yellow plate across the table.

'I don't want this. I'm going to work.' Bitterly she glared at her mother. 'I don't want to end up like you, Mom. Or like Marleen. I'm sick to the back teeth of the pair of you. I want a proper life!'

Picking up her coat, she went out into the grey, overcast morning and slammed the front door behind her with all her strength.

Chapter Three

'Greta – wait for us!'

Dennis's voice rang out behind Pat and Greta as they left the block at the end of their shift.

'Eh—' Pat nudged Greta in the ribs, giving her a mischievous wink as they turned round. 'Look who it isn't!' Though she never went out with boys herself, she was always fascinated by Greta's dates.

Through the knots of people wending their way out from the works towards the tree-named roads stretching away from Bournville Green – Sycamore and Elm, Willow and Laburnum – they saw Dennis's eager figure dashing and dodging round everyone. His jacket was thrown over one shoulder and he was waving. As he drew closer they could see his round, freckled face smiling eagerly.

'Lucky I caught you!' he panted, running up to them and beaming at Greta. 'Hello – you all right, Pat?'

'Yes thanks,' Pat said shyly. She blushed whenever a male spoke to her and seemed to be awed by them. But earlier in the day she had said to Greta, 'He's nice, handsome and that – but he's a bit staid compared with your usual, isn't he?'

'Well, maybe I want a change,' Greta had said. 'Anyway—' She drew closer to Pat and whispered. 'I asked that lady in the wages department to check up on him for me. He lives in one of those big houses on Upland Road – and he's definitely not married!'

Dennis was certainly not like some of the other boys who came chasing after her. He was already twenty and seemed very old and sensible, the way she needed Pat to be sensible and stable too, though she hardly knew it then. With Pat she was always the larky one, the one who needed anchoring. Maybe Dennis would anchor her too. He seemed to offer something she dimly knew she needed. And clearly he had eyes only for her.

'I'll leave you two lovebirds and get home,' Pat said, and as Greta started to protest Pat put her hand on her friend's arm. 'No – I've got to get back – 'cos of Josie.'

'Oh yes – course,' Greta said sympathetically. 'And say hello to your Mom from me.'

'I will.' Pat flashed another brave smile at both of them. 'Tara you two – see yer in the morning.' She glanced up at the heavy sky. 'It's definitely coming on for snow, I reckon. It's bloomin' cold enough!'

'T'ra Pat!' they both said.

Greta watched her walk away, solid and responsible as ever, as she and Dennis began walking together.

'It's hard for her,' she sighed. 'And her Mom.' Mrs Floyd, Pat's mother, was a kindly woman, but she always looked so worn and harassed. And she liked going to Pat's house, where she was always given a warm welcome. The television was forever on, even when it was just the test card. Pat said they always had to turn it off when her Dad got home. He didn't approve of it, but Pat's Mom said she liked the company.

'You coming out tonight?' Dennis said as they headed along towards Selly Oak where both of them

17

lived. 'Thought we could go to the pictures. There's *The Guns of Navarone ...*'

'I dunno ...' Greta hesitated. 'Mom's expecting me ...' Her spirits sank horribly at the thought of that morning and the way her Mom had cut her dead at dinner time. Usually every time Ruby saw Greta at Cadbury's she'd call across to her. ''Ello, bab! Make sure you get 'ome in time!' or 'Watch who you're walking out with tonight!' It was embarrassing but warming as well, and had become a light-hearted joke among Ruby's friends. 'Bringing the whole family to work, eh Rube? Chip off the old block, isn't she?'

Today, even though she was still angry, and sickened by the memory of finding Herbert Smail sitting at the table when she came down, she felt very down and cold inside.

'I know – but after? Oh come on, Gret – we've hardly seen each other ...'

'All right – course I'll come,' she said, trying to sound more cheerful. Unguardedly she added, 'Only – I had words with our Mom this morning. I ought to go home ...'

'Gracious – what about?' Dennis seemed so shocked at the idea of rowing with anyone that Greta immediately cursed herself for saying too much.

'Oh – you know—' Her emotions were too raw about Marleen and about her Mom's chaotic love life, and she was definitely not going to air it all in front of Dennis. What sort of impression would that give him?

Dennis clearly didn't know, but he said, 'Ah well – you can patch it up, can't you? Families always have their moments. But how about meeting me at the end of Oak Tree Lane, seven-fifteen, eh?' He put his lips

18

close to her ear and said playfully, 'I'm yours for the evening, baby!'

Greta giggled, as his breath tickled her ear, excited by his attention. Maybe she had misjudged Dennis!

'Are you now, you cheeky so-and-so?'

He gave a mock salute. 'Eager and reporting for duty with my boots blacked.'

'Well, I'll do my best,' she said, cheered by the sight of Dennis's eager expression. He was in many ways an ordinary-looking bloke, with wavy, ginger-brown hair, and on the chubby side, but his wide mouth, so often drawn into a smile, his hazel eyes and freckled complexion made him very attractive. Greta realized that quite a few of the Cadbury's girls – and others – had their eye on Dennis Franklin. He evidently came from a good family, with money, and she was flattered that he had chosen her.

They parted in Oak Tree Lane, as Dennis's route took him round the back of the hospital. As soon as she was alone, Greta felt herself slow down, her emotions sinking again as she dawdled home. What about when Dennis found out what her family was like? Mom would be back by now. Greta felt disgusted with herself for some of the things she'd said to Ruby that morning, but she still couldn't trust herself not to say them all over again if Ruby started on her. She'd just have to go and face it. It was only a few days until Christmas. Ruby's seasonal work at Cadbury's was coming to an end and she'd be home more. They couldn't go on like this.

As she turned into Kitty Road she realized Pat had been right – there was snow on the way. The sky had that laden, almost creaking look to it, and the flakes were coming down now, large and silent, floating round her face. The sight of it gave her a childlike feeling of wonder that made her feel like skipping down the road. She saw someone halfway up the road, coming towards her, tall and gangling and very familiar.

'All right, Greta?' he hailed her, waving a long, skinny arm.

'All right, Trev?' Greta stuck a smile on her face. 'Scalped anyone today, have yer?'

Trevor gambolled up to her like a stork that only barely has control of its legs.

'What d'yer mean?' His bony face creased, puzzled.

'Never mind, it don't matter. How's it going with Mr Marshall?'

'Oh—' he beamed, enthusiastically. 'It's bostin – I can do everything now – short back and sides, the lot!'

'Good for you,' Greta said, her smile becoming genuine.

She'd known Trevor since the first days of school and he'd been so delighted when Greta and her family came back from America and settled in Charlotte Road, near where Ethel, Ruby's Mom, had lived for years. Greta had a soft spot for Trevor. He was sweet and dopey and she felt as if she'd known him for ever. When they all left school, Trevor had gone to work for Mr Marshall, the barber at the bottom of the street, who said he'd give him a go. Mr Marshall, father of Ruby's friend Edie, was getting on in years, but he had been reluctant to hand the business over to anyone. He was coming to realize, though, that he would soon have to, and he had taken Trevor as an apprentice.

Trevor wasn't top of the league in the brains department but he was sweet and kind and quite handsome in his way. He was very tall and had wide blue eyes and a Tintin quiff of dark brown hair on his forehead that had a life of its own.

'Gret—' He stopped, the trickling snowflakes settling on his hair, and she was sure she saw a blush spread over his face. 'I've been meaning to ask you if you'd ... Well, if you'd come out with me. On a date, like.'

'Oh – well, that's nice, Trev,' Greta said, taken aback. She had known Trevor was sweet on her, he always had been, in a bashful, hero-worshipping way, but she had not expected this. She had never seen Trevor as more than a boy before, a kid brother, even though he was grown to six foot two.

'Thing is — I can't tonight. I'm going out – with Dennis, from the works. It's sort of a regular thing.'

That was almost true. She hoped Dennis wanted it to be true.

'Oh.' Trev's face fell, and for a second Greta saw the little lad he'd once been in his raggedy shorts, a string of snot under his nose.

'Sorry, Trev—' She smiled but set off walking again. 'Maybe another time, eh?'

'Really – would you come out with us, Gret?'

'You never know,' she said, giving him a smile as she made for the gate of number thirty-nine. She didn't want to say yes or no because she liked the feeling of being pursued. She'd just never thought of Trevor like that before. 'T'ra then Trev – see yer.'

Despite her cheerful tone, her heart was heavy as she pushed open the door. Ruby was already home: Greta could hear her in the kitchen at the back as she hung her coat up and there was an inviting smell of frying – onions this time.

21

'That you, Gret?'

Greta assessed her mother's tone. It didn't sound like open warfare.

'Yeah.' On the kitchen table was a bowl with minced beef in it and a pile of chopped swede.

'There's tea brewed.' Ruby nodded to the little tin pot keeping warm on the stove.

Greta poured a cup, glad of it after the bitter cold outside. She went to the table to put a couple of lumps of sugar in.

'Sit down,' Ruby said abruptly. 'Time we got a few things straight.'

Greta pulled up a chair. *Oh, here we go*, she thought. She stared sulkily at the blue pilot light in the Ascot over the sink.

'I haven't always been a good mother to you, I know that.' Emphatically, Ruby chopped the root end off a carrot. 'And I wasn't that much of a mother to Marleen in some ways neither. But times were hard – the war took both your fathers ... It was a terrible time, full of fear and misery. And you can wipe that look off your face! The least you can do is listen when I'm talking to yer!'

'Well I might have guessed you were going to bring the war into it again,' Greta said, rolling her eyes. 'The war this, the war that ...'

Already this was not going well. She knew what her Mom was saying was true, that things had been hard – punishingly hard. She was aware of what her Mom had been through, as well as Janet, Frances Hatton's daughter, and Edie when she was living with Frances and Janet during the war. They'd all had their heartbreaks. Deep down, she knew all this. But what was she supposed to do about it exactly? She'd only been a baby for heaven's sake and it was all in the past now. Why did they have to keep bringing up the war for breakfast, dinner and tea? And what difference did the war make now to the fact that when it came to men her Mom still behaved like some sort of street trollop? What was it she was supposed to understand?

Ruby turned, drumming her fist on the table. 'Your generation won't have to go through all that, at least we hope to God you don't. And we went through it all so you won't have to. But you don't know you're born, some of yer, carrying on as if the world owes you a living with your loud music and your coffee bars and coming and going when yer like . . . You've all got more wages than sense . . . And don't you get up and walk off when I'm talking to yer!'

Greta slumped back down in her seat.

'What's that got to do with it, Mom? What's the war got to do with the fact that I have to come down and find that . . . that bloke here when I get up in the morning! He's *vile*. His eyes were all over me . . . You've never had a moment for me! Why can't you . . . Why can't we . . .'

Suddenly she couldn't find words, didn't know what it was she wanted to say except that she wanted, *needed* things to be different, to have a proper family like Pat, who'd never need to shout at her Mom and Dad, and for there to be something more to life than chasing men and having babies, over and over, round and round inexorably, like the life-cycle of the butterfly she could remember drawing at school.

'Oh, it's no good talking to you,' she snapped, jumping up from the table. 'Whatever I say won't make any difference will it?'

'All I want is a bit of life and family for myself as

23

well,' Ruby shouted after her as she disappeared into the front room. 'And why shouldn't I, after all I've been through?'

'Well, *I'm* your family,' Greta shouted, pulling the door to the stairs open violently. 'Or had you forgotten that?"

And she thumped upstairs, slamming the door. At least Dennis wanted her. She clung to the thought of him.

Ruby cursed over the glowing pile of carrots.

'What's the use in even trying to talk any sense into her, the mardy little bint! When I think of all I had to do for my mother. And if I'd talked to her like that I'd've had a walloping all right!'

Chapter Four

It felt very cosy, walking with Dennis through the falling snow, then snuggling up on seats near the back of the picture house, though it took some time before Greta's feet thawed out. There was already a layer of snow on the ground about an inch deep, and one of her shoes had a hole in and let in the wet. And she felt nervous. Dennis was different from other lads she'd been here with.

'This is going to be good!' Dennis said, settling down. 'Here – d'you want one of these?'

He offered her a bag of misshapen pieces of marzipan coated in chocolate. Like all Cadbury's employees they had a ticket which allowed them to buy cheap misshapes from the reject shop at the factory.

Greta smiled politely. 'Think I might give it a miss, ta.'

They weren't allowed to take chocolate out of the Cadbury factory, but everyone working there was allowed to eat as much of it as they liked while on the premises. Most people, after going chocolate-mad for the first days after they were taken on, soon came to behave in a more moderate way. A few never wanted to eat chocolate again. Greta liked it still, but only now and then.

'Only joking,' Dennis chuckled. 'Have one of these instead?' From another pocket he produced a little white bag of strawberry bonbons. 'I thought they'd be more your thing.'

'Oh – ta, Dennis,' Greta said. 'My favourite!'

'Thought so. I've got some peanut brittle in here somewhere as well.' He twinkled at her and for a moment it felt as if he was more like a Dad than a bloke of twenty, a kindly father giving her a treat, and she liked the feeling. In fact she liked it a lot. He seemed old and capable, and she felt she could sink back and be taken care of. She smiled back gratefully at him, popping a bonbon in her mouth.

'You got a busy Christmas coming up?' he asked, indistinctly.

'Not really—' They both laughed as she tried to speak without drooling. 'You know, just family and a few friends. There's only me and Mom.'

She'd better be damn careful what she told Dennis, at least for now.

'No brothers or sisters?' His tone was pitying.

Greta hesitated. 'No – not really. How many've you got?'

'Three big sisters and one brother,' he said happily. 'I'm the youngest, so it's always a houseful with their husbands, kids and all that. You know – do it all properly, like. My mother's heroic, the way she manages everything. And there might be a new little one arriving for Christmas as well – my sister Maggie's expecting her first.'

'That's nice,' Greta said, enviously. It sounded so lovely, everyone getting together like that, and the way he spoke about it, as if it was the happiest time of the year.

The lights started to go down then. Dennis looked eagerly at the screen, but Greta wasn't that interested in *The Guns of Navarone*: she'd come to please him. Dennis was a real gent, she thought. Nothing pushy or forward, just natural. Not like Reg Wallace, a lad she went out with last year who'd been all over her, fingers prodding and exploring the moment the lights went down. That was when the lads usually made their move.

Every so often she stole a look at Dennis's profile in the silver light from the screen. He was obviously enjoying the picture, sitting with a slight smile on his lips even during the tense parts. It was more of a lads' film, Greta thought. She took her stockinged foot out of her damp shoe and wiggled her toes to warm them. And she tried to decide who was the more handsome, David Niven or Gregory Peck. She decided on Gregory Peck.

But her mind didn't stay on Gregory Peck for long, because something strange was happening to her. She couldn't stop thinking about Dennis. A strange, warm, fluttery feeling was growing in her that she'd never felt before, and it kept growing. Dennis was lovely, wasn't he! She was acutely aware of him sitting beside her and of every time either of them moved and his leg brushed against hers. And although she didn't want to be mauled about she began to wonder why he wasn't paying her a bit more attention.

It was only the second time they had been anywhere together. Last time it had been a Cadbury do where there were lots of other people about and there had been no chance of a kiss or cuddle. This was the first time they had been out alone and he could take his chance to kiss her or at least hold her hand! That was how you knew a bloke wanted you, wasn't it? As the minutes went by she started to feel a bit huffy. What was the matter – wasn't she good enough for him or something? She knew Dennis's family lived in a nice big house – nicer than Charlotte Road, anyway. Maybe he'd already decided that coming out with her was all a mistake.

After a while though, as the action got more exciting Dennis turned to her enthusiastically. 'It's good, isn't it?' he said, then reaching over he added, 'May I?' and took her hand, holding it gently in his warm one.

The warm, fluttering feeling increased and she sat back, gratified now, and excited. Even though he was gripped by the story he turned and looked at her now and then and he held her hand all the way through.

As the adventures on the island of Navarone came to a climax and the credits began to roll, Dennis turned to her, his eyes looking deep into hers.

'That was ever so good. And the best part is being here with you, Gret. You're lovely, you really are.' He hesitated. 'Would it be all right if I gave you a kiss?'

Her heart thudded hard. 'All right.' She nodded, wondering what was happening to her that she wanted him to kiss her so much. With other lads it had felt like something she had to do but hadn't much enjoyed.

Moving closer, he began to kiss her, his full lips warm and caressing as if he really cared for her, and she was just starting to respond when he drew back. People round them were getting up and shuffling out.

'It'd be lovely just to stay here,' Dennis said, 'but the lights'll go on again any minute.'

Feeling breathless, almost dreamlike, she followed him out of the red gloom into the cold.

'My goodness!' he exclaimed when they got outside, still holding her hand. 'It must've kept coming down all the time we were in there!'

While they had been inside, another couple of inches had fallen. The pavements and rooftops were thick with it, and it was still coming. Everything seemed muffled and magical at the same time, the flakes whirling in the beam of car headlights and tickling against their cheeks. Greta ran up the road a little way, frolicking in it, then felt foolish because Dennis didn't join in.

'I think I'd better get you home,' Dennis said. 'We've both got work in the morning.'

He walked her to her door, and on the step, he put his hands on her shoulders and looked into her eyes again. She felt overwhelmed by him, by the speed at which her feelings had come upon her. Even her legs felt a bit shaky and she didn't think she was just shivering with cold.

'Gret – will you smile at me? Please?'

Bashful, she laughed, her lips parting and Dennis threw his head back in pleasure. 'Oh – you're lovely you are. God I love the way you smile.'

He looked very serious then. 'I know it's early days . . .' he started to say. But then he stopped himself.

Greta caught her breath. 'What were you going to say?'

'Best not,' he said. 'Must take things carefully – I like to do things properly, see.' For another long moment he gazed into her eyes, then leaned forward and his lips kissed her cool cheek.

'Don't catch cold – you go in,' he said. 'Goodnight, Greta.'

'Goodnight,' she said, making as if to go into the house, but then she stopped, wondering if he'd call her back for more, but he kept on going. She stood on the step and watched him disappearing into the dark, his footsteps muffled, but the happy sound of his whistling carrying back along the street.

'I love your smile . . .' she whispered to herself, as the sound died away. 'Oh Dennis – I love yours too – and I think I love you.'

Chapter Five

There was no sign of Herbert Smail or anyone else when she got up for work the next morning. Ruby was still in bed, now the Christmas rush was over at Cadbury's. She would have a few weeks off, then be taken on for the Easter egg rush.

Greta flung a woolly on over her nightie and crept down to the freezing kitchen, lit the gas and stood looking out of the snow-swathed back window at their tiny oblong of garden. The sight made her smile. There was a deep layer of snow along the wall and sitting like a drunken hat on top of the dustbin. It must have been snowing for a good part of the night and the sky was a bulging grey again.

She sat down at the table, hugging herself, listening to the hiss of the gas and thinking about Dennis. Memories of yesterday made her feel fluttery and excited all over again. If only she could feel his arms around her now. She'd fallen in love last night, that was what had happened! And Dennis was steady and kind and a good few years older than her – three years felt like half a lifetime – and life was not grim and depressing the way it had seemed all day yesterday but lit up by the look in Dennis's eyes. The snow seemed like a promise of sweet, happy things to come.

She was in such a dreamy daze that the kettle

whistled to the boil in no time, and she mashed a pot of tea.

Better make Mom some, she thought. She'll moan if she wakes and there's no tea on the go.

She poured herself a cup of dark, strong brew and was just shuffling to the stairs in her pink nylon furry slippers when she heard a knocking. Frowning, she put the cup and saucer down.

'If that's greasy Herbert he'll get my sodding tea over him,' she muttered, going to the front. 'It's only seven o'clock in the morning!'

She opened the door a crack and peered out into the whiteness. The front steps were piled with snow, its perfection marred by the imprints of a pair of white plimsolls whose owner stood on the top step. Above the shoes were very skinny legs clad in blue jeans, topped by a jumper with a huge polo-neck in a chaotic blend of red, black, orange and yellow wool. In the person's arms was a small child with big blue eyes.

'Well, open the door then,' the visitor ordered impatiently. 'It's cold enough to freeze a monkey's arse off out 'ere.'

Greta swung the door open, recognition sweeping through her: the narrow eyes, lanky brown hair, pale face, and that voice, only slightly marked by an American twang.

'Marleen?'

'You gonna let me in sis, or what?'

In a daze, Greta led her through to the back. It was only then, when Marleen parked her daughter on the kitchen table and unwrapped the thin shawl from round her, that Greta noticed the child's bare feet and legs.

'She must be frozen!' she exclaimed. 'Why the hell hasn't she got anything on?'

32

Marleen turned and gave her a long, scornful stare. 'Look – you ain't got a clue what I've been through. I was in a hurry, right? She's all right – she ain't making a fuss, is she?'

'D'you want a cuppa tea?' Greta asked, not sure what else to say.

Marleen gave a harsh laugh, standing the little blonde girl on a kitchen chair.

'God, you really are getting like our Mom, aren't you? Have a cuppa tea and that makes everything all right. You sound like an old woman already, Gret.'

'I was only . . .' Greta saw there was no point arguing. Already, though this great sisterly reunion had been going on for only about five minutes, she was having to hold on very tight to her temper. 'Well, d'you want one, or not?'

'Yeah – all right,' Marleen said ungraciously. 'Oh, Mary Lou – you're flaming well wet again!' She laid the child roughly on the kitchen table in a way which made Greta wince, and the little one began to grizzle. 'Well, I ain't got more clean diapers to put you in so you'll just have to shurrup for a bit,' Marleen snapped.

'Shall I give her some milk?' Greta suggested, as the toddler cried miserably.

'Yes, and hurry up with it. Can't stand her grizzling, it drives me mad.' She handed Greta a baby's bottle. It looked grubby and had a rime of old white milk in the bottom so Greta set about washing it.

'So this is Mary Lou?' she asked as Marleen tried to adjust the girl's soggy nappy.

'Yeah,' Marleen said indifferently. 'And a bloody handful she is an' all.'

'She's very pretty.' Though Mary Lou was bawling, Greta could still see how sweet she looked, with wide blue eyes and a round face topped by loosely tumbling blonde curls.

There was no reply, so Greta busied herself making a bottle for the little girl, pouring tea and sneaking glances at her sister when she was not looking. Now she could take in Marleen's appearance she was shocked by it. The reason she had not recognized her at first was because, although she had always been lightly built, she had lost so much weight that she was truly scrawny. Her already pointed features had a narrow-eyed, wolfish look and her hair was unkempt and hung loose. She looked pale and very unhealthy. Despite her thinness, above all, her appearance was of someone worn and tired and much older than her nineteen years. Greta felt a sense of dread looking at her. It was like looking at her Mom all over again, after the effects of Carl Christie. What on earth had happened? Was this what marriage had done to Marleen?

She put Marleen's tea on the table. Mary Lou was still grizzling.

'Here y'are. There's the sugar.' She stood, not knowing what to do next. It was hard to talk over the crying baby. 'Why're you here, sis? You staying long?'

'Oh that's nice!' Marleen snapped. 'I come home after years away and you ask me why I'm here! Ain't I part of the family any more?'

'Well yes, but . . .'

Both of them fell silent then, because they heard a heavy tread on the stairs. The door opened and they saw Ruby's bleary face beneath her bleached hair.

'What the hell's all this racket?' She was tying the belt of a mauve nylon dressing gown. 'Oh!' Her hand went to her heart. 'What's . . . ? Is that you . . . ?'

As Greta watched her mother's face she saw a few seconds of confusion, and then of vulnerable tenderness, pass over it.

'Marleen?' her voice sank to barely a whisper.

'Yes, Mom, it's me – and Mary Lou, your granddaughter,' Marleen said matter-of-factly. 'We've come home.'

Everyone at work was talking about the snow. Thick as a quilt, it had turned everything – the Cadbury's cricket pitch and girls' gardens, the factory blocks and trees, and the old buildings on Bournville Green – into an icing-sugar, Christmas card scene. Everyone was chatting about how they had managed to get in to work, and how it looked as if it really was going to be a white Christmas for once. Heavy snowfalls were moving fast down from the north! But for Greta and her friends, her news had taken their attention away from it. Pat and the others were all ears over this turn of events in Greta's home.

'What – you mean she just breezed in, just like that, after all this time?' one of them exclaimed, now they were on their dinner break, sitting over steaming bowls of soup, and it was the first good opportunity to talk.

'Well – yeah,' Greta shrugged. 'I'd only just got out of bed and there she was, with the kid half-naked, on the doorstep.'

'How did she get there?' Pat said. 'She must've come on an aeroplane. And where's she been? You said she was married?'

'I don't know – I never had time to ask her...'

'And is she staying?'

'Look, I've told you – I don't know!' Greta said,

exasperated. 'She was in a mood and wasn't saying much.' All Ruby's attention had been fixed on Marleen and the child from the second she arrived. Greta hadn't been able to get any sense out of anyone and her longing for a proper sister who she could be close to had come clanging up against the hard reality. 'All I know is that she's turned up and said she's come home for good. Or I think that's what she said. I never had time to ask much – I had to come to work!'

But she rolled her eyes comically to make light of it, and the others laughed. Greta had never hidden the fact that her relationship with Marleen was not a close one. It would have been lovely to think she could go home tonight to a sister she loved and was longing to see. Instead, she was already dreading it.

'Oh, that reminds me,' Pat said as they went back to work. 'My Mom said to ask if you'd both like to come round for tea over Christmas – Boxing Day or something – if you're not busy and that. I mean now Marleen's home maybe she could come too?' But Pat sounded a bit doubtful about that.

Greta was touched. 'That's nice of them, Pat. I'd like to come – course I will.' She liked Mrs Floyd, though she had hardly seen anything of Pat's father. 'I'll ask Mom – if you're sure?'

'Course I'm sure,' Pat said, smiling her sweet, dimply smile. 'And I'd love you to come over. I'll make mince pies! It gets boring over Christmas without a bit of company.'

'I s'pose you spend half the time in church singing hymns,' Greta remarked.

'Well, we do a bit,' Pat said. 'It's not too bad though. It's just once Christmas Day's over the time hangs a bit heavy.'

'You want to put a couple of bottles of summat fiery in their Christmas stockings – that'd soon get them going,' Greta said wickedly, knowing perfectly well that Mr and Mrs Floyd never touched 'intoxicating liquor' of any kind. Seeing Pat blush slightly, although she was smiling, she said, 'Don't worry, chuck, I'm only kidding.'

'So d'you think you'll be able to come?' Pat persisted.

'Yes, course,' Greta said. Her teasing had an edge of envy – she often wished she had Pat's quiet, ordered life.

As they went back to their machines she remembered Dennis's description of his family Christmas. For a second she felt an ache of longing in her chest for the happy family scene he had portrayed to her. And the thought of him made her glow inside. But then came a sinking feeling of doubt. How could she ever be part of something like that? It sounded too good for her – she was too *rough* for people like that, wasn't she? Not sweet and genteel. Someone like Pat would be better for Dennis! But she dismissed the thought. It was her that Dennis wanted to go out with. And whatever happened with Marleen coming home, she had Dennis, the man she was already convinced she loved. Marleen might be one for spoiling things, but at least she couldn't spoil that.

Chapter Six

As soon as the word was out, of course everyone wanted to see Marleen and little Mary Lou. By the time Greta got home from work, her nanny Ethel, Ruby's Mom, was there. She saw the car parked outside as she walked down the street.

When she pushed the front door open everyone was crowded round the fire in the front room: Nanny Ethel, and her husband Lionel, who she'd married towards the end of the war when they were both working for ENSA, Ruby, Marleen and little Mary Lou. There were empty teacups all over the place and the room was muggy and full of smoke.

'Hello Nanna,' Greta said, removing her coat and shaking the latest fall of snowflakes from it.

'All right are you, Greta love?' Ethel greeted her, dragging her eyes away from Mary Lou, who was sitting on the old blue rug by the fire, playing with something. Greta saw it was a doll. Nanna must have gone out and bought it as soon as she heard the news of her great-grandchild arriving home.

''Allo, Greta!' Lionel said chirpily, his leathery face smiling at her through the usual cloud of cigarette smoke. Greta smiled back. At least someone seemed glad to see her, and she liked Lionel. He'd made her Nan happy again after she'd been widowed and depressed and he was always cheerful and good to everyone.

'There's tea in the pot . . .' Ruby began, then leaned urgently downwards. 'Oi Marleen, watch her – she's got summat in her mouth!'

Greta eyed the plate on the low table on which there had evidently been a fruit cake but now there was nothing but crumbs.

'Nice of them to leave me some, she thought, going through to the back to pour a much-needed cup of tea. She found some stale custard creams instead and went to join the others in the front, perching on the stool near the fire as all the other chairs were taken.

'Nice to see your sister home, isn't it?' Ethel said. 'Even if it has all been a bit of a surprise. You had us ever so worried, Marleen – and we've been saying, she's looking very thin and peaky. She wants to look after herself. You can settle back home now, Marleen—' Ethel raised her voice to speak to Marleen, as if she was making a long-distance telephone call. 'Whatever's happened to you, bab, it's all over and you're home.'

'Yeah, thanks, Nan,' Marleen said. She sat huddled in the chair looking cold, her thin arms wrapped round her. She stared blankly at the floor and wouldn't look any of them in the eye. As her Nan spoke though, she managed a thin little smile. Ethel had always been kind to both of them.

'I'm a bit tired now, Nan,' Marleen said, getting up. 'I think I'll go up and have a bit of a sleep.'

Everyone started clucking over her. 'You do that, bab,' Ruby said. 'We'll see to Mary Lou – she's fine down here with us. You have a good sleep.'

'Look at her,' Ethel exclaimed. 'So thin you could snap her in half!'

Without another word to anyone Marleen went off upstairs.

'Where's she sleeping?' Greta asked, a sudden suspicion gripping her.

'In with you of course,' Ruby said. 'She's got the put-you-up in your room and Mrs Robinson's let us have the cot – little Carol's just out of it – she's a good neighbour,' she said, turning to her mother. 'Do anything for anyone, she would.'

'But there's not the room for two beds and a cot in there!' Greta protested. 'We shan't be able to move!'

Everyone was staring at her, shocked.

'Your sister's just come home – I'd've thought you'd be pleased to see her and share your room for a bit!' Ruby said. 'Where exactly do you think she might sleep if not in there?'

Greta went red. She was horrified at the thought of sharing with Marleen, but everyone thought she was being cruel and unloving. Unlike her, none of them had ever shared a room with her sister. They seemed to have conveniently forgotten what she was like!

''Ere, have a fruit jelly – it's Christmas.' Ethel leaned over, seeing Greta's downcast face, holding out a box of coloured sweets. She knew her Nan had always had a soft spot for her.

'Thanks, Nan.'

'Take two while you're at it, go on,' Lionel said, chuckling. 'Makes a change from all that chocolate doesn't it? Do you good.'

'It ain't her that needs fattening up,' Ruby remarked, tartly.

Greta smiled gratefully at Lionel and took a strawberry and a lemon jelly. Lionel held one out to Mary Lou, who stared at it in alarm, then started snivelling. She seemed to cry whatever happened.

'Here, come to Nanna,' Ruby said, and tried to pick

up the child, who screamed more loudly, squirming and kicking. 'Eat your sweetie, darlin'!' She pushed the jelly towards the child's mouth, who went quiet at once when she tasted the sugary coating.

'There, you like that, don't you?' Ethel said in a baby voice. She lit another cigarette and blew out a cloud of smoke across the room. It felt warm and cosy with the snow outside.

'So Marleen won't say anything – about where she's been?'

'Not a word,' Ruby said, draining the dregs of her tea. 'Here – fetch us another cup Gret, will yer?'

Greta got up and did as she was asked and ended up making more tea and filling up her grandparents' cups as well while they talked in low, gossipy voices about Marleen. What had happened to Marleen's husband? He was Mary Lou's father after all. And what about the Sorensons, Greta's grandparents – had they had anything to do with this? Where had Marleen been all this time? No one had any answers. Ethel looked at an old picture of Marleen propped on the cluttered mantel. It was taken in 1959 when they were in America and Marleen was in a pretty sundress, smiling.

'Shame,' Ethel said.

Greta hated hearing them talking about her grandparents, who she was so fond of, as if they might have done something wrong. Whatever had happened, it would be Marleen's fault, of that she felt certain. She didn't want to sit and listen and her feet were still cold and wet. She crept round to the stairs.

'Where're you going, Gret?' Ruby called. 'Don't go waking Marleen will you? She needs her sleep.'

Greta ignored her. In the back bedroom she found

41

the put-you-up bed half folded away and Marleen cuddled up in *her* bed, her eyes closed. Greta felt enraged for a moment at the way Marleen had just helped herself to her bed, but then she found herself feeling softer towards her. She didn't know if Marleen was really asleep or just pretending, but her face, with her eyes closed, looked very young and vulnerable. Suddenly she looked as she had done when she was about six, her dark lashes like two crescents, her skin pale and fragile-looking and her shrewish look relaxed by sleep.

Well, we've never been close, Greta thought, but there were some good times, when we were kids. The old hunger rose in her for her sister, for a proper family. Maybe things could be better, they could be real sisters, close and sharing things.

She moved quietly round the bedroom, finding a pair of socks to put on to warm her feet, and her slippers, and crept downstairs again.

Everyone turned to look at her.

'I hope you didn't disturb her?' Ruby said, busy opening a bottle of port.

'She all right?' Ethel asked.

'She's all right – she's fast asleep,' Greta reported. 'Out like a light.'

Marleen stayed out of the way for most of the rest of the day, leaving everyone else to look after Mary Lou. Ethel and Lionel went off quite early, worried about driving in the bad weather, with lots of 'Happy Christmas' and 'See you before the New Year' greetings. They were going to two of Ruby's five brothers for Christmas, to be with their younger grandchildren. Ruby's family never saw much of them.

As they left, Mary Lou set up a steady mewling, puckering up her little face.

Greta went to her and picked her up. She wanted the little girl to like her – after all, she was her auntie – but Mary Lou bawled even more loudly.

'I 'spect she wants her tea,' Ruby said, almost snatching her from Greta. 'Come on – I'll make her summat.'

Greta gathered up the teacups and plates and took them to wash up. Mary Lou was sitting at the table while Ruby heated some milk at the stove and was still crying, even more loudly now.

'She blarts a lot, doesn't she?'

'She'll be all right with some slops inside her,' Ruby said. 'Must all be a shock, the poor little mite.'

Mary Lou quietened once Ruby sat with her at the table and fed her morsels of bread soaked in sugary milk.

'Pretty little thing, isn't she?' Greta said, watching Mary Lou, whose cheeks were tearstained and her blue eyes still watery.

Greta needed to catch her own mother's attention, to talk, instead of her going on and on about Marleen and Mary Lou. She wished she was close to her mother, the way Pat was, and could talk to her about anything. She would have liked to tell her about Dennis, but she'd never felt she could talk to Ruby. Ruby had always had too many problems of her own, and whenever they talked they always seemed to get on the wrong side of each other.

'It'll be nice having a little baby here at Christmas, won't it?' Greta said, trying to please.

'Ooh yes – lovely.' Ruby laughed at the sight of Mary Lou, her cheeks bulging with food. 'Seems a long time since you two were this size.'

Greta tried to continue this positive wave of communication by adding, 'It's a shame we won't be with Nanna and Lionel. But it'll be cosy, won't it, just the four of us here.'

There was a pause, before Ruby slowly turned her head.

'There won't just be us four,' she said carefully. 'I've said to Herbert that he can come and spend the day with us.' Seeing the look on Greta's face she defended herself quickly. 'It's no good looking at me like that. He's coming and that's that – I don't want any argybargy from you, my girl. Herbert's a single man with no family to speak of and he'll pass a lonely Christmas without an invitation. Now it's up to you to show some Christmas spirit and make him welcome!'

Greta went to the sink and finished washing up the cups. She had barely begun to come to terms with Marleen coming home and what that might mean, and now Herbert Small-Balls would be sitting at the Christmas dinner table with them. Not that anyone ever asked her what she might want, she thought, slamming one of the teacups down hard on the wooden drainer. In this house, she might just as well not exist!

Chapter Seven

It certainly was going to be a white Christmas. There was no let-up in the bone-achingly low temperatures at night. Greta found herself tossing and turning trying to keep warm. In the morning the bedroom windows were frozen on the inside, white patterns like ice flowers. Beautiful, but not much of an encouragement to get out of bed.

'I never thought I was coming home to this,' Marleen moaned. 'It's as bad as America!'

'Oh, so there are some bad things about America are there?' Greta said. Marleen was 'America this, America that,' all the time, until she wanted to say, 'Well, if it's so blooming fantastic, why didn't you stay there?'

Marleen sat up, grimacing. She looked very pale, and with a groan she got out of bed and dragged herself to the bathroom.

Greta got up to mash some tea. She crept out, not wanting to wake Mary Lou, who was still asleep, little mouth half-open. As soon as she woke she always started bawling. Greta got a bottle of milk ready just in case. The child's constant crying grated on everyone's nerves.

It's enough to put you off having any kids, Greta thought, huddled up close to the stove. The kettle seemed to take an age to boil, in the cold.

All she could think of was seeing Dennis later that day. They'd arranged to meet up in town, see the lights and have a bit of a walk round and a drink somewhere before getting back to their families for the evening. And she had a little present for him. She'd asked him what she could give him and to her surprise he'd asked for a book.

'What d'you mean, a book?' She hadn't expected him to say that.

'You know – one of those things with pages with print on them,' Dennis teased.

She felt a sudden longing. She had been clever at school, so the teachers said, and she'd been complimented on her abilities at the Continuation School at Cadbury's where they were released from work for a day of lessons every week until they were eighteen. She'd loved it there and had been sad to leave. But as soon as they had been launched fully into the world of work and the factory, it felt as if things like reading had to stop. She never saw her Mom reading a book. Of course, people round her when she was little read things. When they stayed with Frances Hatton, Janet, Frances's daughter, had read books, and there was Edie, with her painting. Edie's son David, who lived in Israel now – he had always had his nose in a book. But somehow they were different. They weren't like her family. People like them didn't go in for reading. Yet here was Dennis asking for a book!

'I know what a book is,' she retorted witheringly.

'Surely you're a reader, aren't you?' he asked.

'Well . . . Yes.' She was confused. The fact was she barely ever read anything now, but she felt as if really she *was* someone who liked reading, so it was hard to be truthful. 'But what book d'you mean?' she added tetchily. 'There are quite a lot of them out there you know!'

'Nothing expensive – there are second-hand bookshops down the hill in Bournbrook, near the university. I just want something that's a good read – something to get my teeth into.'

On Saturday she had ventured down the hill and found a dark, secretive-looking shop with books displayed in the window. With butterflies in her stomach Greta pushed the door open. It gave a homely 'ting', and she was in another world! There were all those shelves of books all round the room, and free-standing shelves in the middle, and mixed with sweet tobacco smoke was the special smell of old pages that was both forbidding and exciting at once. At the back of the shop, a mild-looking man in half-moon glasses was sitting behind a desk puffing on a pipe and reading a book himself.

'Can I help you?' He looked up rather absently, taking the pipe from his mouth. 'Or are you just browsing?'

'I'm browsing, thank you,' Greta said timidly.

The man seemed relieved to get back to his book and, to Greta's intense relief, soundly ignored her. She looked round in bewilderment. What on earth should she buy for Dennis? A good read, he'd said. That must mean a story, she thought, passing shelves which had books on arithmetic, on religion and the basics of logic. She found poetry, history, books on trains and aeroplanes, books for children. Then she found the literature: Charles Dickens and Elizabeth Gaskell, George Eliot and Evelyn Waugh. Then a title leapt out at her. *Kidnapped* by R.L. Stevenson. That sounded exciting. Dennis had said he wanted a good read. The cover was dark blue and inside the price was marked in pencil at 2/6d. She decided to buy it – otherwise she might be here all day, still not able to make up her mind!

'Ah – very good!' the man said when she handed it to him. 'A nice edition too. That'll be half a crown – no, actually, as it's Christmas I'll let you have it for two shillings.'

'Oh – thank you!' Greta smiled.

'I tell you what—' He looked at her eager face. 'You look to me like a keen reader . . .'

She was about to contradict him but he didn't give her the chance.

'If you give me the half-crown I'll throw in this as well – you might like to give it a try.'

'Oh – thanks ever so much!' Greta said, as he slipped another book into the paper bag.

She left the shop with its tinkling bell, and on the way back up the hill into Selly Oak she pulled the two books from the bag. In the daylight her choice of book for Dennis looked a bit faded, but she liked the gold print on the book's spine.

She turned the other book over, a slim, red-covered volume, and peered dubiously at the spine. *Bonjour Tristesse* it said, by Françoise Sagan. Afraid that the book was in French, she turned the pages, but saw to her relief that it was in English after all. It was a short book. Perhaps she'd give it a try.

Now she just had to worry about whether Dennis would like the book she had bought for him.

She saw him waving, among the crowds in Corporation Street who were out enjoying the lights and

Christmas trees and the bustling atmosphere, before everything closed down for Christmas Day.

'Greta!' he called, and she felt a smile spread across her face. Dennis always looked so happy to see her, and she ran up to him.

'Thought I might miss you,' he panted. 'I got held up back there and there're that many crowds.' He drew her to the side of the street, close to Lewis's department store, and stood looking at her for a moment, in delight, before folding her in his arms.

'I'm going to miss you,' he said, drawing back to look down at her again. 'I wish you could come and spend Christmas with us. You'd love it!'

'So do I,' she said, more sincerely than he realized. She would have loved to be almost anywhere else than with Mom, Marleen and the dreaded Herbert tomorrow. Suddenly it dawned on her that she'd better buy little presents for Marleen and Mary Lou.

'Ah well,' Dennis said, very correctly. 'All in good time. Mustn't rush things.' He often did that, she noticed. He would seem exuberant, carefree when he first saw her, then very quickly he would become rather stiff, as if he had put a brake on somewhere in himself. 'How about we go and find a place to sit down – have something hot to drink? We could go in here.' He nodded at Lewis's.

'All right,' Greta said. 'I'd like that. I'm blooming freezing. And I need to look round.'

Arm in arm they walked into Lewis's, and on the way to the tea rooms Greta picked out a pretty brooch for Marleen with red stones and, in the toy section, a little blue stuffed rabbit for Mary Lou.

'Who's that for?' Dennis asked.

'My sister,' she said airily. 'She was living in America and she's come home with her little girl.'

'You never said you had a sister!' Dennis frowned. In fact he never asked her much about herself. 'Well, that's nice – and just in time for Christmas!' Greta smiled, while shuddering inside at the thought of him meeting Marleen.

They sat down at a table in the warmly lit room, where 'Jingle Bells' was piping out around them.

'What d'you fancy?' Dennis asked.

'You,' Greta said with a mischievous grin. 'But I'll settle for a cuppa.'

'Cheeky minx,' Dennis said. 'D'you always talk to your boyfriends like that?'

'No,' she said truthfully. 'But then I've never had a boyfriend like you before.'

She actually saw Dennis blush. 'Well, there's a compliment,' he said.

They drank their tea, gratefully warming their hands round the cups, and Greta talked a bit about Pat and how they were going to her family on Boxing Day.

'What'll you be doing?' she asked.

'Oh, Boxing Day we always have the Walk,' Dennis said. 'Christmas Day's always a lazy day – nice big dinner, our Mom always does a big turkey with all the trimmings, and all the family squeeze in. And then we talk and sing and play games – well on into the evening, with the kids there – all my sisters' kids – and everyone gets very merry . . .'

Greta remembered the nice times they used to have at Frances Hatton's house and the one really lovely Christmas they'd had their first year in America when things had not been spoilt, with Ed and Louisa Sorenson, and her heart ached. These were the memories of childhood that she treasured, and she held on tight to the past as it seemed so much better than now. If only Frances hadn't died so young and Mom and Marleen hadn't messed everything up in Minnesota!

'Anyway,' Dennis was saying happily, 'by Boxing Day everyone's ready to get moving and walk off the Christmas pud. So we all meet up for a walk – up the Clent Hills. My brothers-in-law have all got cars so there's no problem getting everyone up there.'

'Sounds lovely,' Greta said wistfully.

'Well—' Dennis became solemn and looked at her very tenderly. 'I do hope that eventually, when the time's right, you might be able to join us.'

Her heart beat very fast. What was Dennis saying? That he thought so much of her that he was talking about one day making her a part of the Franklin family? Was that what he meant?

Dennis had a soft, misty look in his eyes as he gazed at her. 'I can imagine you with apple blossom in your hair.'

'Dennis—' To her horror, tears prickled in her eyes. 'I'm not good enough for you.'

He leaned forward, earnestly. 'What on earth are you talking about? You're the most fantastic girl! You're my ideal of all a girl should be!'

'Your family sound so nice . . .' She looked down at the table, flushing with embarrassment. If only she'd never said anything! It wasn't like her to lay herself bare like this. Usually with blokes she was the joker, keeping them at a distance.

'Well, they are . . .' Dennis sounded hurt and worried. 'Look, what's brought this on?'

'You haven't met my family – they're just . . . Well, not like yours.'

'Well, I know your Mom don't I? She's a nice lady.'

'Yes,' Greta conceded. 'I suppose she is.' But she felt inferior, and unsure of herself.

'Don't say that,' Dennis said, taking her hand. 'You're the girl for me – I know that – even from knowing you for just a while. I only have to look at you . . . Come on, cheer up. It's Christmas!'

The sight of Dennis's doting face always cheered her up, although the feeling would not go away altogether. Grateful for his kindness, she gave him her warmest smile.

'Oh—' Dennis made a mocking gesture as if someone had shot him through the heart. 'That smile! One of these days I'm going to get myself a camera so I can take pictures of you. I'd love to have one to keep. I don't s'pose you've got one have you? That you could give me?'

Greta thought. 'No – not recent. My grandparents took some when I was little – in America.'

She'd told Dennis about Ed and Louisa and he had been very interested. She had had her usual Christmas card and brief letter from them.

'Even a picture of you with pigtails would be better than nothing,' Dennis joked.

Once they'd drunk their tea they wandered out into the cold street where their breath billowed in white clouds against the street lights. But the people of Brum were out, determined to enjoy themselves and find last-minute bargains, despite the cold. Greta and Dennis linked arms and strolled through the Christmassy streets, smelling cigarette smoke and cheap perfume and cooked meat from some of the eating places that were still serving. They avoided the Bull Ring as it was full of building work and people doing desperate last-minute food shopping, and walked the gritted pavements round the snow-clad cathedral and along Colmore Row before heading for Navigation Street to catch their bus. All the time they held hands, laughing about day-to-day things and people they knew at Cadbury's. Greta felt dreamy, as if she was walking on air.

When they got off the bus in Selly Oak, Dennis insisted on walking her home although it was out of his way. At the bottom of Charlotte Street he stopped her, in the shadows by the old copper works in Alliott Road.

'I just wanted to say happy Christmas properly,' he said, gazing at her closely. 'And to say ... You're a lovely girl Greta. I don't know what you feel for me, but I'm ... Well, I want to tell you – you do something to me. I love you, that's all,' he finished bashfully. 'And I want us to be together.'

Greta felt emotions welling up in her. She'd never heard him say this before. It made her very happy, but at the same time she couldn't shake off the feeling that she wasn't enough for him – good enough, or clever enough, or something enough that she couldn't even identify.

'I love you too,' she said, in a wobbly voice. 'Oh, Dennis – I can't believe this is happening!'

He pulled her close and held her, kissing her as if she was very precious, and she kissed him back, passionately. She could have stayed there for hours, but soon Dennis pulled away from her.

'Better not get carried away.' He smiled wryly. His hair was looking dishevelled where she had run her hands through it.

'Come here,' she laughed, smoothing it down. 'You

look as though you've been through a hedge back-wards!'

'I've got something for you,' he said, reaching into his jacket pocket. He brought out a little parcel and handed it to her. 'For you tomorrow. Happy Christmas, my lovely.'

Greta reached into her bag for the book. 'I don't know if you'll like this,' she said hurriedly. 'I didn't know what to get . . .'

'Of course I'll like it if it's from you,' he said, already holding it as if it was something precious. He hugged her again for a moment, close and tight.

'See you as soon as we can. Happy Christmas, Greta.'

'Happy Christmas,' she whispered.

He turned to wave at the end of the street as she stood watching, still hardly able to believe it was real. It can't work, she thought, a feeling of doom coming over her even as her heart soared to the heights. Good things like this don't work in my family. They never do. I'll spoil it somehow – I can just see it coming.

She walked in to the sound of Mary Lou wailing. Marleen was pacing up and down the back kitchen with Mary Lou on her hip, jiggling her irritably, a tense, angry expression in her face. The room smelled of liver and onions and another odour which she realized was of dirty nappies.

'Give her to me,' Ruby said, getting up from the table where she was sorting out vegetables for tomorrow's dinner. A ketchup bottle was somehow managing to stay upright, balanced on its lid. 'Let me have another go – quieten her down before we have our tea.'

'Bloody *shurrup*, Mary Lou!' Marleen erupted suddenly. She hoiked the child round and started to give her a good shaking, which only made her cry more.

'Don't be like that with her!' Ruby went to her straight away and took the child, who was now bawling at full volume. 'That ain't going to make her stop is it?'

'I don't know!' Marleen screeched, distraught. 'I don't know what'll make her shut up! She's always been like that ever since she was born – there's no pleasing her. I don't know what to do with her – I wish I'd never had her!'

She burst into tears and ran to the stairs, and they heard her crash up to the bedroom and slam the door.

'Make her a bottle will you, Gret?' Greta could see her Mom was near the end of her tether and she did as she was asked.

The bottle seemed to pacify Mary Lou for a time, and she sat tearstained on Ruby's lap, glugging the milk down. In the quiet that followed they could hear Marleen sobbing in the room upstairs.

'What's up with her, Mom?' Greta asked.

Ruby shook her head. 'If I knew, I'd tell yer – but she's just sat here and hardly said a word all day.' She looked up at Greta. 'Oh – Trevor came round. Said will you pop round and see them tomorrow – teatime?' Despite her weariness a smile played round Ruby's lips. 'He said he had summat for you!' And she gave a big saucy wink.

Chapter Eight

Christmas morning, and the first sound Greta heard when she came to was Marleen being sick.

Dragging herself out of bed into the freezing cold, she listened for a few seconds outside the locked bathroom, then tapped on the door.

'Marleen, what's up? You poorly?'

There was no answer. After calling several more times and hearing more retching sounds emanating from the bathroom, she said, 'Be like that then,' and went downstairs to put the kettle on.

Ruby had beaten her to it and was standing by the stove in her dressing gown. The light was strange because of the snow. Seeing her, Ruby gave a vague smile.

'Little 'un still asleep?'

'Yes, thank God.'

'Happy Christmas, love.'

'Happy Christmas.' Greta perched on a chair by the table. 'I think our Marleen's poorly,' she said, through a yawn. 'She's up there being sick.'

Ruby whipped round. 'What d'you mean?'

'In the bathroom – I could hear her.'

'Oh my God. What about yesterday?'

'What about it?'

'Well, was she sick then an' all?'

'I dunno. I was down here when she got up . . .'

But Ruby was already halfway up the stairs.

'Come out here my girl,' she heard. 'I want to speak to you! You get that door unlocked, *now*!'

There was a pause, then the click of the bolt on the bathroom door.

'What's going on?' Ruby demanded.

Greta didn't hear any reply from Marleen. She could imagine her shrugging in her usual sulky way.

'I asked you a question!' Ruby roared at her. 'Come on – out with it! Are you in the family way again?'

Within seconds Mary Lou gave a great screech which drowned out Marleen's reply.

Greta listened, her heart pounding. Marleen, having another baby? How could she be? Mary Lou was still so young – could you have another one that quickly? She realized how ignorant she was about all that sort of thing. And worst of all was the thought that Marleen might bring yet another screaming brat into the house. She didn't even know how to look after the one she'd got!

Greta filled with explosive rage. Wasn't that just like Marleen, to come home, not say a word, and expect everyone else to put up with whatever mess she'd got herself into? Marleen was so stupid, so selfish! She always had to spoil everything for everybody! Greta thumped up the stairs. At that moment she could cheerfully have given Marleen a good slapping.

In the bedroom though she found her mother and sister sitting side by side on her bed. Ruby had the wailing Mary Lou in her arms, and beside her Marleen was bent over, looking sickly and faint, hair hanging in lank trails each side of her cheeks and obviously feeling dreadful. She also looked very young and vulnerable.

Greta gave her mother a questioning look and saw

Ruby nod grimly. So it was true. She felt her anger drain away at the sight of her sister, to be replaced by a resigned pity. What a cowing awful mess Marleen was making of everything! There wasn't much love lost between them, and probably never would be, but she could still feel sorry for her. Marleen had still not said a word about what had happened to her during her time in America, but it had left her in this terrible low state, and with two children into the bargain.

'Kettle's coming up to the boil,' she said quietly. 'Shall I go and brew up a cuppa?'

'You do that, bab,' Ruby said, over Mary Lou's screams. 'I think we all need it.'

Well, Marleen, Greta thought angrily, hands in freezing cold water, peeling potatoes, you've managed to wreck everything again – you've even wrecked Christmas . . . Jolly music drifted through from the television, which seemed to mock her mood. 'Thanks a bunch,' she growled, throwing the gritty peels savagely into the bin.

They were all trying to take in Marleen's news, and as if things couldn't get any worse, come midday there was the expected loud banging on the front door.

'That'll be Herbert,' Ruby said, as if they couldn't have guessed. She took her pinny off, revealing a new terylene dress in swirls of maroon and white, and patted at her hair, which she had touched up at the roots and sprayed into place. She hissed at Greta, 'Now, listen here – Herbert means a lot to me. You'd better be *nice*.'

From the kitchen Greta heard Ruby greeting Herbert Smail as if she had not a care in the world, laughing and joking with him.

'Oh, you're a tonic, Ruby, you really are!' he said in his smarmy voice, stamping the snow off his shoes. 'A salve and balm for the weary.' She heard the smacking sound of him kissing her mother's cheek, and then he must have noticed who else was in the room.

'Who's this?' Herbert sounded really thrown by the sight of Marleen and Mary Lou on the rug by the fire, near the little Christmas tree. In the background there was music coming from the television.

'Ah, now, Herbert,' Ruby explained, speaking in a light, sparkly way that made Greta clench her fists. 'We had a little surprise a couple of days ago. This is my other daughter Marleen and her little girl Mary Lou – they've come home from America.'

Greta found a wicked grin spreading across her face at the thought of Herbert getting the Marleen treatment. She had to see this. She went and stood in the doorway. Herbert was dressed in a blaringly loud tan and black check suit, the jacket buttons unfastened to reveal an immense, bilious-green shirt.

'Say hello, Marleen,' Ruby said brightly. 'This is my friend Herbert.'

Marleen, still obviously feeling sick, raised her eyes to Herbert as if she had just been asked to inspect a blocked drain.

''Llo,' she grunted.

'How delightful to meet you, Marleen,' Herbert oozed. 'Well what a nice surprise – a familial Christmas festivity. Aren't I a lucky boy?'

Greta wondered whether Herbert had even known Marleen existed. Most likely not, she decided.

'I've had the privilege of visiting the United States of America myself,' he told Marleen. 'Detroit, to be completely precise and accurate. Which part of that great and esteemed country have you been living in?'

Marleen stared at him blankly. 'What?'

'Don't be dense Marleen,' Ruby said sharply. 'Herbert's asking you where you were living in America.'

All he got in reply was another withering stare from Marleen.

'She's not feeling too good today,' Ruby said. 'Any road, here's Greta to see you!'

'Ah, the lovely Greta!' Herbert turned to her. 'Allow me to offer Christmas felicitations by kissing your fair and delectable cheek!'

Before Greta could either decipher this sentence or move away, Herbert had swooped towards her. His wet lips smacked against her cheek.

'Happy Christmas,' Greta said hastily. 'I'll just check on the spuds, Mom.'

She retreated to the kitchen, wiping her cheek. Then she got the giggles and stood snorting helplessly into her hands by the cooker. Herbert kissing her had been like being mauled by a giant slug. God Almighty, what a day, and it was only twelve o'clock!

'Come through and I'll get us a drink, Herbert,' Ruby said. 'I've got some nice cider – I know you like that.'

As soon as Ruby and Herbert came into the kitchen Greta went back into the front room and sat down next to Marleen. She started building a brick tower for Mary Lou.

'Who the bloody hell's that?' Marleen asked.

'Mom's new boyfriend.'

Marleen stared at her. 'What the hell was he on about?'

Within two minutes of sitting down at the table for Christmas dinner, Greta wondered how she was going to get through it, never mind the rest of the day.

Ruby had cooked a sumptuous meal: turkey and trimmings, potatoes, carrots and parsnips and cabbage, and the room was full of steam and the smells of food. There were crackers on the table, which Mary Lou was very taken with and cried when Ruby took hers away.

'You could hurt yourself, bab,' she said. 'We'll have it later!'

Mary Lou was setting up for a big wail when Herbert leaned down to her. 'Coochie-coochie!' he said, blowing cidery breath into her face. 'There's a coochie-coochie little girl, aren't you?'

Mary Lou's mouth opened in astonishment at the sight of his great big red face and she forgot to cry. Greta caught Marleen's eye and for a moment they were on the same side when Marleen smirked back at her.

'You've got a way with children, haven't you?' Ruby said, piling potatoes on to Herbert's plate. 'It's nice to see that.'

'Oh, I do my best,' Herbert said, laughing and looking round the table. 'I'm a bit out of practice, with my own being grown up and gone.'

Greta stopped in the middle of pouring gravy and looking sharply at her mother. *I thought he was single,* her look said. *What's this about children?*

'In America they have Thanksgiving, not Christmas,' Marleen volunteered suddenly.

'That's most true, they do,' Herbert said, and this was his cue to go off on a long speech about the Pilgrim Fathers and the good ship *Mayflower* landing in America in the seventeenth century. 'It's really a harvest celebration,' he finished.

'Ooh, don't you know a lot?' Ruby said, beaming at him. 'Can I top up your glass, Herbert?'

'You can top me up any time,' Herbert said, with a suggestive grin, and he and Ruby laughed for a long time at this.

'You are a scream,' Ruby said, her cheeks very pink from cooking and generous amounts of cider. 'Ain't he a scream, girls? There's no one like Herbert for a good joke.'

As the meal continued, with Herbert boasting about how much money he was earning, about the car he was about to buy, not to mention the new house he planned to buy too, and Ruby's behaviour became more and more flirtatious, Greta sat feeling more and more outraged and embarrassed. She was ashamed of her mother, of her being tipsy, of her past, the way she had to fling herself at men and usually the wrong ones. Men were only after one thing, Ruby often said. So why give it to them all the time then?

The joking and laughing made her feel sick. The longer the meal went on, the more she felt wound up, tighter and tighter. She wanted to get up and run from the house. She looked round the table at her Mom, puce-faced and making up to this fat creep, her sister, sulky-faced and sickly, no more than a child herself and trying to cope with Mary Lou and some other unknown man's brat in her belly. And this was her family.

Suddenly she felt very distant from them, as if she

was seeing them on telly, like a film. She didn't want to be where they were.

I'm never having children, she thought. Never, never, never.

She was the one who was going to be different. She wasn't going to get caught out like that – she was going to get somewhere in her life. But she hated feeling like this about her family: she wanted to be bursting with pride, the way Dennis was over his.

As she was lost in these thoughts, she became aware of a strange sensation in her left leg. As she came back to reality with a bump, she realized it was a hand, stroking her. Herbert was sitting at the end, on her left, talking to Ruby as if with all his attention, but all the time his hand was on her thigh under the table. Greta froze. She tried to move away but there was no space. The hand kept stroking. So she picked up her fork and jabbed the prongs into the back of his hand.

Herbert let out a yelp and pulled his hand away.

'Whatever's the matter?' Ruby asked. 'Have you hurt yourself, Herbert?'

Greta looked up, innocently.

'No, no – it's nothing!' he said, avoiding Greta's eye. 'I just caught my knee under the table, that's all.'

'Well as long as you're all right,' Ruby said, patting his shoulder. 'Now then – who's for plum pudding?'

Chapter Nine

Teeth chattering, Greta rapped her knuckles on the cracked yellow paint of the Biddles' front door. She'd been in such a hurry to get out, and as they only lived a short way down Charlotte Street, she hadn't thought to put her coat on. Icy air bit into her cheeks, snow lay trodden in uneven lumps, and more was beginning to fall.

The door opened a fraction to reveal Trevor's seven-year-old sister Dorrie, a plump, eccentric little girl, who was a smaller version of their Mom. Behind the door she could hear voices and the television and there was a mixture of smells: cooked meat, sprouts, dog and cigarettes.

'Trevor said you'd never come,' Dorrie announced. She was wearing a vivid pink dress with a tiered skirt, each layer trimmed with bands of white lace.

'Well, I'm here aren't I?' Greta said. 'That a new dress?'

'Yes – it's my fairy dress . . .' Dorrie twirled proudly round. By the look of things her podgy arms had only just squeezed into the sleeves.

'Who is it, Dorrie? Is that Greta?' Nancy Biddle conducted most of her front-door conversations from her chair, whether she could see the person or not. 'Hello, Greta, if that's you – let 'er in yer silly wench,

64

she'll freeze 'er bones out there. TREVOR – GRETA'S HERE!'

As she entered the familiar stuffy room she saw Trevor's Mom and Dad, Nancy and Alf, sitting either side of the fire, where the dog, an old brown mongrel called Trigger, lay on the fag-burned hearth rug. April, who was thirteen, was poring over a new *Bunty* annual. There were cups and plates on the hearth and side table, the remains of a fruit cake and a scattering of boiled-sweet wrappers. The Biddles greeted her warmly.

''Ullo, Greta.' Nancy smiled through a haze of cigarette smoke. She was a cheerful woman in her late thirties with chopped, shoulder-length black hair. Freckles dotted her upturned nose, and made her look good-tempered and friendly, which she was. 'Nice of you to call in, bab – I hope yer Mom doesn't mind you coming out?'

'No – it's all right,' Greta said.

'Having a nice Christmas?' Alf asked. He had a long, bony face, a toothy smile, and had given Trevor his long, lean frame.

'Yes, ta.'

Greta could hear feet running eagerly down the stairs.

'Here 'e comes.' Nancy rolled her eyes.

''Ave a chocolate?' Alf said, holding out a box of Roses.

'Oh – no, ta.' Greta smiled.

'Don't be daft, Dad!' Trevor said, appearing from the back.

'Oh – sorry,' Alf laughed, showing his big square teeth. 'You 'ave quite enough of it at work I s'pose! How's yer Mom?'

'All right.'

'I hear she's got company for Christmas,' Nancy said, winking. 'Is 'e nice?'

Greta hesitated and Nancy gave her chesty laugh. 'Oh I see, like that is it!' She stubbed her cigarette out on the saucer by her chair. 'I'm going to make another cuppa – d'you want some, Greta?'

'Yeah, go on then.'

'I've got summat for you, Gret,' Trevor said with eager bashfulness. ''Ere, Mom – I'll put the kettle on.'

Nancy had been about to get up but she sank back with a grin.

'Go on then, Trev – you take Greta through.'

The back kitchen of the Biddles' house was in need of a lick of paint and was in a chaotic state, cascades of greasy pans from Christmas dinner stacked all over the tables and in the sink.

Trevor suddenly seemed overwhelmed at finding himself alone with her and just stood awkwardly the other side of the table, on which the remains of a joint of beef lay in a pool of bloody liquid. Greta saw a cigarette end floating in it. Trevor chewed his lower lip for a moment.

'You look nice,' he said, at last. Greta had on a skirt in red tartan and a cream jumper. 'But you always do . . .'

'Oh – ta,' Greta said. She looked into Trevor's eager face. 'That's a nice thing to say.'

Then they both stood at a loss, until she said, 'You going to put that kettle on for your Mom then?'

'Oh – yeah.'

He filled the kettle and stood it over the flame.

'I got you a present,' he said, going to a shelf where he had hidden something between two storage tins.

'Here – that's for you, Greta. Happy Christmas.' He was holding out a thin, square package. She thought of Dennis's present, a delicate silver chain with a tiny silver flower pendant which was resting now in the cleft between her breasts.

'Oh, Trev!' It was her turn to blush now. She hesitated to take it from him. 'You shouldn't have. I feel bad now – I haven't got you anything.'

'Never mind,' he said, and she couldn't tell if he was really disappointed or not. 'Go on – open it.'

She took it from him. The wrapper had holly leaves on a white background. Inside she found a 45 single.

'Oh!' she exclaimed, doubtfully. 'The Beatles. Thanks Trev.' She'd never even heard of them. The song was 'Love Me Do'. When she turned it over, the B side was 'PS I Love You'.

'It's a really good song!' Trev's face was bashful, but serious. 'I do, you see, Greta. I really love you. I think I always have.'

'Oh, Trev . . .' She was touched and embarrassed at once. She'd always liked Trevor. He was nice in a daft sort of way. But she'd never really thought of him in *that* way – not as someone to go out with or anything. She couldn't think what to say to him, so instead she asked,

'You got a record player?'

'April's got one – it ain't much good. Have you?'

'Yeah – Mom's got an old one. But let's ask April if we can put it on.'

April sprang to life at the thought of hearing the new record and took them up to the room she and Dorrie shared. Dorrie came up as well, not wanting to be left out, and they put the record on the turntable. Soon the four of them were jigging about in the girls' messy room with 'Love Me Do' pouring tinnily out into the room. Greta was glad April and Dorrie were there too because they just had fun and didn't have to talk about anything. They laughed at Trevor's gawky dancing in the narrow space and Dorrie got a bit too excited, twirling round in her fairy dress, and at the end they all fell back laughing on to the beds.

'Thanks, Trev!' she panted. 'That's the best present!'

'Let's put the other side on,' April said.

For the next hour or so they kept playing the record and dancing to the two songs in turn until they knew all the words to them and were pink and hot. Then the two younger girls drifted down to watch the television and Greta was left alone with Trev, perched on the mauve flowery coverlet on April's bed.

'That was good,' she said.

'It's always good when you're around.'

'Really?' Greta blushed, touched by his simple sincerity.

'Yeah. There's no one like you, Gret. You're so nice and so pretty. No wonder everyone wants to take you out.' He looked down at his long fingers. Greta imagined them curled through the handle of a pair of scissors, trimming hair. 'I mean I know I'm not much – but I do love you.' He finished this sentence with sudden passion and looked into her eyes. His were grey and deep. 'I do – honest.'

She looked back at him, drawn in by his adoration of her. Trevor was always seen as a bit of a clown in the neighbourhood, with his long gangly legs and proneness to accidents. But he'd always been a kindly boy, and now he was sitting here all sweet and familiar. She knew she didn't exactly fancy him – not like

Dennis – but if anyone wanted her she usually found she wanted them too, at least a little bit, and she was flattered and didn't want to be unkind.

'Oh, Trev,' she looked back at him, feeling her cheeks burn pink. 'That's nice. I don't know what to say . . .'

'Don't say anything—' He moved closer and she could see he was going to kiss her. She left it just too late to move back and in a second his arms were round her, pulling her close, and Trevor's mouth was eagerly fastened on hers. After a second she realized how nice it felt and she kissed him back. For minutes they were locked together before Trevor pulled away, gasping.

'Oh God – oh, Gret . . .' He looked awestruck, and a beaming smile spread across his face. 'Oh, that's lovely – oh I love you!' Once again he put his arms round her. 'Come out with me? Be my girl, will you? Let's go out together.'

Greta felt panic rise in her. How could she say no to him on Christmas Day, when he'd been so sweet and given her a present? She couldn't tell him about Dennis, not now – it would be so cruel. Maybe if she went out with him once, to be kind . . .

'All right,' she said.

'Will you!' he bounced up and down on the bed whooping with excitement. 'Oh Greta – you're the best!'

She stayed as long as she could at the Biddles' house that evening, playing canasta with Trevor, Alf and April.

'I can't be doing with all those card games,' Nancy

said, sitting back, content to watch them and smoke her Embassy cigarettes. She'd switched to them to collect the gift coupons. 'They get me all in a muddle.'

Then they watched television, Alf's favourite, *Steptoe and Son*, and by ten o'clock Greta said she'd better be off home. Trevor jumped up immediately and said he'd walk her up the road.

It was snowing again and everything felt very cold and still outside, with cosy lights in the windows of the neighbours' houses. He kissed her again on the doorstep.

'Thanks for the best Christmas *ever*,' he said fervently.

'Thanks, Trev – and for this.' She patted the Beatles record.

'See you tomorrow?' he said hopefully.

'I've got to go to Pat's tomorrow,' she remembered. 'Her Mom's asked me round for tea.'

'Soon though – next week? We'll go to the pictures or summat – whatever you want.'

With a pang of guilt, she said, 'OK then. See yer, Trev.'

He backed away down the road, waving, skipping, twirling, until her laughter rang behind him.

Her spirits plummeted at the thought of going back into the house. The light was on at the front, and when she stepped inside she heard Ruby giggling and found her sitting beside Herbert Smail on the sofa, in a high old state, both very well oiled. Herbert's tie had disappeared and his shirt had several buttons open and they were both pink-cheeked and very merry.

'Well that was nice, running off and leaving us!' Ruby said. But she didn't really sound cross. She was having too nice a time to get angry. 'Saw Trevor did yer? You'd like Trevor, Herbert – he's ever such a nice boy.'

'Where's Marleen?' Greta asked, trying not to look at Herbert at all. The sight of him sitting there with his legs splayed apart made her feel sick. He was making himself thoroughly at home.

'Gone to bed,' Ruby said. 'She had a job getting Mary Lou settled.'

Greta rolled her eyes. Another broken night coming up, she thought.

'I'm going up,' she said abruptly.

'Goodnight then—' Herbert made a vain attempt to get off his seat and failing, bowed in a courtly manner anyway.

''Night,' she said, and went to the back, shutting the door with a bang.

Filthy old sod, she thought.

Undressing silently in the bedroom by the light from the stairs, she thought about Trevor, her heart sinking. What had come over her? It was Dennis she wanted to go out with, not Trevor Biddle! What was she going to do now? It would have seemed too cruel to Trevor just to turn him down. She sank into bed – thank God today was over! – trying to block out the sounds of laughter from downstairs. She'd have to go along with Trev for a bit, just to be kind, and then get out of it somehow. Because she was in love with Dennis Franklin, wasn't she, and he with her? And she mustn't let anything spoil that.

Chapter Ten

'You ready you two? Edie'll be here any minute!'

Ruby was fussing at her hair by the mirror in the front room. Instead of peroxide blonde it was now bright copper. They were on their way to Selly Park for the traditional New Year's Eve which they always spent with Janet and Martin Ferris. Edie, who had started work at Cadbury's the same days as Ruby, and her husband Anatoli were giving them a lift. Greta had always liked going to the Ferrises' house, especially when Janet's mother Frances was alive, as she'd been like a grandmother to Marleen and herself. Though she was a bit shy of them, there was something so reassuring about Janet and Edie, and their calm houses full of books. She longed for her own home to be more like theirs.

'Do we have to go?' Marleen said sulkily as they came through for their coats.

'Yes, of course we do!' Ruby snapped through a cloud of hairspray. 'It's what we always do and we've said we're coming. But listen you two—' She turned, looking forbidding. 'There's some things I don't want you saying to Edie and that lot – right?'

Greta put her head innocently on one side. 'What d'you mean, Mom?'

'You know damn well what I mean. I know I go back a long way with Edie, but she's that flaming smug these days ... I don't want you mentioning things about my personal life.'

'You mean Herbert?' Marleen said, insolently chewing gum. If she'd said 'dead rat' instead of 'Herbert' she couldn't have injected more disgust into the word.

'Yes, of course I mean Herbert,' Ruby snapped. 'And for 'eaven's sake spit that stuff out before we go.'

Marleen sulkily obeyed, and they were checking that everything was in the bag for Mary Lou when they heard the car outside. Anatoli had braked his old black Pontiac in the middle of the road, the engine still running, and climbed out, muffled up in a brown coat and rather moth-eaten Russian fur hat. He was born in Russia and had come to England as a small boy.

'I am not going to stop her!' he called to them. 'It is so cold, you never know if we will ever get started again. Come, let me help you!' He greeted each of them by kissing each of their hands with a bow, in his old-fashioned Russian way, and they all giggled with pleasure.

Edie wound the window down and smiled out at them as they stepped over the heaped snow in the gutter. She had her collar up, her vivid ginger hair was swept back and her face was very round and freckly. She was six months pregnant and looking bonny on it.

'Ruby – your hair!' she exclaimed, laughing with surprise. 'God, I hardly recognized you! Suits you! Did you have a nice Christmas?' It was obvious that she had enjoyed hers.

'Oh yes, lovely ta,' Ruby said breezily. 'You get in first with Mary Lou, Marleen.'

'I am hoping the roads have been cleared at the bottom of the hill,' Anatoli said. 'Or this princess of mine is going to struggle.'

Greta loved riding in Anatoli's car. It was long and sleek, with a sun visor over the windscreen, and the radiator grille at the front made it look like a shark baring its teeth. It made her feel as if she was in an American film. She got in last, squeezing in so they could shut the door, on to the slippery old seat. As she did so she felt something against her leg and realized it was a bag with a bottle and some packages in it. Edie and Anatoli had brought presents. Of course Ruby hadn't brought anything for anyone, she thought, with a sinking feeling.

They had to drive extremely slowly down the snow-clogged hill to the Ferrises' house in Selly Park, beyond the big convent. Anatoli chatted cheerfully, mostly about the driving.

'Ah, now we are about to be swallowed up by this drift here . . . No – I have averted a crisis. Ah – now a precipice for us to fall over! Oh – no! I have saved us! You ladies owe me your lives several times over!'

'Anatoli, stop it!' Edie kept saying. 'You're frightening everyone!'

Greta couldn't help smiling. It would have been impossible not to like Anatoli, with his twinkly eyes, his old-world ways and quaint English. Mary Lou jiggled up and down on Ruby's lap, interested in the experience of being in the car. Only Marleen looked glum, her constant expression these days.

Martin Ferris opened the door as they pulled up. He was a gaunt, long-limbed man with a gentle face.

'So – you made it!' he said, with a warm smile. 'Welcome!' As they all scrambled out of the car and slipped and slid over to the house, he teased, 'I say, Gruschov, when are you going to get rid of that old kettledrum you're driving and get yourself a decent English car?'

Anatoli took off his fur hat in the hall to show his magnificent head of steely curls.

'I didn't expect that I would come and live in the city of English car makers, did I?'

'What about Coventry?' Janet said, smiling as she appeared, hearing the men's habitual sparring. She was holding each of the four-year-old twins by the hand and they stared up, awed at the sight of so many people.

'All right – one of the car cities,' Anatoli conceded, kissing her cheek. 'The city of cars and *roads*. Soon, it seems, it will be easier for cars to move round the place than people. Now – you young ladies –' He bent down and kissed Ruth, the taller of the two girls, then Naomi, then briefly held each of their faces lovingly between his hands. 'I do believe you get more beautiful each time I see you.'

It took some time before all the greetings were over. Everyone exclaimed over Ruby's suddenly copper-beech hair, Janet kissed Edie warmly, and laid a hand on her friend's round stomach, smiling in wonder. It was one of the great sadnesses of her life that she and Martin had not been able to have children of their own. They had adopted Ruth and Naomi when they were working in the Congo.

'Only three months to go!' she said. 'I'm so excited for you, Edie.'

'I can't wait,' Edie said, beaming back at her.

Greta found herself kissed by everyone in turn and Marleen, who had stayed uncertainly close to the door, holding Mary Lou, was greeted warmly by Janet.

'Do come in, dear – bring Mary Lou in by the fire. I'm sure Ruth and Naomi will help look after her. They're fascinated by children younger than themselves.'

The light was already fading outside and the Ferrises' big house felt cosy and comfortable. There was a fire burning in the front room and chairs arranged round it. Janet made tea and cut up a big square Christmas cake with reindeer on top, a Father Christmas pulling a sleigh and three Christmas trees. Mary Lou was captivated by the sight.

'I've saved it for today,' Janet said. 'There's always rather too much to eat round Christmas Day isn't there? And look – you girls can each have one of the things off the top. They're made of marzipan.'

'Did you make them?' Ruby asked, amazed.

'Me? No – of course not!' Janet laughed. 'I have a neighbour who makes them. They're lovely aren't they?'

While they sat eating cake, Janet found toys to occupy the little children, moving about the room in her calm way. She was wearing a dress in a deep plum colour which hugged her elegant figure, and court shoes with slender heels. Like her mother, Frances, Janet had always dressed with flair.

'I may be going out to work with the missions,' she had said before she and Martin went to work in Africa, 'but that doesn't mean I have to dress like a missionary!'

Ruth and Naomi sat on the fluffy rug by the fire with some little dolls and a basket of tiny clothes. Every so often they came to the grown-ups, asking for help with a sleeve or poppers which needed fastening.

At first they went to their mother, but then Ruby said, 'Why don't you go and help 'em, Gret? And you, Marleen? Look, Mary Lou wants to have a look what they're doing.'

Greta was glad of something to do, and she and Marleen settled on the hearthrug with the twins. She quite enjoyed dressing the dollies herself because she'd never had anything like that when she was little. And the girls were sweet. Naomi was shyest and looked at her out of the side of her eyes with an impish expression when she wanted help. Ruth was more direct and dumped the doll on Greta's knees, saying, 'Dress doll, p'ease.' Greta had found the African girls so strange at first, their very dark brown skin, the pink palms of their hands and their frizzy hair which Janet had learned to keep oiled and tie in tiny plaits. Now she barely gave it a thought.

Mary Lou sat with Marleen, and there was an occasional squawk when she wanted something the others had, but she wasn't crying so much these days. Tonight her attention was too taken up by all these new people, the toys and the fire.

Greta sat with the young ones, listening to the conversations round her. The men, off to one side, spent a good while discussing medical matters, as Martin was a doctor, with his practice on a new estate in Nechells, Anatoli a pharmacist. Edie was seated next to Anatoli – the two of them were almost inseparable – with Janet and Ruby the other side of her, and they all caught up on Cadbury news. Janet had worked in the offices there and still knew a few people on the secretarial side.

'Oh, it's a wonderful place to work.' Janet sighed.

They all knew she missed working, but she had her children now. 'I hope you're making the most of it, Greta?'

Greta smiled shyly, though Janet's words were like a blow. Was she making the most of it – the way Dennis did? No, not at all. And she felt hopeless.

'Are things settling?' Edie asked Ruby in a low voice. This filled Greta further with shame, the thought of her family. Edie had not had an easy life, it was true, but now she was happily married to a man who was comfortably off. Everything about their big house in Selly Oak was pretty and good quality, and it felt as if Edie was a cut above them, even though she and Ruby had been born on the same day in nearby streets and started work the same week at Cadbury's. Greta always felt a bit grubby and ashamed near Edie, even though she knew Edie would never dream of trying to be superior. Marleen and her carry-on made it all far worse.

'After a fashion,' Ruby said. Greta saw her roll her eyes. Did Edie know Marleen was expecting again? Of course not, she thought. Like she wasn't to know about Herbert Smail or how things really were. Mom had to work hard to keep up appearances in front of Edie and Janet.

'Must be lovely having your granddaughter at home,' Edie said wistfully.

'How's your David?' Edie's adoptive son now lived in Israel with his wife and son, and Edie seldom saw her grandchild.

'Oh, he's doing ever so well,' Edie said proudly. 'He's finished his spell in the army, thank goodness. I couldn't settle at all when he was doing that. It must be terrible for Gila – it's like the war all over again! Now he's getting on with training to be a doctor.'

Greta listened, trying to prise the rubbery arm of a little doll into a red velveteen coat with a tiny strip of white fur round the hood. She hadn't seen David, Edie's son, for years. He was five years older and she remembered him as very bookish and clever. They had played together as children, but as soon as David went off to the grammar school he had become like someone in another world and she had been in awe of him, especially as he had taken very little notice of her or Marleen.

'I just wish they were here,' Edie was saying. 'I know it's where he feels he belongs and everything, all this having to be in the army, and Gila needs more help – I could have Shimon. It just seems such a shame . . .'

'When will you see them next?' Janet asked.

'I don't know. Maybe after the baby's born we could go over – in the summer.'

Greta shifted her position as the left side of her face was getting so hot by the fire.

'Are you all right down there?' Janet asked.

'Yes, ta,' Marleen murmured.

Greta looked up and nodded.

'I'll come and sit with you,' Janet said kindly, moving down on to the rug as well. 'How are you keeping, Marleen? Is it nice to be home?'

'It's all right,' Marleen said. But she spoke politely, not in her usual sulky way. They all liked Janet. She was so kind and sincere that she brought out the best even in Marleen.

'It does take some time to settle back in,' Janet said. 'We still feel as if we've only just arrived.'

'You've been here ages!' Ruby laughed.

'I know – almost three years,' Janet said. 'It takes much longer to adjust to coming back than to going

79

out there in the first place. When I think, this time three years ago . . .' She looked very sad. 'I still think of people there every day and wonder how they're getting on.'

Martin Ferris had been a doctor during the war, in Burma. On his return he had found it hard to settle in England and eventually he and Janet had gone out to work in the Belgian Congo. When the unrest in the country escalated before independence in June 1960, Janet and Martin had stayed and stayed, hoping things would settle. Independence came, with Patrice Lumumba as Prime Minister, but things were no better. Four days later the army revolted and whites were being robbed and killed all over the country. Thousands had to evacuate in a hurry, including Janet and Martin. Already terrified by the appalling stories they had heard of attacks on other whites, they were even more afraid that the abandoned twins they had adopted would attract attention and provoke violence against them. But in a small convoy of fleeing missionaries, they managed to cross the border into Uganda, and from there flew back to England.

'What about Chrissie?' Edie asked. Janet's friend Chrissie, a jungle nurse, had refused to leave and was still in the Congo.

'We did hear from her before Christmas.' Greta could hear the anxiety in Janet's voice. 'She won't hear of leaving. Chrissie always believes that the hand of the Lord is protecting her at all times.'

'That's all very well,' Ruby said mockingly.

'She's right so far though,' Edie said. 'The danger she's been in!'

'She's certainly got nine lives like a cat,' Janet said. 'I suppose I shouldn't worry.'

They all talked as it became completely dark outside. Once the little girls were all put down to sleep, Janet made a nice meal of cold cuts and cheeses and the adults talked and laughed the evening away. Janet found a few magazines for Greta and Marleen to look at and apologized that there was no television. The adults talked about the H-bomb, and how Janet and Martin had just joined the Campaign for Nuclear Disarmament. Marleen fell asleep herself after a while, leaning back in one of the easy chairs, her face looking tense even in sleep.

'Is she all right?' Edie asked. 'She doesn't seem too well.'

'Oh yes,' Ruby said. She was sitting comfortably, lighting up a cigarette once the food was finished. Janet slid an ashtray on to the table beside her. 'Ta, love,' Ruby said. 'Marleen's just tired. Mary Lou takes it out of her.'

Why don't you tell them? Greta thought angrily. She felt differently now towards her sister. A few days ago Marleen had told her, her and no one else, what had happened to her in America. And yet she could see why Ruby hid things from her friends. She'd always been the odd one out. It was only the war that had brought them together really. Once again, Greta found herself feeling angry and ashamed.

Chapter Eleven

Much later, after all the shaking of hands at midnight, accompanied by a warming punch of Janet's making, Anatoli drove them home. Greta knew she would not sleep and she was dying for a bath. After the others were settled she slipped a shilling into the meter and crept past Marleen to the bathroom. Soon the cold room was full of steam and she slid into the water, sighing with pleasure as the lower half of her body turned pink and the warmth seeped into her.

Her mind was in a turmoil of feelings after the last week. First there'd been the shock at Pat's house. She'd been so glad to get out after Christmas Day and had set off expectantly towards Bournville, past the old entrance to the workhouse. Playfully, she trampled fresh snow on the verges. She liked Pat's Mom with her plain, tired face, and their calm home with its little upright piano with hymn-sheet music piled on it, the telly on and Josie squealing at it in excitement. She had been round for a cup of tea now and then after work.

But today it was different. Everything was tidied away, the telly was off, chairs set in a tight circle, and Mrs Floyd, though friendly as ever, seemed almost a different person. She seemed terribly tense, and knocked over a cup of tea as she was carrying it to one of the elderly neighbours they had also invited round. And Greta met Mr Floyd properly for the first time. He was dressed very sprucely in a brown suit, had wavy grey hair and piercing grey eyes, and though he shook her hand and welcomed her in his nasal voice, she felt intimidated by him.

'You've met Greta before, haven't you, Stan?' Mrs Floyd said.

'Yes, I believe so, how nice,' he said. His grip on her hand was surprisingly tight and his eyes met hers, unsmiling. Greta felt a strange sense of dread, as if he already disliked her and she couldn't think why.

He was civil enough, but there was an incident after they had all had tea and cakes and mince pies. Under the window that faced out over the neat back garden stood a table with a jigsaw puzzle half done on it. Greta and Pat broke away from the groups of older people, having a very stilted conversation, and sat at the table with the puzzle, which was a view of a canal with an old narrowboat and a country pub on the bank. On the windowsill, Greta saw a pile of three books, all of which had Holy Bible in gold lettering on the spines.

Greta could feel a bubbling up of giggles inside her because the whole situation was so awkward. What was it about Pat's Dad that made her feel as if she was back at school in the naughty corner? She fought to control herself. She desperately didn't want to offend Pat.

'Ooh it's good to see you,' she said. She realized how desperate she was to be back at work, away from Marleen and her Mom and bloody Herbert. 'You had a nice Christmas?'

Pat nodded, wide-eyed. 'Oh yes,' she said – as if she'd say anything else. Greta thought how innocent she was, and how sweet. For devilment she leaned in closer to the table.

'Guess what? Trevor's asked me out!'

'What? Trevor Biddle?' Pat said far too loudly, and she made a face, looking round to see if they'd disturbed everyone. She and Greta had gone to the same primary school together, with Trevor.

Greta nodded, enjoying the impact of her words. Her eyes danced.

'You never said yes?'

Greta giggled. 'I did!'

'But you're going out with Dennis, aren't you?'

'Well, yes . . .'

'Whatever are you going to do?' Pat said, shocked.

'Thing was, I couldn't say no. I was round his house and he'd just given me this record, the Beatles – it's ever so good. And he was being nice. We were dancing and everything . . .'

Pat raised her eyebrows. 'Oh, it's like that is it?'

'Like what? No!' Greta protested. 'April and Dorrie were there . . .'

'So why did you say yes?' Pat brought her back to the point.

'Well – 'cause I didn't say no,' Greta said. The two of them were getting the giggles. In the restrained atmosphere of the room almost anything would have seemed funny.

'But what about Dennis?'

'Dennis is lovely,' Greta said, tittering. 'Really he is. But I just thought if I went out with Trevor once – to the pictures or summat – that'd keep him happy.'

'Well, I hope you're right, but aren't you leading him on?' Pat said drily.

'Oh, I'll soon sort Trevor out,' Greta said, putting on a woman-of-the-world tone.

'Gosh,' Pat said.

They were silent for a moment, looking at one another as the laughter bubbled up and burst out. It was like getting the giggles in the classroom. Greta saw Pat glance anxiously across at her father, who was eyeing them.

Seeing that made them giggle even more until Pat said, 'Ssshhhh.'

But it was too late. Greta looked up and jumped, suddenly aware of a brown-clad body standing over them at the table. Mr Floyd laid his hand on Pat's arm and Greta remembered the tight grip of his handshake.

'I think we're all getting a little bit out of control over here, don't you?' he said, in tones of sweet reason.

Pat sobered up instantly. 'Yes – sorry, Daddy.'

He did not move away instantly, but looked at each of them in turn, a penetrating look deep into each of their eyes as if in warning, before he moved slowly away to sit down again. Greta felt quite shaken by the intense expression in his eyes.

'Blimey,' she said, grimacing.

'Oh dear, sorry,' Pat said. Greta could see she was mortified. She had seen Pat's household in quite a different light this afternoon, and afterwards she tramped through the snow as glad to get out of there as she had been to escape her own house. All this time she'd envied Pat her home, seeing it as calm and loving and everything hers was not. And she liked Mrs Floyd. But this time, seeing how it was when Mr Floyd was there, the way Pat and her Mom were so nervous with him, had opened her eyes. They seemed almost afraid of him. Things were nothing like as ideal as she had thought.

Then that night, when she got home, she'd found Marleen up in the darkened bedroom, howling her eyes out. For a moment she had been afraid to go near her, but the crying sounded so heartbroken that she groped her way to sit on the creaky folding bed and said timidly,

'What's up, sis?'

There was a silence for a moment, followed by sniffles, then, in a high baby voice, Marleen wailed,

'I thought he loved me. He told me he loved me!'

'Who?' Greta said.

'Brett . . . He said he loved me and he'd be with me for ever!'

Her face appeared, mascara smudged, over the bed-clothes. 'I just wanted someone to love me – to be mine!'

Greta was touched by the sight of her at that moment. With her hair hanging loose and her tear-smudged cheeks she looked about ten years old.

'What happened, sis?'

Marleen lay back on the pillow in the dim light from the landing and it came pouring out. She had met Brett Stewart when she was just seventeen and couldn't stand any more of the Sorensons. They were too good and sweet, too kind and Christian, and anyway, they were not her grandparents, only Greta's, and she was jealous. She didn't say that exactly but Greta understood and remembered how it was.

Brett had a car. He was nineteen and they whisked off together, got married in a registry office and soon she was expecting Mary Lou. There followed a dismal tale of living in a broken-down trailer on the edge of town which belonged to Brett's uncle, of Brett's dis-appearances. He would go for a week or so, come and go unpredictably, expecting to sleep with Marleen and be fed whenever he turned up, until she was almost out of her mind with it. He brought money, though she didn't know how he obtained it. Mary Lou was born and she hoped that would make the difference, but things only got worse. She couldn't get shot of Brett because she needed the money and she clung to the hope that he would come back and love her again the way he had at the beginning. Finally he didn't come home at all and she heard he'd been arrested. He and two other boys had robbed a house. One had a gun. Brett was given four years in the State Penitentiary. Only as she picked herself up and went to the Sorensons to beg the money to come home – Greta's heart sank to her toes as she heard this – did Marleen realize she was carrying another baby by Brett.

'So you see – what else was I s'pose to do?' Marleen's chin jutted as she said this. 'I had to get home.'

Swallowing her fury with Marleen for bringing yet more shame and sorrow to her grandparents, Greta managed to say, 'Well, whatever's past is past. It's nice to have you home, sis.'

At that moment, seeing Marleen soft and vulnerable, she had meant it.

She soaped her arms and legs, breasts and stomach, and lay back again. It was so quiet, felt very late. Condensation was running down the windows. In those moments, she felt strong. She could look at Pat's family and see that not all was as contented as Pat tried to make out. And as for Marleen, God knows she could hardly do worse than that! She thought about Dennis with a surge of excitement. She'd seen him in the week, thanking him for his gift, and he'd been sweet and said he was ever so pleased with the book and was reading it already. She told him about the book the man in the shop had given her and that she was reading it and he looked impressed. She couldn't wait to see him again. He felt like something hopeful and positive in her life, someone she could learn from, who could get her out of the oppressive sense of chaos which was home. Her dreams took shape as the bath water developed cool edges along her body. She and Dennis would take off together and travel. They'd set off with no destination, on the open road, to see the world. They would get away from these suffocating rooms, these families and babies and all the things that tied you down. They'd be free!

Chapter Twelve

As soon as the New Year celebrations were over, Trevor was on at Greta to go out on the promised date. He came round to the house, huddled up in an old black gabardine, hands pushed down into the pockets.

''Llo, Mrs Gilpin,' he said to Ruby. ''Llo Marleen. Nice babby you got.' He seemed drawn to Mary Lou, and winked at her.

Marleen, whose moment of softness at Christmas had soon passed, said hello with a look of amusement, as if to say, you must be desperate, going out with *him*. That was the trouble, Greta thought. They'd all known Trevor too long.

'D'you wanna come to the flicks then, Gret?' he said at last.

'Yeah, all right.' She folded her arms, in defiance against Marleen's mocking expression. 'When?'

Trevor shoved his hands further into his pockets. 'What about tonight?'

'All right, then.' She was going out with Dennis the next night. She'd better get Trevor over with, now she'd promised.

Trevor seemed so overcome that she'd agreed that he was lost for words.

'I'll come down at seven, all right?' she said.

'Your Mom and Dad all right are they?' Ruby said, struggling to put up the ironing board.

'Yes, ta – here, let me do it.' Trevor yanked the wooden-framed board into place with surprising competence, then said, cheerily, 'Tara then. See you tonight, Gret!'

'Ooooh, wish I was coming with you,' Marleen said sarcastically.

'You shut it,' Greta snapped. *You'll be lucky to go out with anyone now*, she felt like saying, but buttoned her lip.

'He's a nice lad, that Trev,' Ruby said. 'You could do a lot worse.'

'He's a prat, that's what he is,' Marleen said poisonously.

Greta felt as if she was going to explode if she stayed in the room. It was so crowded, what with the clothes horse and ironing board, the furniture that was too big for the room and the old pushchair one of the neighbours had passed on for Mary Lou and other baby stuff, that you could hardly get across it. And Mom and Marleen seemed to take up all the space anyway. It was too cold to go out, and all she could do was take herself off upstairs and sit on the bed, fists clenched.

'Snow's still 'ere then,' Trev said as they struggled towards the picture house through the freezing fog, the mucky whiteness under their feet jaundiced under the street lamps.

Trev had always had a way of stating the obvious, but Greta knew what he meant – it had gone on a bit. Now Christmas and the New Year were over it felt like time for a thaw, but if anything there were even harder frosts at night, and even in the day it felt as if everything had frozen solid.

'I get fed up with slithering and sliding about,' she said. 'Makes getting to work take twice as long. It's all right for you.'

'Yeah.' Trev grinned. 'I s'pose.' He only had to walk a few houses distance down the road to Mr Marshall's barbershop.

'I brought you these,' she said as they settled in the red plush seats, handing him a bag of misshapen chocolates. 'Caramel squares – or not so squares.'

'Oh!' Trevor looked stricken, 'I haven't got anything for you.'

'Good,' Greta said. 'You gave me that nice record. You eat 'em up, Trev. I don't want any.'

'Oh, Gret . . .' Trevor turned in the gloomy cinema and gave her a look of such melting adoration that she was quite thrown by it. A funny feeling came about in the pit of her stomach and she had to pull herself together. She had already decided she wasn't going to let him hold her hand or any of that carry-on, not when she was going out with Dennis the night after. She was Dennis's girl and this was just a friendly trip to the flicks – she was being kind to him, wasn't she?

They were showing *A Kind of Loving*, and once the lights had gone down, Trevor sat happily munching chocolates. He didn't try to hold her hand and Greta found she had almost forgotten he was there. In the cosy, smoky darkness she got drawn right into the story. It took hold of her, the doomed love affair between Vic and Ingrid, the way everyone seemed to have a say in their lives except them – especially when Ingrid got pregnant. Sometimes she felt she was right in the picture and she wanted to stand up and give some of the old gossips a piece of her mind!

When the lights went on at the end she was so full of it, she burst out before they had even stood up.

'I never want to have babies. It's a trap – it spoils everything!'

Trevor looked at her, startled.

'But Gret . . .'

'But nothing!' she stormed at him. 'I want to be able to decide things on my own – to have some life. Not get saddled with babbies and washing and nappies all the time! Look at Marleen – she's got Mary Lou and another on the way . . . She's not even twenty . . . It's horrible. There're more things to do, there must be!'

'Yeah – yeah, there must.' Trevor nodded vigorously. 'That's right, Gret. I mean . . .' He couldn't seem to think what he meant, but she was at least gratified that he seemed to agree with her. It calmed her down a bit. Then he had to go and spoil it by saying, 'So Marleen's expecting again? That's nice really, ain't it – babbies, family and that. 'S what life's for, ain't it?'

'Huh!' Greta looked down mutinously at her feet. Not if she could help it, it wasn't! 'It'd help if she was married at least, don't you think?'

The rest of the audience were all on the way out and it was quiet and warm and fuggy.

'You're so fiery, ain't you?' Trevor said, fondly. 'You make me think, you do, Gret. You never was anything like Marleen.'

This softened her and she smiled fondly at him.

'You're the most lovely girl I know,' he went on, with sweet seriousness. 'I wish—' His face twitched for a second. 'I mean – I want you to be my girl.'

'Oh, Trev—' She laughed a little. He was sweet and

92

kind and she could let off steam with Trev. He knew everything there was to know about her family, there was no use hiding anything. But as for being his girl – well, it seemed daft. He wasn't Dennis, was he? Being with Trevor was like wearing a warm old cardigan that she'd had for years when Dennis was like a new fur coat. There was no comparing the two!

'Gret –' Trevor looked at her very seriously. It was quiet round them now. 'It was lovely dancing with you . . . It was the best thing . . . Can I kiss yer?'

She wanted to say no, Trev, we can't get into that! But he was already leaning towards her. He wrapped his arms round her and in a second he was kissing her, his lips full and wet and tasting of chocolate. The way he kissed was awkward and sweet and for a second she froze, before giving in and kissing him back. What was the harm anyway? Lots of lads had kissed her and she knew they didn't care! It felt nice and reassuring.

He drew back and looked at her for a moment, deep in her eyes, then rested his forehead against hers so that their noses touched. She felt as if he was a little boy.

'I do love you, Greta. I really love you.'

She pulled her head back sharply. Now this had gone too far: she had led him on, he was getting all serious! She had to get out of this. Giving him a cheerful smile, but with no special meaning in it, she said,

'That's nice, Trev.' She squeezed his hand for a second then got up. 'We'd better get going eh, before they lock us in!'

*

93

'So who's this other bloke you're going out with?' Marleen demanded the next evening. She had still been lying queasily in bed when Greta left for work. Now she was huddled up in an old woolly of Ruby's, her hair looking lank, as if neither brush nor comb had been near it all day. Feeling ill and fed up only made her more spiteful.

'Just someone,' Greta said, standing by the fire still in her coat, to try and thaw out her hands and feet. Everything outside was painful to touch: door handles, iron gates, the icicles hanging from gutters and railings. It all burned the hands and seeped its cold into the body.

'Well who?'

'What the hell's it got to do with you?' Greta flared.

'I'm your sister, that's what.'

'What – all of a sudden? Funny kind of sister you've been all this time.'

Greta flounced off. Why should she tell Marleen anything? She'd only throw it back in her face. She knew Herbert would be round that night, as he was more and more these days, and she was going to get out of there as fast as she could. Marleen could get stuffed.

She bolted down the sausages Ruby had done for tea.

'What's the flaming hurry?' Ruby asked.

'I'm going out,' she said, scraping up the last of the mash and gravy.

'Who with this time?'

'Dennis – Franklin.'

'She wouldn't bloody tell me,' Marleen complained.

'Oh, him again. What's the carry-on with Trevor then?'

'Nothing.' Greta got up and put her plate in the sink. 'That was just a bit of fun. T'ra – see you later.'

Marleen's moaning followed her out. 'That's right – just go and leave us the washing up!'

Dennis had said he'd call for her and she wanted to get out before he arrived. She didn't want him anywhere near Marleen. A sister with two kids born out of wedlock didn't seem to fit into Dennis's sunny ideas about family. So she hurried out into the street to see him just coming up Charlotte Road. He raised his hand and beamed in greeting.

'Thought I'd save you the trouble of calling,' she said, struggling towards him. It was hard to walk on the ice.

'It's no trouble – it'd be nice to see your family.'

'Ah well – another time, maybe?' she said. 'They're still having tea.'

'I wondered if you'd fancy a drink?' Dennis said. 'We could just go down to one of the pubs over the bridge.' There were no pubs in Bournville of course – they had to stay in Selly Oak or go to Stirchley if they wanted a drink.

'That'd be nice.' She smiled.

A lot of other people seemed to have had the same idea, and the pub was crowded. Greta asked for a lemonade shandy and she and Dennis managed to squeeze close together on to a bench in one corner. It felt cosy, even though they had to speak up to make themselves heard over the piano and all the other talk and laughter. There was a rowdy game of pool going on nearby as well. Greta took her hat off and laid it in her lap, patting her hair. She tried to put on the calm, intelligent demeanour she thought Dennis required.

'It's ever so nice to see you,' Dennis said, smiling at

her in that way which made her quite giddy. 'I've missed you, Greta – only we've had such a lot going on.'

'So you had a nice Christmas, then?'

Dennis beamed. 'Oh, it was lovely! Maggie, my sister's, had a baby boy and they've called him Mark – he's such a great little lad. They're astonishing, babies are! You should have seen Mom's face! He was the centre of attention all the time of course. Even while we were eating dinner and having games and all the usual sort of thing. We have all sorts of things we do at Christmas – rituals you'd call them, I s'pose. There's a meal on Christmas Eve and we gather the presents together all round the tree. And when we all get up in the morning we always have boiled eggs. Nothing fancy – just things we always do.' He took a sip of his pint. 'It makes you realize – there's nothing like family life, is there?'

'No – no, there certainly isn't,' Greta said, her heart sinking. 'Only mine isn't a big close one like yours.'

'We're very lucky – but we can't all be the same,' he said, turning to her. 'Look, I'd like you to come home, soon – meet everyone. Or at least the ones who are around. Maggie and Don live in Wolverhampton now of course. He works on the *Express and Star*.'

'I'd like that,' Greta said, feeling excited. If Dennis thought she was good enough to meet his wonderful family, then things must be going all right.

'We'll sort it out then. You can come round for tea or something, at the weekend. It's very important to me – and so are you.'

They sat chatting about the book she had given him and how he'd enjoyed it. She told Dennis a bit about

Bonjour Tristesse and he said he'd like to borrow it when she'd finished.

'We'll have to go and have a browse in that shop together,' he said. 'He's a great bloke, the one who runs it.'

'Yes, he seemed very nice,' Greta said. She suddenly felt Edie's words wash through her, the feeling that she had wasted her opportunities at Cadbury's, that there were so many more things she could be doing. Dennis seemed to be in so many clubs: the film club, cricket and football, and he even went to German classes on Mondays.

'I went on one of the trips,' he told her. 'When I was sixteen. We went walking in the Austrian Alps and it was absolutely marvellous. I'd never heard German spoken before and everyone seems to hate Germans anyway, but the Austrians were ever so kind and hospitable to us. I've been learning for a few years now.'

'Oh,' Greta said, shrinking inside. Cadbury's offered trips to everyone of course, but somehow she never seemed to have taken these opportunities. Whereas Dennis just took life head on and did things with straightforward enthusiasm. Somehow, for herself, things always seemed to be more twisted round. Why did she not want to do more things to improve herself? She knew there was a competition at the factory – Cadbury Girl of the Year. When she'd heard she'd felt a bitter pang of envy knowing that she couldn't enter herself. What did she have to offer? Nothing.

'I don't do many club things,' she admitted. 'But I think it's time I took up some more.'

'Good idea,' Dennis said. 'It's marvellous, I think,

all the things we can do. I wouldn't miss it for the world. Some people even go on to the university.'

This seemed so completely over the horizon to Greta in terms of ambition that she could think of nothing to say.

'It's so nice talking to you,' Dennis said suddenly. 'I always feel that you really understand what I'm saying.'

Greta blushed. Suddenly she was filled with a longing she couldn't explain. 'Do you?'

'Yes. You're sweet – lovely.'

Everyone seemed to keep telling her she was lovely, but she didn't feel it.

They walked home very slowly in the icy darkness and Dennis took her arm on the slippery pavement and walked her all the way to the front door.

'D'you want to come in?' she felt compelled to ask, praying that he would say no. Herbert Smail was there no doubt, and she could hardly bear the thought of Dennis seeing him. She breathed out with relief when he said, 'Better not. Another time when it's not so late.'

For a moment he stood, just looking at her, then put his hands on her shoulders. She thought he was going to take her in his arms and kiss her as she was dying for him to, but he didn't.

'God, you're lovely.' He looked solemnly into her eyes, and what he said next brought her to tears. 'And you don't think well enough of yourself, Greta.'

She could not speak.

'Goodnight, love. See you very soon.' And he kissed her cheek, and then he was gone into the dark street, leaving her aching for more.

Chapter Thirteen

Everyone kept harking back to the winter of '47. The sea was frozen, it said on the telly, and the Thames. Every day the roads had to be cleared and Greta met snowploughs as she struggled along Bournville Lane in the mornings.

'D'you know,' Pat said one day when they were on their break, 'Mom said she saw a bird in the garden this morning. It was sitting on the washing line, very still, and then it fell off, just like that – dead! She's been putting food out in our garden – crumbs and nuts and stuff. She says it's the only way they'll stay alive.'

'Well, it's not working very well, is it?' Greta joked.

'Anyway—' Pat said. 'How's Dennis?'

'All right. I'm going for tea to meet his Mom on Sunday,' Greta said, realizing as she said it how nervous she was. Carelessly, she added, 'And I'm off to the pictures with Trevor tonight.'

Pat's eyes widened. 'What – again?'

'Well, yeah.' Greta rather enjoyed Pat's look of shock. 'He wants me to go with him, so . . .'

'But you're going out with Dennis aren't you?'

'Yes, but . . .'

'Well you can't just string poor old Trev along, Greta! You're such a flirt – it's not right.'

'I'm not! I'm just . . .'

'Yes you are! If it was just for a laugh it'd be

different, but he's ever so keen on you, you know that.'

'Well I know, but . . .'

'It's not very kind, is it?' Pat had a way of holding her hands, primly, one clasped over the other, which irritated Greta, and she did it then.

'What the hell do you know about it?' Greta's temper flared as she knew she was in the wrong. She got up, scraping her chair back. 'You're not exactly an expert are you?'

They couldn't discuss Pat's love life because she didn't have one. Even if anyone offered she felt she couldn't leave her Mom to look after Josie on her own. Greta was sorry for her, but sometimes Pat's goody-goody ways got on her nerves.

She went angrily back to work, slamming the bars of chocolate so hard off the belt that she dropped several on the floor and was told off. She was seething. Who was Pat to tell her what to do? Pat didn't have a clue what it was like living in Charlotte Road! She needed Trevor as an excuse to get out, when the house was full of Marleen, as well as her Mom's carry-on with Herbert Smail, who seemed to be there most of the flaming time now. He kept staying over, and the next thing, Greta saw, would be wedding bells and him moving in. All her life she'd been at the mercy of Mom and her blasted men!

But deep down she was ashamed because she knew she *was* playing with Trevor. She liked the sense of power she had over him because he wanted her. It was very gratifying when blokes wanted her – and plenty of them did. But she knew Pat was right, and that made her anger burn even more fiercely as it was a hard truth to swallow. She'd have to tell Trevor the truth – that she was really not his girl, but Dennis Franklin's.

By Sunday afternoon she was desperate to get out and go to Dennis's. Herbert was asleep by the fire, mouth hanging open and apparently oblivious to Mary Lou's grizzling and Marleen's snappish outbursts to her.

If the weather doesn't change soon we're all going to go mad, Greta thought, slipping and sliding round the back of the hospital towards where Dennis's family lived, in one of the big houses on the hill. They were all so cooped up she felt as if she was going to explode half the time.

She was shaky with nerves. She had to make a good impression on Dennis's family, make them like her! Dennis was like a door opening, her chance for a way out, for a better life. She wasn't clear exactly what it was she wanted, only that she ached for things to be better. Of course, she had to try harder with Dennis than she did with Trev – it didn't all come quite naturally. But Trev – he was just like her . . . All she'd get with him was more of the same.

But Trevor's face when she'd told him on Friday that she wasn't going to go with him wouldn't leave her. She'd braced herself and gone down to the Biddles' house. A delighted grin had spread across his face when he saw her standing at the front door. A thin beam of late afternoon light shone on them along the street. She had to brace herself.

'Trev – I've just come to tell you I can't go out tonight,' she said, once he'd shut the door behind him. Trev's smile was already fading and she killed it dead with, 'Or any night. Thing is Trev – I've got to tell you. I'm going out with Dennis Franklin from the Fitting Shop. So I can't go out with you as well . . .'

Trevor suddenly looked about six years old again, with his slicked-back hair and crestfallen expression. For a moment she thought he was going to cry.

'Oh,' he said, rubbing at his hair so it stood up in spikes. Just for a moment Greta wanted to put her arms round him.

Then he looked at her solemnly, not like a little boy now and said, 'Thing is Gret – I'd've married yer. I would. I'd've been good and kind to yer – but I s'pose I'm not good enough, am I?'

Greta felt terrible. She realized that up until then she'd never really taken Trevor seriously. He'd been a bit of a joke, the snotty-nosed kid who was no good at football.

'No – it's not like that . . .' She trailed off, knowing it *was* like that, that was just the trouble. 'I'm sorry, Trev,' she said gently. 'I really am.'

He'd heaved a big sigh which pulled his shoulders up to his ears, and just said, 'Oh well. I thought it was too good to be true.'

Thinking about it now as she went to Dennis's, she felt very ashamed that she'd led him on.

The Franklins' house was high and gabled, with well ordered flower-beds at the front, the rose bushes laden with snow. Dark, shiny windows stared down at her and she felt she was being watched. In the front door was a window edged with glass flowers and fruits, and the front steps had been carefully scraped and swept clear of snow. Altogether it felt very posh and intimidating. She pulled her shoulders back. Dennis had obviously been waiting for her.

'Hello!' he said, beaming as ever. He was wearing

brown corduroy trousers and a thick dark green jumper. 'Just on time – and that's no mean feat in this weather! Come on in and meet the gang!'

In the hall, on the plush crimson carpet, he pecked her on the cheek.

'Is that your visitor, Dennis?' she heard a voice call from the front room. 'Bring her through!'

'Coming, Mom – I'm just taking her coat!'

'She's here then?' A man's voice came from the back of the house somewhere.

A further woman's voice joined in from upstairs.

'Who's that? Is that that friend of yours Den?'

Blimey, Greta thought, overwhelmed. Was it always like this?

A woman appeared then out of the front room, very small in stature, with her blonde hair swept off her face. It was immaculately pinned back, just as the pleats in her skirt hung perfectly straight and true. She was delicate-featured and fair, with freckly, fragile-looking skin, and she didn't look at all like Dennis. But in seconds, Greta saw that beneath the tissue-frail appearance was a personality of steel. Greta found herself examined by a sharp, blue-eyed gaze. Something about Mrs Franklin made her shrink inside.

'Mom – this is Greta,' Dennis announced proudly.

Greta smiled shyly. 'Hello, Mrs Franklin.'

To her surprise Dennis's Mom put her hand out and Greta responded. As they shook hands, Mrs Franklin smiled, but Greta could feel a shrewd appraisal going on.

'It's nice to meet, you Greta.' She had a soft, well-spoken voice, and Greta realized she was not from Birmingham, but somewhere further north. 'Dennis has told us a lot about you.'

'Oh,' she said stupidly. 'Has he?'

'Oh yes,' Mrs Franklin assured her. 'He talks to us, our Dennis does – about everything he's doing. You're a pretty lass, aren't you? What lovely hair.'

'Hullo there,' a voice said before Greta could reply, and she found herself shaking hands again, with Dennis's Dad, a bulky man who did look very like Dennis, with the same wide mouth and cheerful eyes, and a brisk, businessman's manner. Greta realized then that she recognized him from Cadbury's.

And then from upstairs came a young woman who Greta knew was older than Dennis, but she was very small and fair like her mother, except her blonde hair was cut in a short bob which made her look very neat and crisp. She had her mother's sharp stare.

Dennis said, 'Greta, this is my sister Lorna.'

Lorna gave her a long appraising look, said hello and disappeared upstairs again.

Greta was starting to wonder whether they were ever going to get out of the hall when Mr Franklin said, 'Come on now – move through,' an order more than an invitation.

'Yes, do come through to the back,' Mrs Franklin said. 'We've got tea ready.'

'D'you notice anything about this house?' Mr Franklin asked as they took their seats.

Greta fumbled for an answer. *It's big and posher than any house I've ever been in before and you've got thick carpets and you've obviously got lots of money* was what sprang to mind.

'It's very nice and warm,' she chose to say.

'Yes! Yes indeed!' Mr Franklin slapped his knees. She'd lit on the right answer by fluke. 'And d'you know why that is?'

The huge, hissing gas fire under the chimney breast seemed too obvious an answer. Greta shook her head.

Mr Franklin leaned forward, triumphant. '*Central heating.* Throughout. If you look around you'll see radiators in every room. You can't beat it.' He sat back as if able to relax having imparted a vital piece of information.

'Oh,' Greta said. 'That's nice.'

'It's more than nice, young woman. It's the future.'

Greta was taking in the lavishly decorated room with its red carpet and wallpaper with clusters of red flowers. The room was stifling hot and exceptionally tidy. The furniture all looked new and there was a table to one side with a great spread of sandwiches and cakes. On the mantel was a brass clock which ticked very loudly, the gas fire hissed powerfully, and in front of it was spread a white, very fluffy rug. Soon after she had sat down, Greta was startled when the rug began to move and she found a yellow-eyed face looking at her and realized there was a huge, fluffy cat lying on the rug!

'That's Fifi,' Dennis said, laughing at her surprise.

A few moments later the white cat separated itself from the rug and came towards her, sniffing her. Then it leapt up on to her lap.

'Aah!' Mrs Franklin said, enthusiastically. 'She's taken a liking to you, Greta. Well aren't you lucky?'

'Oh, yes, isn't she?' Mr Franklin said, and Dennis laughed. They were all staring at her.

Greta blushed, looking down at the cat, which turned itself around on her lap a few times, stuck its claws in her leg and finally settled with the apparent intention of going back to sleep.

'Well, you are privileged!' Mrs Franklin remarked. 'She hardly ever favours anyone like that!'

Greta smiled and stroked the furry body. It felt nice but she wasn't really used to cats. She felt very much on her best behaviour and very scared of saying the wrong thing. As she'd wrapped up well to come out she was also beginning to feel very hot, and she wished desperately that she could fade into the corner and they'd all stop paying her any attention.

'Don't mind her,' Dennis said. 'She'll just sleep.'

'Now, Greta, would you eat some pikelets?' Mrs Franklin asked.

Seeing her hesitate, Dennis said, 'They're a bit like crumpets.'

'Yes, I know,' Greta said. 'Yes please.'

Mrs Franklin handed out little flower-edged plates She seemed to be full of wiry, restless energy and kept getting up and down and offering more food – cups of tea with little silver tongs to pick up the sugar lumps, buttered pikelets, bread and butter, little iced cakes and fruit cake . . . Each time she offered a plateful to Greta, she said, 'You will have one of these, won't you?' and Greta only felt she could say no once she was so full she couldn't face any more.

'So tell us all about yourself, Greta,' Mrs Franklin said when they were still on their first pikelet. She leaned forward in her chair, with keen attention.

Greta swallowed. 'Well, I work at Cadbury's,' she said, barely above a whisper.

'You'll have to speak up, wench,' Mr Franklin said, a hand behind one ear. 'My hearing's not what it used to be.'

'Your mother works there too, doesn't she?' Mrs Franklin continued her interrogation.

'Yes,' Greta agreed. She was starting to feel a slight itching in the corners of her eyes and put her plate down to try and rub them without smudging her makeup.

'I'm in my twenty-fifth year with the company,' Mr Franklin said proudly. 'I joined in '37, when I'd done my apprenticeship in machine tools, and I was there all through the war when it was made over to Bournville Utilities for the war effort. Course, that's when I met Rita . . .'

'I came down during the war of course – from Burnley . . .'

Mr Franklin took up again. Greta looked from one to the other as if they were a double act. 'I said to Dennis as he was growing up, Dennis, you want to get an apprenticeship at Cadbury's – it'll set you up for life. Michael should've done the same of course – he's our older boy, but he wanted to go into the motor trade. Still, he's done well for himself . . .'

'Oh, he has that . . .' Mrs Franklin chimed in.

'And I've had my finger in a few other pies as well. You have to learn how to invest wisely, that's what I tell our Dennis . . .'

Greta soon realized that she was not going to have to tell them anything more about herself because the Franklins were quite capable of talking for the whole of teatime about their family: Michael and his wife and two children, and Dennis's sisters, Angela, the eldest of the family, and her three, Maggie and the new baby, about Lorna, the frosty young woman upstairs who was training to be a nurse. Dennis sat smiling at this catalogue of successes, and Greta listened politely, eating and feeling inadequate and all the while feeling the itchiness in her eyes grow worse and worse. She was finding it difficult to concentrate. More than anything she wanted to rub furiously at her eyes.

She dragged her attention back to Mr Franklin, who was now telling her about the caravan they kept parked out beyond Redditch.

'Nothing like it, getting into the country of a weekend – out in the fresh air, good long walks and no one else to please. We all go down when we can, Lorna, all of us – in the fairer weather of course. Marvellous.' Mr Franklin sipped his tea.

'Yes, that must be nice,' Greta said, desperately blinking to try and clear her agonized eyes. She looked at Dennis, hoping he would notice she was in trouble, but he was watching his father, eyes shining with pride. For a moment he glanced at her and smiled, as if to say, see, I told you my family is special.

'You'll have to come out with us one weekend,' Mrs Franklin said. Once more, this was an order more than an invitation. 'We know how to show people a good time. You'd love it.'

'That'd be nice,' Greta said politely, half repelled, half attracted by their absolute belief in themselves. 'I expect I would.'

Then, unable to stand the terrible itching any more, she put her plate down and rubbed at her eyes one by one, hoping desperately that she wasn't rubbing mascara and eye-liner all over the place. Mr Franklin was talking about the difficulties of towing caravans.

'What you don't want at any price is them fish-tailing,' he was saying.

Greta, with tears beginning to spill down her cheeks, shot a desperate look at Dennis, who at last paid her some attention.

'What's the matter, Greta?' He jumped up. Suddenly everyone was watching her. 'Has something upset you?'

'Gracious!' Mrs Franklin cried. 'Whatever's the matter?'

'Nothing – I'm not upset – it's just my eyes.' She was screwing them up, trying to ease the dreadful irritation. 'They've gone all itchy – I don't know why.'

'That'll be the cat,' Mrs Franklin said. 'Oh good heavens, I never thought! You should've said you were sensitive that way! None of us are, you see.' She made it sound like a weakness. 'Fifi, get off, you naughty girl! Now you come with me, love, and we'll bathe your eyes.'

She led Greta upstairs to a very smart, clean bathroom with blue lino on the floor and a woven white rug over it.

'Here – cotton wool. Let's get plenty of water on them to ease them. Oh dear – you should've said, love.'

'I didn't know,' Greta said, in immense relief at the feel of the water on her burning eyes. 'I don't have much to do with cats, you see.'

Mrs Franklin fussed round her and was kind and motherly and Greta warmed to her a little more, though she still found her intimidating. Dennis and his father fussed over her when she went downstairs. They even got Lorna to come and check if there was anything seriously wrong.

'She's a nurse, you see,' Mrs Franklin said proudly.

Lorna's piercing blue eyes stared into Greta's for a moment. 'No – she'll be all right,' she said. 'Have you washed your hands? Yes, well don't touch your eyes again.'

'I'm sorry to be such a nuisance,' Greta said, mortified.

'Not at all – now you sit down and I'll make another cup of tea,' Mrs Franklin said. 'You still poring over your books up there, Lorna? She's still at her books, Bill,' she informed her husband.

They fussed over her so much that Greta was amazed. She had never known a family who seemed to be so much all over each other. Everything anyone did had to be remarked on by everyone else and chewed over. But they did take care of her and that felt very nice.

When Dennis said he'd walk her home there was a great to do about getting home before it was dark and did she need to borrow any boots? At last they stepped out into the dusky afternoon.

Dennis turned to her, beaming. 'So – you've met my family. Marvellous, aren't they?'

Greta smiled, gratefully. At that moment they did seem rather marvellous, and things hadn't gone too badly despite her reaction to the cat. And she'd fixed on Dennis, she knew that now. He made her feel as if she'd been invited into a magic circle. 'Yes. They're very nice,' she said. Of course they were! 'Sorry about all the fuss.'

Dennis squeezed her hand. 'Don't you worry. You were in the best hands. Now – my turn to come to yours for tea next, eh?'

Chapter Fourteen

The freeze went on and on. In February, a thirty-six-hour blizzard hit the West Country, and villages and farms were cut off by gale-force winds and twenty-foot drifts. Sheep and cattle starved in the fields and barns. Later in the month, a massive snowfall hit the northwest of the country.

Birmingham, though more sheltered, was still buried deeply. The streets had to be ploughed or shovelled almost daily. Pipes burst, coal in the factory stores froze so hard that it had to be loosened with steam jets and hacked out by pickaxes. Though everyone got browned off with it all pretty quickly, there were compensations.

'Have you seen the Girls' Grounds?' Pat said one sunny morning, arriving at work rosy-cheeked and smiling broadly. 'It's just a wonderland – absolutely beautiful!'

Greta was glad to find any chance to get out of home, and there were socials still laid on at Rowheath, the Cadbury recreation grounds. In the evenings there was skating under floodlights and she and Dennis went sledging. She perched behind him on a sledge, her arms round his waist, and they both laughed and screamed, whizzing along and just managing not to fall off at the bottom. They stood in the freezing evening, amid crowds of people enjoying themselves and clouding the air with their breath.

'Shall we have some chestnuts?' Dennis said.

The chestnuts were roasted on coke braziers and they stood savouring their delicious singed taste, watching everyone enjoying themselves and tapping their feet to music from the loudspeakers and smelling the tantalizing whiff of hot dogs and fried onions from another stall. Dennis put his arm round her and Greta snuggled up to him. She felt proud that he was claiming her as his girl. She looked up at him and he smiled, and popped his last chestnut into her mouth.

'Warm enough?' he asked, protectively.

Greta nodded. 'Just about.'

'We don't want you getting cold. Shall we go soon?'

She nodded gratefully. It was a long time since she'd been able to feel her feet. Dennis was considerate like that, she thought. He took notice of things. Not like at home, where no one seemed to notice her at all.

On the bus, which crawled slowly along, Dennis kept his arm round her. They had been out and about together, a drink here, a visit to the pictures there. Dennis had liked the book she gave him, and one day when they were in a coffee bar, warming their hands round the cups, she'd talked about *Bonjour Tristesse*.

'It was sad,' she said. 'She was very close to her Dad and he was about to get married. She didn't like it – well, in a way she did like it, that was the sad thing, 'cause she liked the woman he was going to marry – but she just mucked it up for them . . .'

'Why?' Dennis frowned.

Greta thought about it. 'She was always pulled this way and that, inside herself, I mean – wanting one thing and doing another – as if she had to do the opposite of what was really going to make her happy.'

Dennis frowned. 'Seems pretty daft to me,' he said.

112

Greta watched his face. She knew he hadn't a clue what she was on about. She drained her cup and put it down.

'Maybe it's not your sort of book.' But she knew she'd understood it, even if he didn't. And it made her want to read more books.

The thing she couldn't work out was whether Dennis really fancied her or not. He said he did, but apart from kissing her hello and goodbye, he held off. It wasn't what Greta was used to. Other lads had always been pushy, forever wanting kisses, hands trying to find their way to places they shouldn't. Dennis is a gent, she told herself. But in a way she felt rejected and was confused by it. Didn't he want more? And if he did, why didn't he show it? Sometimes he felt almost like a brother. She didn't want to seem loose but she expected him to want her. She knew he was well brought up and thought he was too shy. Maybe he needed her to make the first move.

One night when they had been out for a drink together, sitting pressed close together in the warm pub, they came out into the icy street and Dennis put his arm round her, as usual.

'Can't have you slipping over, can we?'

Greta giggled. 'You don't want me turning into a fallen woman, you mean?'

'Steady on – that's not exactly what I meant,' Dennis said, though from his tone she could tell he had a twinkle in his eye and it encouraged her.

As they came up the hill and under the darkness of the railway bridge, she stopped him.

'Oh Dennis – I don't want to go home yet . . .'

'What's wrong with home?' he asked, teasingly. 'You don't seem very keen to invite me in.'

'I mean, I want to stay with you.'

She reached up and put her arms round his neck, drawing him towards her. 'Give us a kiss.'

She heard him give a faint chuckle in the darkness and he held her in his arms. 'There's an invitation,' he said. 'Oh, Gret – you're lovely, you are.'

He kissed her on the lips, enthusiastically but also politely. Greta remembered the urgency of Trevor's kiss. But Dennis was much more of a gent, she told herself. She gave a little moan of pleasure. She wanted Dennis to be fiery, to *want* her. She wasn't sure what she'd do about it then. She hadn't thought that far, but she wanted to make something happen.

As she and Dennis kissed, she pressed herself against him, and she could feel that he was aroused. It made her feel excited and powerful. He did want her!

'Ooh, Dennis,' she murmured, hardly thinking what she was saying. 'Let's go further ... Let's find somewhere to go ... I want to go all the way with you.'

The second she spoke she felt Dennis's arms slacken. He pulled back and there was a long, horrible silence. She couldn't see his face in the darkness.

'What's up?' she whispered eventually.

He let go of her completely then and spoke to her, gently but firmly. 'I'm shocked, frankly, Greta. I didn't have you down as that sort of girl. You know – fast, like that. I mean, we've got to get this straight. I don't hold with that sort of thing. My Mom and Dad, they courted for nearly six years before they got married. They were young, and they never ... Well, I mean, they waited. They did the decent thing. And that's what I intend to do. That's the proper way to do things, in my book.'

Her cheeks were blazing, if he could have seen, and she felt cheap and dirty and utterly mortified.

'I'm sorry, Dennis,' she said, tearfully. 'I just got a bit carried away.'

'Well, I know it happens,' he said stiffly. 'But let's not let it happen to us, all right love? You're worth more than that.'

This thought filled her chest with a bursting ache, and the tears spilled silently down her cheeks.

'Come on now,' Dennis said, as if he was a teacher and she a wayward six-year-old. 'We'll forget about it. You're a lovely girl, so let's not hear any more of that, all right? Let's get you home now.'

Her embarrassment stopped her tears and she wiped her cheeks in the dark. On the doorstep he gave her one of his polite kisses.

'Goodnight, love.'

'Goodnight, Dennis.' She wondered again why he had anything to do with her.

And then he said, 'Remember, you're lovely. You're a bright girl. You just need a bit of guidance.'

She watched him walk away again, tears in her eyes at being called lovely, yet wild with rage, like a child after a telling off.

Two weeks later she went up to her room at home, desperate to find a place she could be on her own. It was March now and the thaw had come at last. Icicles and snowmen which had hung around for weeks were finally seeping away. Lumps of ice lay stranded on bigger and bigger patches of emerging green. But at home there was no let-up in the stifling atmosphere.

She sat on the bed, in the small space between the cot and the folding bed. The room was full of a slightly sweaty-smelling clutter of Marleen's clothes, stockings draped over the chair, and baby things all over the bed. Through the floor jarred the sounds of Marleen snapping at Mary Lou as she had her tea. Marleen had stopped feeling sick now, but it hadn't eased her temper. It was worse if anything, now she had no sickness to distract her from her fury at the fact she was pregnant again. All she wanted now was to be out gadding and not tied down by babies.

On her lap Greta had a copy of the *Bournville Works Magazine* which she had brought secretively upstairs. It contained news and articles about the Cadbury factory and employees and she usually had a look through it, like everyone else. But today she had a special interest in it which she would have been very hesitant to admit to anyone.

Her fingers turned straight to the page. She already knew, of course, what would be there, but she had to see. It felt almost like a way of tormenting herself.

'"Girl of the Year" Final,' she read. 'Miss Hilda Hurlbutt, the winner.'

The competition was sponsored by Wallis Fashion Shops, and as part of the final there had been a fashion show. The prize included a trip to Paris and a set of new clothes and luggage.

Above the photographs of the contestants at various stages of the competition there was a photograph of Hilda Hurlbutt in a stylish suit, her dark hair swept back, smiling happily.

Greta stared at her. 'You cow,' she murmured. 'You lucky, lucky cow. I wish I was like you.' She thought about going on an aeroplane and about all the visits

116

Hilda had been promised: Paris, Versailles, visiting dress designers and perfumeries, being treated like a VIP. 'I'm going to Paris in May,' Greta murmured, in an affected voice. 'To the Louvre, and to visit a couturier, you know . . .'

'What the hell are *you* going on about?' Marleen demanded.

Greta was so jarred by her bursting in like that when she'd been in another world altogether that she jumped, her heart pounding. She slammed the magazine shut at once.

'What're you doing?' Marleen wanted to know, her eyes narrowing. She rushed at Greta and snatched the magazine off her, holding it above her head as Greta tried to pull it away from her again. 'Let me see!'

'No! Give it!' Greta exploded with rage. 'Give it me and mind your own cowing business!'

'It's only the stupid factory magazine,' Marleen said, looking at it in disgust. 'What're you making such a fuss about, you prat?'

'Nothing – just give it me!' If Marleen saw what she had been looking at she would have mocked even more.

Marleen threw the magazine down on the floor in contempt. 'Take it, you bloody nutcase. I only come up 'cause *he's* here again, the fat old git.'

In the pause, Greta heard Herbert's voice and rolled her eyes. For a rare moment, the sisters were allies.

'I'm off out,' Marleen said languidly. She rummaged among the litter of clothes for her cardi, then leaned close to the mirror on the dressing table, pulling her jaw downwards as she stroked mascara thickly on her lashes.

'Where?'

'I dunno. Anywhere.'

And she picked up her jacket and was gone downstairs. Ruby's raised voice followed her to the front door, before it slammed behind her.

Greta picked up the magazine and opened it again to read the rest of the article about Hilda Hurlbutt. She was sick with envy, but what chance did she ever have of winning anything like that? What did she ever do with her life? She'd done so well at the Continuation School, but now she never did anything, even when there were all these opportunities available that Dennis was always going on about, his language class on Monday, cricket and football. Even Pat played hockey every Saturday morning at Rowheath. But she'd let everything pass her by!

She gave a deep sigh, staring out through the window at the grey sky. Dennis must think she was pretty feeble, as well as a fast worker. The thought of what had happened under the bridge still made her feel queasy with shame, even though Dennis had said they should put it behind them. She must try and do more, be more interesting. She should join some of the Cadbury clubs, get out more – set her sights on something!

But at that moment everything felt useless. She lay back on the bed. It was no good even going downstairs in this house. She could hear Ruby and Herbert laughing together. Even through the floorboards she recognized the flirtatious tone her mother used with him, with men in general. No wonder she knew no other way to be, with a Mom like that!

Clamping her hands over her ears, she turned on her side, staring at the wallpaper. How could she get out? Eyes fixed on the faded rosebuds on the wall, she knew, in a sudden flash, that the only way out was to have a man of her own. And that man was Dennis. If it was marriage Dennis wanted, then that was what they must do. They could set up on their own, out of the clutches of her family and of Dennis's: nicc as they were to her, she found them overwhelming, interfering. She and Dennis would be free of them – they'd make a better life all on their own.

Chapter Fifteen

A couple of days later, Greta arrived home from work into the middle of yet another row. Marleen, dressed in clothes far too skimpy for the weather, apart from a pair of black patent boots, and made up to the nines, was trying to prise a screaming Mary Lou from round her legs.

'You can't just keep taking off and leaving her!' With a grunt Ruby squatted beside her granddaughter. 'Come to Nanna, Mary Lou – Nanna'll look after you, pet.'

Mary Lou just screamed all the more.

'I could hear the pair of you from outside,' Greta remarked, but no one took any notice.

'You're a disgrace!' Ruby shouted over the screams. 'You damn well stay in for a change, yer little minx!'

'You can't stop me going out!' Marleen hoiked her coat off the hook and put it on furiously. 'Anyway, what do you care? You've got yer fancy man round here all the time. Makes no difference to you if I'm here or not, does it?'

'Poor little bugger. She's your daughter!' Ruby managed to pick Mary Lou up.

'And your granddaughter . . . So you look after her for a bit!' Marleen fastened the last of her buttons. 'And don't you carry on at me as if you're better than me, with all the blokes you've had!'

'Don't you talk to me like that!' Ruby began but Marleen wasn't listening. And although Ruby shouted and carried on at Marleen, Greta could tell she didn't feel in control or know what to say because she felt guilty about all that had happened, especially them having to live with Carl Christie and all he'd put them through. It often felt as if Mom wasn't solid inside, and it wasn't a very nice feeling.

'Anyroad, I can't stop in,' Ruby changed tack, desperately. 'I've got to go out . . .'

Marleen already had the front door open.

'Well, tough tits – get *her* to stay in then. She never lifts a finger to help. I'm sick of it all. I'm off, and you can't stop me!'

The door slammed, shaking the house. Mary Lou buried her face in Ruby's shoulder and wailed all the more.

'What the hell am I going to do with her?' Ruby groaned. 'Gret – can you mind this one for a bit? Edie's had her babby – a little boy. I promised I'd go up the hospital to see them . . .'

'Oh, all right,' Greta said sulkily, thinking, more flaming babies!

'Anatoli's pleased as punch – he said they've called him Peter,' Ruby said, settling Mary Lou at the table with a rusk. 'I'm happy for her really – thank God it's not me, that's all.'

'Are you going to marry that Herbert?'

Ruby was standing at the cooker, heating milk, and for a second Greta saw a hunted look on her face. Then her expression hardened.

'That's my business.'

'How can you even go near him?' Greta persisted.

Ruby turned back briskly to the pan of milk and in

a hard voice she said, 'Beggars can't be choosers at my time of life.'

And Greta suddenly found she wanted to cry.

Marrying Dennis felt like her only way out. You had to have a man, otherwise you were a sad, dried-up spinster, and marrying was the only way she could see to leave. Dennis was a classy bloke, his family had money and he wanted her, didn't he? He was the answer to all her problems – except for one. In everyone else's eyes, it seemed, the whole point of marriage was children and family. And at the moment that was the last thing she wanted. The very thought filled her with panic.

'You can get these pills now . . .' She remembered a whispered canteen conversation. 'It's the woman who takes them and it stops you having to have a baby . . .'

The thought that she could be in control of whether or not she would have babies felt like a miracle. She could get married but it wouldn't all just be that endless round of babies and nappies and washing! She could do other things! She had no clear idea of what those things were, only that her whole being rebelled against everything she could see around her about being a woman and a mother. Marriage to Dennis would be a way out of home all right – but she would marry and be different. Look at the mess Marleen was in already! Anything was better than that.

On her dates with Dennis now, she tried to be what she thought was his ideal kind of woman. She dressed prettily but in a demure style and was careful never to be forward with him in any way. She talked about her family as warmly as she could and told him about Dr

Ferris and Janet, and Edie and Anatoli, talking about them almost as if they were relatives. Her fears about Dennis insisting on coming to her home soon faded. She always had some ready excuse when he asked: Mom wasn't well, there was no one in or they already had visitors. It wasn't hard to put him off. It soon became clear that Dennis was so wrapped up in his own family that he only had a passing interest in hers. She was always enthusiastic about the Franklin family, even though she found them very hard going.

Spring arrived, the verges in Bournville scattered with cheerful yellow, purple and white crocuses and clumps of daffodils, and Dennis's Mom and Dad started going out to their caravan again. Dennis invited Greta to come too.

The site was in the country near Redditch, a long, sloping field edged with trees and with a stream running through it. As the caravan needed a scrub out after the winter, Greta helped Sonia Franklin, Dennis's Mom, and his sister Lorna to give it a spring clean. Lorna was still not very friendly, but Dennis's Mom seemed grateful for her help. Sonia Franklin, Greta learned, was always nice as pie as long as you did everything the way she wanted. Underneath the warm exterior she was as hard as nails and completely dominated her family, whether they could see it or not. Dennis had not said much about his mother's life except once, when he let slip that she had come from a background of gruelling poverty and hardship. Whatever had happened to her, Greta could see it had left a rod of steel where her spine was, and chips of ice in her eyes.

On that sparkling spring afternoon, while Dennis and his Dad attended to things outside, the women scrubbed the ceiling and walls and the doors of the little cupboards and swept the place out. Mrs Franklin gave the orders, correcting the way Greta and Lorna were doing things. Greta had no choice but to do as she was told, so keen was she to please, but Lorna argued sometimes and there were flare-ups.

'Oh, Mom – just leave me alone!' Lorna would say, tossing her head so that her ponytail swung fiercely. 'I know how to do it. I'm not six years old any more you know!'

Then, from being hard and overbearing, Sonia Franklin could change in a second to being warm and sweet again. That afternoon, as she scrubbed the wall of the caravan, she reminisced about her sisters in Lancashire and their childhood. She obviously enjoyed an audience and, whatever the grim elements of her past were, she did not disclose them. She described how she had come south for an adventure and to look for work, and met Dennis's father.

'I'll never forget the first time I set eyes on Bill,' she said, pausing with the cloth in her hand. She had a blue scarf tied over her hair and looked quite starry-eyed, a soft smile on her face. 'I took one look at him – it was on the Green, in Bournville – and I knew he was the one. I must be one of the luckiest women in the world. I know it doesn't happen for everyone like that.'

And she gave a Greta a sudden, penetrating look with her blue eyes, as if to say, *Don't imagine you can match up to that for Dennis – oh no!*

But then she smiled. 'Oh – many years ago now, that was. When we were young and foolish.'

'Sounds lovely,' Greta said. And it did. But even though there were these softer intervals, or moments of laughter, she found it hard to warm to Sonia Franklin. She felt that deep down the woman didn't like her and looked down on her. She talked endlessly about her family, especially Dennis, the high hopes they had for him, about his learning German and all the cricket he played, and Greta felt she was saying: *You may think you've got your talons in my son, but he's far better than you.* She was the sort of person, if she'd met her, that Ruby would have said, 'Oh, all her geese are swans.' But Greta felt woefully inadequate. She *was* honoured that Dennis wanted to go out with her!

When they had finished washing the walls, Sonia asked Greta to wash the flowery curtains which she had taken down from the windows. Greta enjoyed squatting on the grass in her old pair of black slacks and her little pea-green blouse, a scarf tied over her hair, pounding the curtains in a big bucket of soapy water. As she was pegging them out on a line strung between the end of the caravan and a tree, she saw Dennis watching her, a smile of pleasure and approval on his face. Greta beamed back, genuinely enjoying herself. She was fitting in and it felt nice! At that moment she really began to believe she could be part of Dennis's family, even if she had to become what they wanted her to be.

After the work was done they all sat out on deck-chairs and drank tea and ate cherry Madeira cake, watching what other caravanners were up to on the field, reminiscing about other caravan holidays they'd had and how marvellous they'd been, and even Lorna became more talkative.

'It's nice out here, isn't it, Greta?' Dennis's Dad called across to her. 'Puts the colour in your cheeks all right! You must come again.'

'Oh yes,' Sonia decreed, though there was a hard edge to her voice. 'She must.'

She did go again, several times. And she began trying to improve herself. She applied for a ticket for the library in Selly Oak, and at Cadbury's she joined the Girls' Athletic and Social Club and went to some classes on cake decorating, which she found she was quite good at. She made sure she told Dennis and his mother all about it.

'That's a good idea,' Sonia Franklin said. 'Our Angela's a dab hand with decorating cakes. She's quite a girl. Makes quite a bit of money out of it too.'

Oh, she would, Greta thought.

'Blimey,' Pat said when she told her. 'You're getting a bit domesticated aren't you?'

Greta smiled mysteriously. She had not mentioned her plan even to Pat.

As the weeks passed, Greta worked hard at impressing Dennis. At home Marleen was growing bigger and bigger. The baby was due in June, and as the days grew warmer she became heavier and even more evil-tempered.

'I wish I could just get it over,' she snarled, sitting hunched on the folding bed in their room one evening. For a moment her face became scared and vulnerable. 'What am I going to do, Gret?'

'Well it's a bit late to ask that now,' Greta said. *You got yourself into it, so what do you expect?* she thought. But she tried to find something kind to say.

'I 'spect it'll be all right, Marl. And it'll be company for Mary Lou, won't it?'

It didn't stop Marleen going out and about either, bump on her belly or no, and there were constant battles over this with Ruby. Greta watched her swelling up with horror. She had to get away from here before the whole house was taken over with Marleen and babies and all the racket that went with them – not to mention Herbert Smail, who seemed almost to have moved in already.

Dennis still treated her very fondly but seemed in no hurry for anything to go any further, and Greta was getting frustrated. Now and then she brought up the subject of marriage.

'It must be so nice to be settled and that,' she might say. 'You know – married with your own home.'

'Oh yes,' Dennis agreed in his rather ponderous way. 'Nothing like it.' But he said nothing further.

Another time, she said, 'I don't think people should leave it until they're too old when they get married, do you, Dennis?'

'No – not if they're sure,' he said. 'Although courtship's a serious thing – look at my parents.'

Greta looked deeply into his eyes. They were sitting across a table in a coffee bar that afternoon. 'I'm sure, Dennis,' she said hopefully.

Dennis smiled and took her hand across the table. 'That's sweet,' he said, stroking the back of her hand. 'I'm a lucky man. But we mustn't rush.'

She almost said something then, but stopped herself. When she lay in bed that night, hemmed in by Marleen's bed and Mary Lou's cot, she felt overwhelmed with longing and frustration. What was holding Dennis back? He said he wanted to be with her, so why didn't he say something? What was the point of waiting if they'd both made up their minds? How long was she going to have to hang on until Dennis popped the question?

Then a thought came to her which made her heart pound with excitement. Did it always have to be the man who proposed? It might seem very forward, but why could she not say something – perhaps help him along?

She lay rehearsing lines in her head. 'Dennis – I'd like to ask you to marry me . . .'

Chapter Sixteen

A couple of nights later, she was woken by a piercing yowl of pain. She leapt out of bed, heart racing.

'Marleen?'

'It's the babby – it's coming!'

'Are you sure?'

'Course I'm sure!' Marleen gasped. 'Get Mom!'

This was not right – it was only the beginning of June and it wasn't due to arrive yet. Surely she wasn't going to have it here!

'Aren't you going to have it in the hospital?'

'I don't bloody know – just get our Mom!' Marleen roared at her.

Ruby took one look at Marleen writhing on the bed and said, 'Gret – go down the phone box and call an ambulance. Quick!'

Greta ran outside, a jumper thrown over her nightie, up to the telephone box at the top of the road. Please, she thought, don't let it be too late. She wanted Marleen's baby to be born away from there, somewhere where she didn't have to see or know much about it.

'I hope they flaming well hurry,' Ruby said, throwing a few things into a bag for Marleen. 'I don't want a repeat of the night you were born. I'm not up to that, not like Frances was.'

Ruby had given birth to Greta at Frances Hatton's

house during the blackout, but at least Frances had once worked as a midwife.

The ambulance soon drew up outside and Marleen was taken away, moaning with pain, to Selly Oak Hospital. Ruby went with her. Mary Lou had miraculously slept through the whole thing. Greta dozed, her nerves jangled, and was eventually woken by the sound of the front door closing. Getting up, she found Ruby downstairs, eyes ringed with tiredness but a soft look on her face.

'It's over,' she said. 'Quite quick really. She's had a little lad. Says she's going to call him Elvis. Make us a cup of tea, love, will yer?'

While Ruby sank on to the kitchen chair, Greta put the kettle on and digested the news.

'She all right?' she asked.

Ruby nodded proudly. 'She's not one who has it too hard – she's a natural.' She was twisting her wedding ring round her finger. Greta realized she wasn't even sure which man had given it to her. 'We'll have our work cut out here though.'

They were in Bournville Park when she asked him, the next day. It was a beautiful early summer evening, May blossom in flower and the leaves a fresh, exuberant green. It was a Thursday and they'd finished work, so they were snatching a bit of time together before going home, walking along the little stream which ran the length of the park.

She'd told Dennis that her sister had just had a baby.

'Wednesday's child is full of woe,' Dennis said, squeezing her hand. 'Well, let's hope that's not true. A boy eh – I bet her husband's pleased?'

'Oh yes,' Greta said vaguely. 'And I'll go in and see her a bit later tonight.' The more she got to know Dennis the more she had realized how horrified he would be if he knew the true details of her family. There was time for that later, she thought, when they'd got settled and it wouldn't matter.

They wandered along, hand in hand, talking about this and that. Greta knew she was going to push things forward today. She couldn't resist. She was in too much suspense. Marleen would be out of hospital and she needed to know she had a means of escape.

Dennis was talking about some of his mates at work, telling her jokes and what had happened in one of the departments that morning. She hardly heard what he was saying, she was so distracted by trying to think how to steer the conversation her way.

'Dennis!' Playfully she faced him and put her arms round his neck.

'That's my girl,' he said, smiling. 'Ooh you are lovely.'

'Am I your girl?' she asked, suddenly serious.

'Course you are.' He was still speaking lightly. 'What d'you mean?'

'Well—' She put her head on one side. It was now or never. 'It's just that sometimes I wonder – if I really am your girl, you see.' She could see she had his attention now, so she just kept talking. 'I mean, if we're really serious – if I'm your girl and you're, well, you're my man, sort of thing – then why don't we make it legal? I'm asking . . . I mean, I think . . . Would you marry me, Dennis?'

For a moment he looked stunned, and then Greta saw him recoil. He stepped back so that she had to release him, a look of absolute disgust on his face.

'That's . . . Oh God . . .' He was almost speechless. 'What on *earth* d'you think you're doing? You can't . . . I mean, you don't propose to me! We spend time courting . . . Years if necessary. Do it properly! That's not how things are done at all! I can't believe you'd behave like this . . .'

'But Dennis—' Greta felt sick at the look on his face. 'I'm sorry, but I . . .'

'I can't possibly marry someone who thinks like that . . . I mean, I've had some doubts – your family don't seem to be very close, to offer much. But I thought mine could make up for that. They're very strong and they have a way of taking in waifs and strays and keeping them on the right track . . .'

'Waifs and strays?' Greta's temper erupted. All the things that had irritated her about Dennis's family welled up now. 'Who the hell d'you all think you are, you and your flaming family? You all think the sun shines out of each other's backsides don't you? Everything the Franklins do is *so* marvellous and perfect . . . Well, I've got news for you Dennis: not everyone thinks your precious family is as bloody wonderful as you do. Your mother's a bossy, interfering cow just for a start!'

She was so stung by his rejection that she could have said a lot more, but she stopped herself.

'I see.' Dennis's face went pale with rage. He looked at her like a blind person seeing for the first time. 'I've obviously had a lucky escape here. I thought you were getting well in with my family, after all their kindness to you, but obviously I was wrong. You're not who I thought you were at all. You're . . . You're cheap and superficial. I'd certainly never marry you.'

He turned and began to walk back through the park. 'See you around, Greta.'

She watched him disappear across the grass, every line of him giving off righteous indignation. She boiled with rage and humiliation.

'You smug bastard,' she said aloud. 'Good riddance – to you and your bloody perfect family!'

A few minutes later, as she began to walk home, she began trembling in shock, and the tears came.

'Oh God,' she sobbed, not caring who saw her. 'What have I done?'

Part Two

Jerusalem, 1963

Chapter Seventeen

David lay naked, half covered by a sheet. Thin blades of sunlight knifed in between the slats of the blinds and already he could feel the heat building up, sense the glare from the strip of concrete outside the block of apartments. Beyond it grew a dusty row of cypresses, separating it from the scrubland round the neighbouring set of raw new blocks of tiny apartments like theirs. Their development was on the far-flung edge of southwest Jerusalem.

Sometimes he woke still expecting the camp after his years in the army, even though he had been home now for weeks, and as he surfaced was convinced he could smell hot canvas and male sweat. Occasionally, even now, he woke thinking he was in England, that he was still young and unmarried, with Edie cooking him breakfast downstairs and the lush Bournville gardens outside. Then he would open his eyes and find himself back here, in the place he now called home.

The boy from the apartment below was bouncing a ball on the concrete outside. Once David had taken notice of the sound it began to irritate him. Very soon it was more than irritation: he experienced one of his moments of weariness, of revulsion at this country and the exhausting, anxious difficulties it presented him with daily. This feeling came to him as tightness in the chest, a queasiness in his stomach, and he had to turn his thoughts to something else to escape it. He rolled on to his side, aware of the sheen of sweat on his body, and lifted himself up on his elbow, looking down at his wife.

At once the sick feeling subsided. Gila was sleeping soundly, curled on her side, facing away from him, her blue-black hair tucked neatly round her head, just one strand lying across her cheek. Very gently, he lifted it between finger and thumb and smoothed it back, stroking her head. She stirred, her body neat and athletic, even after the child. The curve of her buttocks rubbed, arousingly, against his thigh. He loved her waking, fresh, a little bewildered, like a child herself.

'Doodi,' she murmured, opening her eyes. Her name for him: English David crossed with Rudi, his real birth name in Germany. Her eyes opened wider, startled to see him looking down at her, and she began to sit up. 'Shimon – he's OK?'

She was forever nervous about the boy. There was no real reason, as Shimon was healthy and strong, but since his birth she saw danger everywhere.

'He's still sleeping. I checked just a few minutes ago.'

They almost always spoke in Hebrew, though he had taught her a little English.

Gila smiled, more awake now. 'Well – that's very nice and kind of him, for a Saturday morning.'

Usually Shimon, who had passed his third birthday back in March, was up at first light, chattering and jumping into their bed with its noisy springs. He slept on the sofa in the little living room, as there was only one bedroom.

Gila's dark brows pulled into a frown. 'He doesn't have a fever? He was hot last night . . .'

'He's fine. Really. Don't worry so much.'

She cuddled up to him, his arm round her and her head resting on his chest. Their skin stuck clammily to each other's. Gila raised her head, looking into his eyes.

'You want a drink?'

'Not yet. Stay.' He was full of desire for her and he stroked his hand across the small of her back. He loved the dip at the base of her spine above the muscular slope of her buttocks, and the steep curve from her waist up to her hips. 'You are like a guitar,' he joked sometimes. 'Curving and beautiful.'

She kissed him. For a second she drew back, taking him in solemnly, and then, eyes filling with mischief, she climbed on top of him. David gave a groaning laugh, pretending to surrender. 'So – you're not getting up?'

Gila grinned. Her two top middle teeth crossed over slightly, which seemed to add mischief to her smile. She tweaked the tip of his nose. 'Do I look as if I'm getting up?'

'God, woman . . .' already he could feel himself slipping off into that place of desire where there was nothing but the two of them and all their tenderness. Then for a second, cold thought intervened and his eyes opened again.

'You took your pill?'

'Yes,' she said impatiently, reassuring him, and angry with him all at once. Angry too at herself.

Always now there was this between them – their longing for another child mixed with their dread of it. Every other young woman in the young state of Israel seemed to be pregnant. It was a good thing, and smiled upon. And neither of them had a brother or sister themselves, so that the idea of not giving Shimon a brother or sister soon was terrible. But they had so many demands on them already. David had at last begun his medical studies after army service and Gila was burningly frustrated because she could not yet begin her own training. So Gila took the tablets, day after day, trying to keep doing the practical thing. She was a child of the kibbutz, conditioned to being of use, to act for the greater good. As soon as she could she would begin her studies to be a dentist.

When they had made love, she padded away barefoot and brought back tall glasses of water with chips of ice floating in them. She had on a blue cotton frock but was naked underneath. A few moments later they heard a chuckle from Shimon.

'I'll fetch him!' Gila bounded from the bed with that special, excited smile that meant she was to see her son. 'You rest – you are studying so hard.'

David tried to protest, but she flapped a hand at him to quieten him as she went out. And he did feel tired, as if a weight lay on him and he could not get up from the bed. The weight was all the physiology he knew he must learn for his classes, added to the responsibility of fatherhood. He lay drowsily listening to the sounds of his family: Gila's happy greeting and his son's chortles of delight. After his first words, *ema*, *abba*, mummy, daddy, the rest had come in a torrent. Gila carried him to the kitchen and made him some food – he was crazy about eggs – and he heard her soft voice and Shimon's replies. For some reason this morning David was acutely aware of how precious it all was, as if at any moment his little family could be snatched away. In Israel there was constantly a feeling that life was built on eggshell.

'Doodi?'

He must have dozed because he had not heard her coming.

'There is some mail for you.'

'Not my mother again?' he joked. The frequent letters from Edie in Birmingham were a gentle joke between them. *I wish you lived over here, David. Wouldn't it be easier for you if you brought Shimon to England and you could study here?* . . . And so on.

'No.' There was an edge of worry to Gila's voice which made him sit up and reach for the thin envelope. 'It's from Tante Annaliese.'

The letter was addressed in deep blue ink, in Annaliese's looping script, to Mr David Mayer. They had agreed that he would be called David, the name he had known all his life, but that he would take his true surname, Mayer, and he had changed his name in his British passport. He opened the envelope. As he read he could imagine Annaliese writing the little note at the table in the living room in the flat in Haifa. She wrote in German:

My dear David,

    I am writing, my boy, because I am worried about your father's health. Each day he is growing weaker and really he should be in hospital, but I promised to him that he will never be taken away from here. He is more frail daily. I thought you should know and perhaps it is possible for you to come and visit him.

I hope your studies are progressing well and that
you and Gila and our little Shimon are in the best
of health.

Loving greetings from your,

Aunt Annaliese.

'It's my father.' David leapt out of bed. 'I shall have to
go.'

Gila nodded, her wide brown eyes full of anxiety. It
was serious if Annaliese was asking for him. There was
no telephone in their apartment, but she knew the
number of one of their neighbours and could have
called. But how like Annaliese it was to write a letter
and wait in patience even if she was deeply worried!
They both held Annaliese in great respect and gratitude. It was she to whom David had gone when he
first arrived in Israel in search of his father, Annaliese's
brother, and she had welcomed him immediately as her
lost nephew, with a warmth and affection he felt he
could never repay.

'Should we go together?' he called agitatedly, from
the bathroom where he was already sluicing himself
with water. 'All of us? Would Shimon be too much for
them?'

'I think it is better if you go alone,' Gila said. 'You
can't stay for long can you? Your lectures . . .'

'But if Annaliese needs my help?' He appeared in
the doorway, hair dripping. 'What if I have to miss
weeks of lectures?'

'But that is not what will happen,' Gila said firmly,
taking the towel which hung uselessly in David's hand
and drying him like a child. 'Stop panicking! Annaliese
would not let you disrupt your studies. She will be on
your back about it if you stay long. She just wants to

142

see you. You go! Shimon and I will be OK. I will make you food.'

An hour later, David stepped out into the baking hot morning in faded blue trousers and an old short-sleeved shirt, the small haversack, packed by Gila, hanging from one shoulder, and the sensation of kisses from his wife and small, curly-haired son still fresh on his cheeks. He walked through the streets, with their dusty, fledgling eucalyptus trees, to the main road to catch the bus in to the main bus station in Jerusalem.

Chapter Eighteen

Before he lived in Jerusalem, David had dreamed of it as a city full of scholars. He imagined squares edged by crumbling stone apartments where educated people from all over Europe and further afield sat debating life's deep questions, where the sweet notes of pianos drifted from open windows on the warm breeze. And there were parts of the city like that, even though there were forever soldiers scattered among the intellectuals. But this was not the Jerusalem where he lived.

He caught the bus to Haifa from the Jaffa Road before eleven o'clock, and pulled his books out of his haversack, planning to revise his most recent notes on the nervous system. But he could not concentrate and sat with the notebook in his lap, looking out at the passing streets. He did not travel away from home much since the army, except to the hospital a short ride away at Ein Karem. His life shuttled back and forth between classrooms and hospital corridors and the apartment block with its echoing staircases. There was scarcely time for anything else. He felt immersed in their featureless neighbourhood of young couples and elderly people, the main inhabitants of the apartments. When he first came to Israel he had worked on a kibbutz in Galilee, where he met Gila. There he had felt part of something bigger, as he had in the army.

Now it felt as if life had shrunk and he found it hard to see a bigger picture.

The bus roared round a corner on its way north. Sunlight flashed off windows. And on a dirty white wall, painted in faded black Hebrew characters, were the words, 'EICHMANN MUST HANG!'

David felt the words like a blow. Oh they had hanged him all right, Adolf Eichmann, the man who had come to be known as one of the key orchestrators of the Nazi death camps and the 'final solution to the Jewish problem'. The anniversary of his death had just passed, in June. The trial had gone on in Jerusalem for much of 1961 and had electrified Israel and the world. Set against the early months of David's marriage and the second, tender year of his son's life, from their little transistor radio had poured a horrific torrent of detail about the death camps from surviving witnesses. Blame for many of these atrocities was laid at the feet of this nondescript-looking little German who had been fished out of hiding in Argentina, when the vengeful fury of the Israelis found voice against him.

The trial had shaken David to the core. For the first time since he had settled in Israel, full of idealism and a new sense of belonging, he began to question. Amid all the baying for Eichmann's life, pleas for clemency were coming in from round the world. Should another life be taken? he had found himself asking. How did this advance anything? Gila, however, had no such doubts. They argued about it again and again.

'Doodi,' she said, emphatically tapping a finger on the table between them during one such dispute. 'Think of the ghetto in Warsaw. Think of the shootings, the starving of thousands of people. Think of the camps, the pits full of bodies, the ovens at Auschwitz . . .'

Her voice choked, her eyes brimmed with angry tears. He knew that her anger was both utterly reasonable and utterly beyond reason. 'Thousands, millions died because of this man. What is his one life in return for that? What?' She snapped her fingers. 'It is a straw. It is nothing! He is a piece of scum!'

'Yes,' he nodded, sick at the thought. 'There is nothing that can compensate for that. His life is nothing. But . . .'

'But *what*?' She was ablaze with emotion now and he was afraid. He had always been an emotional man, but she touched the edge of hysteria in a way that made him recoil. 'But nothing! You think they should spare him? Keep him to live out his life in some comfortable cell?'

'No, but . . .' He wanted to talk about the Quaker teaching of his childhood, about non-violence, but he knew she would dismiss this as the luxury of those living in safety. And Eichmann, what he had done was so enormous, almost beyond compare . . .

'You think he should be treated with mercy when all those people remember him, remember what he did to their wives and husbands, their sons and daughters?' Gila was shouting now and Shimon started to wail, hearing her voice raised. Gila leaned down and scooped him up on her lap.

'It's OK, little one.' She kissed his curls, smoothing a trembling hand over his forehead. '*Ema* is just a little bit worked up.' She glared across at David over the top of their son's head. 'I can't *believe* you would say something like this . . .'

'But I haven't said anything!' David burst out. 'You haven't let me get a word in! Look, I know all those people need to see Eichmann dead – that nothing else will do. I can feel the rage and hatred for him, for the evil things he has done. The thought makes me sick to my stomach. But I'm just asking, *asking*, that's all—' It was his turn to bang on the table. 'What kind of example is Israel, or any other state, making by executing criminals? What kind of people are we if we just do what they do?'

Gila got up, completely enraged, still clasping Shimon, who stared anxiously into her face, his eyes full of tears. 'Criminals? I can't believe you Doodi! As if he is some thief, or pickpocket, not the cause of the massacre of millions of Jews! This is not an ordinary case. You are Jewish, Rudi . . .' He heard her emphasize his birth name. 'Think what they did to your father . . .'

His father . . . He only had to think of his father . . .

They made up their argument, of course, but the anger had bitten deep. He understood, he felt it in himself also, the blood lust for Eichmann, for Dr Mengele, the doctor who committed so many atrocities in Auschwitz in the name of research, and for all the others who had done things from which the mind recoiled in horror. But this hatred and vengefulness was set to go on and on . . . Was this what being an Israeli meant – an endless cycle of vengeance against the Nazis, the Arabs . . . ?

Such thoughts were usually buried under the business of his life, but today as he sat on the Egged bus, they flooded through him. Perhaps he was too much of an outsider, not having known he was a Jew until so late in his life. Sometimes a feeling of panic would flow through him, a whirling feeling of being lost, untethered to anything. What did being a Jew mean? It was a thing of blood, his link with his family, his German mother. But he had not known his mother and had no memory of her. He was not religious. Gila, like many others on the kibbutz, would say, 'We don't need religion, not in Israel. We have the land. That is our place.' But this too meant violence, the displacement of others. And instilled deeply into him, through his upbringing, had been the tenets of the Quaker way of life: the peace testimony, which said that violence was the wrong course of action.

He remembered with longing the passion and certainty he'd had in his teens, when he first found out about his mother, when he met Joe and Esther Leishmann, who helped him in Birmingham, and when he first when to Kibbutz Hamesh. Everything, for the first time in his life, had felt so clear and strong. This was who he really was – Rudi Mayer! A German Jew who would become an Israeli! Whose father had survived the concentration camps. But now who was he? Sometimes now he was overwhelmed with longing for England, for a milder life, for the quiet decency of the Society of Friends. Where did he really stand or belong?

Unable to bear his confused thoughts any longer, he leaned forward and rested his head on his arms on the seat in front and went to sleep.

The journey up the slopes of Mount Carmel in Haifa always reminded him of the first time he came looking for his father. How long ago that seemed! He wondered, as he stepped out of the bus at the top of the hill, whether this would be the last time he would ever come and find him alive.

'*Shalom, shalom, mein Liebchen . . .*' Annaliese

kissed him and reached up to rumple his hair as if he was a little boy, and he was deeply touched by it.

'Tante,' he spoke with her in German. Annaliese, now in her mid-fifties, was a handsome woman with dark, lively eyes, her hair greying but still containing much rich chestnut brown. She had the pronounced cheekbones of a once very beautiful woman, her eyebrows plucked to thin lines and pencilled in and her dress deep green and elegant. She moved without stiffness and appeared calm, though her face held sadness and the crinkled skin round her eyes showed fatigue.

'How is he?' David spoke very softly, in the familiar lobby of the apartment.

Annaliese beckoned him into the kitchen, just as she had done on his first visit there, when she had not wanted Hermann to hear them.

'Here—' She passed him a glass of orange juice with ice in it. The peelings were still on the side: she had obviously just squeezed it. They sat at the little Formica-topped table.

'He is dying,' she said, again with great calm.

David watched her. He had guessed really, but his father was often ill. It was hard to be sure.

'What happened?' he asked.

'Oh – it came on very quickly. A cold, his chest, pneumonia. The doctor has just left – they are sending me a nurse. He wants me to move him to the hospital, but that is unthinkable. I had to explain . . . He understood of course . . .'

For a moment her face crumpled, and she put her hand over it. When she removed it, her expression was composed again. 'Hermann is sedated a little. Without the drugs, he is—' She made a helpless gesture. 'He is

149

overcome with memories. He is back there again – he is tearing at himself, pulling out the catheter ... Terrible.'

'I can stay,' David said. 'As long as you need ...'

But already she was raising her hand to stop him. 'No. That is not necessary, *Liebchen*. Your life is very full – your lovely Gila and Shimon, your studies. I wanted you to see your father, but then you go. You hear? There is no point in your staying – he will not know you.'

'But for you,' he started to protest.

She would not hear of it. 'I am all right. I have help. Just now I need a doctor who has already passed all his exams!' She twinkled at him so that he did not take offence.

'You come back and see me soon – all of you, when it is over. That would make me very happy. Now, you will want to see him. He may be sleeping. He mostly sleeps now.'

She led David to Hermann Mayer's room. David realized that in all the times he had visited the little third-floor apartment he had never been in his father's bedroom, and he felt like a nervous intruder.

The room was of a modest size and cramped. Hermann's bed lay under the window, which looked out from the side of the apartment on to the buttery stone of the apartment next door. Close to it was a very large armchair which took up much of the room. It was upholstered in a heavy, brown hessian, and its arms and the place where the head rested were threadbare and slightly greasy. There was little else in the room except some clothes folded on a wooden chair in the corner, and a little table by the bed which held the staples of Hermann's life: the radio, his glasses, a folded newspaper, medicines. There was a strong smell of eucalyptus oil, which overpowered everything else.

The first thing was the sound of laboured breathing. The figure on the bed looked very small. Hermann was covered neatly by a sheet and a light brown blanket, his chin resting on it as if the bed had just been tidied. What remained of his hair was white, his cheeks sunken and the skin so thin that the purple forking veins could be seen through it. It was the face of an eighty-year-old: Hermann was in fact fifty-three, younger than Annaliese.

'Come – just sit by him for a while,' Annaliese encouraged him. 'Take this chair. He may not wake – but you can take your leave of him, darling.' He heard her voice catch, despite her attempts to be matter-of-fact.

She slipped out of the room and David sank into the big brown chair.

He felt a sense of awe in the face of the enormous, quiet event unfolding in front of him. Hermann's death, he realized, did not feel sad. What tore at him was the life his father had endured. Death had been this close before, when Anatoli, Edie's husband, then in the British army in 1945, had gone with the liberating forces into Bergen-Belsen transit camp. He had rescued Hermann from among a pile of the dead and taken him to the camp hospital, where he survived malnutrition and typhus.

As he watched his father struggling for breath, David tried to see him in his youth, a gifted scientist in Berlin who had married his love, a beauty called Gerda, the mother he had never known. What followed in his young life then was Theresienstadt concentration camp, Auschwitz-Birkenau, Bergen-Belsen, and even one further camp after the liberation. These years of brutality broke his health, mental and physical, and it was Annaliese, reunited with him after the war, who had looked after him ever since.

He listened to his father breathing, thinking of all the places he had breathed before.

'I don't know you . . .' David whispered. 'I shall never know you.'

Tears filled his eyes for a moment, but he wiped them fiercely away. *I am crying for myself*, he thought angrily. *Out of self-pity!* Then he was less hard on himself. *No, I am crying for you too, for the suffering of your life.*

Hermann Mayer had reacted with pathetic emotion when he first realized his son was still alive, and David had visited him regularly ever since. He remembered the warning of the lady who had directed him to Hermann Mayer before he had met him: *You should not expect too much of your father.* It had been the wisest of advice. He and Hermann had met, both needing and wanting, but finding themselves to be like two planets that pass and never touch. It was too late for anything much, for a real father. But at least, after all those years of uncertainty about his background, David had met and known Hermann. For that he was grateful.

For a moment he leaned over and gently brushed his hand over the wisps of white hair. Hermann's scalp gave off a dim, papery warmth.

'Rest now,' he whispered. 'Be at peace. Shalom, *abba*, shalom.'

He stayed talking for a short time with Annaliese before she shooed him out to catch the bus back to Jerusalem.

'I do not think he will regain consciousness,' she said solemnly. 'Go, boy. Live your life. Study hard and be a great doctor. I will let you know when the end comes.'

And she kissed him fondly and waved him down the steps of the apartment block. She was watching, smiling, as he turned again to look at her.

Chapter Nineteen

David expected to receive news of his father's death almost immediately, but several days passed and there was nothing.

He worked hard at the medical school, returning exhausted from his long day of classes to the cramped apartment and the pleasures of his little family. In the evening Gila always had food ready, baked aubergines or mutton, and chopped salads of tomatoes and small fat cucumbers. He loved the return home to what felt like safety.

One afternoon though, a week after he had been to Haifa, there was an extra anatomy class that he did not need to attend and he came home early. He was restless, finding it hard to concentrate on his studies as he waited for a telegram or letter from Annaliese.

The apartment seemed very quiet as he pushed the door open. If Shimon's voice could not be heard laughing and chattering he must be napping, David knew. He closed the door very carefully and peeped into the living room. Sure enough, Shimon was sprawled on his back on the old sofa, arms flung out and his closed eyes fringed by immensely long lashes. David stood smiling down at him. The sight of his son always melted him. He longed to pour over him all the safety and love he had never had from his real parents: to heal the wound in himself.

He realized Gila must be resting too and thought to join her. Sure enough, she was lying on the bed, and thinking her asleep, he sat down gently on the edge to take off his shoes. As he undid his laces he felt her stirring and heard a sob.

She was lying curled on her side, hands over her face.

'Hey, my sweetheart . . .' He knelt over her, a little afraid when he heard her weeping. What on earth could have brought on such emotion? He dared to touch her shoulder. 'What is it my love?'

She gave way to her tears then, curling up more tightly. Only when he lay beside her and held her against him did she turn to him.

'Oh, Doodi – you're going to be so angry with me!'

'Am I?' he was trying to humour her a little, because there was a wildness in her expression which disturbed him. 'Why's that? What have you done that's so terrible?'

'I'm bleeding,' she said, weeping even harder.

He stared at her, trying to make sense of this.

'I had to go and see Dr Hirsch this morning. He said I am losing again – a child. It is not very heavy now, but if it gets worse I should go to the hospital . . .' She looked fearfully at him, her face seeming very young and vulnerable.

'But . . .' David put a hand to his forehead. 'I don't get it. You were taking the pills – I mean, you weren't pregnant . . .'

But Gila was shaking her head. 'I'm sorry Doodi – I'm so sorry – but I was.' Tears spilled down her cheeks. 'I just wanted – I don't know . . . It was for Shimon. I need to do my studies, but I wanted to have another baby so badly. I have not been truthful with you, that is the worst of it.'

David looked at her, feeling his face set into a stony expression. 'When did you stop taking them?'

'A while ago – three, four months? I don't remember.'

Ablaze with fury he removed his arms from round her and rolled off the bed, to go and stand by the window. For a moment he wished that he smoked. It felt as if the harsh scrape of cigarette smoke across his throat would be soothing. He looked out at the row of cedars, the hazy sky over the apartment blocks, sickened by its rudimentary ugliness. Gila was crying softly behind him.

'Doodi,' she said eventually. 'Don't – don't be so hard. Please come back here.'

His anger flared. 'What – for you to tell me more lies?'

'I'm sorry,' she said bitterly. 'But I am not having a child. So there is something for you to celebrate.'

The words cut through him. He was furious and very hurt at her deceiving him, but he knew how much she longed for it, as he did. For a moment he felt like weeping himself.

'Are you in pain?' he asked, more kindly.

'A bit – not too bad.'

He went and lay beside her again, their faces almost touching, but he did not reach out for her.

'You didn't have to be so sneaky. Are you afraid of me?'

'No, of course not.' She looked into his eyes, grief and longing in hers. Sometimes she looked so lost and bereft, this woman who he had thought was all strength. 'Only you're always working so hard and I know I should be finding a way to work and study as well. But then there's also something in me – something that takes over. I just felt as if we had to make a baby. *Had* to!'

He reached out then and pulled her tenderly to him, stroking her head, then laying his hand on her belly, aware of the tearing process taking place in there.

'Should we have a child now? Are we wrong?' he said.

'Well, we know my body is tricky and choosy with babies,' she said bravely. Shimon had originally been a twin, but Gila miscarried the other child. 'So something is saying to us that the time is not right. Maybe I should put away this crazy idea until later on.' She was reverting back to being brisk and practical.

They lay for some time, gently holding each other, discussing what they must do for the future. Things felt warm and right again. David hated quarrelling.

It was only when Shimon woke from his nap that he got up, leaving Gila to rest, and made a drink of juice for his little son, full of thanks for his existence.

Despite his frailness, Hermann Mayer did not hurry into death. It was not until ten days later that David received the letter from Annaliese, telling him that his father had slipped away in his sleep. He had been kept heavily sedated and had never come to full consciousness again. She told him that Hermann would be buried in one of the Jewish cemeteries in Haifa and she would take David to pay his respects when he next came to see her, but he was not to disturb his routine by travelling there again now.

On hearing the news David abandoned his studies

for the afternoon and caught a bus into Jerusalem. Entering the Old City through the Jaffa Gate, he wandered through the narrow streets and bazaars of the western side of the city, which was Israeli: the eastern side was in Jordan. The streets were lined with stalls selling round soft breads, tomatoes, cucumbers, aubergines and bunches of mint. When the sun was sinking low in the sky, he found a place to climb up on to the walls and stood looking over the pale stones of the city, its domes and towers and minarets and the golden glow reflecting from the Dome of the Rock. A church bell tolled somewhere, and as evening came the call to prayer would go up from the mosques – yet still he knew he was standing in the beating heart of Jewish Israel, its very purpose, *Yerushalaim*, founded back in the very earliest history by the Canaanites. His people, he told himself, the home of the Jews, where he belonged. But as he looked across the hot, bustling city with its alleys and markets, its spice sellers and donkeys, its peoples gathered from Vilnius and Odessa, from Paris and Berlin, the Yemen and Warsaw, he asked himself how close he really felt to the Canaanites or to the history of this torn piece of land. It was not even the land of his parents: it would have been quite foreign to them. Was he not just as close in his heart to Edie, who had brought him up, to the place he had once called home? For a moment he longed to hear the soft, familiar tinkling of bells across the leafy spaces of Bournville.

He felt a shock of emptiness, almost of panic. With his father's passing he had lost one of his very few links with his real blood family and their history, tragic as it had been. Now there was only Annaliese. Without her, he was cast adrift in this country of refugees. At this moment, being a part of the land did not seem enough.

With powerful longing he thought of Gila and Shimon, and a passion filled him. They were his all, truly his home! He was making a place to belong, with his loved ones, his family. He cursed himself for his stupidity. Why had he been so angry when he found out Gila had been pregnant? She had deceived him of course, that was the real reason for his hurt. But why should they not have more children and build a family? Wasn't that what he really longed for? And the state of Israel wanted lots of healthy Jewish babies. He pushed all the difficulties aside in his mind. They would manage, somehow. They would have children – lots of them! – and they would flourish and belong, all children of the state of Israel and he the father of the household. They would be both his roots and his branches.

He hurried down the steps from the walls and through the shady alleyways of the city, longing now to be home, to tell Gila his thoughts, to lie with her, holding her close in his arms, and share this vision of what home could mean.

Chapter Twenty

'Doodi – I have been thinking.'

He had come home bursting to talk, but decided to wait until Shimon was in bed, since conversation with the child around soon became like a pile of shredded paper.

Gila had cooked his favourite dinner of chicken with tomato salad and he knew she was pampering him because of his father's death. She fussed round him and insisted he rest while she helped Shimon wash and prepare for sleep. Tonight she seemed brighter and energetic.

The living rooms of the apartments gave out on to tiny balconies with just enough room for two chairs close together, or for a rack of washing. These spaces, cut into the mass of the building and enclosed by railings, ran up the side of the block like a row of missing teeth. David sat in the balmy darkness holding a glass of mint tea, listening to the sounds of older children playing and to other voices: the high nagging of the Lithuanian lady in the apartment below, and occasional grunts of reply from her husband, the raucous Yemeni family sitting outside by the main entrance, a baby crying somewhere further along the block. In the room behind him, Gila was humming softly to Shimon.

He had a speech prepared in his head but she spoke

first, coming to sit on the other chair when he had scarcely realized she was there, rubbing her eyes sleepily after being in the darkened room with Shimon. Her hair hung loose on her shoulders.

'Today, of all days, I want to speak clearly with you.' In seconds she became the tough, resolute Gila, the kibbutz Gila. Reflected in her eyes he saw dots of light from the lamp across at the edge of the concrete strip.

She's so beautiful he thought, and with his whole being he wanted to take her and hold her, but she was not in the same soft mood as he.

'I'm so sorry, Doodi darling, for what I did. For stopping taking the pills. I don't really understand myself, except that I am in conflict. Sometimes my heart wants something that my head tells me is wrong and I don't know how to manage it. But now I feel strong and I have come to a decision. It will be better for our future – for all of us – if I begin my studies as soon as possible. I am going to apply to the School of Dentistry and study to get my qualifications quickly. Then I will be useful and we will not be so poor. It all makes perfect sense.'

David watched her earnest face. All the things he had been dying to say on the way home from the Old City seemed pushed aside by the clear, hard-headed thoughts of his wife. But he tried to regain them.

'Or, we could just carry on and have a family,' he said. 'Children – lots of children . . .'

Gila's face softened and she leaned forward and stroked his cheek. 'My darling, sometimes you are so romantic, and so stupid. Where exactly are we going to put these children? On the roof perhaps? And what are they going to eat, or wear – especially when you

161

are off being an army doctor? We have no money – we should starve!'

'We'd manage,' he said stubbornly, knowing all the same that she was right.

In the shadows he could see the tender laughter in her eyes. 'Of course we would, you silly boy,' she said lightly. 'No, please, Doodi – I have been thinking about it all day. It will be hard – very hard – but we can manage. In the term times I could take Shimon to my mother.' She held up her hand against his protest. Gila's mother was frail, nervy. 'It would be good for him to be at Hamesh – he will have company on the kibbutz, and learn about the life. If my mother cannot cope, he can stay with Auntie Miriam in Tel Aviv – she adores him. And in the vacation we can be with him all the time.'

He could hear that she was struggling with her emotions, being brave, when the thought of being separated from her son for such long periods would almost break her heart.

'Love, you don't have to do this – not yet,' he argued. 'Wait at least until Shim is in school . . .'

But she was shaking her head, tears welling in her eyes. 'No, Doodi – it's for the best. We cannot just carry on like this, or have more children now. It is just too difficult. My training will give me a sense of purpose and afterwards I can work and have more children. We are still young.'

He knew she was right, and relief flooded through him, yet at the same time his vision was evaporating: of himself at the head of a great family which would nail him down into this place, this rough, spiky country. He would have to work it all out in a different way.

He stood up and took Gila's hand, drawing her to her feet, and held her warm, curving shape in his arms.

'You are so brave,' he said. 'You will find it hard, leaving our little one. I will find it hard too.'

'I know,' she said, tears running down her cheeks. 'But I am thinking for the future: it is best to do the hard thing first.'

He kissed her wet cheeks, stroking away her tears with his thumbs.

'I love you so much.' He was so moved by her. 'Come inside, will you – to bed?'

She nodded at him, trying to smile.

He hesitated for a second.

'You've taken your pill?'

Her smile broadened, teasing a little now. 'Yes, my lovely tyrant. I have taken my pill.'

Part Three

Birmingham, 1965–7

Chapter Twenty-One

Spring 1965

'Gret! You there?'

Greta rolled her eyes in irritation, hearing Trevor come crashing in from work. Sometimes she thought he'd break the door off their little house in Glover Road. And there was always the shout as he came in.

'What?' she called, not moving from the cooker. Trevor seemed to expect her to drop everything and come running like an eager puppy whenever he called, even though she was cooking their tea.

'Hey, bab—' Trevor burst into the kitchen, dressed as ever in his black gabardine, even though it was a warm spring day. He threw his arms round her from behind, cupping his hands over her breasts. 'Let's go out tonight, eh? I got a good couple of tips today. There was some bloke, from Manchester he was, said he was just passing and he gave me five bob! Said he's never had a better hair cut! I thought we'd go down the boozer . . .'

Greta squirmed, half annoyed, half amused.

'Trev, get off! That tickles – look, you've brought me all up in goose pimples!' She freed herself from his grip. 'You know I can't go out – it's my club night.'

'Oh, Gret!' Trevor threw his coat angrily over a chair. 'You're always cowing well out these days – we never go out no more – not just the two of us!'

'Yes we do . . .' She tried to think, as she said it, of the last time they'd been out together, but realized with a shock that it was a long time. 'But you know these are my nights out – French Monday, club tonight. That's all. We can go out any other night if you want.'

'Make us a cuppa tea then,' he said, sitting down sulkily on top of his coat. 'At least you can do that for us.'

Greta put the kettle on, biting her lip. Trev was envious, she knew that. Her going to the class on Monday seemed to annoy him the most. 'What d'you want to learn French for?' he'd say. 'You're not going to France, are you?' The Seven O'Clock Club at Cadbury's, a social club, just seemed to wind him up because she had somewhere to go and he didn't. She liked dancing too, but Trevor said he couldn't dance. And he thought she was getting full of high-flown ideas, reading books and all that.

'Why don't you go down the Old Oak with your mates?' she'd ask. 'You know – while I'm out. You might as well go and enjoy yourself.'

The plain truth was Trevor didn't really have any mates. He hadn't been very pally with anyone at school and now he just worked with Edie's Dad, Mr Marshall, and he was old enough to be his grandfather. Trev just wanted to go out with her and no one else. Or better still, stay in and watch Dick Emery on the telly. He was a proper Derby and Joan sort, whereas she still went out with Pat now and again, as well as to her clubs at Cadbury's.

'Look, we'll go tomorrow,' she said.

'It'll be too late then,' Trevor said morosely.

'Too late for what?'

'I want to go tonight.'

Greta could feel herself beginning to lose her temper. All Trev could ever think of to do was going down the pub! Even if she suggested anything else he'd just shrug and say, 'Oh, I dunno. No – let's just go down the boozer . . .'

And there was she doing all sorts. Two weeks ago the Seven O'Clock Club had gone to the Alpha TV studios in Aston to see them recording *Thank Your Lucky Stars* – and the Beatles had been on! It was ever so glamorous, the cameras and bright lights! Trev had been green over that, her seeing the Beatles in the flesh. But there were all sorts of other things going on – talks and sketches, music and outings, and he just poured scorn on them or said, 'What d'you want to go and do that for?'

Sometimes, she thought, all Trev ever wanted to do was sit in a pub with a pint and stare at the wall. More and more it made her want to scream. She took a deep breath, telling herself she was being unkind. After all, Trevor had good reason to be fed up with her as well.

'Look, love—' She went and stood behind his chair, hands on his shoulders. 'We'll go tomorrow. It's a date – all right?'

Trevor twisted round, his pale face eager, like a little boy. 'Shall we, Gret? Eh – come here.'

He pulled her round to sit on his lap.

'Trev, the kettle's about to boil – and I'm all grease down my front!' She tried to get up, but he pulled her down.

'Sit here – I want you to.' He cuddled up against

her, a hand on her breast once again, then ran his tongue along the lobe of her ear. 'That's my girl. Eh, Gret, before you go, can we...? You know ... You've got time, ain't you...?'

'Trev! No I haven't! You're terrible you are!'

Trev grinned in a sort of 'Well, it was worth a try' sort of way. Then his face became serious again.

'I don't s'pose ... Is there any sign of ... You know...?'

Trevor had no words for anything that went on with women's bodies, periods, pregnancies, the very names of anything. He always trailed off, leaving her to guess what he was trying to say. But this time she knew exactly what he meant. It was what he always meant.

The kettle started to whistle and she jumped up.

'No,' she said softly, her back to him. 'There isn't. Sorry, love.'

She could feel him staring at her.

'Our Mom says you'd oughta go and see the doctor,' Trevor said. 'You ain't taking anything, are yer?'

'What d'you mean?'

'Our Mom says there's pills you can have now to stop it...'

'*No!* Why would I be doing that?'

'She says no one takes this long to catch for a babby if there ain't nothing wrong.'

Greta put the tea and a mug on the table, still not looking at him, but her heart was pounding and she knew her face had blushed a guilty red. Two years they'd been married and Trevor had been patient at first and he hadn't got a clue anyway. She kept telling him that it often took a long while.

But *two years*! Of course they'd all be on about it –

170

Ruby, Trev's mother, even Marleen. *Hasn't our Gret caught for a babby yet?* Ruby had said things to her, but Greta had fended her off. What business was it of Mom's whether she became instantly pregnant the minute she got married? Didn't anyone have anything else on their mind?

But poor Trevor – she knew he longed for children. That was the whole point of getting married so far as he was concerned. He wanted a wife who was always in the kitchen with a gaggle of kids round her, and so far he had neither.

'Maybe I will,' she said gently, pouring milk into his cup. 'That's a good idea.'

She knew she wouldn't. There was no point in going to the doctor because Dr Lonsdale knew exactly why she wasn't having a baby. It was he who prescribed the little cards of pills that she kept in a secret little soap box with a sprig of lavender painted on the lid, in the kitchen cupboard, behind the tins and packets, the pills she had been taking since the very week they got married.

When she said 'Yes' to marrying Trevor, that summer, after things had ended with Dennis, everything seemed to happen very fast. She had gone running back to Trevor, to all that was easy and familiar, needing his adoration after her humiliation with Dennis, and Trevor had obliged with gleeful willingness.

They married at the registry office. She found a long, pretty white dress in C & A and Trevor wore a suit which hung loosely on his skinny frame. He had beamed with delight the whole day long.

'I can't believe my luck!' he kept telling everyone.

'The prettiest girl in the world and she's going to be Mrs Biddle!'

Alf Biddle found them the house for rent in Glover Road.

'Nice and near Trev's work and yours, Gret,' he said kindly.

Greta had forced a grateful smile. She had hoped that getting away from home would entail going further afield than just round the corner in Glover Road, but still, the rent was reasonable and it was better than nothing. At least she'd got away from Marleen and Mom and flaming Herbert Smail. By the time she moved out he was starting to leave his slippers in the house.

Forty-six Glover Road was owned by a fat, lazy landlord who did not keep the place in good repair. There were big patches of damp on some of the walls and both the front step and door frame were broken. Trevor, handier with his hands than Greta expected, was delighted with it.

'We can soon sort it out,' he said, arm round Greta's shoulders as they first went in with the key. 'Our little castle, that's what it is.'

Greta went through that whole time in a shocked daze. Ruby was pleased, of course. That was what you did, marriage and kids, and it was at least one of her daughters off her hands. She also liked the Biddles. Trevor was a good lad, she said, now he'd grown up a bit. Marleen just shrugged and said, 'You might as well, mightn't you?' Pat tried to look pleased for her.

'You sure about it, Gret?' she asked once, as they walked home from work together. She sounded concerned.

But Greta just said, 'Yeah, course. Trev's all right.

Anyway – at least it's not like the old days at Cadbury's when they gave you a carnation and a bible and a wave bye-bye if you got married. I'll still be here, you know!'

'Oh, that's what you think. It won't be long before you'll be up to your eyes in nappies and bottles,' Pat predicted.

Greta had already decided that this was not going to happen, but she didn't say anything. She squeezed her friend's arm.

'I expect it'll be the same for you soon. But I'm not going anywhere, Pat. We've practically been brought up by Cadbury's, haven't we? All those days in the school and factory, and all the swims we've had – well, we still will!'

Pat looked a bit comforted by this. They had often had lunchtime dips in the Girls' Baths, where they had been taught to swim as youngsters.

'Me getting married won't make any difference – honest it won't.'

She knew, in a vague way, while she was in town buying her wedding dress, and she knew even as she stood in front of the registrar making her wedding vows, that this was all a terrible mistake. Trev loved her, that she did believe. She needed someone to love her and want her, and in a spirit of hoping for the best, she bet on that being enough. She knew she didn't love him and felt badly about it, so she tried to be affectionate. After all she *liked* Trevor. He was a mate, someone she knew through and through. But she had barely yet admitted to herself that she'd married him on the rebound because she was angry: with Dennis for his snobby, superior assessment of her, with her Mom and Marleen and the way everything was at home.

And she was angry with herself, for not doing more with her life, for not achieving more for herself.

A few days before the wedding she went to Doctor Lonsdale for the pill. He was not a thorough doctor, and when she said she was about to marry and wanted to delay having a family, he said, 'Very well,' and handed her the prescription. She never said a word to Trevor.

Marriage felt like a game, as if she and Trevor were playing at it like children, even if they were married solemnly, in the eyes of the law. But there was one thing she was sure about: there would be no babies, not for a long time.

Chapter Twenty-Two

She couldn't complain that Trevor was unloving. Not at first, especially. He practically worshipped her. Whenever he came in from work the first thing he always did was fling his arms round her and kiss her. And she was flattered and, for the first time in her life, enjoyed being at the centre of someone's adoring attention.

There was the new experience of having their own home, even if it was tatty and the landlord never seemed to bother with anything. It was all a bit like playing house, like children, having fun buying pieces of furniture from second-hand shops and painting and covering the walls with papers in bold, bright, patterns, orange and brown circles in one room, green leaves with big pink flowers in another.

They bought a second-hand record player and Trevor started talking about saving up for a car. Greta suddenly felt very grown up, having her own front-door key, able to make her own decisions without her Mom bossing her about at every step. Best of all, she didn't have to come home to a house full of Mary Lou's tantrums, the squalling of Marleen's new baby, Elvis, or Herbert Smail's oily presence. And Trevor was her mate, she'd known him much of her life and was comfortable with him, as she was with his Mom and Dad. There wasn't anything she had to make too much effort about. She didn't feel all the time that she was trying too hard, the way she had with Dennis.

In fact she didn't feel much for Trevor at all, except a familiar fondness. Certainly there was no passion, although when it came to the bedroom, she was touched by his enthusiasm in that department. Trevor couldn't seem to get enough of her.

'We'll soon have us a nice little family, won't we, Gret?' he used to say in the early days, as they lay in their little bedroom overlooking the street, where they heard the postman whistling along from house to house in the mornings.

Greta would smile at him and say something like, 'Well, we'll just have to wait and see, won't we, love?'

After a few months had passed she started to say, 'There's no hurrying Mother Nature. She takes her time.'

Trevor was very patient to begin with. 'I suppose it's nice to have a bit of time on our own,' he said. 'Once kiddies come along there's no turning back – that's what our Mom always says. All the same – it'd be nice if summat happened soon.'

'Oh I 'spect it will,' she said, comfortingly.

Six months after Greta and Trevor's wedding, Ruby had persuaded Marleen to have a christening for Mary Lou and Elvis. Both Greta and Marleen were puzzled by her making an issue out of this, and it only became clear why later in the day.

It was February, and they all gathered at St Francis's Church on the Green in Bournville huddled up in warm coats. Herbert Smail was there, to Greta's disgust.

'Anyone'd think he was part of the family,' she complained to Marleen.

He seemed to have put on even more weight and his jacket buttons were under strain. His hair was combed over his bald patch and even in the cold he looked hot and bothered, yet also very pleased with himself.

Marleen was still as thin as a rake and had on a short dress in black and white diagonal stripes which made Greta's eyes go funny every time she looked at it. Marleen had bleached her hair and back-combed it up into a big beehive and she was heavily made up with eye-liner and mascara. Even with all the makeup on, she looked exhausted.

Greta and Ruby had to help her keep Mary Lou and Elvis under control while the ceremony took place. Meanwhile Ruby stood smiling proudly, holding Herbert's arm. Elvis was a proper little bullet-headed bruiser, who was just beginning to crawl and wriggled and squirmed constantly, wanting to be put down, and Mary Lou kept yanking at her mother's skirt, trying to get her attention. They had to keep a tight hold on them by the font. Eventually their small party emerged out of the church into the cold grey day.

'Right now, you lot,' Ruby said. 'We'll all go back to ours and wet Elvis's head.' They walked back to Selly Oak, and almost as soon as they were through the door, coats still on, Ruby seemed bursting to speak.

'Just listen a tick before you all start.' She was pink-cheeked. 'This is a double celebration. We've got a surprise for yer.' She eyed Herbert, taking his arm with a coquettish smile which made Greta's stomach lurch with embarrassment. 'Thing is, Herbert and I have a surprise for you . . .' She paused dramatically and Herbert beamed with revolting bashfulness. 'He and I got married yesterday – on the quiet with a couple of witnesses. We just wanted a quiet wedding – no fuss. So – we're now man and wife!'

Greta looked at Marleen, who mimicked being sick. But everyone else tried to sound pleased, and soon Ruby was opening bottles and putting out plates of sausage rolls and there was nothing they could do about any of it anyway. Greta even felt sorry for Marleen.

'It's a bit much,' she said to her, 'Mom making you have a christening so she can take it over and tell us about her and Herbert getting married by the back door!'

Marleen rolled her eyes. 'I just let them get on with it. Here – take him off me a minute. Give over, will yer!' she snapped at Elvis, who was throwing himself backwards as she tried to hold on to him. They were all in the front room, the small family and a very few of Ruby's Cadbury's friends. Greta noticed that her mother had not invited either Edie or Janet. Wouldn't they have approved of her marrying Herbert? Was that why she didn't ask them, even though they were such old friends – they knew her all too well!

She was sitting on the sofa holding a squirming Elvis, amazed at his eight-month-old strength, when Trevor came over in his baggy suit. He squatted down beside them.

'Come 'ere mate – I'll take him for a bit, shall I? Give Marleen a rest.'

Greta felt a pang of guilt and she saw Elvis look up awestruck at Trevor and move eagerly into his arms. Trevor was good with kids, it was obvious. And she was depriving him of having any. But the thought of it, of being stuck with it all and with Trevor, appalled her, she was shocked to realize how much. That wasn't how you were supposed to feel, was it?

Marleen sat smoking and watching without much apparent interest as Trevor played with Elvis, holding him high in the air until the little boy let out delighted chuckles. Marleen had calmed down a bit since having Elvis. Either calmed down or had the stuffing knocked out of her, Greta couldn't decide which. She just seemed rather lifeless now.

A burst of laughter rang across the room. Ruby, Herbert and one or two others were sharing a joke. She watched her Mom, laughing, self-satisfied yet somehow vulnerable as well, and the sight dragged her down. Was this the fate of women in her family – to keep marrying any old bloke who came along? Her own wedding had only been six months ago, and hadn't she done just the same thing? She pushed the thought away. She and Trevor were OK! They were happy enough weren't they?

But hard as she tried to persuade herself, a sinking, desperate feeling came over her as she watched her mother link her arm through that of a man who none of them could stand and who she didn't think Ruby loved either. He was just someone, anyone in trousers to have around the place. Watching her mother that day, it was as if she had suddenly woken up and found herself in a place she didn't expect. How had she come to be married to Trevor? How could she have done it all so lightly, just rushing into it? How could she ever make anything of herself now? She had slipped somehow into marriage and now there was no turning back.

This thought, as she stood there on her mother's

third wedding day, a match so ghastly that even Ruby had kept the ceremony a secret, made her feel utterly desolate.

When they got home later, Trevor was all lit up. He had spent most of the afternoon entertaining Mary Lou and Elvis, making them laugh, tickling them and clowning around. They kept hearing Elvis's gurgling laughter.

'Wasn't that lovely?' he said as they got into the house. Greta went wearily and put the kettle on.

'Umm, s'pose, so.' She slammed it down on the hob.

'What d'you mean, s'pose so? Your Mom's done well for herself there, I reckon. That Herbert's all right – and he's got a bit of money behind him.'

'Has he?' she asked, indifferently. 'Maybe *that's* why she married him then.'

Trevor looked shocked. 'That's not a very nice thing to say, is it? They looked very happy together.'

'Have you *looked* at him, Trevor? Can't you see, he's just vile!'

'No he's not! And anyway – you're the one who's always saying looks aren't everything!'

Greta stared at him furiously, wanting to lash out in her frustration. Damn Trevor and the whole bloody lot of them! All she said was something she had been thinking about all afternoon. It was when she had decided for certain.

'I'm going to go to French lessons,' she announced.

'What?' Trev's brow crinkled. 'What're you on about? I don't get it.'

'No,' Greta snapped. 'I don't s'pose you do, Trevor.'

Chapter Twenty-Three

The other thing that had finally propelled Greta into attending classes and trying to better herself was a chance meeting with Edie one day, in the girls' dining room at Cadbury's. Edie was carrying a bowl of soup on a tray, her russet hair tied up neatly.

'Oh hello, Greta!' Edie greeted her warmly, her smile including Pat as well. 'How are you, love?'

'All right,' Greta said, blushing. She liked and admired Edie.

'Come and sit with me,' Edie invited, and Greta followed her small but robust figure to a table where they all sat together.

'They've taken me on for seasonal work now I've got Peter,' Edie said, 'so I'm back along with your Mom – just like old times! We work three days together – she's off today and I'm off Fridays. They've taken me on for the great Easter egg rush – I'm packing them into the Waddies.' The Milk Tray eggs were packed into Waddington's cartons. 'Oh it's really nice to be back, I can tell you. I've missed it.'

Her freckly face was full of enthusiasm and Greta saw she was looking at someone who was radiantly happy.

'How is Peter?' Greta asked.

Peter was a handsome little boy with a magnificent head of black curls and obviously like his father,

Anatoli, in appearance. Greta thought what a handsome pair of boys Edie had brought up. She remembered that David had been a looker as well. In fact David had been rather awesome in every way, very clever and, once they had grown out of childhood, she had always felt he was way above her.

'Oh, Peter's full of it,' Edie said happily. 'I can hardly believe he's three already – it won't be long before he's at school. And he goes off to the shop and helps Anatoli while I'm at work. I was worried to death when he first started taking him down there, in case he swallowed any of the pills or anything by mistake. But Anatoli says he's very sensible. He's starting to teach Peter the violin as well ... He's such a grown-up little chap already – he knows all his letters and he's learning to read.'

Greta listened enviously to Edie's pride in her son. If only she'd had a Mom and Dad who had spent time with her and taught her things! She felt handicapped by ignorance and awkwardness, a sense of wanting more but not knowing what to do about it. She went to her classes and read any book she could get her hands on, but she never really felt she knew what she was doing.

After Edie had asked after Pat's family, Greta plucked up the courage to say, 'Are you still going to the art school?' Ruskin Hall was another provision by the Cadbury foundation.

'Oh *yes*,' Edie enthused. 'I've had one of my paintings chosen to go in the exhibition again this year. And I've been doing some sculpture, which is all new to me. Oh, it's marvellous there! I don't think Anatoli would let me stop even if I wanted to – and I certainly don't!'

She looked at Greta intently. 'Why – are you interested in coming to the Ruskin as well?'

Greta blushed. 'I'm no good at drawing,' she said. *I'm no good at anything* was how she felt.

'You were always the clever one,' Edie said. 'I remember when you and David were little he used to read to you sometimes. Marleen always got bored and wandered off, but you used to sit there, your eyes almost out on stalks listening to him.'

'Did I?' Greta blushed. She could remember, dimly, sitting at David's side, his thick jumpers and wayward curls. 'I 'spect he read very well.'

'Oh yes – but so did you, later. You were a bright little spark. Janet always says you could have gone far.'

Though she didn't show it, Greta was glowing inside. She felt like getting up and doing cartwheels round the dining room. Someone believed she could do and be more! But she stumbled on the words *could have gone far* . . . Was it too late now? After her rebuff by Dennis she had fallen into marriage as if it was a refuge from everything else and an answer to all her problems.

It was then she made up her mind that she was going to take up the opportunities that working at Cadbury's offered her.

She joined the Monday French classes. Ever since she'd seen the picture of Hilda Hurlbutt, the Cadbury Girl of the Year, standing smartly dressed outside the church of the Sacré Coeur in Paris, where she had been taken for her prize, Greta had seen France and French as something romantic and desirable. Of course she had never learned French at school – not at the

Secondary Modern. In the eleven-plus she'd barely bothered to answer any of the questions – what was the point? That was how she had felt at the time. And then they'd gone to America anyway, where everything was different, and trying to study in any house where Carl Christie lived was impossible. So everything had drifted, any feeling that she might be good at anything or capable of more, even though her grandparents had told her that her father Wally had been a clever boy at school. That was how it had been for so long, even if they had thought she was the studious one. Anyone was studious compared with Marleen!

When she started the French classes she was afraid she would not be able to keep up. Dennis had been so proud of himself for learning German. She could never do that, she had thought at the time! She even saw Dennis from time to time, coming out of his German class. The two of them acted as if they didn't know each other, just looking away. The first time it happened Greta had a pang of sad regret, but it passed. Who needed that stuffy prat? she thought. He'd only liked her because he thought she was something other than she really was.

And she wasn't going to let him put her off her classes. Nervous as she was, she found the teacher patient and good at explaining, and Greta's hungry mind absorbed the new words quite easily and was always left longing for more.

'You're a natural at this,' Miss Davis, the French teacher, told her when she had been in the class for a few weeks. 'Well done. We'll expect great things of you.'

Great things! Greta felt she was almost going to

burst with excitement. She was learning and achieving something and someone expected something for her. From then on she felt she would do almost anything for Miss Davis, and she worked very hard at learning all the new vocabulary and verbs. She felt like a sponge, soaking it all in.

That was when she joined the Seven O'Clock Club and persuaded Pat to join as well.

'It'll do you good to get out for an evening,' she said. 'You can't stay in all the time with your Mom. Surely she wants you to enjoy yourself a bit?'

'Oh she tells me to go out and enjoy myself,' Pat said. 'Only I feel bad going out when she's been in with Josie all day. And Dad says it's my duty.'

'Well what about him stopping in?'

'He has a lot of church meetings,' Pat said loyally. 'It is very important you know.'

'Well I'd've thought you should get out sometimes,' Greta said, thinking what a grim, selfish man Mr Floyd seemed. Pat never said a word against him though, and Greta was amazed how much she was still under the thumb of her parents. They could hardly expect her to stay at home for ever, surely?

But apparently it was all right for Pat to go out the night of the club, so the two of them joined and began to enjoy themselves a lot, with the talks and out-ings and socials which the club organized. They had gone carol singing at Christmas and put on a play, and over the months Greta could feel herself expanding almost daily into someone different, who could learn and master new things, who wanted more, expected more from life ... And who was growing further and further away from her sweet, homely husband and his family, who, though kind and easy to be with, expected nothing much from life either.

They went to Trevor's Mom and Dad's every other Sunday for their dinner. When she first went, Greta had felt relieved to be in the familiar little house, after Dennis's family, where she always felt she had to try too hard and still couldn't match up to the glorious Franklins. With Nancy and Alf, and Trevor's sisters April and Dorrie, she was used to them and knew what to expect. She knew everyone could sit around for minutes if not hours at a time without saying anything, that she wasn't expected to perform and impress anyone. Nancy was partial to the boxing and Alf slept in his chair for half of Sunday afternoon then went down to his mate Jonno's house, where the pigeon coop was squeezed into the back garden.

''Ere, Gret – give us a hand,' Nancy would say when they got there. Even if it was already dinner time sometimes Nancy had not got round to putting the potatoes on and they never knew what time dinner would be. At first Greta enjoyed helping with April, but April became sulkier the older she got and Greta grew fed up with it all as well. You never knew when dinner would be done and in the end most of the afternoon got used up by cooking and eating, and then Nancy would sit back by the television with her fags and her pools coupons and say, 'Well the cook doesn't wash up,' so Greta and Trevor ended up doing it even though they'd helped cook most of the meal as well.

And every week no one had anything much to say and everything was the same: telly on, the gas fire pumping out in the front room so that the place was always blazing hot and their cheeks were burning red and everyone smelled sweaty, and she soon found herself desperate for reasons not to go. But she couldn't hurt Trevor's feelings by saying so. In her way, she knew, she was already hurting him enough.

Chapter Twenty-Four

'Where're you off to now?'

Trevor stretched out on his chair in front of the telly. The theme tune of *Z Cars* filled the room and he had to shout to be heard over it.

Greta already had her coat on.

'Out.'

'Out where?' A sudden surge of energy hoisted Trevor from the chair. He clicked off the television and the room went quiet. 'Where d'yer think you're going this time?'

'I told you...' Greta fished in her pockets for her gloves. It was only October, but a cold snap had arrived. 'I said earlier – I'm just meeting Pat – for a coffee, that's all.'

'Oh – a coffee!' Trevor mocked. 'Tea not good enough for you now then? What the hell're you meeting her for? You work with her all bloody day – what more can you have to say to each other?'

Greta kept calm, but she wanted to scream at Trevor. *What d'you want me to do? Stay in with you for ever more, when you haven't got a word to say about anything?*

'She just asked me to come. I think she'd got something on her mind.'

'Oh – summat on her mind eh...' Trevor made a mocking, sinuous movement with his body which was somehow more insulting than his words. 'Well it must be nice to know a woman with summat on her mind . . .'

'Don't be so horrible, Trev,' Greta snapped. 'That's disgusting.'

'Ooh – since when have you been so prim and proper? Why can't you stay in for once?'

'You'll just watch telly. You don't want me here anyway, do you? You never say a word when I am here.'

He looked upset now. 'No, but we don't have to talk – we could cuddle up, watch Z Cars. Go on, Gret – just for once.' He came towards her, putting his hands on her shoulders, trying to seduce her. 'It's a long time since we had a proper kiss and cuddle. Go on, stay in.'

Looking up at him she thought what nice eyes he had. She knew that really, that his eyes were big, grey and somehow innocent; it was just that these days she didn't look at him very much.

'Look, I've promised,' she said. 'I can't let her down . . .'

His hands fell from her shoulders and he backed away. 'You can let me down all right though, can't you? OK – suit yourself.' He switched the telly on again and threw himself down in the chair.

Sergeant Bert Lynch was saying something urgent on the screen. Greta thought about apologizing, promising they'd stay in together tomorrow. But he was lost in the programme.

She went to the front door and slipped outside.

They decided to take the bus into town, found a coffee bar near the end of Bull Street and sat with their espressos in the steamy warmth with other young people, mostly couples, around them on the high stools by the counter and at the tables. In the background The Seekers were singing 'I'll Never Find Another You'. This was more like it, Greta thought. A bit of life and freedom!

Pat hummed along, then started giggling.

'What's up with you?' Greta asked, though it set her off as well. It was a way of letting off steam after her argument with Trevor. For a moment the two of them sat and laughed. Pat's eyes were dancing with life and Greta had never seen her look so much as if she was bursting with news.

'Go on – what's up? Spit it out!'

Pat beamed. 'I think I'm in love!'

'What? You're never!' Pat, who never had boy-friends or anything like that. Not that she wasn't pretty in a sweet way, but she barely ever got out to meet anyone. 'Who on earth with?'

'His name's Ian, and he's ever so good-looking, and he's . . .' She hesitated, blushing even more deeply. 'Well, he's a few years older than me.' She looked anxiously at Greta as if waiting for her approval.

Greta was laughing with astonishment. 'How did this come about then, all of a sudden? I thought they never let you out!'

'It was that wedding we went to on Saturday, over at Kings Heath . . .' She was girlish with excitement.

'Oh – someone from the church then?'

'Well no – not exactly.' Pat looked bashful. 'It was after the service: we were all standing round outside while they had their pictures taken and all the confetti and that, and I was at the edge of the crowd and suddenly I realized there was this gorgeous bloke standing next to me. I sort of looked round at him and he smiled and I smiled back and then he said, "Are you one of the family?" I said "No," and he kept looking at me and he told me he was one of the drivers, taking them to the do afterwards. Well, we went off to the hall they'd hired and of course he was there and one way or another we spent most of the afternoon together. I kept out of Mom and Dad's way – she was busy with Josie, Dad was hobnobbing and there were too many people there for them to pay me too much notice. And by the end, he asked me out!'

Pat was blooming, Greta could see, as if all her natural prettiness had been brought into flower by this attention.

'So – you going with him?'

Pat's face clouded. 'Thing is, Mom and Dad don't know. I daren't tell them. They're touchy enough as it is . . .'

'But they must want you to have a life of your own?'

'They wouldn't like Ian – he's not a Christian and he's older than me.'

'How old?'

Pat looked down at the red Formica-covered table. 'He's thirty-one.'

'Hmmm,' Greta said. 'Well, they'd have a point.'

Pat looked sharply up at her. 'I thought you'd be pleased for me.'

'I *am*. Don't get me wrong. But ten years is quite an age gap.'

'It doesn't feel like a gap when I'm with him,' Pat said dreamily. 'He's lovely to me. I've never felt like this before.'

'Well—' Greta sat back, holding up her coffee cup, taken aback by the pang of envy that shot through her. 'Lucky you.'

The music in the bar changed to the Beatles singing 'Help!'

'I think it's the Real Thing,' Pat was saying breathlessly. 'God, Gret – I just can't stop thinking about him. D'you know what I mean?'

Greta looked into Pat's eager face. Did she know? Yes, she had been besotted with Dennis all right, or thought she was. Never with Trevor.

'Yeah – I think I do,' she said.

And she ached inside as she said it.

Ian Plumbridge, as he was called, was all Pat could talk about at work now. One minute she'd be working at manic speed, pulling the chocolates off the belt, the next, standing there as if she'd forgotten what she was supposed to be doing and getting left behind.

Often the radio was tuned to *Music While You Work* in the mornings and everyone sang along. One morning soon after the forewoman, Janice, wandered along the long rows of women working in their white overalls and caps, most of them singing away, and then she went over and clicked the radio off. There was a great collective groan.

'Hey – what's that for?'

'What's happened to the music?'

'Bit of a break, I thought,' she said, looking hard at Pat. 'Some of us've got their heads up in the clouds!'

'Aw – come on, Jan,' someone else moaned. 'We want our music back again!'

'We were listening to Shirley Bassey!'

Pat looked mortified and turned back to work with renewed vigour.

'What the hell's got into you?' Greta demanded at the break. 'You're a proper Little Dolly Daydream.'

'Ooh, I feel in a right tizz,' Pat said. 'I can't sleep and I'm all sort of floaty. Thing is, Gret—' She stared at Greta, obviously daring herself to speak. 'It's very difficult for Ian and me to meet, what with Mom and Dad and all that. Ian lives out at Barnt Green as well so it's a bit of a way. I was wondering . . .'

'Ye-e-s?' Greta could already guess where this was leading.

'Well I thought, maybe if I said I was coming to meet you, and Ian and I could meet instead?'

'Thanks,' Greta said drily.

'Oh, I'm sorry, Gret! It's not that I don't want to meet you but I want to see Ian so much and I can't say anything to them. They'd go mad at me – they'd never let me out again!'

'For God's sake, Pat – you're twenty-one years of age!'

'I know – but you don't know what Dad's like . . .'

'Yeah, yeah – course I don't mind,' Greta said. 'Tell them what you like. I just hope this fella of yours is worth all this.'

Pat's face lit up. 'Oh, he is, Gret. Really he is!'

Chapter Twenty-Five

A few days later a raw wind was driving across Bournville Green as Greta left work. The sky was a heavy grey, the grass edged with the remains of the last soggy autumn leaves. She walked head down against the stinging wind, and as she passed the old Day Continuation School she heard the bells of the carillon in the tower across the Green.

When she reached the road she was in another world, thinking about Pat and this Ian bloke she never seemed to hear the end of at the moment, when she suddenly realized a car was crawling alongside her by the kerb.

'Greta!' Edie was winding down the window of Anatoli's black Pontiac. 'You all right, love – like a lift? You could come for tea if you've got the time!'

Greta hesitated, seeing the car was almost full, with Anatoli and Peter and also Janet and her girls. And Trevor would be expecting her home. But there was something in the way Edie called out to her as if she was an equal. She felt a sudden longing. She wouldn't be late – they were only going for a cup of tea. And she liked the idea of being seen climbing into their big, swish American car!

'Well yes, thanks – that'd be nice,' she said.

Anatoli came round and ushered her into the back seat in his gentlemanly way and she found herself next to little Naomi, who gazed solemnly at her.

'Hello, dear,' Janet said warmly. 'How're you and Trevor getting on?'

'Oh, all right,' Greta said flatly.

She saw Janet looking at her rather intently, but she didn't ask any more. *No children yet . . . ?* Greta could feel her thinking.

Edie and Anatoli lived in a big house across the road from the university. It felt cosy inside on this dark winter day, a fire burning in the front room, where there were comfortable chairs, Anatoli's grand piano and violins, along with a comfortable scattering of sheet music. There were a large number of pictures on the walls, some of Edie's – a landscape over the mantelpiece on which there were family photographs – and some Russian icons in gold and other rich colours, and colourful Persian rugs covered the floorboards.

Peter and the twins ran straight to the piano and started hammering out a proper racket on it.

'No, not now, loves,' Edie protested. 'We'll go into the kitchen and find you something nice to eat, shall we? Do sit down, Greta – I shan't be long.'

Anatoli helped make the tea in his usual solicitous fashion, carried in angel cakes and biscuits and then said, 'If you'll excuse me ladies . . .' and disappeared off to his snug at the back of the house.

At first Greta thought she would fall into her usual role of playing with the children, almost as if she was still one of them, and she was down on the floor with the three of them, Peter, and Ruth and Naomi, who were six now and had started school. But then Edie said,

'Here you three – *Play School*'s about to start. They can sit and watch that, Greta – give you a break.'

The television was in the back room, and soon the

three of them were settled in front of it, all trying to squeeze into one armchair and pushing biscuits erratically towards their mouths, eyes fixed raptly on the screen.

Greta felt awkward then, unsure where to sit, but Edie beckoned her kindly, handing her a cup of tea.

'Come on, love, come and sit with us. I should've bought some crumpets to toast if I'd thought.'

'Never mind – it was all a bit spur of the moment wasn't it?' Janet said. She smiled encouragingly at Greta. 'It's lovely to see you, dear. We don't see very much of your mother these days.'

'No,' Greta said. 'I s'pose not.' She wasn't sure what to say. Ruby was so caught up with Herbert and Marleen and going to work that she scarcely had time for anything else. And she knew her Mom felt left out with Edie and Janet, now Edie had gone up in the world and was living in a big house.

'She seems all right though?' Edie said, sitting down, balancing a plate with a cake on it on the arm of her chair.

'I think so,' Greta said. She didn't see much of Mom either, even though they only lived round the corner, but that suited her very well.

'You look tired, Jan,' Edie said.

'Ah.' Janet's kindly face smiled wearily. 'Just middle age creeping up on me.'

'Is he having bad nights again?'

'Yes – off and on. It's not too bad at the moment.'

Edie looked at Greta and explained gently, 'It's the war, you see. Martin and Anatoli – some of the things they had to see – it doesn't leave you.'

'How's Anatoli?' Janet asked.

'Oh, he's all right. It's not nightmares so much for

him – it's just, he's so moody and changeable. Sometimes he gets very down, goes all silent on me. He says I'm not to take any notice, it's not my fault or anything. It's as if he gets these attacks of gloom and then comes out of them. I feel ever so shut out. But he does come out of them and it's all right then.'

'At least we know what it is,' Janet said. 'And actually, that's not what's been on my mind. It's the girls – school and everything.' Her eyes filled. 'Oh sorry – I didn't come to be miserable.'

'Don't be silly,' Edie said, squeezing her friend's arm. 'What's happened? People being rude?'

'Yes – the stares, the comments. I mean it was bad enough when they were babies but at least it was just directed at me then. All those "Oh, she's been with a black man" sort of smirks and remarks. People can be nastier than you could ever believe. Calling the girls golliwogs and all that sort of thing. Well they couldn't understand then, not when they were babies. I mean they're not the only coloured children in the school, but the others are from Jamaica and Trinidad, and at least when their mothers come to collect them they're the right colour. Poor little Naomi had some vicious, bullying little boy pinning her up against the playground wall the other day, demanding to know why her Mum wasn't a golliwog and making her open her mouth so he could look inside, as if she was a horse!'

'Oh, how awful!' Edie said. 'It's so terrible the way people pick on anyone who's different. I know Anatoli had a bit of it when he first came here, but of course he soon learned English and blended in. But poor Ruth and Naomi . . .'

'The thing is, they're only little . . .' Janet wiped her eyes. 'And up until now they've just sort of accepted

Martin and me as their parents. But now of course we're having to explain about being adopted and being Congolese and everything all at once.'

'Ah,' Edie said. 'Poor little mites. It's a lot to take in at their age isn't it? And with people being so unkind . . .'

Greta felt uncomfortable, thinking of things Ruby had said, and Nancy Biddle, about all the blacks who were coming in these days. If she said, 'But what about Ruth and Naomi?' Ruby would say, 'Oh well that's different.'

'Not everyone's unkind,' Janet said. 'Some people have been very good and accepting. But you can't help feeling it when people are so ignorant and cruel. We're all human, after all. Thank goodness for the Friends – they always have a lovely welcome at the Meeting House. Anyway—' She rallied herself. 'That's enough of my woes. Your little Peter is looking full of beans. And how's David?'

Edie's face clouded. 'Well – he's certainly working hard. And Gila. She's still pushing on to be a dentist. I know it's what they want and in the long run it'll be good for them – but I don't like it. It seems all wrong to me, having Shimon up on the kibbutz or in Tel Aviv. He's with Gila's aunt mostly now – goes to school in Tel Aviv. I don't know how Gila can stand it. It feels all wrong to me. They should be a proper family, not living all over the place like this. I worry about them – it's all such a strain.'

Greta listened, intrigued by any mention of David, whose life was so unimaginably different from her own. An image came to her of seeing him, aged eleven or so, walking home from school with his satchel and his serious, studious expression, which suddenly broke into a beaming smile when he saw her. They'd been play-mates then, equals, before he grew a few years older and transformed into a superior being who went to the grammar school and hardly spoke to girls any more.

'I've begged and begged him to think about coming over here,' Edie was saying. 'Anatoli thinks it would be better too. He worries for him. But David won't hear of it.'

She turned to Greta. 'D'you ever hear from him, love?'

'Sometimes – at Christmas usually.'

'Yes – he's good like that. Keeps in touch with his family.'

Greta was touched by the way she said 'family' so proudly. Edie and David were not related by blood in any way, but she had brought him up.

'Nothing like family,' Edie was saying. 'I thank God every day for Anatoli and Peter . . .'

She stopped suddenly and leaned forward to put more coal on the fire, perhaps realizing she had not been tactful. Janet and Martin had not been able to have children of their own, and Greta knew everyone was beginning to wonder about her.

They turned their attention to her now, asking how things were. As the two older women looked at her she realized they were in some way concerned about her but were too tactful to ask. Is everything all right? How is your marriage? Is there a problem over having children? These questions were in their looks, but they would not have voiced them. She felt the same concern that she knew they had always had for her Mom, for Ruby's men troubles and her erratic life.

'I'm doing French lessons.' She spoke shyly, afraid of being mocked. When she told her Mom, Ruby had said, 'Huh – don't s'pose you'll stick at that for long. You've never even been to France, have you?'

'Oh that's marvellous!' Janet exclaimed.

'What a good idea!' Edie agreed.

They asked her about it and wondered whether she might think about taking up any other classes. When Anatoli came into the room to suggest a lift home, he was told about it too.

'French lessons! Ah – what a very good thing. Well done, my dear. Keep it up!'

When he dropped Greta off at the end of Alliott Road and she walked the brief distance home in the dark she felt uplifted and glowing from Edie's and Janet's encouragement. She felt warm inside, and understood, and bubbling with excitement.

'Oh – so you finally made it!'

Trevor was in a right state when she came in. He was sitting in front of the gabbling telly. Glancing at the clock she saw to her horror that it was a quarter to seven. She'd had no idea she was going to stay so late!

'God – sorry, Trev,' she said, sincerely. 'I lost track of the time – I'll get the dinner on.'

'Too bloody late – I've been down the chippy.' He got up, glowering. Only then did she take in the fishy, vinegary smell in the room. 'Thought I'd better, since my *wife* wasn't going to bother turning up.' He didn't even bother to ask where she'd been, and for a moment she thought he was going to hit her.

'Edie asked me back for tea, that's all,' she said, backing away, trying to calm him. 'They gave me a lift down to the Bristol Road and I had to wait for him to give me one back . . .'

Trevor's face was closed and sulky and he sat back down by the television.

'I had our tea half ready anyway – the rest of that stew. You could have had some ... Done some potatoes to go with it ...' She couldn't hold back her sarcasm. 'Or is boiling a few spuds beyond you?'

There was no reply for a while. Then eventually, like a sullen child, he said, 'I don't care where you've been.'

Trevor sulked all evening and barely said a word. At first Greta felt apologetic, then impatient. And she didn't like him ignoring her. She sat by him on their old sofa and Trevor, sprawled with legs stretched out, wouldn't even look at her.

'I've said sorry, haven't I? What more d'you want? All I did was go out for a cup of tea.'

'*All?*' Trevor snapped.

'Well it's not the crime of the century is it?'

He folded his arms more tightly and kept staring ahead.

'Trevor!' she protested, suddenly wanting him to be nice to her, to forgive her. She tried cuddling up to him, undid the top buttons of her blouse, and in the end he gave in and put his arm round her.

'You shouldn't keep going out all the time,' he said. 'I want you here – you're my wife.'

'I know I'm your wife.' She spoke to him seductively. 'I never meant to stay out so long ...'

'Well, what d'you want to go and see them for anyway? They're not your age are they?'

'No, but ...' She couldn't easily explain. They'd known her always, but also they had things she

201

wanted, they had lives full of interest, better lives than hers. But all she said was, 'They're a bit like aunties I s'pose.'

Trevor soon came round. She knew he loved it when she cuddled up to him, wanting something from him.

'Let's go up shall we?' he said after a while, giving her a wink.

That night things were good. Trevor got into bed and immediately snuggled up and started making love to her. She cuddled him back, knowing she could please him easily and make things better between them. He lay on top of her, grinning with pleasure as he moved inside her, and when he'd finished he lay back, panting.

'There – I bet that's made us a babby,' he said happily.

'Yes, love,' she said, stroking his chest, glad he was happier now because she needed to feel loved and held by someone. 'Maybe it has.'

Chapter Twenty-Six

Pat was changing. Ever since she and Greta started at Cadbury's she'd always been the quiet one. Greta had always felt like the lively one who took the risks, and she knew she was safe with Pat. Now it was as if her best friend was living a double life.

Before Christmas she asked Greta if she could use their house as a place to get changed before meeting Ian.

'Thing is, I've bought myself a new outfit and I don't want Mom and Dad to see,' Pat said bashfully. 'They think I'm coming to see you anyway, so that sort of makes it true, doesn't it?'

'Well, I s'pose so,' Greta said. They were standing outside at the end of work, in the hot, chocolatey breath of the factory.

'You don't sound very sure,' Pat said, disappointed. 'I thought you said you didn't mind if I said I was with you? I know it's not very nice lying, but . . .'

'No – it's all right,' Greta said. 'Course you can.' It would have been hard to explain to Pat that she was much less bothered about her telling fibs to her Mom and Dad than about the way she seemed to be moving on so fast. She needed Pat to be her old, sweet, reliable self. 'Anyroad—' She forced a cheerful note into her voice. 'I want to see this outfit of yours.'

That night Pat got changed in their bedroom and came down wearing a knitted Orlon dress, in black and orange stripes, with a black belt nipping her in at the waist and matching shoes with kitten heels. She stood in front of Greta and Trevor, blushing but pleased with herself.

'Well – d'you like it? I got it at C&A.'

Trevor said, 'It looks nice, Pat.' And he seemed genuine.

'It's lovely,' Greta said, though she was a bit taken aback. Pat had put black eye-liner on and her long hair was hanging loose. Instead of appearing mousy she looked suddenly quite glamorous.

'Blimey,' Trevor said when she'd hurried off to meet Ian. He looked a bit disapproving. 'What's happened to her?'

'She's in love,' Greta said.

'Looks a bit fast to me.'

Pat started coming round once a week, more if she could get away with it, changed her clothes and went eagerly off to meet Ian, who would drive over in his Ford and pick her up. She was full of him all the time, especially at work: Ian's taking me to the Hippodrome, Ian says this, Ian says that, all over the Christmas period, until Greta wanted to say, 'Can we just talk about something else for a change d'you think?' But she never said it. Pat was on cloud nine and she didn't want to shoot her down. Lucky Pat.

It was Christmas when Nancy Biddle had a proper go at her. They'd gone round to have Christmas dinner with them. Greta was coming to dread it more each time. She found it so boring.

'D'you want some help?' she asked Nancy, as usual.

She didn't mind doing the veg or whatever was needed. It was better than just sitting around!

'Oh ta, bab – we could do with yer,' Nancy said. 'In fact you're more help than these two—' She nodded at April and Dorrie. 'Dor – go and let the dog out to cock his leg, will yer, before he has an accident on the floor. And April – you go and set the table.'

Having got rid of her two daughters, Greta realized, had given Nancy the chance to start on her.

'Here—' Nancy circled the kitchen, a cigarette burning at the corner of her mouth, screwing up her eyes against the smoke. Handing Greta a big bag of potatoes and a blunt knife, she said, 'You'd better get started on these. Sit at the table there, bab – I'll bring you a bowl of water.'

Nancy was a kindly sort, and Greta set to work happily enough while Nancy chopped lumps of lard into the roasting pan and pushed it into the oven. There was a huge joint of beef waiting on the table.

'Want a cuppa tea, bab? There's some in the pot.'

'Oh – yes please,' Greta said. Nancy fished out a packet of custard creams.

'Go on – have one. The dinner won't be ready for hours yet.'

April and Dorrie, having done as they were asked, were now drifting in and out of the kitchen and Nancy shooed them out. She sat down at the table with a grunt, stubbed out her cigarette and spooned sugar into the tea.

'Now then,' she said bluntly. 'I've been meaning to have a word with yer. I'm not being funny with yer, bab, but – is there summat wrong with you and Trevor in the bed department?'

Greta stirred her own tea, looking down at the table as a thick blush spread through her cheeks.

'What d'you mean?' She looked up, trying to make her expression as innocent as possible.

'What d'you think I mean, wench? You and our Trevor have been married for more than two years now, and no sign of a babby on the way. I know not everyone goes for having them straight off, but Trevor says he wants kids and you're trying for 'em.' Her tone softened a little. 'You know love, there might be a problem. Have you thought about going and seeing the doctor?'

'Well . . . no,' Greta stumbled, trying to think what to say. 'I mean, I s'pose I thought . . .'

'What, bab?' Nancy was motherly now, her freckly face sympathetic. She lit up another cigarette. 'You thought things would come right in the end?'

Greta's cheeks were absolutely burning now. She felt guilty and panic-stricken all at once. 'Yes, I mean, I thought maybe it takes some time . . . I don't know really.'

Nancy leaned over and touched her hand for a second. 'Course you don't. You're only young. That's when you need a bit of advice. Your mother said anything?'

'A bit.' Of course Ruby had hinted at things occasionally, but she was wrapped up in her own life and Greta thought she seemed quite relieved not to have any more grandchildren to deal with just yet.

'Well look, love. You might well be right: sometimes it does take a little while. I mean I've had long enough gaps between mine, and not for want of trying. But I've got a bit of a tilted womb, the doctor said. It might be nothing, but maybe you should go and get yourself looked at?'

Greta saw that she had no choice but to go along with it, so she smiled gratefully and said, 'All right. I'll go – soon as Christmas is over.'

Later that evening, once the meal was over, they went to call on Ruby and the rest of the family for tea. Ruby had the house all decorated with tinsel and streamers. Mary Lou and Elvis both squeaked with excitement when they saw Trevor and he was immediately in his element, throwing Elvis up in the air and trapping Mary Lou between his legs and tickling her while she giggled in delight.

'Don't overdo it,' Ruby warned. 'Or she'll be sick.'

But Mary Lou was on at him all evening. 'More tickles Uncle Trevor, gimme more!'

'That's what those children need,' Herbert remarked. He had settled in the big chair by the fire with his slippers on and a good supply of ale, and he didn't move all evening. 'They need a father figure.'

Who asked you anyway? Greta thought, furiously. She saw Marleen rolling her eyes.

'Pass us another one of those pies, Rube,' Herbert commanded. Ruby got up and handed him the plate of mince pies.

Why does she do that? Greta wondered. Why not tell that fat slob to get up and get them himself?

'Maybe you're the father figure round here now then,' she said nastily.

Herbert laughed, undoing his huge cardigan. 'Oh I think I'm a bit long in the tooth to be able to help with that.'

'Or with anything, by the looks of it.'

'*Greta!*' Ruby said in a warning voice.

Within a few minutes of being in the house, with the stifling front room, the sight of Herbert Smail, of her Mom being used by him, of Marleen, whippet-thin and sulky, and Trevor obsessed with the kids, Greta was desperate to get out again. It was like walking back into the same old trap. There must be more to life than this, surely? But she was so confused. What did she want? One minute she longed for a cosy family like Edie, the next she wanted to be Cadbury Girl of the Year, learning French, off travelling the world!

She watched Trevor guiltily as he helped Elvis roll in a backward somersault off his lap. Marleen was watching too, smiling at Elvis's excitement. Both their faces were lit up and Greta hadn't seen Trevor look so happy in a long time. He looked sweet and boyish as he always did when he smiled. What she should do was stop being so selfish and give him reason to smile more often. She should give in and let him have the babies he longed for so much. After all, she had married him, for better or worse. She surrendered, that afternoon. Why try to be different? Everyone was on at her. She'd stop taking the pills and just give in, let it happen. She'd do what everyone else wanted and maybe it would all come right.

Chapter Twenty-Seven

The next morning she went downstairs as usual early, to make a cup of tea. This was when she usually took her pill, while Trevor was still safely upstairs out of the way. Shivering in the cold, she lit the gas under the kettle then fished around in the cupboard for the little soap box, with the picture of a sprig of lavender on the lid, where she kept her pills. She was intending to throw it in the bin, have done with it.

'Then I'll wait and see what happens,' she said to herself.

She perched on a chair by the table, the little card with the pills in front of her. ENOVID, it said along the side. She stared at it, only realizing how long she'd sat there in a daze when the kettle boiled. She knew she couldn't bring herself to do it. Not today. Maybe tomorrow – or next week ... Getting up quickly, before she could change her mind, she fetched a cup of water and swallowed today's pill down, feeling relief surge through her.

He's the one who should have been a woman, she thought. If he wants a babby that badly, he could just get on with it!

The first day she was back at work after Christmas and in the swing of things, she wondered how she could have even thought of doing anything else.

'Ian bought me a coat for Christmas,' was the first

thing Pat said when she saw her. 'It's beautiful – it's black and ever so elegant.' She was full of it, pink-cheeked, her eyes sparkling.

'That's nice. He must have a bob or two to spend,' Greta said morosely. She was sick of hearing about Ian Plumbridge – he was all Pat ever went on about these days.

'He has,' Pat said, almost purring. 'And he's ever so good to me.'

Pat talked about Ian all through the coffee break, and it was only as they were heading back to the conveyer belt with its regiments of Dairy Milk bars that she said,

'Did you have a nice Christmas, Gret? I bet it's lovely now you're married and everything. All the families together and that.'

'It was all right,' Greta said, remembering that, what now seemed like an eternity ago, she had thought getting married and away from home would solve all her problems. She knew Pat was desperate to get away from home, even though in her loyalty to her Mom and Dad she could never admit it.

'Ian's taking me out to a New Year's party,' Pat said before they parted to go to their workplaces. 'I don't know where I'm going to tell Mom and Dad I'm going. Could we pretend you're having a party at yours?'

'Oh, I expect so,' Greta said wearily. She wondered why she felt rubbed up the wrong way by Pat's starry-eyed love affair and realized that she expected it to end in tears one way or another. That was what happened with men and love.

*

210

She spent the next few weeks being Pat's pretend chaperone and avoiding Trevor's Mom so that she couldn't keep going on at her about whether she'd seen the doctor. She felt very distant from Pat, and as the weeks went by Pat seemed to withdraw a bit as well. Greta wondered if things with Ian were going downhill. By February Pat was looking pale and drawn. She didn't like to ask.

One day she turned to look at Pat along the line where they were working. She was white-faced and seemed to be struggling with tears.

'I don't want to be nosy,' Greta said to her during their break, 'but you look ever so miserable. Are things not going too well with lover boy?'

She kept her tone light and joking, but Pat glowered at her from under her cap.

'Of course everything's all right – why wouldn't it be?'

'You just look a bit down, that's all.'

Pat forced her face into a smile. 'I'm not – I'm perfectly all right. I've just got a bit of a cold.'

'Everything all right at home – Josie?'

'Josie's much as ever.'

And she wouldn't say any more, but Greta was uneasy. She felt quite sure there was something up with Pat when all her rosy, happy appearance seemed to have drained away so fast.

A few days later, Greta found out why.

It was Valentine's Day and she and Trevor had intended to go out. Out of guilt she was trying her best to make the best of things and be kind to Trevor.

'It's horrible out there,' Trev said, coming in from work out of a night of pelting rain and having to towel his hair dry. 'Let's just have our dinner in front of the telly, shall we? You know, just you and me, have a cuddle?'

'OK,' Greta said, relieved. She didn't especially want to go and sit in some beery pub staring at Trevor over his pint, though she would have done to try and please him. 'I've done us egg and chips.'

'Lovely!' Trevor said happily. 'I'm starving. Bring us the ketchup, love.'

They settled down together on the old sofa and watched *Blue Murder at St Trinian's.* Trevor thought Joyce Grenfell was very funny. Greta wondered what real boarding schools were like. Full of posh girls in funny clothes learning all sorts of things like Latin and Greek and reciting Shakespeare all the time. She wondered what it would be like to be one of them. She couldn't imagine it.

The room was warm and cosy and they had hot cups of cocoa on the little rickety table in front of them. It felt nice not to have to go out in the wet. Trevor put his arm round Greta and she felt a rush of affection for him and snuggled up to him.

'That's nice, love,' Trevor looked down at her, delighted, pulling her even closer. It wasn't often these days that she was all soft and cuddly with him. She so often seemed to be rushing off somewhere. He kissed her and leaned round to stroke her breast, his eyes glazing with desire.

'Shall we skip the end and go to bed?' he murmured.

'Oh, let's just watch the end,' she said sleepily.

'Sit on my lap, then . . .'

She snuggled up on Trevor's lap. This was all right.

It was nice to be wanted, to have someone to come home to . . . In a moment of softness she nuzzled against his cheek. Rain blew against the windows.

'Ah, Gret,' Trevor said dreamily, squeezing her tighter. He slipped his hand inside her blouse, then her bra. 'Ooh, come on – let's go on up.'

The credits were just beginning to roll as the jaunty theme music played and Trevor kissed her hungrily.

'I don't think we're going to make it upstairs, are we?' Greta teased him, but her words were cut off by an urgent hammering on the front door.

'Who the bloody hell's that?' Trevor groaned as Greta jumped up.

'No idea . . .' Her heart was pounding with shock. 'Sounds like the fuzz, banging like that . . . You haven't been up to anything have you, Trev?'

'Course not!' he said as the thunderous banging came again.

She opened up, and outside in the soaking darkness saw a stranger with dark hair and a lean, handsome face. She had no idea who he was.

'Are you Greta?' He was obviously in a state, eyes roving nervously from side to side.

'Yeah . . . Who're you?'

He jerked his head towards the road. 'I've got Pat Floyd in the car. She told me to come here. She's been taken bad.'

Greta was glad to feel Trevor standing in the hall behind her.

'What d'you mean? Are you Ian?'

'Yes – give me a hand will you? She's really bad. Said she couldn't go home and I was to come here . . . I didn't know what else to do.' She could tell he couldn't get rid of Pat fast enough.

Without even thinking of a coat, Greta followed him to the car. Through the wet windows she could just make out someone slumped inside, on the passenger seat. Ian opened the door.

'Pat?'

Even in the gloom she could see the terrible pallor of Pat's face. She was lying across the seat, barely even conscious. She managed to open her eyes.

'Gret?' Her voice was slurred. 'Help me, for God's sake . . .'

'Trevor!' Greta shouted, only to find he was already beside her. 'We'll have to take her in – put her to bed . . . Both of you, get her out,' she instructed the two men. 'Sit her in the front room and I'll get the bed ready.' She caught Ian's arm as he went to obey. 'How long's she been like this?'

He wouldn't look her in the eye. 'It just came on this afternoon,' he said.

He and Trevor gently took Pat from the car, and half carried, half dragged her into the house. She gave terrible moans as they moved her, especially as they jerked her up the step into the hall.

It was only once they were in the front room, in the light, that they could see the full horror of the situation. Greta, following them, gave a sickened gasp.

'Oh my God, what's happened?' she cried.

Pat's clothes and all the backs of her legs were drenched in blood, so much that it was seeping down into her shoes. Her head lolled and she passed into unconsciousness.

Chapter Twenty-Eight

Greta grabbed a towel and flung it on the chair as they struggled to sit Pat down. She was a dead weight and her head rolled back, eyes closed. There was a smear of blood down her cheek.

'Trev, go and call an ambulance!' Greta fumbled frantically in her bag for change.

'No – you mustn't!' Ian tried to stop him. 'No one's got to know about this . . .'

'What're you on about!' She was screaming at him in panic. A creeping tide of blood was seeping through the towel Pat was sitting on. 'For God's sake, look at her – she'll bleed to death – *go on*, Trevor!'

Ian tried to stop him but Trevor flung him off, cursing, and ran for the phone box. Greta seized Ian Plumbridge's arm, sinking her fingernails into him.

'What've you done to her you bastard? She was perfectly all right and *now* look at her!'

'It was . . .' The man looked scared and almost tearful. 'We went to someone – a doctor – paid him. They said he was a proper doctor, it'd all be all right. I mean she was all right earlier on, just a bit pale, and then this started, this evening. And it just got worse and worse. She kept saying not to tell her Mom and Dad and then it was just blood everywhere . . .'

'Doctor for what? What're you on about?' Greta raged at him.

215

'The baby – she was having a baby . . . She said her Dad'd kill her . . .'

'Oh my God.' Greta was stunned. 'Oh, Pat – you poor, poor, stupid girl . . .' She went to her friend, taking her hand and gripping it tightly. Pat moaned, barely conscious. 'It's all right love – we'll get help. Oh, you poor babby – we'll look after you . . . Pat love, can you hear me?'

There came a tiny moan from Pat's throat, then her eyes flickered open, full of fear and anguish.

'What – I can't hear you?' Greta leaned closer.

'For God's sake . . . don't . . . tell . . . my Dad . . .'

Greta visited Pat the next afternoon in Selly Oak Hospital. She found her at the far end of the long Nightingale ward, looking as if she had been put in the corner in disgrace. And that was how it felt, the way the doctors and nurses treated her, as a dirty, fallen woman. She had had a huge blood transfusion, and lay under the covers, eyes closed, her face a ghastly white, and too weak to move. Greta only just managed to stop herself weeping at the sight of her.

'Pat . . .'

Her eyes opened with the same look of terror Greta had seen in them before.

'It's OK – it's me, love.' Greta found herself saying things a mother might say. 'Look, I've brought you some flowers . . .' She had some bright bunches of daffs and freesias. 'And some chocolate for when you feel a bit better – home from home, eh?' Pat was especially partial to Crunchie and Fudge, so she'd gone and got some misshapen ones from the factory shop for her.

She had been speaking in what she hoped was a

chirpy, cheering tone, but when she turned to Pat she saw there were tears streaming down her cheeks. And Pat was shielding her face with her hands as if she couldn't stand anyone looking at her.

'Oh, Pat!' Greta sat down and reached for her friend's hand again, unable to stop her own tears as well now. 'Your poor thing.' She leaned closer, seeing that Pat was trying to speak.

'I killed my baby,' Pat sobbed weakly, 'and all these people think I'm terrible . . .'

'I don't s'pose they do,' Greta tried to say, though she could see really that Pat was right.

'You should see the way they look at me – as if I'm dirty and wicked And one nurse called me a murdering bitch . . .' Through her sobs, she said, 'I expect you think that too, Gret?'

'No!' Greta squeezed her hand. How could she think such a thing when she was taking pills day after day to stop babies from being born! 'Course I don't. You had to . . .'

'It was Ian's babby and I love him, and . . .' Crying even more, she choked out the words. 'They said they'd be informing my next of kin and I said no, they mustn't! But they said they have to and they'll have told Mom and Dad. He'll kill me – I know what he'll say . . .'

'Has your Mom been in to see you?' Greta asked.

Pat shook her head, miserably. 'Maybe she won't want to see me – or Dad won't let her . . .'

Greta's heart ached for her, seeing her friend in such a low state, physically and mentally.

'Are you going to be all right?' She squeezed Pat's hand. 'You gave us the most terrible fright.'

'They say I should be . . .' Tears rolled down her

217

cheeks again. 'But they don't know if I'll be able to have a babby again . . .'

'Oh, Pat, I expect you will . . .'

'And they keep on at me wanting me to tell them the name of the doctor who did the . . . Who took it away . . .'

'Well you'll tell them, won't you? He wants stringing up, whoever he is!'

Pat shook her head, and to Greta's disbelief, whispered urgently, 'No! He was kind and he was trying to help us. He didn't charge that much – not like some. And he did his best. He said things should be easier for women when this happens . . . I don't want to get him into trouble.'

Before Greta could argue, she caught sight of someone coming in through the double doors at the far end of the ward and a second later she saw Pat register it as well – her Mom, Mrs Floyd, was walking between the other beds towards them. She looked even more drab in these surroundings, her brown coat pulled protectively round her, the collar still up and her face, never adorned with makeup, was dreadfully pale and pitted with worry and grief. Greta wondered whether to get up and leave, but there wasn't time. Mrs Floyd had seen her and hesitated for a second, but then came towards them.

'Hello, Greta,' she said flatly, stopping a few feet from the bed.

'Hello, Mrs Floyd . . .'

But her eyes were fixed on Pat's face and Greta saw in Pat's eyes the defenceless, frightened longing for her mother not to reject her. Mrs Floyd came closer, almost on tip-toe, gazing wide-eyed at her daughter as if she was a monster.

'Pat ... We've only just heard ... Dear Lord, what have you done? *What have you done?*'

'I'm all right, Mom – I'm going to be all right,' Pat assured her, weeping weakly as she spoke. 'I'm so, so sorry ...'

'How could you *do* something like this to us?' The words choked out harshly. 'You've never been like this ... You were a good girl ... Your father is in a dreadful state ... He's been praying, praying, with no let-up until I'm afraid he'll make himself ill!'

Greta could feel herself beginning to boil. Why did everything always revolve round Stanley Floyd, as if no one else ever had any feelings? Who cared if he was praying or not? And she knew Mrs Floyd was afraid of her husband.

'Pat's very weak,' she pointed out. 'She's lost a lot of blood.'

This seemed to penetrate through Mrs Floyd's frozen exterior to the real kindliness which lay beneath. Suddenly, she fell to her knees by the bed, tears welling in her brown eyes.

'Oh, my poor dear!' she cried, weeping now and not seeming to care who saw. 'My poor little girl ...'

'But Daddy?' Pat's expression was terrible.

Mrs Floyd closed her eyes. It was a moment before she opened them again. Her silence seemed to say everything there was to say and her tears continued to flow. They were all crying, Greta as well. A nurse walked down to the bottom of the ward, gave them all a distasteful stare, then turned on her heel and went away.

'What did he say?' Pat sobbed.

Mrs Floyd wiped her eyes, but her face creased again with terrible grief.

'I don't know if he'll ever be able to forgive you.'

Chapter Twenty-Nine

Pat stayed in hospital for almost three weeks, very low after all the blood she had lost and fighting an infection that sent her temperature soaring. Greta visited her often, but Pat swore her to secrecy.

'I don't want anyone else knowing,' she said, her face pinched with worry. 'Just tell them I'm poorly.'

She was in a dreadful state all the time she was in there. Although her mother came to visit, she did so secretly: Pat's father would not countenance her coming back into his house. She had broken one of the Ten Commandments in the most wanton and shameful of ways, and so far as he was concerned, his daughter was dead to him.

And just when other Cadbury girls might have been able to give her friendship, Pat refused to let them know. She was popular in her quiet way and they kept asking after her. Greta found it difficult bearing the burden of Pat's secret tragedy and having to make up stories about her having had appendicitis, which is what they decided on. Despite all that, it did not stay a secret.

One Saturday afternoon when Pat was still in hospital Greta opened the door to find Marleen on the doorstep with the kids.

'Oh!' she said startled. It wasn't like Marleen to call. 'What're you doing here?'

'Just thought I'd come. Don't you want to see me?' Marleen responded in her usual aggressive style.

'Well, yeah – I just wasn't expecting you, that's all. Hello, Mary Lou, Elvis! Trev – we've got visitors!'

Trevor was on the sofa watching the football and Elvis, who was toddling now, ran in and flung himself roaring into his lap.

'Oi mate!' Trevor gave a pretend groan and rolled his eyes, which made Elvis gurgle with laughter. 'You're like the human cannonball!'

'You be careful with your Uncle Trevor,' Marleen said. 'You'll do him an injury.'

'No, he's all right.' Trevor laughed. 'D'you wanna watch the football, Elvis?'

The kids gravitated towards Trevor, and Marleen buttonholed Greta in the kitchen. She leant up against the back of a chair. Greta could see her looking round, sizing the place up to see if there was anything new.

'Nice outfit,' Greta said. She always got on better with Marleen if she complimented her.

Marleen smiled smugly. She'd got a job now, parttime in a clothes shop in town, and she had a bit of spare money for clothes. Today she had on a straight pinafore dress in big black and white checks over a white roll-neck jumper, her hair swinging long with a fringe. Marleen fancied herself as looking like the model Jean Shrimpton.

'Ta.' She flung her hair back, then looked down at the floor, rubbing the toe of her black shoe round a rough hole in the lino. '*Shame*,' she said. 'I'd've thought you could run to a new bit of lino, couldn't you, Gret? It's not as if you and Trev have got kids as a drain on yer.'

'No,' Greta said drily, making the tea. She wasn't

going to be drawn on that subject. Marleen was ever so nosy about it. But she had other fish to fry today.

'So—' she eyed Greta slyly. 'What's this I hear about your mate Pat?'

'What about her?' Greta said sharply.

'Why's she in hospital?'

'She had her appendix out,' Greta said. 'I've only got Rich Tea, sorry,' she added. 'Trev's eaten all the others.'

'That's not what Trev's Mom said,' Marleen persisted.

'What – that he's polished off all the Bourbons?'

'No. She said . . .' Marleen whispered the words importantly, eyes agleam. 'That Pat went to a *backstreet abortionist*.'

The blood rushed to Greta's cheeks. 'Is that why you came round? To spread lies and gossip?'

Marleen narrowed her eyes. 'It ain't lies though, is it? I heard Nancy Biddle telling Mom that Trevor came to her saying Pat had turned up with some bloke and was drenched in blood from head to foot, and that he had to go and call an ambulance because she'd had a botched job. She said Trevor was in a right state . . .'

Greta knew this was true. Trevor had come in from seeing the ambulance off, trembling and white as a sheet. It was partly the sight of all the blood, of course.

'I've never seen anything like that,' he'd said, sinking down on the sofa. 'How could she do it? Killing her own child? She ain't the type.' He put his hand to his head. 'I feel all funny – that was horrible that was.'

Greta was furious with him. She had asked him not to tell anyone and he had gone running to his Mom, and now Ruby knew as well and soon everyone would because Nancy Biddle was leaky as a cracked bucket.

All she said to Marleen was, 'Don't you go spreading evil gossip about my friend. You just shut it – right?'

'So it's true then?' Marleen smirked triumphantly. 'Little Pat, eh? Not such a Holy Joe after all then is she?'

Trembling with rage, Greta poured the tea and swept past Marleen into the front room, ignoring her. She didn't trust herself to speak. Marleen followed, a smug smile on her face.

'You all right, Trev?' she asked, as he romped with Mary Lou and Elvis. 'You like your Uncle Trev, don't you kids?'

This wound Greta up even more, and as soon as Marleen had gone, she erupted.

'Why did you go and tell your Mom about Pat? What the hell did you think you were doing? She'll tell everyone under the bloody sun now!'

'No she won't – I said not to. Anyway –' abruptly he turned nasty, 'why shouldn't I? She turns up at our house looking like summat from a slaughterhouse . . . I can talk to who I like, I don't have to ask your permission.'

'For God's sake, Trevor – she's telling everyone! My Mom knows, and Marleen – she'll tell the world just to be spiteful . . .'

'No – she ain't like that!' Marleen was always sickly sweet to Trevor because he'd spend hours entertaining her kids.

'Oh, yes she is! She's a mean, scheming cow. God—' She wanted to punch something in her frustration. 'I could kill you for spreading that. I told you not to!'

'Don't cowing well keep on at me!' Trevor threw

himself down in front of the telly again. 'Serves her right. You and your mates think you're a cut above everyone else. You're just not normal – you're not a proper woman, are you, swanning off, going to all these classes instead of being a proper wife and mother. And that stuck-up little cow shouldn't have got herself into that mess in the first place, should she?'

Greta stood watching him, her jaw clenched, as he stared at the television. Just then she could have hit him with all her strength. Instead she went into the kitchen and filled the yellow plastic bowl to wash up. Seething with feelings, she stood for a long time with her hands resting in the soapy water, staring out at their tiny strip of garden with the old privy at one side. Trevor made her so angry and frustrated, but at the same time she longed for him to love her, for everything to feel right. Marriage was a lonely place and she was filled with longing. She saw the years stretching ahead. Couldn't it be better than this?

Chapter Thirty

When Pat came out of hospital at the end of March, Mr Floyd had still not relented. She was forced to take up lodgings in a bedsit in Selly Oak which she and Mrs Floyd hurriedly found.

Greta was disgusted by this.

'So much for Christians!' she raged to Trevor. 'His own daughter and he's treating her like some kind of whore!'

'Well – she asked for it.'

'*What*?' Greta shouted at him. 'What're you on about, you prat? Pat was as innocent as anything – she was taken advantage of!'

'That's what they all say,' Trevor said angrily. He seemed determined to disagree with whatever she said these days.

Greta went to see Pat in her new place, and it wasn't bad: an upstairs room in a house off the Bristol Road, quite newly painted and not too dark. Mother and daughter had set it up the best they could, and Pat made Greta a cup of tea on a little gas ring.

'My Mom's been so kind,' she said.

Apart from looking pale she seemed quite recovered, and was putting a brave face on. 'I think it's brought us closer. And she says she's sure Dad'll come round in the end.'

She looked very anxiously at Greta. 'No one knows

225

except you, do they? At work, I mean?' She was due back the next week. 'If they found out, I'm sure I'd get the sack. Thanks for being such a good pal.'

'Why wouldn't I?' Greta said, with a pang of guilt. She knew perfectly well that she wasn't the only person in on the secret. Her Mom knew, and probably Edie, at Cadbury's, and the Biddles and Marleen, but it seemed to have been contained and none of them were spiteful enough to report Pat and make her lose her job. At least, fingers crossed, that was the way it seemed to be.

'I just want to forget all about it,' Pat whispered, perched on the edge of the pale green candlewick bedspread with her cup of tea. 'And about *him*.'

Ian Plumbridge had come to the hospital to visit just once, at the beginning. He hadn't a clue what to say to her and Pat had not heard another thing from him.

'Useless bastard – what a way to go on,' Greta said. 'And you were ever so keen on him, weren't you?'

Even now, Pat's eyes filled when she thought about it. She nodded. 'I really loved him. He was obviously only out for what he could get.' Wiping her eyes determinedly, she said, 'I won't make that mistake again. I just feel so guilty about Mom, having to manage Josie all on her own and everything.'

'Well, what if you'd got married?' Greta said. 'You'd have to move out then, wouldn't you?'

Pat shook her head, miserably. 'I s'pose so. That's not going to happen now, is it? I've let them down. Disgraced them.' She looked seriously at Greta. 'I owe them, Gret. I don't feel as if I deserve a life of my own. Not until Dad can forgive me, anyway.'

Greta looked at her friend's sad face. Knowing what

Stanley Floyd was like, she thought her friend might wait for ever for forgiveness.

As the spring passed into summer, Greta tried to forget about her own feelings and look after Pat. She worried about her, with her pinched face and sad eyes, and tried to do nice things to cheer her up.

'We may not be able to afford a holiday,' she said to Pat, 'but at least we can sunbathe here!'

She encouraged her to get out in the fresh air, walking round Bournville Green and the Girls' Grounds, and groups of them sat out to eat their dinner on hot days by the lily pond, where they could sprawl on the grass and drink in the sun. At weekends they took their costumes and went to the Lido at Rowheath, the recreation ground for Cadbury's workers. Pat had always been a keen swimmer, and a good splash in the water always put a smile on her face.

One day, in the heat of August, they went shopping in town and found themselves walking across the end of Pinfold Street and found it was all blocked off. Across the street big white banners were draped, saying, 'Birmingham's Boy, Steve!'

'They're filming,' a man told them. 'Some film called *Privilege*.'

'Let's go and see!' Greta said. 'Blimey, a film – we might be in it!'

They caught glimpses of the film crew hurrying along behind a clutch of motorbikes, and they hung about for a bit, wondering if the cameras had swept across their faces.

'We'll have to go and see it,' Pat said. Her cheerfulness was returning more now, even though Ian's and her father's treatment of her were a permanent sadness. 'We might see our ugly mugs flash past!'

'Huh – speak for yourself!' Greta said.

When she got home that day, Marleen was waiting on the doorstep.

'You again?' Greta said sarkily, because Marleen seemed to be turning up a lot these days. 'Looking for a free babysitter again?' Marleen wanted someone to mind her kids on a Sunday afternoon and Trevor was ideal for the job. Sometimes she even came and just left the kids and went off. Greta got sick of it, but Trev said he didn't mind. And the way he said it now was always touched with bitterness. *You* may not be able to give me any kids, was the message, but at least I can play with Marleen's.

'You've taken your time,' Marleen said, but Greta saw she was really anxious. 'You'd better come, Gret. Mom's up the hospital. It's Herbert – he's collapsed.'

They didn't have long to wait. Soon after they got round to Charlotte Road, Ruby walked in, and her face told them everything. They both stood up, unsure what to do.

'Well—' Stopping just inside the doorway, Ruby made a helpless gesture with her hands. She looked much older suddenly, her hair limp and straggly, the dark roots showing. Greta felt a pang for her. 'He's gone. Just like that. His heart, they said. He didn't even make it to the hospital.'

'Sorry, Mom,' Greta said softly.

Ruby put her hands over her face and her shoulders began to shake. Greta and Marleen helped her to a chair, but she gathered herself, not giving way to it, and looked up at them.

'I can't take it in. He was just there, right as rain.

Then he said he had a pain, he sat down ... Thought it was just indigestion. There's one thing, he didn't suffer long.'

'I'll put the kettle on,' Marleen said, softer and kind for once.

'Yes bab, ta.' Ruby sat on, staring ahead of her, obviously in shock.

Greta sat on the chair close to her. The clock ticked loudly.

'Well,' Ruby said, eventually. 'That's him gone now as well.'

And then she began to weep.

Herbert's body was cremated at Lodge Hill cemetery on a boiling hot day. Greta didn't feel too well when she got up in the morning, and by the time they reached the crematorium she was feeling quite sick and dizzy.

'I don't know what's the matter with me,' she said to Trevor. 'I must've eaten something bad. Must've been that fish last night. Are you feeling all right?'

'Yeah,' Trevor shrugged. 'I'm fine.'

Greta felt there was nothing she would have liked better than to crawl back into bed but she couldn't miss the funeral. As she sat in the little chapel for the brief ceremony, she felt more and more sick and faint.

Everyone was there of course: Edie and Anatoli, and Janet and Martin Ferris, lending support to their old friend. Greta could see them thinking, *poor old Ruby*. And while she couldn't stand Herbert herself, she felt sad for her mother. She'd had such a cursed life when it came to men! With a pang of gloom, in her sickly state, she realized she had no real idea how things were supposed to be between a man and a woman because she'd never seen it – not when it was good and happy. The sick feeling got worse, a cold sweat passed over her and she put her head in her hands.

She just managed to get through the short service, but by the end she was feeling so bad she had to run outside and was sick in one of the flower-beds.

'Greta?' She heard Janet's voice behind her as she was struggling to recover. 'Oh dear, you poor thing! I thought you were looking groggy!'

'I think I'd better go home,' Greta gasped. 'Oh, I feel dreadful!'

'Let's get you some water, and then Martin can drive you,' Janet said, taking her arm. 'Come along, dear.'

Greta felt so ill she hardly remembered the journey home, just the relief of being able to lie down at last and give way to being ill.

'I don't know what I ate,' she said to Ruby two days later. As soon as she was feeling better, she went round to her Mom's. 'Whatever it was turned me inside out, I can tell you! I'm sorry for missing the rest of it, Mom.'

'Can't be helped,' Ruby said. 'Your face was nearly as green as the grass, bab! It went off all right – and Edie and Janet were a big help, bless them.'

She looked pale and sad, as if the life had gone out of her.

'He wasn't the love of my life or anything, Gret. If anyone was that, it was your Dad. But he was all right – and he was company.' She managed a wan smile. 'Ah well. Seems to be my bad luck, doesn't it?'

Greta smiled. Her Mom could bounce back, that

was one thing for sure, and one thing she admired about her.

'Maybe your luck'll change one day,' she said.

But Ruby found she had another bitter pill to swallow on the reading of Herbert's will. He had made no provision in the will, she told Greta and Marleen shamefacedly, and there was nothing left to her at all.

The girls were completely confused. 'But if you're his wife you get his money don't you?' Marleen frowned. 'I thought that was how it works?'

Ruby was shaking her head, looking hurt and embarrassed. 'Thing is – we weren't married.'

'But Mom what're you on about?' Marleen argued. 'You got married – the day of Mary Lou's christening!'

'No, bab – we didn't' Ruby gave a ragged sigh. 'We told everyone we was wed so it wouldn't look bad us living together. But Herbert was never properly divorced from his first wife. They just never got round to it somehow. And I thought he'd altered his will, but I was wrong as it turned out.'

Herbert had had a bit of money put away, but in law it was all due to go to his estranged wife and their two children who had both moved away from Birmingham.

'Did he tell you he'd altered his will?' Greta asked. She could hardly take all this in.

'Well, not in so many words . . .'

'What a bastard!' Marleen said.

Ruby tried to rally. 'It's not that I begrudge it them really,' she said soberly. 'His wife and kids I mean. She

231

was married to him for a long while. But he could have made some effort for me ... I feel as if he's used me and not bothered to think of me at all. It's not a very nice feeling.'

Greta felt for her, however much this confirmed her opinion of Herbert Smail. Her Mom always talked as if she ran men for what she could get, but really she was romantic and seemed to get used again and again.

'Oh, he'll look after me,' she'd heard her say so many times. When it came down to it that had never been true.

'I wasn't expecting a fortune or anything, but a little nest egg would've been nice.' Ruby sighed, wearily. 'Ah well – at least I can work, eh? Back to square one again – story of my life!'

Chapter Thirty-One

A few days later Greta woke feeling groggy. Oh no! I can't have eaten something bad again, she thought. She had still barely recovered from the memory of the upset stomach which had started the day of the funeral. She'd never felt so ill in her life. Surely it wasn't that again!

'P'raps it's my cooking,' she said wryly to Trevor.

Trevor, who was sitting sleepily on the edge of the bed, grunted in reply. She wasn't going to get any sympathy there, Greta could see. When they first lived together Trevor would have been sweet and concerned, but these days they were growing further and further apart.

'I'll go to work and hope it doesn't get any worse,' she said, dragging herself out of bed. 'If it does, I'll just have to get home somehow.'

She felt queasy all morning, but once she'd had her lunch it wore off and by the evening she was feeling better.

'I haven't poisoned myself quite as bad as last time!' she joked at work.

But the next day it happened again, and the next.

'I don't understand it,' she complained to Pat after a few days. They were sitting out on the grass by the lily pond. 'It's not like a bug – I think I'm over it and then it just comes back again.'

Pat's eyes were searching her face. 'So you just feel sick in the mornings?'

It took Greta a moment to catch the meaning of her words. She burst out laughing.

'Yes ... But I mean, not like *that* ... I just don't feel too good, that's all!'

'You sure?' Pat said in a low voice. 'You couldn't be ... ? That's just what I had ...'

'No!' Greta said. 'I can't be!'

She'd been making her regular morning visits to the little lavender box in the pantry. She and Trevor still made love every so often, even if things between them weren't very good in any other way. She found it kept him happy and she quite liked it too. It was their best time together, when they could snuggle up and feel loving, even if it all quickly wore off afterwards. Sometimes she thought it was the only thing holding them together.

'Well, sounds as if it could be,' Pat said solemnly. She leaned closer and whispered, 'The doctor could give you a test.'

A few days later she emerged from Dr Lonsdale's office, in shock.

'But I can't be!' she gasped, when he gave her his opinion.

'You seem very sure,' Dr Lonsdale said. 'But you say you've missed your period, you're feeling sick in the mornings ...'

'But I'm taking the pills, Doctor ... The ones you gave me.' She found herself half whispering even talking to him about it, and her cheeks were burning.

Dr Lonsdale was a kindly, middle-aged man with a fatherly manner.

'Well, my dear – what could have happened? Perhaps you have forgotten on some occasions. Or have you been ill, by any chance?'

'What d'you mean? I did have a bad stomach upset – oh, about six weeks ago. I was ever so sick and that.'

'Ah, well, that'll be it,' he told her. 'If you experience diarrhoea and vomiting when you're taking the contraceptive pill it can make it ineffective. Did you have, er, relations, round that time?'

Blushing even more, Greta tried to remember. 'I 'spect so,' she said, staring at the blotter on the doctor's desk.

'Well,' he said. 'Then congratulations are due, Mrs Biddle. Do cheer up – it's not the end of the world, is it? You're a married woman, and after all, that's what marriage is for. Off you go, and prepare for motherhood!'

She didn't say anything to Trevor then. She was having enough difficulty herself, coming to terms with the fact she was pregnant. All day at work it was all she could think about, especially as she was battling with feeling queasy in the mornings, something she tried to hide from Trevor, as she didn't want him putting two and two together.

She went through the working days like a robot.

'Greta. GRETA!' Pat tried to get her attention at times. 'Hello – are you down here with us or up in a moon rocket?'

More privately she asked, 'Is anything wrong? You're not . . . ?'

But Greta shook her head. 'Course not,' she laughed. She couldn't face the truth herself yet, let alone tell anyone about it.

At first her main, shameful impulse was to get rid of it. The pregnancy was a problem she had to solve. Quite quickly, though, her attitude started to soften. The second night after she had the news she lay in bed beside Trevor. He always slept easily and she could hear his steady breathing.

Little does he know, she thought.

For a moment she imagined telling him, and how happy it would make him. Then she thought about the baby, the real, unseen, tiny creature inside her, and felt suddenly overwhelmed with tenderness. A baby – which would turn into a little person like Edie's little Peter, and Ruth and Naomi and Mary Lou! She stroked her hand over her stomach. Suddenly she felt older, as if in seconds she'd grown into a mother.

From then on it didn't seem so bad and she felt herself beginning to adjust. She didn't mind as much as she'd expected to.

Next Saturday she went shopping, late in the morning when she was feeling a bit better. She decided to take the bus into town to get meat and fruit and veg from the market. People were getting used to the new Bull Ring now they had rebuilt it, although there were plenty who moaned about it being nothing like as good as it was before. But Greta quite liked the new Market Hall and having a mooch round the market outside, all the activity and colour of the veg and fruit stalls and the man selling willow pattern crockery. She bought a milk jug off him because she liked its shape.

She took her time, glad to be alone for a bit, and sat down and had a cup of tea in the Market Hall, as a rest from carrying the heavy bags of carrots and spuds. She had a currant bun with her tea, and by the time she'd eaten it she felt completely better. The café was full of Saturday shoppers, and she saw one woman over the other side with a young child on her lap. He was a pale, brown-haired toddler who kept squirming, yanking at the collar of her blouse and whining, but the woman was very patiently feeding him pieces of toast.

She really loves him, Greta thought. The way Edie loved Peter, with utter devotion. For a second she felt like crying. She was being offered that too! In that moment everything changed. She picked up her bags and set off in a hurry for the bus stop. She would go home and tell Trevor and it would make everything sweet between them because this was what he wanted and they could have a family and be happy. And suddenly that was what she found she wanted more than anything else in the world. She could hardly wait to get back, now everything felt so clear.

The bus crawled along. From the university clock she saw that it was almost three o'clock and she was in a fever of impatience.

Weighed down by her bags in each hand, she hurried down Alliott Road and home as fast as she could. She went along the entry and round the back: it saved having to get her keys out as the back door was nearly always open when it was warm.

She put the bags down thankfully in the kitchen and hurried through.

'Trev?'

What she saw was like a slap in the face.

Trevor was on the sofa, Marleen beside him, and

they jumped apart as she came into the room. But she'd seen them, locked together, kissing. They couldn't hide it: they both looked guilty as anything.

'Gret!' Trevor got up, trying to act normal. 'Hello – you're back early.'

Marleen stood up as well, smoothing down her tight blouse and little short skirt. Her skirts seemed to get shorter by the week. She looked smug and defiant.

'No – I'm not early, as a matter of fact,' Greta said, injecting as much venom as she could into her voice. She could feel herself beginning to tremble with shock and rage. 'I've been out ages – but I don't s'pose you've noticed, you've been enjoying yourselves so much!'

They didn't deny it. Both of them stood there looking both shame-faced and pleased with themselves at the same time.

'Sorry, Gret,' Marleen said. 'Only – we've been wanting to tell yer for a while now . . .'

'Yeah,' Trevor nodded. 'We have. Only we didn't know what to say.'

'Tell me what?' A terrible dead feeling came over her. Things were far worse than she had thought. How had she not noticed?

'Thing is,' Marleen announced pertly. 'You and Trev aren't happy in any case, are you? And Trev wants kids and that, and you're never here, and . . .'

'We was just *driven together*,' Trevor announced urgently.

'What d'you mean I'm never here?' Greta asked. But she felt helpless. Things had already been decided, she could see, and she had been asleep and not noticed what was going on under her nose.

'Thing is, Trev and me, we're really two of a kind . . .' Marleen said.

Greta felt she was drowning. She couldn't think to argue or plead.

'But what about . . . Ron?' She groped for the name of Marleen's latest date. 'I thought you were with him . . .'

Marleen shrugged with a look of distaste. 'Nah – I chucked him ages ago. He were no good.'

'Sorry Gret . . .' Trevor said. 'Only me and Marl – we want the same things, see.'

'So—' She groped for words. 'You're just chucking me?' She stared Trevor straight in the eyes. Should she tell him now, that she was expecting his baby? With a flare of pure rage, she thought, *No!* I'm not giving him the satisfaction.

'Sorry, Gret,' Trevor said again. 'I think it'd be better if Marleen moved in here. At least you can go and live back at yer Mom's.'

'Yes,' Marleen said. 'You're lucky to have some where to go.'

'Well—' Greta looked from one to the other of them, completely despising them. 'You've got it all nicely worked out, haven't you? Well, sod you both – you deserve each other.'

And without so much as picking up her bag, she walked out of the house.

Chapter Thirty-Two

She walked and walked for hours.

All she could think of at first was how stupid she'd been. How could she not have seen this coming? Then the hurt and rage started to course through her. She stormed along paying no attention to where she was going, noticing no one, crossing roads without even looking.

What was so shocking was the way they had had it all worked out. She could just go back and live with Ruby, as if she was nothing, just like a piece of furniture to be moved around. All this time – how long? – they'd been carrying on under her nose and she'd had no idea. Her husband and her sister! And just at the moment when she had been ready to give Trevor what he wanted, she had to walk in and find that! Her heart thumped so hard that several times she had to slow down and catch her breath.

All those soft feelings she had had only this afternoon towards Trevor, the thought of having a family with him, how pathetic they seemed now. Thoughts swirled in her mind. Trevor had betrayed her . . . She was alone and carrying his child. For a second she imagined doing what Pat had done: looking for someone who would help her be rid of it. But immediately there came the memory of Pat that night, the terrible haemorrhaging. Heavens, no! Shuddering, she knew she could never go through that. And her tender feelings towards the little being inside her had not all vanished, despite her fear and upset.

As the afternoon waned into evening and she had wandered round and round the back roads of Selly Oak, she sat down on a bench at the edge of a park. Some boys were playing football across the green and their shouts carried to her.

'Well,' she whispered, a hand on her stomach. 'It's you and me now.' The thought made her feel both strong and terrified.

She sat in the gathering dusk, sick with anger towards her sister.

'Course, you think you can just move in on my husband, don't you, Marleen,' she murmured out loud. 'You and your kids can play happy families with Trevor and you pack me off back to Mom's– all tidied up, out of the way to suit you, just like that. 'Cause you never think of anyone else except yourself even for a second, do you, you selfish little bitch. Well I've got news for you – I'm not being pushed around by you . . .'

Going back to Mom's would be like landing right back where she started, trapped and frustrated – only worse, now she was pregnant. For a second she thought of her grandparents, Ethel and Lionel. But they didn't want her, she knew that. And they lived so far away. Ruby's was the only realistic place to go.

'Wild horses wouldn't drag me back to Mom's,' she said. 'I'm not bloody going back there just on your say-so . . . I'm going to manage on my own, and sod the lot of you . . .'

The thought drove her to her feet, but utter weariness came over her. Her legs felt wobbly and a wave of nausea hit her. The tears came then, and she slumped back down on the bench, hands over her face, shaking with sobs. She knew her pride was terribly battered. All those times Trevor had said he adored her, when they were first married, had said he'd do anything for her. She'd never really wanted or appreciated him, had taken him for granted. And hadn't she dreamed of leaving him and starting again without being burdened by a man and marriage? But it still felt bitter now that he'd made a fool of her – with Marleen of all people! How much more could he have betrayed her? Well, she wasn't going to show him she cared what had happened. What did stupid Trevor matter – she wasn't going to have to keep house for him or wash his bloody socks any more! And she wouldn't tell him about the baby either, not until she could avoid it no longer. She wanted to hurt him as he had hurt her.

But in the meantime she was the one alone, feeling ill and exhausted. She wiped her eyes, but more tears kept coming. No wonder she felt so low. She had not eaten anything since her tea and bun at the market, and she was supposed to be eating for two! Then came the realization that she hadn't even a penny on her. Her anger seeped away and she began to feel really frightened. What on earth was she going to do? There were homes for girls like her, weren't there, who were 'in trouble'? It was a desolate thought. All she'd ever heard whispered about them was grim and frightening. No – she wasn't going anywhere near one of them – and she couldn't stand the thought of running back to Ruby even for the night. She must manage alone somehow.

Feeling very groggy, she got up and walked on and on, still crying exhaustedly. After a time she crossed the Bristol Road, seeing the lights of the cars blurrily through her tears, and kept on walking, having no real idea where she was going. Overwrought and exhausted, she scarcely knew any more what she was doing.

She glimpsed the university clock across the road and to her right were large houses set back from the road, lit up and seeming to shut her out by their cosiness. All these people had homes and she had nowhere to go. But a little while later she saw one that she recognized. It was quite a large house, the lights were on and it looked very homely. The sight of it filled her with longing, and in desperation she walked up the path.

Pulling the bell cord produced a gentle clanging inside. She leaned exhaustedly against the front wall and closed her eyes.

'Greta – Greta love?'

Afterwards she realized she must have lost consciousness for a moment, because she had not heard the door open. Edie's arm was already round her shoulders, trying to guide her into the house.

'Are you all right love? What're you doing here? Oh dear – you don't look very well at all! Anatoli – come and help me, love – quick!'

Within a few moments, Greta had been led through the crimson-carpeted hall of the Gruschovs' warm house, to the couch in their sitting room, and collapsed on to it. She must have fallen asleep again, because the next thing she heard was a voice saying,

'Here my dear – Anatoli's very special scrambled eggs. Come now – eat. You look half famished.'

Greta sat up, dazed, taking in that she was in the Gruschovs' warm living room, with the piano at one end, curtains drawn across wide windows at the other, vivid coloured rugs on the floor and photographs on the mantelpiece. She could scarcely remember how she got there. Edie was sitting opposite her, looking anxious. Greta thought how lovely Edie looked. Though she was a homely woman, she had her hair smoothed back in a bun in a way that was not fashionable but looked softly elegant.

Anatoli was laying a tray on her lap, on which were a plate of scrambled eggs on toast and a big mug of tea.

'Sugar in your tea?' He offered her a delicate china sugar bowl.

'Oh – yes please,' she said, stirring in two lumps. 'What time is it? I fell asleep.'

'It's after nine,' Edie said gently. 'You've been asleep for an hour but we thought we'd better wake you.'

'Now – tuck in, and *bon appétit*,' Anatoli said, retreating with a little bow.

The eggs seemed to have tiny green bits in which she realized were spring onion, and they were the most delicious thing she had ever tasted. She wolfed the plateful down while Edie and Anatoli looked amused at her hunger and left her in peace. Once she'd downed the sweet tea as well, she felt much better.

'That was lovely,' she said shyly. 'I'm ever so sorry . . .'

Edie moved over and sat beside her on the sofa, while Anatoli tactfully took the tray away and stayed out of the room.

'You were in quite a state when you arrived,' Edie said. 'What's going on, love?'

Seeing her kind face, a huge aching lump came up in Greta's throat, and her tears flowed as the whole sad story came tumbling out. As she explained about Trevor and Marleen, and then about her baby, she saw Edie's expression turn to one of shocked sympathy.

'Oh, you poor, poor girl . . . How terrible . . . And you've been wandering about all afternoon?'

Greta nodded, sobbing. 'I didn't know what else to do . . .'

Edie was trying to piece it all together. 'But have you told Trevor about the babby, love? Surely he'd have to think again? . . . And Marleen . . . And what about your Mom – what've you said to her?'

'Marleen just said, "Oh, well I'm moving in with your husband, so you can go and live back with Mom . . ."' She mimicked Marleen's pert tones and saw Edie grimace. 'I mean who the hell does she think she is, marching in, taking my husband and telling me what to do! And I don't want to go and live with Mom again . . . I know it's the only place I've got to go, but I just can't stand it – even now *he's* not there any more . . .' She knew Edie had not taken to Herbert Smail either.

Edie's eyes searched her face. Without her saying anything Greta knew Edie understood. Edie and Janet had both watched Marleen and Greta's patchy childhood with Ruby, the lost fathers, the men coming and going, the disastrous stay in America. They were very fond of Ruby but they knew she had not been a reliable mother, or given her girls much guidance.

After a moment Edie said, 'Look – it's Sunday tomorrow. We'll all have time to talk. But in the meantime you're all in, aren't you? I'm going to put you to bed in the room next to Peter's. We've got plenty of space here. You get a good rest, and don't worry, all right pet?'

She led Greta up to a pretty spare bedroom where the bed had a cheerful flowery coverlet and there were bookshelves along the walls and a chair for her clothes. There was even a washbasin in the corner.

'This house was a guest house for a while so we've got lots of washbasins!' Edie said.

'It's lovely.' Greta was tearful again with gratitude.

'I'll lend you a nightie,' Edie said. 'And here's a towel and flannel. I expect we can find a toothbrush . . . Then you can tuck up and get some sleep.'

Greta got ready for bed, wearing a white nightdress of Edie's. It was a warm night and she pushed the window open, feeling the balmy night air drifting in. She couldn't think about the future any more, not tonight. Once she was washed and in bed, she lay feeling like a child, an all-embracing sense of being more cared for and snug than she ever had in years.

She was woken by Edie bringing her a cup of tea, girlish-looking with her hair down, wrapped in a pale blue dressing gown. As she came and perched on the edge of the bed she looked much younger than her forty-six years.

'How're you, love?'

Greta grimaced. 'Bit groggy. I'll feel better when I've got some tea down me.'

'Two sugars.' Edie passed her the mug and the comforting aroma met Greta's nostrils.

'Anatoli's giving Peter his breakfast.' There was a pause, then, her face serious, she went on, 'We've been talking – Anatoli and me . . . Look, I don't want to tread on your Mom's toes – I can have a word with her for you. But what we wanted to say was, you can lodge with us, if you like – for as long as you need. Till you get back on your feet, sort of thing.'

'What – stay here?' Greta gasped. 'But I can't . . . I mean, I'm having a baby and everything . . . I mean, I'd be a nuisance . . .'

Even while she was protesting, she was full of hope. Could they really mean it? It truly hadn't occurred to her that she might be able to stay here, but now it felt like a dream come true!

'Yes – that's all right, love,' Edie said gently. 'Look, I know what it's like to be expecting and left on your own. All I'm saying is, you're welcome here if that's what would suit you. You can pay us a bit of rent – maybe look after Peter now and then if we go out . . .'

'Course I will,' Greta said eagerly. Suddenly there was nothing she wanted more. She was full of joy. 'Oh, I'll help you all I can. You're so kind – I was at my wits' end, not knowing what to do!'

Edie patted her hand. 'You're almost like one of my own,' she said. 'Course we'll help you. But you will have to go home and get your things, if everything's as you say. And Greta – you must talk to Ruby – and tell Trevor about the baby. Whatever else he is, he is the father.'

Chapter Thirty-Three

She couldn't face seeing Trevor straight away, but she did manage to get into the house the next day while he and Marleen were still at work and hurriedly bundle up some of her things. Anatoli came and fetched her in the car.

'That boy is a fool,' Anatoli said as they drove away, and Greta could hear that he was really angry on her behalf.

'It's not just his fault,' she said wearily. 'Takes two, doesn't it?'

'Well, you have a generous spirit,' Anatoli said. 'But I still say he's a fool.'

Greta sighed as they drove away from her marital home. She knew she had plenty to reproach herself with for not paying Trevor enough of the attention he wanted, for not giving him a child, for not really wanting him in the first place. She had to face the fact that she had married him under the law, but never in her heart. And as well as sadness and worry, the humiliation of what had happened, there was also a sense of relief, of excitement, like a cheer getting louder and louder inside her head. However angry she felt with Marleen, she was free of Trevor! The corners of her lips twitched into a smile.

She saw Anatoli's glance settle on her for a moment, then he looked back out through the windscreen. She wondered if he was thinking she was terrible to look happy.

'Soon,' he said distractedly, 'I shall have to bite the bullet and get myself a proper English car.'

She didn't go to work for the next few days. She was in shock, licking her wounds. And she felt sick a lot of the time and had to rest at the Gruschovs', who were kindness itself. It was a few days before she could face Trevor, but she knew it would have to be done. That weekend she braced herself and just marched over to Glover Road. When she walked in, Trevor, Marleen and the kids were all there. Mary Lou was grizzling loudly, and Marleen was shouting at her. They all looked very startled to see Greta.

'Sorry to barge in on your domestic bliss.'

Greta was glad to see that Trevor was looking pale and rather irritable.

'What're you doing here?' Marleen said nastily. 'You've already been in and taken everything that's yours, haven't you?'

'Actually, if you've forgotten, this is my house and I've come to see Trevor, deary. So what you can do is piss off out of here with your screaming brats while I talk to *my husband* – all right?'

She stood with her hands on her hips. *No arguments*, her stance said. *Get out and leave us alone.*

'Trev?' Marleen said plaintively. 'You gunna let her talk to me like that?'

'You'd better go for a bit, Marl,' Trevor said. 'Just take 'em out round the block, eh – or to your Mom's or summat?'

'I can't go to Mom's,' Marleen said in a low voice.

Greta laughed. 'Why's that then, Marl? She not too impressed with you? Running off with *your sister's husband*? Maybe even our Mom thinks it'd take one hell of a bitch to do that?'

'Aren't you gunna stand up for me, Trev?' Marleen whined. 'Letting her talk to me like that!'

But Trevor was silent.

Greta stood waiting while Marleen huffily gathered up the kids and went out, slamming the door.

Trevor stood there helplessly, by the kitchen table.

'D'you wanna sit down, Gret?' he said eventually.

She stared at him. She had begun already to feel quite sorry for him. At the same time she felt triumphant. 'God, you are a stupid prat, Trevor.'

'What d'you mean?' he said defiantly.

'Going off with *her*! You won't last five minutes with her, no one ever does, 'cause she's a selfish cow who never thinks about anyone but herself.'

'She's selfish is she?' Trevor came to life suddenly, full of emotion. 'What about you, Greta, calling everyone else selfish. What d'you call this then?'

He strode over to the pantry and came back with something in his hand that she recognized with horror. It was the little box with the sprig of lavender on the top. He opened it and shook the card of contraceptive pills in her face. The word ENOVID swam in front of her.

'How long've you been taking these?'

Greta felt an ugly blush spreading through her cheeks.

'I never realized what a prize clown you'd taken me for!' He was shouting now, truly upset. 'Go on – how long've you been on them?'

'Quite a while,' she admitted, unable to look him in the eye.

'You deceiving bitch!'

'Trev!' she looked up, in appeal. She certainly didn't feel superior any more. 'I'm sorry – only I just didn't want all that – not yet. I didn't want to settle down like Mom and Marleen and just be tied down by a whole load of kids all the time. Not when I was so young. I wanted to do other things!'

'Well what about what I wanted? You never seemed to give me a thought, did you, when you were off with your mates, doing your *French* lessons and all that . . .' He finished with bitter mockery. 'If there's anyone who only thinks about themselves, I'd say it was you, Greta. You're a selfish cow and that's all there is to it.'

'The thing is, Trev . . .' As his words hit home, she felt herself turn hard and angry. She wanted to hurt him, the way he was hurting her. 'I've got something to tell you. I was going to tell you the day I found you with Marleen, only it was too late. It wasn't like you thought. I hadn't always been taking the pills . . .' A little white lie suited her purposes just now. 'I'd stopped. And I'm expecting, you see.' She left a little pause to let her words sink in. 'Your baby, Trev. I'm pregnant. Only now you've thrown me out, taken up with another woman. So what was the use in telling you? I wonder what our babby will think of his Dad when he grows up? He'll be like all the other bloody useless fathers in this family!'

'What?' Trevor came towards her, his face taut and serious. 'What're you saying to me, you scheming cow? You're making up stories now, aren't you – just to get your own back. Well it won't get you anywhere!'

251

'No – it's true, I swear to you! The doctor said . . .'

'You're just full of bloody lies!' he pushed her away. 'Coming here, mixing me up! Go on – get out!' Face twisted, he came at her, ready to push her out of the door.

'All right, all right I'm going!' There was no use in talking to him now. 'But it's true, Trevor. I'm carrying your baby. I'm living with Edie and Anatoli. So when you see me about with a big belly on me, you'll know whose it is.'

She marched out and stormed round to Charlotte Road. While she was in fighting mood, she might as well see her Mom and get it over with.

'Oh – so you've turned up at last, have yer?' Ruby said. 'You'd better come in.'

She waited for Greta to get through the door then shut it with a slam.

'Well I don't know what you're talking to me like that for,' Greta retorted. 'I'm not the one who's run off with someone else's husband.'

Ruby went ahead of her into the back kitchen and filled the kettle.

'You needn't think I'm happy about that either.' She slammed the kettle down. 'But you are the one who disappears off the face of the bloody earth without bothering to tell anyone. And I have to hear it from Edie of all people . . . No one else bothered to tell me what's going on!'

Ruby turned, hands on hips, a thunderous frown on her face. Although they were friends, she was always touchy about Edie. It was as if she thought Edie had got above herself just by being happy.

'Mom,' Greta got in before her Mom could start. 'I've not been well. I'm having a babby.'

Ruby's arms dropped to her sides, her expression changing from anger into shock.

'What? Whose is it?'

'Mom! What d'you mean whose is it? Trevor's of course!'

'Well, does he know?'

'He does now – I've just been round and told him.'

Ruby gaped at her. 'What did he say?'

'Not much. You know what Trevor's like.' She sank on to a chair.

Ruby made tea, digesting this information, and sat down with the pot and cups between them. Greta saw that her face looked pasty and unhealthy.

'He doesn't want you back then?'

Greta shook her head, tears coming then. She realized she wanted to enlist her mother's sympathy.

'No – he's playing happy families with Marleen.'

'Huh,' Ruby rolled her eyes. 'Good luck to him, with that little bitch. Brazen as anything. I'm sorry for yer, bab. You didn't deserve that. Marleen thinks of no one but herself – always has, and now she's done one of the worst things a sister could do.' Then she looked hurt. 'But why didn't you come to me, instead of going to them? You could've come and talked to me – I'm your Mom! I've just lost my husband – then I lose both my daughters in one week . . .'

Impatient with her self-pity, Greta said, 'You haven't lost us Mom – either of us. Try seeing it from my point of view, just for once. I just wanted a bit of time to come to terms with it, that's all.'

'But you'll be coming to move in with me? I'd like you to, bab – now Marleen's gone. I'm all on my own.'

Greta swallowed. 'Edie and Anatoli have said I could stay there for as long as I want. They've been ever so kind . . .'

'Oh, I bet they have,' Ruby said bitterly.

'I said I'd stay on for a bit.'

'But what about when the babby comes? I'm its Nan, not Edie!'

'Course you are, Mom. You always will be. But I've left home. They said I could stay on then too, if I wanted.'

'Well . . .' Ruby said, with a mixture of wonder and bitterness. 'You've all got it worked out, haven't you?'

Greta felt guilty now, but she'd had to say it. Her Mom was looking tired and sad and sorry for herself, but she couldn't move back in there. Somehow in Edie and Anatoli she knew she had found people who could help lead her into something different. And that was what she hungered for more than anything.

Chapter Thirty-Four

The first day she went back to work, she caught up with Pat in Linden Road.

'Hey!' She tapped Pat's shoulder.

'Greta!' Pat pulled her urgently aside. 'Where the hell've you *been*? They said you were off sick but no one seemed to know anything: I've been worried half to death about you! I went round to your Mom's and she said she didn't know where you were either, and neither did Trev. There's not much I haven't been imagining!'

'I'm all right . . . It's not what you think . . .' Greta felt bad, seeing the worry in Pat's face. She should have let her know what had happened. After all, Pat was having a miserable time of it too, getting used to living in her bedsit all alone and creeping home to see her Mom and Josie when Mr Floyd was out.

'But are you . . . ?'

Greta nodded, finding her eyes suddenly full of tears. She kept finding herself crying these days.

'Yes. And Trevor's gone off with Marleen. I'm not living with him any more . . .'

Pat's mouth opened in shock. 'God, Gret – he never told me that.'

'No, I don't s'pose he did.'

They walked slowly downhill, towards the Friends' Meeting House on the Green.

'Oh, Greta – that's awful. What're you going to do?'

'I'm living with Edie and Anatoli. And I'm having the baby. I couldn't go through what you did . . .'

Pat turned to her, wide-eyed. 'Well, you are married . . . Sort of, anyhow . . .' She lowered her voice even more. 'D'you want it, Gret?'

'No.' Greta walked on, thinking about it. 'Yes. I don't know. At first I was horrified, but then, when I'd thought about it, I started to feel different. I've never wanted children, not really. But I started to think about it inside me and . . . Well, it's just him, or her, and me now against the world . . .'

She smiled sadly, and hearing her words, Pat burst into tears. 'Oh, Gret!'

Greta pulled her in close to the entrance to the Meeting House, away from other Cadbury workers who were passing, and put her arm round her. Words spilled out, full of raw emotion, that Pat had obviously needed to say for a long time.

'I never let myself feel anything like that!' she sobbed. 'I was so frightened and Ian never for a moment let me think I might have the baby. He told me I had to get rid of it. I feel so terrible – like a murderer. I killed my own baby – and my father's never going to let me forget it!'

Greta felt terrible for her. All she could do was try her best to be comforting.

'You just did what you had to do, that's all,' she said, rubbing Pat's back. 'Your Dad'll come to terms with it in the end. It wasn't your fault. If Ian had really loved you he would have been behind you and he'd never have forced you into something like that.'

'Well, that's the worst of it!' Pat was distraught. 'I

thought he did love me! How could someone be like that, all lovey-dovey, and then turn on you the way he did? I'm never going near another man so long as I live – ever!'

It was nice to be back at work, but she felt different. The baby made everything that had gone before seem a long time ago, as if she had become a different person. She worked away quietly, her heart aching for Pat, and also trying to take in the strangeness of her own feelings. All that had happened had made the two of them closer, and more grown up.

At the same time she couldn't wait to get home. The Gruschovs' house on the Bristol Road already felt like the home she had always longed for. She loved living with Edie and Anatoli. There was the warm welcome, the cosiness of the place and the sense of a settled family, of their happiness and interest in so many things. Thinking back, she realized how Edie had changed. Seeing her now from an adult point of view, she could recognize how difficult Edie's past life had been and she felt a deep respect for her. It had been news to her that Edie had lost a baby herself, when she was young and working at Cadbury's. It had happened shortly after she was widowed, when her first husband was killed in an accident just after joining up in 1939. And after that she had taken in David, a foundling of the Blitz, and brought him up as her own, loving him passionately, while constantly afraid that someone would arrive to claim him as theirs and take him away from her again. She had relied on the help and kindness of Frances Hatton and the other Quakers, since her own family had been so unsatisfactory. In a way she was passing on the same kindness to Greta. And Greta could see that now, with Anatoli, Edie had found a deep happiness and was grateful for it every day of her life.

When she got home that evening, Edie let her in.

'Oh, hello, love!' she said smiling. 'We must get a key cut for you. Come on in – Janet and the girls are here.'

Greta went in, glad to be offered a cup of tea and a biscuit and to be included in the general homey chaos, with Peter, Ruth and Naomi playing with little Dinky cars all over the living-room carpet. Janet was down there with them, in a floral cotton dress. She had taken off her white sandals and they were beside her on the floor. As Greta walked in, Peter lobbed one of the cars and it got caught in Janet's curly hair.

'Ouch!' she cried, disentangling it. 'You little monkey – no throwing, please!'

'Sorry.' Peter grinned, full of his father's handsome charm.

'That's all right – just don't do it again! I think I'll get up – it might be safer. Hello, Greta,' Janet said warmly, still rubbing her head. 'How are you?'

'All right, thanks,' Greta said, shyly. She didn't know if Janet knew she was pregnant, or about Trevor and Marleen, but then Edie said,

'I've explained the situation a bit, love. I hope you don't mind. Only it could be a little bit awkward with your Mom if Janet was to meet her . . .'

'No, that's all right,' Greta said, blushing.

'I'm so sorry to hear about all your troubles,' Janet said tactfully. 'But congratulations on the baby all the same! It seems awful for the thought of a child to be met with gloom and despondency, doesn't it? How're you feeling?'

258

'Not too bad – a bit queasy, off and on.'

'Come on, sit and have your tea,' Edie said, guiding her to a chair. Greta realized that Edie loved being at the centre of a family, fussing round everyone. She sat and gratefully nibbled biscuits and drank the sweet tea.

'How's Ruby taken it?' Janet asked.

'Well – she was shocked, of course. Especially about Marleen and Trev. And she wanted me to move in with her.'

'And you don't want to?' Janet asked cautiously.

Greta looked at the teacup on her lap. 'Not really.'

There was a silence, but not a critical one. Greta sensed that both women were somehow on her side and understood.

'We hope she'll settle in happily with us for the moment,' Edie said.

Greta looked up and smiled. She was too shy to be able to say how much she loved it there. She hoped they could see.

As ever, Edie and Janet chatted in a relaxed way, not seeming to mind her presence at all. They talked about their families and Janet told Edie about one of Martin's patients who he was desperately worried about. They talked a little about politics and about the subject nearest to Janet and Martin's hearts – the Campaign for Nuclear Disarmament and the way its aims had been betrayed by Harold Wilson's government.

'We're spending more than four hundred million pounds a year now on the army and weapons, thanks to this dreadful government,' she said hotly. 'It's an absolute disgrace – inhuman.'

She and Martin were staunch members of the local CND group.

A little later they heard the sound of the front door.

'Dad!' Peter cried, and he and the twins raced through to the hall.

'Oh my goodness, hello, hello, and hello again!' they heard Anatoli laughing and the three children flung themselves at him. Greta saw Edie's face light up.

'Hello, love,' she said, going out to greet him. 'I'll make a fresh pot of tea. And Janet's here.'

'Hello, my dears,' Anatoli greeted them. 'No don't get up,' he said to Janet. 'I'm sure these two make you run about far too much as it is.' He sat down with a grunt of weary pleasure and Peter, Ruth and Naomi all settled near his feet to play.

'And how's our lovely Greta today?'

'All right, thank you,' Greta said, smiling up at him. Anatoli had such a fatherly gift for making people feel loved, and she, like everyone, blossomed in his presence. As soon as he arrived he lit up the room with his amiable personality, and the sense that he had all the time in the world to sit and chat. Greta felt like a child with him, as if she was having a second childhood after missing out on the first. And he already treated her like a daughter.

'You ventured back into work today, did you? How is the making of chocolate progressing?'

Greta laughed. 'Oh, same as usual!'

'I never tire of free samples you know. Even with Edith working at Cadbury's from time to time now, I still feel we have been rather deprived!' He leaned over and asked gently. 'And are you feeling all right?'

'More or less, yes thanks.'

She saw Janet, who had never been able to have a child herself, watching her with a fond but wistful smile.

Chapter Thirty-Five

So began some of the happiest months Greta could ever remember, living with the Gruschovs, in their cheerful, homely household.

'D'you know, it's an awful thing,' she confided to Edie one cold autumn night as they sat by the fire. They were both already in their nightclothes and Anatoli was upstairs having a bath. 'I've been married to Trevor for three years, but I don't miss him at all. I barely even think about him.'

'Does he know where you are?' Edie asked.

'Yes, I told him, like you said.'

'Well he hasn't gone out of his way to come and see you, has he, love?'

'Not much of a marriage,' Greta said gloomily.

Edie's face clouded. 'Well, I think, to be honest, with my first husband it would have been like that in the end. I didn't know what it was like, not a really good marriage, until I met Anatoli. That's the thing isn't it? How're you supposed to know? My Mom and Dad's marriage didn't give me much to go on.'

Edie didn't say it, but Greta knew she meant that Ruby hadn't given her daughters much to go on either.

'I don't want to get married again,' Greta said, staring into the glowing fire. 'It's not worth it. I'd rather do other things than bother with men.'

Edie smiled, gently. 'What other things?'

261

'I dunno. Just something. There must be more to life than working in a factory and having babbies.'

'I suppose having babies – a family – was what I wanted most . . .'

'Oh, I didn't mean . . .' Greta was embarrassed. 'It's lovely. All your family and everything. But you're one of the lucky ones who's got a good marriage and you're happy. There aren't many are there?'

Edie sighed. 'No. Maybe you're right. But don't think it doesn't take effort.'

As the weeks passed, Greta understood more of what she meant. Though she loved Anatoli like a father, and he was always kind to her, she began to notice the dark, depressive moods that she had heard Edie and Janet talking about. For days at a time he could be withdrawn and silent, seemingly sucked down into some dark place where none of them could reach him and he would barely speak. Often he took refuge in music. Though he played the piano and violin to entertain them, at these times it was different: it was as if he was playing only for himself, and the tunes he played were in melancholy, minor keys which tore at her heart when she heard them. He seemed to lose himself in the music as if there was no one else in the house, even if they were close by, or in the same room. At these times, Greta found him forbidding, and his grim silence, when his face seemed carved sternly out of granite, made her feel miserable. Edie and Peter also trod carefully with him.

'It always passes,' Edie told her. 'He can't help it. You just have to give him time to come out of it.'

'Is he angry?' Greta asked the first time it happened when she was living there. 'He seems angry.'

Edie sighed. 'I don't know. Maybe partly. But not with you or me. He finds it hard to explain even to himself. He says it's to do with memories, atmospheres that come back to him and overwhelm him but he can't put it into words at the time. He says it's like wanting to crawl off into a dark forest for a few days. He calls it his lone-wolf time.'

All Greta knew was that she found Anatoli's wolf times desolating, and it was an enormous relief when the days had passed and the wolf turned back into a daytime, friendly hound.

In his more summery moods, he was wonderful. The children loved him and he would sit and tell stories to Peter and the girls if they were there. Greta loved to hear them too. Often they were old Russian fairy tales which involved deep, impenetrable forests, and snow and bears, witches and lost children, and which he told magnificently in his slightly accented English, building up the tension until Peter's eyes almost popped out of his head.

Greta enjoyed living with the Gruschovs so much that Edie even had to remind her to go and see her own mother. She did see her at work sometimes, but when she went round, Ruby was often a bit short with her to start with.

'Nice of you to bother turning up,' she'd said, the last time. 'I s'pose you've got time for a cup of tea?' Greta knew she was jealous of her living with Edie, but wild horses would not have made her move back.

'Yes, ta.' She sat down at the kitchen table. 'You could come and see us sometimes you know,' she pointed out. 'We're only down the road.'

'I'm not sure I'm wanted, am I?' Ruby said huffily,

banging about with the teapot and cups. 'I never see you.'

'Well, you are wanted, all right?' Greta felt she had enough problems of her own, being left with a child, for a start, without Mom having to be always the one who needed looking after. 'You could come round any time if you'd just swallow your pride. And I'm here now, aren't I?'

Once they were sitting talking Ruby thawed out a bit. She was never good at staying in a paddy for long.

'Seen Trevor?' Greta asked, sounding as casual as she could. She didn't miss him, it was true, but she did feel bitterness and sadness about what had happened. Above all she was very curious as to how on earth it was working out with Marleen.

'No. *She's* been round a few times though.' She held the tin out to Greta. 'Biscuit?'

'Ta. And? She driven him round the bend yet then?'

Ruby looked a bit bemused. 'According to her they're getting on like a house on fire.'

Greta gave a bitter laugh. 'House on fire's probably about it!'

'Well, time'll tell.' Ruby's face softened. 'How're you? Keeping all right?'

'Yes. I don't feel so sick now – it's wearing off.'

'You're a brave 'un, I'll say that for yer.'

Greta was touched by this unexpected compliment.

'You can't rely on men, that's what life's taught me. If you can make it on your own, then all power to you, I say.'

Greta was tempted to ask why, if men were so awful, Ruby had gone in for quite so many of them, but she held her tongue.

'Well, I don't know what I'd do without Edie.'

As she said it she realized it was the wrong thing to say, but instead of getting huffy again, Ruby looked thoughtful. She seemed to be coming to terms with it.

'I suppose Edie's taken on the mantle of Mrs Hatton. She was ever so good to Edie, she was. She was a lovely lady, no one would say otherwise. She helped all of us out during the war. So you're lucky, bab. She going to let you stay on after the baby's born?'

'Yes, she says so,' Greta said.

Ruby looked wistful, but Greta could also sense relief that her house was not going to be full of the chaos of babies again.

'Well good luck to her. But don't forget I'm yer Mom, will you?'

Greta didn't see Trevor until just before Christmas.

It was evening and a few flakes of snow were whirling in the air.

'Greta?' She heard a gentle tapping on the door of her bedroom where she had been having a lie-down, and opened the door to find Edie, looking troubled.

'Trevor's downstairs, to see you.' She spoke very quietly. 'I said I'd see if you were in, just in case . . .'

'Oh, thanks, Edie.' Greta pushed her feet into her slippers. 'If he's taken the trouble to come over here finally then I'd better see him.'

'You can ask him in – take him in the back room if you like . . .'

Greta found herself feeling very calm. She hadn't seen Trevor in four months, so she certainly didn't need to get wound up about him now! It did cross her mind to wonder if he'd come to tell her what a dreadful mistake he'd made and to beg her to come home. In which case she'd be able to turn him down!

A draught was blowing through the open front door. She saw him watching her come down the stairs and she felt very conscious that the baby was showing now. He was standing on the step with flakes of snow in his hair.

'Hello, Trev. What're you doing here?' She addressed him in a casual, jokey voice.

'Come to see you, ent I?' Trevor seemed to sag, as he always did when unsure of himself.

'That's nice. D'you want to come in?'

'No.' He looked cold, but also uncomfortable and at a loss what to say.

There was a silence. She saw Trevor staring.

'How are you?' she said.

'All right. Yeah. Fine.'

'And my sister?'

'Yeah. She's fine too. You know, going along...'

'Good,' she said sharply. As usual Trevor was not going to contribute anything much and she was already impatient. 'So we're all fine then.'

'I just wanted to see—' He nodded in the direction of her belly. 'How you are and that.'

'The baby you mean?'

'Yeah.' He looked into her face then, and she could see the hurt. 'You should've told me, Gret. Should've told me earlier.'

'How could I've told you when I didn't know myself?'

'That's my babby in there.'

'Yes,' she put her hands on her hips. 'But you went off with my sister. So what d'you want, Trev?' To her annoyance her eyes filled with tears.

'Can I see him – when he's born?'

'Don't see why not. It might be a girl though. Some of them are you know.'

'The thing is . . .' He looked down, obviously uncomfortable. 'It's not just you . . . Marleen's expecting an' all.'

'But I thought she said . . . !' She remembered Marleen's past declarations that she'd never, ever, have another baby.

'Well she is. Three month gone.'

'Blimey, you didn't waste any time, did you?' She blinked her tears away, the soft moment completely over.

She was longing to ask him, almost as if he was still just a pal: So how're you finding it, Trev? What've you let yourself in for, living with Marleen and her kids? D'you wish you'd never started with her?

As if he could read her mind, Trevor said,

'We're all right, Marleen and me. She's not like you. She just wants me. We're a family. And we're going to get wed, soon as we can.'

'Well, bully for you.' She was stung by that. It didn't sound like the Marleen she knew at all. 'Pity you never married her in the first place then, isn't it?'

'I want to see my kid,' Trevor persisted, suddenly turning nasty. 'You can't stop me.'

'No,' she said pertly, her hand on the door, ready to close it. 'Well, you know where I am, don't you?'

Chapter Thirty-Six

As Christmas drew near Greta could see that Pat was getting more and more down, even though she put on a brave face.

'What're you going to do at Christmas?' Greta asked her. 'Surely your Dad'll come round? He can't keep this up for ever.'

'I don't know that he will,' Pat said gloomily. 'So far as Dad's concerned, right is right and wrong is wrong and there's nothing in between. He's got very high ideals.'

'Hmmm,' Greta said, thinking she far preferred people whose ideals weren't quite so lofty if they made you so cruel. She didn't like to criticize Pat's father to her, but she thought he was awful, Bible in hand, nose in the air, and unable to show kindness to his own flesh and blood.

'I know Edie'd be happy for you to come to us,' she said. 'Mom's coming too – everyone together – well, not Marleen . . .'

'That's nice of you – and her,' Pat said sadly. 'I'll just have to see if Mom can talk our Dad round.'

A couple of days later she came to work looking as if she was about to burst with news.

'Guess what!' She pulled Greta aside as everyone was putting their overalls on to start work. 'My Mom came round to see me last night and said she'd spoken to Dad. She said, if he didn't let me in the house for our Christmas dinner, she was going to take Josie and come and have it with me in my room!'

Greta laughed, astonished. 'She never!'

'She did!' Pat looked tearful, torn between laughter and sadness. 'I'd've loved to be there and seen his face.'

'So he said yes?'

'He had to – swallowed his pride.'

About flaming time, the mean old hypocrite, Greta wanted to say. Instead, she said, 'Well, good luck to you. And I'm glad for you, Pat.'

Christmas was a very happy occasion that year. Greta always loved Bournville in the winter, the factory all lit up like a great palace as they went home in the dark, the shine from its long windows falling across the recreation grounds in front. She loved seeing the big Christmas tree twinkling near the Meeting House, the glow from the windows of cosy houses and glimpses of Christmas decorations inside. A group from the Seven O'Clock Club went carol singing in town and collected money for charity.

In the evenings she went back to the warm welcome of Edie and Anatoli's. Their house, with its open fire and Christmas tree and streamers made by the children, swirled with visitors over the Christmas break. They were a very sociable couple, and as well as Ruby and Janet and Martin and the twins a whole stream of other friends and relatives visited, among them Edie's brother Rodney. Greta couldn't help noticing, though, that although Anatoli had two older children from his first marriage, there was never any sign of them. She knew his son lived abroad somewhere, but why didn't he ever see his daughter? But she didn't like to ask.

Edie and Anatoli treated Greta just like a daughter, and were also sensitive and welcoming to Ruby. Pat and her Mom and Josie came round at New Year as well, and though they put on a cheerful front, Pat said Christmas had been a strain.

'He let me into the house,' she told Greta quietly. 'But it was awful. He just carried on as if I wasn't there. He barely even spoke to me. And poor Mom was trying to keep everyone happy and smooth everything over.' Her eyes filled with tears. 'I don't mind for myself, 'cause at least I can go back to my little room, and go to work. But Mom's just stuck there day after day and I can't give her enough help.'

Obviously Mr Floyd never helped. He had to be fresh for his important work in the daytime, for Birmingham's education department, as well as for the Lord.

The next month was an uneasy time for Pat, because Josie was ill for a time and Mrs Floyd wanted Pat to move back home. Pat was torn.

'I ought to go back because Mom and Josie need me and I miss them,' she said. 'But I don't want to live with my Dad – not the way he is. I know I did a terrible thing, but my God I've paid for it too. And if he can't forgive me, I don't want to live there.'

Greta didn't know what to say. She felt desperately sorry for Pat and Mrs Floyd, both under the thumb of this heartless man.

Chapter Thirty-Seven

Easter 1967

'So why don't you come with us?' Edie invited. 'There'll be room in the car – we can squeeze up.'

She laughed, seeing Greta's surprised face. *Her*, go all the way down to London? She'd never been to London in her life! And for a demonstration or march or whatever, with all those strange people Edie and Janet seemed to know, who wore duffel coats and had strange eating habits like being vegetarian. Ruby said they were all cranks.

'CND needs our support – and there'll be lots of young people,' Edie said. 'It's vital that we protest – the H-bomb is a terrible evil; surely you think so, don't you?'

'Well, yes . . .' Greta agreed. 'But . . .' What did it have to do with her? All these things were decided by politicians weren't they?

'But what?' Edie asked gently. 'Everyone should be able to have their say, you know. This isn't Russia. And anyway, it'll be fun. We're not going on the march or anything – some people walk all the way from Aldermaston in Berkshire. We'll just go and join them in London. It'll be fun – we'll take all the children and a picnic. I mean—' She eyed Greta's

271

stomach apologetically. 'That's if you think you can manage? I'd have my doubts if I were you.'

Greta smiled, more worried about what she was letting herself in for in general than about being nearly eight months pregnant. She was carrying the child neatly, a small, round bump at the front, and she felt very healthy. 'It's all right, I'll come! I'm sure I'll be OK.'

So on Easter morning they set off, all in Anatoli's capacious car, Martin Ferris in the front beside Anatoli with Naomi on his lap, and Edie, Janet and Greta taking it in turns to hold Peter and Ruth on their laps.

'I don't know if they usually have many children on the march,' Janet said, sounding nervous.

'Well, in that case,' Anatoli called breezily over his shoulder, 'it's time they did. After all, we are marching on behalf of the future, are we not?'

They played 'I-Spy' with the children, and read some story books to while away the time. Edie kept up a supply of mints to suck and biscuits. Every so often she whispered, 'You all right, love?' to Greta and Greta said, 'I'm fine.' She was happy to sit staring dreamily out of the window while the others talked, taking in the journey south to London, through towns and villages she had never seen before. Life was expanding, she felt, a delicious feeling.

When she thought about the baby and the birth, she felt very scared. Most of the time she pushed thoughts of it away. At least she knew that once it was over, she could stay with Edie and Anatoli.

They found the stream of people moving towards Trafalgar Square, a solemn, soberly dressed crowd holding home-made banners with the CND symbol on them and the words 'London to Aldermaston'.

For a few moments they stood watching them pass. Greta looked round her, seeing the grand, high buildings of London, dwarfing the drab column of marchers with their macs and serviceable, unglamorous clothing, their sensible shoes and little haversacks. Scattered among the earnest-looking men with spectacles, the women in tweed skirts, walked clergymen in black cassocks. All of them looked determined and serious.

'Look, here's a gap,' Janet said, steering Ruth, whose hand she was holding, into the crowd.

Greta and Edie followed with Peter between them, each holding his hand. Behind them a group was holding a banner which read 'Leeds Campaign for Nuclear Disarmament'.

'Feels a bit of a cheat just squeezing in at the last moment!' Martin Ferris said.

'Ah well, we've got children to deal with,' Janet replied.

Greta felt self-conscious at first, moving along in the crowd of protesters while passers-by stared at them. She noticed the curious looks they received because of Ruth and Naomi, and realized how much of that Janet had to put up with all the time. It made her feel proud, and defiant on Janet's behalf.

Every so often someone would call out 'Ban the H-Bomb!' or 'Make Peace not War!' and there would be a ragged cheer of agreement. Somewhere ahead someone was strumming a guitar and singing. As she looked round Greta saw that there were quite a few people her own age on the march. Students, she thought. They looked different, educated and intelligent, and she felt intimidated by them.

But it was exhilarating as the crowd gathered in Trafalgar Square for the speeches, more and more filing in until the middle of the square round the fountains was a sea of people, sending the pigeons scattering out of their usual haunts towards the grey sky with an alarmed flapping of wings, and she gazed across at the sunlit faces of the buildings. They had all changed places and now Greta was squeezed in between Anatoli and a young man who she thought was from the Leeds group behind and facing the grandest building she had ever seen.

'That's the National Gallery,' Anatoli told her. Smiling wistfully, he added, 'Edith and I spent some fine afternoons there when we were courting, when I still lived here.'

There was a ripple of applause through the crowd.

'Ah now – we are supposed to listen.' Anatoli winked down at her. 'Are you feeling all right my dear?'

Greta nodded, but suddenly she did feel rather weary. She wished she could go and perch on the side of the fountain, but she didn't like to push through the crowd, so she stood still, hoping the speeches would not go on for too long. She looked round the square at the statues, leaning back to catch the soaring height of Nelson's Column.

'Where're you from?'

The young man standing next to her, wild-haired, with black-framed spectacles and dressed in a dark blue duffel coat, repeated the question, smiling down at her.

'Who me? Oh – from Birmingham,' she said, flustered.

'I didn't see you on the march,' he said. She heard his northern accent. 'Have you just joined us today?'

'Yes – we just drove down. Cheating a bit, I suppose.'

'Well,' he laughed, and Greta saw that he had a handsome, kindly face, 'better than not coming at all. I joined the march because I've stayed down here over Easter. But I've joined in with the Leeds lot because that's where I come from.'

Greta wasn't sure what to say, but she didn't want to look like a dumb cluck, so she asked, 'You're a student then?'

'Yes – at the LSE. London School of Economics. I'm studying French and Economics, second year. It's hard work, but I'm glad I came.' He seemed happy to have someone to talk to. 'My Dad's not so sure about it all – they never had much education. It can drive a bit of a wedge between you at times. We don't really see eye to eye. They treat me a bit like a stranger when I'm there now. Tiptoe round me, like. That's why I stay down here for the holidays if I can. I've got a friend who lets me lodge with his family.'

'Oh,' Greta said. 'That's nice.' She liked the way he was talking to her, like an equal, and the way he had told her about his family. He leaned closer.

'Are you a student?'

'No.' He had not noticed that she was pregnant either. 'I'm out at work.'

'Ah – what sort of work?'

'In a factory,' she admitted. 'I work at Cadbury's.'

'Well, that's what I'd be doing if I hadn't ... Well, I s'pose I just went for it. Tried for summat else. I didn't want to be like my Dad, see?'

'Yes,' she said.

'Must be a nice place to work though? Not like the

275

factories round us.' She realized he was worried about sounding like a toff because he was a student.

'Yes – it's all right,' she said. 'I've been there since I was fifteen.'

The young man looked thoughtful. 'Sometimes, when it's really hard down here, I think I should have just stayed. Done what they wanted. The work's hard, least I find it is. And I don't find it easy to fit in, being a northerner. Bit of a fish out of water. Anyway, damage is done now, I reckon.'

He laughed at himself and she laughed with him.

Before too long someone else in the crowd beckoned him and he moved away with a goodbye nod in her direction. Greta realized she had not even asked his name, but she had liked the way he talked to her, as if she was someone worth talking to. Although he was a student he didn't seem so different from her really, struggling to work out where he fitted in. It made her feel better about herself.

As the marchers dispersed later that afternoon, Edie suggested they go and find some fish and chips before driving all the way back to the Midlands.

'You must be starving, Greta,' she said.

'Yes, I am a bit,' Greta said, though in fact she did not feel all that hungry. Instead she felt a bit sick, her body stretched and heavy from all the standing and walking around. As the afternoon wore on she had kept getting niggling pains through her, her muscles tightening painfully. Edie had warned her that this would happen towards the end.

'It's your body getting ready for the birth,' she said.

'Like practice contractions. Anatoli used to say it was like an orchestra tuning up!'

Some of these 'practice contractions' had started coming on late in the afternoon, and the last one had almost taken her breath away.

She couldn't finish her fish and chips. Not liking to say anything, she longed to be back in the car, able to sit and rest. Surely then these sharp pains which seemed to turn her body into a tight muscular drum would let up and she could have a doze and feel better.

At last they reached the car and the children crawled in thankfully, exhausted by the day. Peter and Naomi fell asleep almost immediately; Naomi huddled in Janet's arms. Ruth, awake and bright as a button, sat on Martin's lap in the front, chattering to him. Greta sank on to the seat, more grateful to sit down than she had ever been in her life. She took a deep breath, and as she did so her body contracted again so that it took her all her self-control to keep quiet. But she was beginning to feel really frightened and her thoughts whirled. Please make it stop! She gripped the leather strap inside the door. What was happening? It was too early for the baby to be coming, so why was she having all these pains? She must have just overdone it today, walking around London. The pain eased off again and she sat back and closed her eyes as Anatoli drove off. If only she could just sleep through the journey and be safe home in bed!

There was a lull and she sank thankfully into the darkness.

'Poor Greta – we've really worn her out,' she heard Edie say, and then she was unaware of anything, and must have dozed for a few moments, until another pain jerked her awake and she gasped at the force of it.

'Are you all right, dear?' Janet asked, next to her.

'Yes ... Thanks ...' Greta managed to say. Maybe this would be the last, she thought. It would all be all right. But she was close to tears of pain and panic. How could this be happening when she was stuck here in a car in the middle of London?

More pains came, and soon there was one so bad that it made her cry out.

'Oh goodness, Greta – whatever is it?' Janet cried.

'You're having contractions, aren't you?' Edie said, leaning round. 'I thought so! Oh my goodness, I knew you shouldn't have come!'

The pain took its grip in her again, built until it was like being clenched between enormous jaws. She felt sweat break out on her forehead and back, and then it began to die again.

'Oh God!' Greta cried. 'It's the baby – I think I must be starting!'

Chapter Thirty-Eight

Once she had admitted what was happening, the pain seemed to take her over, coming in wave after wave. She was aware of Janet trying to help loosen her clothes, tugging at the little sash on her smock blouse, and her voice saying,

'It's all right dear, you'll be all right. We'll look after you . . .'

One of the children was crying somewhere, and she heard Martin saying, 'The only one I can think how to get to from here is St Mary's . . .'

It was dark in the car, lights from the street flashing past, and then suddenly there was a muddle of being lifted from the car and everything was very bright. She was on a stretcher and being rushed along a white, glaring corridor. Everyone she recognized seemed to have vanished. They took her to a room, lifted her on to a bed, and as the pains came and went, searing through her, a nurse undressed her and she was draped in something pale and rather stiff. Everything felt like a bad dream.

In a lull between the pains, a black face loomed over her, framed by a rounded bowl of black hair.

'I am your midwife,' she said in a calm, deep voice. 'Now, let me have a look at you.'

'Where is everyone?' Greta cried, panic-stricken. 'I don't even know where I am.'

'Ah now – you need not worry.' The midwife pronounced every word very precisely and slowly. 'You are in St Mary's Hospital, Paddington. And you have someone waiting for you outside. Your father, is it? He is very worried about you.'

'I'm not supposed to be having it yet!' Greta wailed. 'It's too early.'

'Don't worry,' the woman said, as if nothing on earth could throw her from being calm and steady. 'You're doing all right. It's going quickly, dear – it won't take you long I don't think. You just do your breathing exercises, all right?'

Greta had had a few instructions on breathing in labour, and she tried to put them into practice. But at the height of each of the contractions the pain wiped any thought of counting from her mind and she just wailed and groaned.

In a calmer moment she wondered who was waiting outside. It sounded like Anatoli, or Martin perhaps. He was a doctor after all. But she hoped, longingly, that it was Anatoli. She just yearned to see someone familiar between these frightening white walls.

And then she could think of nothing as the pains overwhelmed her and there were other people in the room and she was being told to *push!*

But there was something wrong, more people there, and she felt her lower body being lifted, and when she looked up there were someone's legs being held up in the air in stirrups and she thought, I wonder whose legs those are, and then a voice said,

'We're going to give you a bit of help here . . .'

There was a terrible tearing, stretching feeling, as if she was going to crack apart, and then, in the silence, a tiny snuffle.

'Oxygen,' someone said curtly, and the baby was whipped away.

Greta heard herself moaning. Then there was silence.

'My baby . . . ?' she whimpered.

The midwife appeared, looking solemn. Greta felt her hand taken and held with a gentle pressure.

'You have a little girl,' the midwife said softly. 'But she is small – she came early. They are just doing some work on her to help her breathe.'

'Will she be all right?' Greta tried to sit up.

'No – don't move! We hope so, dear – now lie still.'

The eternal minutes which followed were an agony. She felt the midwife washing her.

'I want to see her. I want my baby!' she said, sobbing. There seemed to be nothing else in the world at this moment, except her bond with this tiny creature after all the two of them had gone through together. She could hardly bear it that they had taken her away and that the midwife looked so worried. What was it they were not telling her?

'Ssshhh, it will be all right,' the woman said in her strange, springy English.

Greta lay, weak and frightened, tears running down into her hair.

There was a flurry of activity and a man appeared and brusquely called the midwife away. Greta realized he was a doctor, and lifting her head, she saw a small, bundle being handed over. There was no sound from the bundle, only a terrible silence. She watched, paralysed, as the midwife turned to her, her face terribly solemn. Greta couldn't breathe . . . *Oh God . . . Oh God . . .*

The woman looked across at Greta, and after what

281

seemed a terribly long time her face broke into the most beautiful smile.

'Here she is,' she said. 'Your little girl . . .'

All pain forgotten, Greta pushed herself upright, her heart pounding with excitement. The bundle was laid in her arms and Greta saw a crinkled, yet somehow familiar face. She felt she recognized her at once, and her heart expanded out to her in a way it had never done to any other being before. Almost as soon as she was in Greta's arms, the little girl began to snuffle and cry.

'Is she all right?' Greta said anxiously.

'She has had some oxygen. They were worried because she is a little premature,' the midwife told her. 'But she seems very strong. Now she wants to drink – offer her your breast, dear.'

As the baby began to suck, everyone was smiling, the midwife, the nurse who turned from clearing up the room to watch, and above all, Greta.

'She is almost six pounds,' the midwife told her. 'That's a good weight. If you had carried her to term she would have been a very big size!'

Greta couldn't stop staring at the little being sucking confidently on her nipple. She and Trevor had made this little miracle! She felt a pang of misery – how Trevor would have loved seeing her. He would have been so happy! More tears ran down her cheeks.

'Oh you little love,' she said, wiping one of her tears from the little girl's cheek. 'You're mine – you're my little girl!'

'Now – we need to take you to the ward, and she must go to the nursery. It is far too late to have a visitor on the ward.' She eyed the clock on the wall, which Greta was amazed to see said one o'clock. It was the middle of the night!

'Just before you go, there is someone to see you. You must be quick, this is not really allowed!'

She went to the door and spoke to someone outside. Anatoli's face appeared round the door, a little anxious and then, at the joyful sight of mother and child, his face bloomed into smiles as well.

'My dear girl – what a marvellous thing! A little daughter!'

He came straight to her and kissed her, perching, quite oblivious of hospital rules, on the side of the hard bed, his arm round her shoulders. Greta's tears began to flow again.

'You waited all this time!' she said, overwhelmed. She felt so full of love for him, and gratitude, this man who was more than a father had ever been to her. Fancy his caring enough for her to wait out there faithfully all these hours!

'Of course!' he said. 'We would not desert you my dear, at such a time.' He smiled fondly at her.

'You're so kind,' she told him, tears and smiles coming at the same time.

Anatoli gave her a squeeze. 'Not at all. I was worried about my girl . . . !'

She was so touched by this she couldn't say anything for a moment. Then she wondered,

'Where are the others? Not out there, surely – the kids and everything?'

'No – I persuaded them to go back to Birmingham. After all, we couldn't all clutter up the hospital corridors could we? So our friend Dr Ferris is suffering the indignity of driving my much-despised car! I am in a position to stay down here because I have friends in London who will put me up. So that was that. All the same,' he twinkled at her, 'I'm not sure that Edith will ever speak to me again after this – her having to miss the birth of a baby!'

It was almost impossible to sleep that night, in the strange hospital ward, and full of the strain and excitement of the birth. And in the night they brought the baby for her to feed and she was able to hold her, gazing on her in the dim light, and fall even more deeply in love with her.

The next day passed in a round of feeds and bed-makings and other ward routines. The other new mothers were all local, and were amazed by Greta's story of almost giving birth on a car journey back to Birmingham! Anatoli came to visit later on and they were all very curious about him.

'Is he your dad? He's ever so handsome, isn't he, for an older bloke!'

Greta just said yes, he was her father. It was easier than explaining and it felt very nice.

He came to see her the first afternoon, bearing a beautiful bunch of pink tulips before him and a big smile. Greta felt very spoilt, and was delighted to see him, but said she was sorry to put him to so much trouble.

'Yesterday was in any case a holiday, remember?' he said. Greta was amazed to remember that it had been Easter. 'And I am able to see my friends and have a little extra vacation, thanks to you. And to make acquaintance with this little lady.'

'The thing is, I don't know what to call her,' Greta

said. 'I've thought about naming her after my Nan – well, both of them. But Ethel's such an old-fashioned name, and if I call her Louisa I s'pose I'll offend someone. Or there's Frances Hatton, but I'm not sure about Frances . . . Maybe something more modern . . .'

'Hmmm,' Anatoli pondered. 'I can see it's a problem. Louisa is pretty . . . And Frances – of course we all remember Frances with such affection . . .'

'I like Louisa – I like names ending in "a". They sound all Italian and romantic don't they?'

'Ah!' Anatoli beamed. 'In that case, I have the solution! Why not call her Francesca? Then you have a lovely, dignified name and the best of both worlds!'

'Francesca . . .' She tasted the word on her tongue and broke into a smile. 'Yes – that's lovely. Little Francesca – that's very pretty!'

She stayed in hospital for three days, by which time they seemed sure that Francesca had no problems with her lungs and was feeding well.

On a chilly March morning, Greta carried a well wrapped up Francesca with great care, and with Anatoli constantly fussing, into a taxi to Euston Station. Everything felt so strange – being out of hospital, being in London, being suddenly a mother. She felt like someone else, older and much changed. Even the CND march felt as if it had happened months ago.

Sitting on the train with Francesca in her arms she alternated between gazing out of the window and down at her daughter's snugly sleeping form. She had given her a good feed before they left the hospital, so it was fingers crossed that she would last the journey.

'You're coming home to Brum,' she whispered to

her, excited at showing her to Edie and her Mom and Janet. She tried not to think about Marleen and Trevor.

Another anxiety seized her.

'You know,' she turned to Anatoli. 'I shall go back to work – soon as I can. I don't want to take advantage – sponge off you or anything.'

Anatoli leaned round and looked very seriously at her.

'Greta – listen to me. I know you are not one to take any kind of advantage. And I am serious when I say you are like a daughter to me.' He touched her hand for a moment. 'You will have realized, I do not have much relationship with my own girl. Now, you are to go back when you are ready, and not before.'

'Oh – thank you,' she said, her eyes filling with tears. She turned to look out of the window, wanting to sob. Here was she, always longing for her father, for a loving family, and life had given him to her in a way she never expected.

Part Four

Jerusalem, 1967

Chapter Thirty-Nine

June 1967

'Stop – this is far enough.'

David climbed out from the back seat of the car in a dusty suburban street in Jerusalem, hauling his pack out after him.

'*Todaroba*,' he said curtly. 'Thank you. Shalom.'

'It's an honour.' The elderly man leaned across the front seat to shout fervently through the window. 'For one of our fighting boys. What a victory – and in six days! *Shalom, shalom.*'

The ceasefire had been agreed on 11 June. For the first time in the two weeks since the reservists were mobilized, David found himself alone, standing in the street in the mellow light of late afternoon. There was the usual sense of anticlimax when released by the army, a floating feeling of loss of structure and routine, as well as that of renewed freedom and exhilaration at going home. But it was different this time. For a short while he needed to be alone, much as he longed to rush back to the flat. Only now, in this pause, could he begin to take in that he had been, for these intense days, at war: that the war was now over.

His solitude lasted only a moment. His army uniform drew passers-by towards him.

'Are you back from the Front? Where you been – the Golan, Sinai?'

'You boys have done a great job – you are the jewel of the state of Israel!'

'When you think what might have happened . . .'

'. . . if the Arabs had won . . . God knows . . .'

An elderly lady hurried from the shade of her doorway and David found himself clasped against her diminutive form as she pulled him down to rain kisses on his cheeks, chattering all the while in a blend of Hebrew and Russian before letting him go on his way.

But there was no mood of exhilaration, not then. Just a deep, sober relief, after this nation of refugees had faced the old fears of being driven out once again. The build-up of hostilities had been terrifying: the border skirmishes with Syria and Jordan, the chilling threats from Nasser in Egypt that he would drive the Israelis into the sea, of genocide. During those six days in June, the Israelis had managed to destroy most of the air power of Egypt and Syria and take control of the Golan Heights, the Gaza Strip, the west bank of the river Jordan including eastern Jerusalem, the Western Wall, the Temple Mount, and the whole of the Sinai Peninsula. It had been an astonishing victory.

But any excitement was dampened by exhaustion, a numbness which enveloped him now. His own unit had been in the north of Sinai, under Major-General Ariel Sharon. The last three days had been of constant fighting until they had broken through the defences at Abu-Ageilah, south of El-Arish. The Egyptians had retreated in panic and the Israelis were able to sweep through the Gulf of Suez. One of the finest moments had been the yelps of joy as his unit flung themselves into the waters of the Gulf, fully clothed, soaking themselves after the parched desert, in the waters of victory. It had been sweet indeed, a victory won with merciful speed. But now his greatest desire was for home: for peace and normality, and to see the faces of his wife and son.

On the way to the apartment, though, he stopped at a call box and dialled the number of his aunt in Haifa. She had a telephone now.

'Who is it? Rudi? David – is that you?' Her voice was shrill with nervous tension.

'It's OK, Auntie,' he told her. 'It's me. I'm safe – and almost home.'

'Oh, thank God! I have been so worried – I couldn't eat, or sleep . . . And poor Gila – how is she? She has been worried half to death as well.'

'I'm just going home,' David told her. 'I won't talk now – I just wanted to let you know I'm OK.'

'You're all right? Not injured? Nothing?'

'Nothing. I'm fine – really.'

'You are miraculous,' she said. 'And now Rudi . . .' She could not resist calling him that, the name he was called originally, in Germany. 'You go home and see your wife . . . And telephone Edith. I spoke to her. Of course she is worried sick too. In fact, I know you – you are in a call box somewhere with no money left . . . I shall call England for you – let them know that you are OK . . .'

'Thank you, Auntie . . .' He rang off, smiling. He enjoyed her fussing. And her concern for Edie, so far away in Birmingham. He knew Annaliese was deeply fond of Edie and Anatoli, and grateful to them. And she had kept him strictly in touch with them at times when he had found the tensions of his identity too difficult. At times in the past he had wanted to forget his Englishness, simply to lose contact with them and pitch himself in totally as an Israeli with no other ties. Annaliese understood him all too well.

'You think no one else has to struggle with where they have come from – with living in this thorny country? She has been as a mother to you, and don't you forget it!' Yes, he would telephone, or write very soon.

Now he felt ready for home. A year ago he and Gila had moved to a slightly bigger apartment in the same settlement. Standing outside, now it seemed to him an immensely long time since he was last there.

'Doodi!' She had seen him from the tiny balcony and as he went to the door he heard her sandals slapping on the stairs, and Shimon's eager voice. The two of them erupted into the little hallway.

'Daddy, Daddy!'

Laughing, David bent down next to the apartments' mailboxes and scooped Shimon up into his arms.

'Oh, you big boy, you are so heavy! You have got bigger just in a couple of weeks!'

Gila was more joyful, more girlish, than he had seen her for a long time. Maybe things would be OK now, he thought. But he could see the strain in her face, the tightness of the skin round her eyes. Once he could put Shimon down they fell into each other's arms and just held each other. She pressed her face against his chest and he stroked her dark, wiry hair. He felt her begin to shake.

'I was sure you were going to die . . .' And then she was sobbing, the fear and anguish pouring out, and he held her helplessly.

'But I did not die, I'm here. I'm here – don't get in

such a state . . .' As time went by he could fathom her emotions less and less.

He felt Shimon clinging to his leg, silent, understanding the seriousness of the moment. He was seven now, physically strong, but emotionally fragile.

After a few moments, Gila looked up, face crumpled, tears rolling from eyes which held a wild look. 'I had a bad feeling. Very bad.'

'Ssssh – it's OK now.' He was moved, yet a little frightened as well. Less and less did he see the tough sabra girl he had married. But her vulnerability stirred him. Holding her close aroused him at once, and he wanted her.

Much later, after making love, when Shimon was sleeping in the tiny second bedroom, they lay awake together long into the night.

'Are you not tired?' she asked.

'Absolutely exhausted,' he said. 'But I'm still primed for action.'

'I noticed.' She was able to tease now, stroking his side, fingers playing his ribcage like a piano. 'Plenty of action.'

'Once I sleep, I expect I will sleep for ever.' He wanted sleep to block out the images of the past days. Over and over in his mind he saw the fleeing Arab refugees, possessions in bundles like those of the Jews before them. What were they doing to these people? Where were all their high-minded kibbutz ideals of equality now?

'He's wetting badly,' Gila said. 'Worse than before.'

Shimon's bed-wetting had been a problem for some

time now. Auntie Miriam had said, 'I expect he is anxious, living away from you. When he moves out from here back to you, it will stop.'

But he had been back home for a year and still he woke often, crying in the night with wet sheets, or they found him sodden in the morning. His new school, they told each other, that must be the problem. He had started school in Tel Aviv, then moved to one in Jerusalem. He had had too many changes.

'My being away. The war,' David said. 'Everyone has been talking about nothing else. It's bound to unsettle him.'

'Dr Hirsh says he will grow out of it. That we should lift him in the night . . .'

She fretted about her sensitive boy. David understood that she was also worried that he would be a nerve case like her mother, Mrs Weissman. No, he would reassure her. It was her life that made her like that. Shimon will be different.

They lay close, facing each other. It was a long time, he realized, since they had last lain and gazed like this, into each other's eyes. He told her she was beautiful and remembered how much he loved her thin, dark-browed face, the sweet unevenness of her little white teeth. Here was this glimpse of love, the freshness of it again for a few moments. In the dimly lit room he could not see the lines on her forehead which he noticed in the daylight. Sometimes she looked girlish, at others much older than her age of twenty-seven. Growing up Israeli you had to be tough, to take on responsibility beyond your years. They heard about the 'Swinging Sixties', the carefree and outrageous goings-on of young people in Europe and the USA. But mostly they had been too busy, too much under pressure from his studies and hers. They had had to struggle with juggling where Shimon was to be, missing him dreadfully and quietly blaming each other for his absence even though they knew really that neither of them was at fault.

When Gila began to train as a dentist, Shimon had gone to Kibbutz Hamesh for a time, to Gila's mother. But Mrs Weissman suffered with her health, having black periods of depression and instability. Gila came back one evening from Tiberias pale and strained, bringing Shimon with her.

'I can't leave him with her – even at Hamesh.' There were plenty of other people about, but it wasn't working. She was afraid for Shimon.

That was when they decided he must stay in Tel Aviv with Auntie Miriam during the term times. Miriam, Gila's aunt, was a spirited lady who worked at home as a potter and seemed quite able to absorb the company of a small boy into her life. Gila went back and forth as often as she could to see him. But the past three years had been a time of hard work and strain, and David was called up for the army reserve every year as well. There had been very little time or money to be carefree and young. The most they could ever afford was a trip to the cinema now and then.

It was as if they had not seen each other for a long time. And when they did not see each other, and the stresses of life pressed in on them, the bond between them loosened and it felt as if they were strangers.

Chapter Forty

For a few days in August, once exams were over, they went to Haifa to stay with Annaliese.

It was their chance of a holiday and Annaliese was always delighted to have them there. Often she would join them on the beach, a bus ride away, down the Carmel, sitting under an umbrella to protect her fragile skin, determined to watch every moment of Shimon's play and swimming.

David knew they needed some relaxed days, away from all the pressures of work and study. Things were tense between him and Gila. Whereas after Shimon was born Gila had longed for another child and he had tried to persuade her to wait, now it was he who thought they should be trying for a brother or sister for their son. This time though, it was Gila who was holding back, who seemed to have lost the desire for more children that she had felt so burningly before.

'If we don't have another baby soon, it will be a different generation from Shim!' David would say, exasperated. He still had the same sense of insecurity and need for family when he had so little.

'Oh, don't exaggerate,' Gila would fire back at him. 'This is my first job. I have to get established. I can't just take time off. And you're not qualified! We need the money, Doodi. We have to be practical.'

'We can manage,' he would argue, galled that she

was the one bringing in the most money, though he did not want to admit it. 'We can't sacrifice everything for work – what about family – what about *life*?'

'Oh – you mean it's my work that should be sacrificed, not yours! I know it would be much more convenient for you if I was at home all the time cooking and cleaning for you and having your babies. But don't forget, I'm the one earning a proper salary just now . . .'

And so the arguments went on. And David realized, secretly, that this was just what he did want. It would be so good to come home in the evening when he was tired from a day of classes and laboratories to find his wife less tired than he, less under pressure, his son happy and secure, not wetting his bed, a meal on the table . . . The tender welcome he had received once back from the Front in June had waned quickly and they were back to normal, having hardly the energy for each other again.

But they did their best to be united in front of Annaliese, and it was easier to be relaxed there, since she longed to mother them and look after them, urging them to rest. In the mornings they all went down to the crowded strip of sand dotted with coloured umbrellas, where they swam and played with Shimon, buying cool drinks from the kiosk at the top of the beach. Usually, when the heat became very intense after midday, they caught the bus back up to the Carmel, sat under the big single tap in Annaliese's bath and washed the sand off themselves with caressing, tepid water. Then they would eat bread with cheese and hummus, cucumbers and tomatoes, and lie down in the musty-smelling apartment with the blinds closed against the glare, to nap until the fiercest heat was past.

This was utter luxury, being able to sink into sleep in the daytime, to wake, sometimes before Shimon, who seemed drugged by the heat and worn out by leaping in the waves. If this happened, they sometimes made love, slippery with sweat like two seals. It made them much better friends for a time.

Annaliese would wake them with mint tea, or juice, or David would get up and slip out to make something for her. And as they woke one by one they would sit out on the balcony, where the sea was a hazy blue in the distance, and talk softly in the lazy late afternoon.

David soon noticed that there were changes in Annaliese. There was a new liveliness. If anything, she seemed young for her fifty-eight years, whereas before, while she was caring for Hermann, she had seemed prematurely aged. She pencilled in her eyebrows, fastened her mostly grey hair up in a simple bun and dressed in elegant cotton frocks. And she seemed more animated.

One afternoon David sat with her at the shady end of the balcony while Gila and Shimon were still asleep. He lounged in the cane chair, barefoot and wearing only a pair of faded shorts, enjoying the tickling breeze on his tanned skin. The two of them sipped mint tea. Annaliese wore a mauve shirtwaister dress and had slipped her knobbly feet out of her sandals. Both her hands and feet had swollen, arthritic knuckles. In the breezy silence she looked fondly at him.

'How are you, my boy?' When they were alone together they nearly always spoke German. David's German was basic but he tried to keep it up to please her.

'It's good to be here – to have a change of scene,' he

said, stretching out luxuriously. 'And be with you, of course.'

'Ah – you are charming to me!' she laughed. 'Your hair looks nice short. Though I suppose I still prefer you with your curls.'

David ran his hand ruefully over his army-cropped hair. He had thick hair which became wavy when he allowed it to grow.

'I suppose they're not really the thing for a doctor though either,' he smiled. 'There are so many rules about controlling infections.'

'You didn't answer me.'

'Answer you what?'

'How things are. How you are.'

Just sometimes, occasionally, he confided in Annaliese about his feelings, his dilemmas. Sometimes she laughed them away – 'You think you're the only Jew with a crisis of identity?' – but at times she listened with gentle sensitivity.

'You don't give up, do you, old lady?' he teased her.

Annaliese sucked her cheeks in, pretending she had no teeth. 'No, we old people have to beg for any information,' she said in a quavery voice. 'No one tells me anything!'

David laughed. 'You look very well. Not in the least old.'

'Ah—' Smiling, she held up a finger. 'I shall tell you, since you remark on it. But don't think I have forgotten my question to you. I shall be coming back to that.'

There was a pause for a moment, then, looking away from him, out over the pines and the sandy-coloured town towards the sweep of the Mediterranean, she said, 'You know that all the time until Hermann passed away, I was here with him, looking after him. He was my life all those years, since we had no one else remaining. I had a couple of cousins who survived the Nazis but they went to America. Here, there is no one else – well until you came along, *Liebchen*. So after Hermann had gone, I had a crisis—'

She held up a hand against his expression of concern, that he had not known.

'There was nothing you could have done, darling. Your existence here was the greatest help to me. Some things have to be lived through, that's all. I had given so much of myself to Hermann for most of the time that I had been in Israel, on top of all that happened in the war, that I did not know who I was any more. Annaliese Mayer – who is she? I used to sit in front of the mirror sometimes and ask that question. I was in a state of being lost, utterly.'

She took a sip of her tea, cradling the glass between her hands. David had a struggle to follow some of her German, but he caught the meaning of what she was saying.

'So, I thought, I must find a person who can help. I went to a lady to whom I could talk, week after week. She was a psychotherapist, they call it. Not a psychiatrist – not a doctor. She was someone who specializes in the cure of talking, of listening and interpreting one's ills. She helped me a good deal – for two years. And I started to feel better. Then, recently, I met a new friend. His name is Pierre.' She gave a darting, bashful smile and lapsed into silence.

'Go on,' David said gently. 'Tell me about him.'

'Well – he was born in Paris. His parents made *aliyah* in 1920 when he was in his teens. He had a wife and has three grown-up children and he has been living in Haifa since his wife died five years ago . . .' She gave an impish smile. 'And what else do you want to know? You will meet him – that is the best thing.'

Before David could get a word in she leaned forward and laid her hand on his arm for a second.

'And now, you are going to talk to me. Tell me about your life, your studies. What are your thoughts?'

'To be honest, I don't seem to have many thoughts these days,' he said ruefully. He drained his tea glass and put it down on the tiles. 'The last couple of years I've had my head down, non-stop, study, study – except for the war . . . And Gila has been studying too . . .'

Annaliese was giving him a penetrating look which David found disconcerting. She had a gift for seeing deeply into anything he said.

'You are settled – you and Gila? You are an Israeli?'

These were the questions David tried hard not to think about these days. He had made his aliyah, his migration to Israel. He must stand by that now. Looking down at the floor, at the little water outlet at the end of the balcony, he said, 'I live here. I fight in the army. My wife is a sabra and my son was born here . . .'

The prickly pear, the sabra, was the name given to native-born Israelis. They were said to be hard and spiky on the outside, but soft within. How frail and vulnerable were his two prickly pears, he thought, Gila and Shimon.

'But . . . ?'

He looked up at her. He could not answer her because he did not know the answer himself. All this time he had thrown in his lot, his life, his whole identity with Israel. It had given him a sense of himself when he was young and lost. And the war had been a triumph, he had been part of it all. He could not understand, at this time, the shifting feelings inside him.

In this moment of their gazing at one another there was a little rattling of the door behind them and Shimon's face appeared, wide-eyed and tender after waking from sleep. Annaliese's face broke into a smile.

'Hello, my little darling – come to me, here!'

Shimon walked over to her in his little shorts and shirt, utterly trusting, and David's heart bucked inside him. His son was so beautiful and vulnerable that he felt burningly protective. What did his own confusions and misgivings matter when it came to looking after this child, and making sure of the safety and happiness of his life?

Part Five

1967–9

Chapter Forty-One

October 1967

'It's only me, Mom!'

Greta elbowed open Ruby's front door, holding Francesca in her arms, and managed to shut it behind her with her foot.

'Is that my granddaughter you've got there?'

Ruby hurried through from the kitchen. She sounded welcoming, but Greta knew her jealousy and resentment were never far from the surface. Even though she put on a good front, Ruby was feeling it, having been left on her own. She'd never been one to be alone for long, and Herbert's death and Greta and Marleen moving out so close together had left her feeling lonely and unwanted. She looked faded too, her hair a scrappy mixture of blonde and brown and scraped back. Ruby wasn't making the best of herself.

'Look, Franny – there's your Nan!'

The little girl pumped an arm in excitement, her round face all smiles.

'God—' Ruby said, gazing at her. 'She really is the image of yer Dad. I see it more every time . . .'

'I know,' Greta said, smiling. 'Even I can see it!'

A photograph was all she had ever seen of her father, Wally Sorenson, but Francesca clearly favoured him in looks. She had a lovely round face with big blue eyes, fair hair which sat in pretty waves across the top of her head and a sunny temperament. Everyone loved her, and life had taught her to smile and bathe in the attention. Greta adored her.

'If Wally was like her, I can see why you wanted to marry him, Mom,' she said, going to put Francesca down. Ruby had acquired a little wooden playpen for when she came round.

'Oh, don't put her in there – let me have a hold! You go and put the kettle on, bab.'

Ruby kept hold of the baby as they drank their tea. She gave Francesca a finger of bread to chew, and every few moments she kissed the top of the child's head and Francesca chuckled at the tickly feeling.

'She's very like you were, you know,' Ruby said.

'Only better-tempered?' Greta reached for the packet of sugar and dropped three lumps into her tea. She was weaning Francesca now she was six months old, but she still needed all the energy she could get.

'You were all right. Only life was harder – me on my own and the war on. We didn't have time for miniskirts and all this stuff you all go in for.' The usual tone of self-pity crept into her voice.

'Well, I'm on my own,' Greta reminded her.

'You've got plenty of help. I didn't have the likes of Edie and Anatoli and all their odd friends dancing attendance.'

Greta could feel the conversation running off the rails already. By 'odd friends' she knew Ruby meant people from the Society of Friends, the Quakers. She took Francesca to the Sunday Meeting quite regularly now with Edie and Anatoli. The Meeting was held mainly in silence, but children only stayed in for a little while and then went out and did activities, depending on their ages, and Greta carried Francesca out with them and lent a hand where she could. She had felt very shy going there at first, but everyone was very kind and she had made some new friends. Her Mom's remarks about them stung. What did Ruby really know about it anyway?

'Well, you had help too, from Frances Hatton. She was so kind, and you didn't seem to be so fussy about whether she was a Quaker or not when you needed her!'

'Huh,' was all Ruby replied, busying herself with Francesca. Then she fired out the words that Greta always dreaded.

'Look, bab – you really ought to move back in with me and not be living off them all the time. I'm ashamed to think of it, with you not working, and me here all on my own . . .'

'That's what I've come to tell you, Mom,' Greta said quickly. She didn't want this conversation, yet again, about her moving back. How could she explain how much she loved living with Edie and Anatoli? And she genuinely believed they enjoyed her living with them. She had found the parents she'd always wanted, but she could hardly say that to her Mom!

'I'm going back to work – next week. Seasonal, for the moment, till Franny's older. I'm going to do three days and Edie's doing two. We'll look after the kids the days we're not working . . .'

Ruby's face darkened. 'You mean Edie's going to be looking after *my* granddaughter three days a week?'

'Well, I'd ask you, Mom, but now you're back on five days a week you're not here to have her, are you?'

'Well, some of us have to work don't we, not just

go in for a bit if fun when we feel like it? I don't have a big house and a husband where I can take in all and sundry like Lady Bountiful!'

'Well you've had kindness in your time, plenty of it!' Greta flared. 'And you could have hung on to it instead of mucking it all up with the way you've carried on. With my grandparents for a start!'

'Oh don't go on about that again, it's water under the bridge,' Ruby snapped, her cheeks flushing. She struck a match, angrily and lit up. 'And it's Marleen you want to blame for that, not me.'

Greta bit her lip, already regretting losing her temper. She knew her Mom's marriage to Carl Christie had wrecked everything as well. But there was no point in keeping on.

Instead she said, 'And how is Her Majesty?'

'Well the babby seems all right.' Two months after Francesca was born, Marleen had had another baby boy, and Trevor had insisted they call him George after George Harrison. Ruby gave a chuckle suddenly. 'Looks ever so like Trevor, he does!'

'Poor little bugger!'

'Well at least one of them looks like its Dad anyroad – I don't see much sign of him in her!' She nodded down at Francesca. They both laughed and things eased. 'What you going to do about her knowing who her Dad is?'

'Oh, she'll have to know,' Greta said. 'I'll cross that bridge when I come to it.'

'You know, you'd be surprised,' Ruby mused. 'But Marleen seemed to be all right with him. Least, for the moment.'

'Well, Trev's got what he wanted. Lots of babbies.' Greta drained her teacup.

'You seen him?'

'Not since that one time he came, early on.'

He'd turned up when Francesca was a fortnight old and had been quite emotional when he saw his daughter, told Greta he was sorry and everything.

'I expect he's forgotten about her now he's got another baby of his own,' Greta said briskly, standing up to go. 'Better be on my way.' She lifted Francesca from Ruby's reluctant arms. 'I 'spect I'll see you at work, Mom.'

'Bring her round to see me, won't you?' Ruby said petulantly. 'Don't let her forget who her *real* Nan is.'

Going back to work was very hard at first, even for two days. For the past six months her life had revolved round her little one, and Greta felt as if she was being torn away from her. To her surprise she found she had loved looking after her, washing and feeding and rocking her, in a way which she had never imagined for a moment in all the time she was trying to avoid having babies!

But once she made the break it was fun to be back in the swing of things. She was not in the same section as Pat, who was still working full-time. Pat had come to visit her at home and see Francesca after she was born. Greta had wondered if it would upset her, seeing a lovely new baby, but Pat certainly didn't show it. She was delighted at the sight of Francesca and brought a pretty pair of white bootees as a present.

'That's an attractive name,' she said on her first visit when Greta told her what she was planning to call her. 'It's unusual that. I like it.'

Greta told her that it had been Anatoli's suggestion. Pat looked up at her.

'He's very good to you, isn't he?'

Pat had moved out of her one room now into a tiny little flat not far away, and went round to help her Mom, keeping out of the way of Mr Floyd. She seemed resigned to how things had turned out.

'I suppose I'd've had to make the break sometime,' she said. 'Although I feel terrible about Mom being left with it all. But I look at my Dad and I think, however much I did something wicked and awful, he's still in the wrong. I'm his daughter, and if he can't forgive me, well, that's his loss.'

Greta was impressed at how strong Pat seemed these days. And Pat was delighted that Greta was coming back to Cadbury's.

'It hasn't been the same without you,' she said, when they met to walk to work the first day to begin the morning shift.

'Well it won't be the same now either,' Greta said, half her mind still wondering how Francesca was. When she left, Greta had had to hand her over to Edie to finish giving her her bottle, and it felt like one of the hardest things she had ever done. 'I'm on seasonal – no holiday pay or sick pay or anything. And they'll lay us off once the Christmas rush is over. But it'll give me time to be with Franny again and I'm desperate to give Edie some money. They're ever so kind, but I've lived off them long enough.'

When she went back this time she was put on Milk Tray. The women working seasonal shifts were mainly mothers and the atmosphere was chatty, with the radio on, but the work was very fast and you had to keep alert. Hands covered by white gloves, they worked either side of the belt, while the chocolates streamed past endlessly after their journey through the enrobing machine, then into the cooler room to set the chocolate. They scooped them off the belt on to trays fast and furiously, to ready them for packing. When you got there early enough in the morning you could have free cocoa and bread and butter, but Greta did not think she would ever be organized enough for that and tried to eat something at home with Francesca first.

It was wonderful to go home at the end of her first shift and find her baby happily asleep.

'You'll be able to pop in for a swim after work if you feel like it,' Edie said. 'She's no trouble. Now Peter's at school, looking after her is ever so easy.'

She still had plenty of days to spend with Francesca, and on the days Edie was working she sometimes went and picked Peter up from school. He practised his violin and piano while she played with Francesca, or snatched a while to read when the little girl was happy playing near her. Edie and Anatoli had quite a few books and told her to dip in and read whatever she liked. Best of all she liked Thomas Hardy, and had read *Tess of the D'Urbervilles* twice already. And he encouraged her to read bits of French, even though she no longer went to her lessons.

Things settled into a contented, almost dreamlike routine, and when she stopped to think about it she realized how happy she was. As Christmas drew near again, Greta realized with surprise how much she was looking forward to it.

Chapter Forty-Two

Greta's favourite time of the day was the early evening when Anatoli came home after closing the pharmacy. The shop was almost a mile away and he always chose to walk home, shaking rain from his big black umbrella on wet winter nights, or anxious to get down to his shirtsleeves in summer. In his old-fashioned way he would never dream of removing his jacket until he was inside with the front door closed, restored to the informal realm of his family.

As soon as he came home Edie made him tea, bringing it to him in his favourite wide-rimmed willow-patterned cup and saucer. He always drank it sitting in his chair in the living room, stirring in plenty of sugar and sipping it with relish, the big blue and white saucer resting in the palm of his hand. Edie always slipped a couple of biscuits in beside the cup as well.

'Aaah!' he would say, closing his eyes with pleasure while he swallowed the first mouthful of tea. 'The taste of home! Where I am treated like a Prince!'

It was a ritual which Greta loved and it was when Anatoli held court to his family. The children were always excited when he came home. Peter would hurry in with a book or some Meccano and bask in his father's attention. Later it would be time for serious things, like violin lessons, but now was a time for fun.

At the moment Peter's favourite books were the adventures of Thomas the Tank Engine, and Anatoli was good at mimicking different voices for the characters of the trains, which made Peter laugh or gasp in fear at what was going to happen next.

Greta was coming downstairs one evening, deep in the winter, with Francesca in her arms, when Anatoli arrived. His breath streamed white on the freezing air as he came in, then shut out the cold and dark. At first he did not notice her. He closed the door and turned to take off his coat, reaching up to hang it on the hooks near the door. But instead of backing away he held on to the hook and leaned his head against his woollen coat for a few seconds, as if in extreme weariness. This small private action sent a chill through her, though she did not know what it meant. Then Francesca let out a squeak of excitement at seeing him and Anatoli immediately drew back, lowering his arms, and turned to smile at the two of them.

'Hello young lady!' He took Francesca's hand and shook it as she gurgled happily. 'And hello to you, my dear. Have you had a good day?'

'Yes thank you,' Greta said. 'Did you?' She wanted to ask if he was all right but she felt shy.

'Oh yes,' he said in his light way, as if to say, what other sort of day might he have had?

'Hello, love,' Edie said, coming through from the kitchen. In her dark brown skirt and pale blue, ribbed polo-neck jumper, her hair pinned up in a pleat, she looked warmly cosy and comforting. She kissed Anatoli and he put his arm round her shoulders and drew her to him. Greta watched with a pang. How wonderful to have found love like that!

As soon as the children heard that he was home,

Peter came rushing out of the living room and Anatoli said, 'Ah – it must be story time!'

'There's tea in the pot,' Edie smiled. 'I'll bring it through. D'you want one, Greta?'

'Oh, yes please!'

Greta sat and listened to the stories too. She remembered Frances and Janet reading to her and Marleen and David when they were little, and how much she had loved it. Edie sometimes stayed in the room if she was not cooking, and she did today. Francesca sat on the floor or on one of their laps. Normally she was very active, now she was ten months old, crawling around and into everything, but during story time she already seemed to know to keep still and watch with huge eyes, giggling at Peter's laughter, and waving and clapping her hands. The sight of her joining in was one of the loveliest things Greta had ever seen. It made her glow with happiness.

'Look at young miss,' Anatoli said as he closed the book on another of Thomas's adventures. 'She takes in everything doesn't she? Every detail.'

Edie went out to check on the cooking, but Peter was not satisfied. He sat straddling Anatoli.

'Will you read another one Daddy?' he begged.

'Ah, now you know, you young rascal, that we only read one story!' Anatoli tickled him, and Peter squirmed happily. 'That is your ration for the day. And anyway, you know you can really read them yourself as well now . . .'

'Oh please – just this once!' Overexcited, Peter began to pummel Anatoli's chest.

Greta, who had been looking down at Francesca, jumped in shock as Anatoli suddenly let out a yell.

'I said no! All right? You heard me – now get off and stop this! Go!'

Peter scrambled down from his father's knee, lips aquiver, looking as if he was going to explode with upset as he ran from the room. It was almost unheard-of for Anatoli to react like this and raise his voice.

'Now just leave me!' Anatoli shouted after his son.

Greta took this to mean her as well, so she got up and went to find Peter, who was curled in a sobbing ball at the bottom of the stairs.

'It's all right, love—' She went and put her arm round the bewildered little boy who was used to a father who, even in his darker moods, was calm and kindly to him. She felt upset herself, almost as if she was a child and Anatoli had yelled at her as well. 'Daddy must be tired or something. I'm sure he didn't mean to frighten you.'

'Mom,' Peter said, pulling away and running for the kitchen. There was hurt and outrage in every line of his body. Greta picked up Francesca and went after him.

Edie was checking the boiling potatoes to see if they were cooked.

'What on earth's the matter?' she said, putting down her knife as Peter plunged at her and buried his head in her skirt. 'That's not like my big boy!'

'He had a little run-in with his Dad,' Greta said awkwardly.

'Anatoli?' Edie frowned and bent down to her son. 'What happened?'

'Daddy shouted at me!' Peter cried.

Face stricken Edie looked up. 'Why on earth?'

'I don't really know,' Greta said. 'Peter just wanted another story.'

'Oh,' Edie said, baffled. It was so unlike Anatoli. 'Well, maybe your Daddy's tired today love. Or got a toothache. Come on – you come and stir the stewpot for me, will you?'

Greta was surprised not to see Anatoli coming into the kitchen to make amends. He and Peter were usually so sunny with each other. She carried Francesca from the kitchen, thinking to go and see Anatoli. She wanted to see him in a happier mood again to make herself feel better.

But when she put her head round the door of the living room, Anatoli was stretched out in the chair with his eyes closed and his face looked tired and sunken. Frowning, she left again, quietly closing the door.

It happened gradually. Edie started teasing Anatoli, telling him he must be watching his waistline because he didn't seem to be eating much.

'It's because you're going to be sixty this year, isn't it?' she said, patting his comfortable tummy. 'You're starting to get vain.'

'Yes – I am going to be like Twiggy,' Anatoli said, fluttering his eyelashes. 'These young models have made me start to feel ashamed.'

But as the weeks went past, it was impossible to hide that he was losing weight fast and that something was seriously wrong. Edie confided her worries to Greta. The two of them were very close now, sharing the daily routines of work and each other's children. They spent a lot of time together in the big kitchen of the Gruschovs' house, preparing meals or sitting at the table over cups of tea with the children around them.

'I've begged him to go and see the doctor,' Edie said one gloomy February afternoon. 'He's usually quite sensible about things like that, but he keeps saying he's perfectly all right. He doesn't look all right at all to me. And d'you know what he said to me this morning? He said, "I think I'll take the car into work today – just for a change." He *never* drives!'

Greta wanted to reassure her but she was very worried as well. Anatoli's thinness was upsetting: he was gradually beginning to look like someone different. And she saw, from his small movements, in the effort it seemed to take for him to climb the stairs, to hang his coat or lift his small son, that he was tired and weak. One afternoon she found courage while she was sitting with him, Francesca cruising round the room, pulling herself up to stand by the chairs and chuckling.

'Anatoli?'

'Umm?' He looked up at her from his newspaper. The whites of his eyes seemed yellowish, she thought. Or perhaps it was the light.

'It's just – you don't look very well. We're all worried about you.'

'Oh!' he gave a dismissive laugh. 'Not you as well, umm? Edith keeps fussing ... You don't want to be worrying about me.'

'But I do ...' She felt tongue-tied. 'Why won't you go and see the doctor?'

Anatoli looked down at his hands. They were bonier than they had been.

'Perhaps I should ...' he said vaguely, as if to himself. She was sure she saw a look of fear pass across his face and she found she had tears in her eyes. She had never seen him look like that before and she wanted to put her arms round him and tell him everything would be all right.

'It might be better,' she said. 'You know – just to make sure there's nothing serious.'

'Yes, my dear,' he said, thoughtfully. 'I suppose I'm being silly.'

A few days later she came home from Cadbury's, bringing her white gloves to wash as usual, and she went straight to the kitchen to soak them. Edie was standing by the sink, looking out of the window, and she didn't seem to hear Greta come in.

'Edie?'

When she turned, her face was wet with tears. She looked shrunken, as if something in her had collapsed. Greta's heart seemed to stop.

'It's Anatoli isn't it?'

Edie crumpled, nodding. She leaned back against the sink, hands over her face, and started to sob. Greta went and put her arms round her. The age gap between them, which had mattered less and less over these months, was nothing now. This was a man both of them loved.

'He came in earlier...' Edie brought her hands down and felt in her sleeve for a hanky to wipe her nose and cheeks. 'He's gone back to work now ... I asked him not to, but he said he had to. He wouldn't know what to do else...' She turned to Greta. 'He's ill – very ill, Greta. The doctor said it's cancer – of the pancreas ...' She struggled to say it, looking as if she'd been punched. 'I don't even know what a pancreas is ...'

'Oh my God,' Greta breathed. She didn't know

what a pancreas was either. It was the word cancer which filled you with dread.

'He said ... They're going to do an operation – soon. He'll have to be in hospital and they'll take out some of the tumour. I think that's what he said.' Her eyes started to pour tears again. 'But he said...' Her face contorted again. 'There's no cure. Nothing much they can do, in the end. Oh God, Greta – he's going to die. My lovely Anatoli's going to die!'

Chapter Forty-Three

Greta was afraid of facing Anatoli. She was afraid of breaking down. The thought of losing him was unbearable. And today, of all days, she planned to keep out of the way so that Anatoli and Edie could be alone together.

When he came home, she was upstairs. She heard the door open and close, and she was in such a state that she couldn't seem to do anything except perch tensely on the edge of her bed, cuddling a wriggly Francesca. Softly, from downstairs, came the sound of voices. There was an ache inside her, like a heavy stone sitting in her chest. It was awful to dread seeing Anatoli. It was as if his illness had turned him into a stranger and she had no idea how to talk to him.

But within a few moments she heard his voice.

'Greta? Are you coming to join us for our cup of tea?'

Cup of tea? As usual! How could anything be usual when the sky had fallen in? But his voice sounded much as ever. And it came to her that precisely because the sky had fallen in, Anatoli might want things to feel normal. She must pull herself together.

'Yes – just coming!' she called, getting shakily to her feet.

In the living room, Anatoli was already holding his teacup, and there was a Madeira cake on a plate, cut into slices. Peter lay on the hearthrug by the fire with his Dinky cars, close to Edie's chair, and everything seemed just as it always did. Perhaps it was! Greta clutched at the idea. Perhaps it was all a mistake!

'Here you go,' Edie said, passing her a cup of tea. 'Have some cake if you'd like, love.'

Edie's face had the freshly washed look of someone who has wept for a long time, but she was calm and not crying now.

Greta sat down, trying to keep her hands from shaking, and was about to say something bright and conversational, when Anatoli put his cup down and looked from one to the other of them.

'You both know the news that I have been given today.' He gave them a moment to nod. 'I don't want to hide anything from you or for this to be something we have to whisper about, or pretend it is not true, that there is really nothing wrong and so on. I have been pretending to myself for too long. I have not been feeling well for some time, I know that now, but somehow it has crept up on me and I find that I am much sicker than I thought.'

Greta felt a lump forming in her throat and swallowed hard. She wanted to be calm, like him. She glanced at Peter, wondering if he knew what was happening, but he was playing, trying to stop Francesca pinching his cars, and did not seem to be listening. Every now and then Francesca let out loud roars of indignation as he tugged cars away from her, which made them all smile and helped the situation.

'I shall go into hospital some time fairly soon. They can delay things a little, by an operation, but so far as I understand, that is really all they can do.'

Both Edie and Greta were fighting back their tears,

and Peter suddenly looked up and saw his mother's face. Without saying anything he climbed on to her lap and stared up at her. Edie held him tight and kissed his curls.

'It's all right, love,' she said gently.

'I just . . .' Here, Anatoli's own eyes filled with tears and the ache in Greta's chest became so sharp she felt it might burst open. He wiped his eyes on his handkerchief, and looking at Edie, went on. 'I have a life with you which is so good, so happy – all of you.' He encompassed Greta in his loving gaze as well. 'All I want is that, until I am too ill . . . Until I die . . . I just want to live, you understand? To carry on just as we are and be with you all – my loving family.'

Greta couldn't help it. The tears flowed down her face. Edie was crying too, quietly, and Peter had buried his face in her chest. The only one in the room chatting happily to herself was Francesca, now she had all the toy cars to herself, and this made them smile through all the tears.

'Now there is someone who knows what I mean,' Anatoli said, wiping his eyes again. There was a pause, as he pushed his handkerchief back into his pocket. 'I still have to let this sink in – we all do. And I'll try not to be a dreadful nuisance of a patient . . .' He held up a hand against their protests that they would look after him whatever, that they would do anything for him. 'Let us try to be of good cheer.' He gave a watery smile. 'Life is for living while you have it – that is my way of looking at it.'

They continued as usual then, swallowing down their tears, Anatoli calling Peter to him and reading his favourite Thomas story. Greta sat with Francesca and enjoyed it all. Afterwards though, she went up to her room, lay on the bed and sobbed and sobbed. She had lost one father, now she was about to lose another, a real flesh-and-blood person, not a smile from a blurry photograph. Anatoli had been so kind and loving to her. It felt as if everything was falling apart. But it was so much worse for Edie, she knew, losing a husband who she loved so much. She resolved that she must be strong for Edie and help her as much as she could.

Within a short time, Edie had another shock. On one of the days she was at home, there was a knock at the door. When she found Trevor on the doorstep, still in his white overall from the barber's, she knew there must be something wrong.

'Greta's not here,' she said, leaning on the doorframe. She didn't intend to ask him in, whatever he wanted. Edie didn't think much of Trevor. 'She works on Thursdays.'

'No – it's you I've come to see, Mrs Gruschov – it's about yer Dad . . .'

Edie only noticed then that he looked pale and shaken.

'He's collapsed, just a while ago. They've taken him up the hospital.'

Edie's father, Mr Marshall, had run the barber's shop in Charlotte Road all her life.

'Oh my goodness – is he going to be all right?' She was putting her coat on, ready to go straight up to the hospital.

'I dunno,' Trev shrugged. 'They took him off in the ambulance.'

*

323

Mr Marshall had had a stroke. It was a serious one and he only lingered for one day, dying in the small hours of the following night.

'I suppose it was a mercy,' Edie said to Greta. 'He would've hated to be paralysed or anything like that.'

'I'm ever so sorry,' Greta said. She hadn't heard until she came home from work. 'You are having a rough time, aren't you? Look, let me make the tea and everything tonight – you've got enough on your plate.'

'No – I'll do it with you, love,' Edie said, as they went into the kitchen together. 'I've only got a bit of liver. I thought it might build Anatoli up a bit. Tell you the truth I'd rather keep busy.'

She filled the kettle and then turned, her face thoughtful. 'I wouldn't want to give you the wrong impression. I was never close to my Dad – nor Mom. She was worse. A bitter, cruel woman she was, and I never found out why till she was dying herself. My dad had been through it with her all right. But he and I were never close either. He never said much.'

'Yes – Trevor said that. It was the customers did nearly all the talking. Your Dad just told them how much they owed him!'

Edie laughed. 'Yeah – that was our Dad all right. Funny thing was, he had quite a few pals. I s'pose he never argued back to them! It's no wonder our Rodney has hardly a word to say for himself either. There was never anyone to teach him how to do it.'

'He was still your Dad though,' Greta said. That must mean something, she thought. Having a father at all still seemed something to envy.

'Yes,' Edie said flatly. 'I suppose it's the end of an

era. He's always just been there, in the same place, ever since I can remember.'

Greta went to the funeral, at the Crem at Lodge Hill. In fact Anatoli asked her to.

'I want Edith to have as much help as she can,' he said. 'She has so little family now.'

It was a small occasion, the day very cold. A few customers came, who had had their hair cut for years at Marshall's 'Gentleman's Barbers'. The family contingent was small. Edie's younger brother Rodney was there with his wife, and Edie and Anatoli, and of course Trevor. Marleen stayed away, with the children. Dennis Marshall was dispatched quickly and with the minimum of ceremony and they were all outside again, walking off along the tree-lined path to make ready for the next funeral party.

Anatoli was with Edie of course, and Greta found herself beside Trevor. It was funny how familiar he felt, and yet she could hardly believe now that she was married to him and had lived with him all that time.

'So,' she said to him. 'You'll take over the shop now I s'pose?'

'Yes,' he said proudly. 'Mr Marshall always said I'd step into his shoes managing the business.'

Greta saw that Trevor seemed to have grown in the past days. He was standing more upright, looked actually physically bigger.

'Well,' she said, with the usual mixture of fondness and irritation. 'Good for you. Your own business.'

'Yes—' Trevor drew himself up even taller. 'And

325

Greta – Marleen wants us to get married. So you and me – we need to get a divorce. Do things properly.'

For a second she felt a pang of loss, then dismissed it. Of course they had to get divorced. She didn't want to carry on being married to Trevor did she?

'Our Marleen wants to get married does she?' She was amazed.

'She's having another babby. It's time we made it legal, like,' Trevor said proudly.

They reached the road and Greta could see Anatoli waiting for her with the car door open.

'All right then, if you want,' she said lightly.

Chapter Forty-Four

Anatoli did not give up work at first. He went to the pharmacy in the mornings as he had always done. But he drove to work now, and more and more often he came home at lunchtime looking drawn and exhausted and had to rest, leaving the work to his trusted assistant.

Everything kept going almost as before – but nothing felt normal or the same. They knew they were waiting for Anatoli's operation, clinging to the hope that this could make him better and save him. His face told the story of his increasing illness even though he was almost always cheerful and courageous.

Edie tried to carry on as usual too, and with Anatoli she was gentle and loving and put on a happy face. When she broke down it was often when she and Greta were alone. Sometimes she would come in and sit at the kitchen table and just put her head in her hands.

After a moment she would say, 'If only he could eat a little bit more – I can't bear to see him wasting away.' Or, 'When I look at him, the way he is, it breaks my heart.'

Then they would look at each other, with a deep, knowing look, then wipe their eyes and carry on. What else was there to say?

*

Anatoli's illness was the agonizing chorus that ran through their lives now. The routine continued, with work and children and Greta trying to make sure that Francesca saw something of her Nan. Soon after Mr Marshall's funeral, she went round to see Ruby. It was a Saturday afternoon and there was a fog which had barely lifted all day, making the little terraced streets seem ghostly and quieter than usual.

Greta pushed Francesca up the hill in the little pushchair. As she went through Bournbrook she passed the second-hand bookshop where she had bought the Christmas present for Dennis Franklin and where the man had been kind to her and given her a book.

She had walked past the shop again many times and hardly given it a thought. What a long time ago it seemed that she had spent her time running after Dennis, trying to impress him! Occasionally now she saw Dennis at the works. She had heard that he had married recently, though he could still barely bring himself to acknowledge her. She still remembered what had happened with Dennis with burning embarrassment, but she could see now that he was stuffy and self-important, even in the way he walked round the factory looking so full of himself.

'Pompous prat,' she said, out loud. 'Who the hell does he think he is?'

When she got to Ruby's she found her in a mood.

'Thought you were coming earlier than this,' she snapped as Greta hoiked the pushchair up the two front steps into the front room and started to get Francesca out. 'I've been waiting since eleven. Hello, *sweetheart . . .*' she greeted Francesca.

'Sorry,' Greta said, to keep the peace, even though

she didn't think she was late. Under her breath she couldn't help adding, '*Yes and it's nice to see you too.*'

Holding Francesca she led the way into the kitchen. There was a tall coffee pot on the table, in an orangey-brown pottery, with a long spout and patterns on it like snowflakes. Greta had never seen it before.

'That's nice,' she said. 'Where d'you get that?'

'Mavis got it me cheap somewhere,' Ruby said. Mavis was one of her pals. 'Nice, ain't it? It's meant to be for coffee but I'm going to use it for tea . . .' With Francesca on one hip she put the kettle on with one hand.

Greta waited for her to ask how Anatoli was. She knew Ruby had had her differences with Edie, but surely when something so sad and serious was happening she could put that aside. But when she had first told Ruby that Anatoli was sick, that it was serious, for a second she had seen an expression creep over her mother's face which looked like triumph. *Huh*, it seemed to say. *Time something went wrong for little Miss Perfect.* There was spite in her face which sickened Greta. Could she not put her envy of Edie aside even when something as bad as this was happening? Ruby recovered herself and made the right concerned noises, but Greta could not forget it and it made her feel even closer to Edie.

Instead of asking about Anatoli, Ruby turned to glare at Greta.

'So – he's divorcing you?'

'Who?'

'Who? Trevor, yer silly bleeder, who else?'

'I think you'll find I'm divorcing him,' Greta said pertly, sitting down at the table. 'After all, he's the one who's committed adultery.'

Ruby was frowning at her, pouting almost.

'What's up with you? We can't exactly go on with him married to me and my sister popping out one of his babies every five minutes, can we?'

'We've never had a divorce in the family before,' Ruby said, pursing her lips primly. 'It's not very nice, is it?'

'*What*?' Greta exploded, astonished. 'What're you on about? You're a fine one to talk! You divorced Carl Christie, didn't you?'

A haunted look came over Ruby's face and she turned red.

'What's the matter, Mom?' Greta pressed her.

Ruby turned back towards the stove. 'I didn't divorce Carl Christie . . .'

'But . . .' Greta stuttered. 'How could you . . . ? You mean you married Herbert when . . . ? But that makes you a whatsitsname – a bigamist! Oh no – of course! You *didn't* marry him!'

Ruby's cheeks were puce.

Greta stared at her incredulously for a second, then started to laugh. 'Oh my God, Mom! . . .' She put a hand to her head, wondering if she was going crazy. 'But – hang on, you *did* marry Carl! That weekend . . . You were having a quiet, romantic wedding, by that lake in Virginia or whatever it was – that's what you told Marleen and me. And we cried because you wouldn't let us have new frocks and be your bridesmaids. You said you wanted no fuss . . . We stayed with Ed and Louisa and they took us to the farm show and we had corn on the cob . . .'

'Yes, well . . .' Ruby looked down, taking refuge in fiddling with Francesca's little socks. 'That's what we told them. They were so churchy, Bible this and Bible that – I thought it would keep them happy. I loved Carl, or I thought I did, and I thought he loved me. Only I didn't want to get married again. Not in America. It was all too far away from home.'

'Mom!' Greta said, laughing now. After all, what could you do but laugh? Two pretend weddings! Sometimes she felt as if she was more grown up than her own mother. 'You're terrible, honestly you are. So stop giving me lectures about me and Trev – you can't exactly talk, can you!' Another thought struck her. 'Hang on though isn't Marleen still married? To that Brett bloke?'

Ruby looked stricken. 'Oh my God – I'd never thought of that! Well she'll have to get that sorted out before she even thinks about marrying Trevor, how ever many kids they've got!'

It was a relief to be at work and try to forget the heartbreak of the Bristol Road house, of watching Anatoli become more drawn and yellow-skinned by the day.

She was taken on again at Cadbury's with the other seasonal workers for the Easter rush and was put to work filling Easter eggs. The endless parade of Dairy Milk chocolate half-eggs, with their smooth, shiny insides, slid towards her along the conveyor belt. She had to drop the five chocolates inside, the orange cream first, then the others on top and a piece of tissue paper, before it moved on for the other half of the chocolate shell to be added, before it was wrapped in tinfoil, then encased in the colourful 'Waddies' for the shops.

She soon got to know the other women and enjoyed being there in all the company and chatter. And it meant that at least sometimes she saw Pat, who was always over the moon to see her.

'Hello, Gret!' she'd call across the girls' dining room, whoever else she was with. 'Come and sit here!'

Pat's life had settled into a quiet, quite dull routine, but she seemed content with things.

'I don't want any excitements,' she said. 'I've had quite enough of that. Come to work, go home and have a bit of peace – that's me.'

Greta worried for her sometimes. There was something closed down about Pat, as if she had shut the door on life after the tragedy of what happened with Ian. But then, she thought, her own life wasn't so very different. Neither of them had the cosy marriage and couple of kids that seemed to be held up as the perfect life. And Pat's predictable life felt comforting at the moment, when other things were changing in a way that was sad and frightening.

Chapter Forty-Five

Anatoli went into Selly Oak Hospital on a bleak March day. Martin Ferris came and drove him, bringing Edie back home afterwards, where Greta was waiting.

The wind gusted through the front door as Edie and Martin came in. Daffodils lay flattened on their stalks on the front garden and the door closed with a slam. Martin smiled hello to Greta.

'Can I make you a drink?' Edie asked, after thanking Martin distractedly several times. 'Tea, coffee?' Greta could hear what a state she was in, as if her wits were scattered.

'No thanks, Edie – I'd love one really, but I'd better get back to the surgery.'

Martin, who was normally very reserved, put his hands on Edie's shoulders and looked down at her with gentle eyes. 'He's in good hands.'

Edie nodded, trying not to cry. 'I know.' She looked down, the tears falling anyway.

'Janet will be round later,' he promised, on his way out.

Edie sat down at the kitchen table with a ragged sigh saying, 'Dear oh dear . . .' She seemed smaller, her hair less bright, as if she had faded since this morning.

Greta wanted to comfort her, to say everything would be all right, so she didn't say anything, just put the kettle on and arranged cups and saucers, milk and sugar. The familiar ritual felt comforting.

She could feel Edie watching her. 'I'm glad you're here, Gret,' she said.

The doctors said the operation had gone well. Edie went in to visit the first few times, while Anatoli was at his weakest after the surgery. The first day she came back looking very pale and worried.

'It was terrible,' she told Greta, 'seeing him lying there, with that thing in his arm. He looked so poorly, so *old* all of a sudden. When he opened his eyes...' And here her own filled with tears, though she was smiling at the same time. 'He managed to give me a little smile and he said, "So, I assume I am looking my age at last?"'

Despite her worries, Anatoli rallied quickly. Soon she came home from visiting and said that he had been asking for Greta.

'Me?' Greta felt a great surge of happiness. 'He actually asked for me?'

Edie looked fondly at her. 'What he actually said was, "So where's that lovely girl of mine?" And I said, "I thought I was your lovely girl," so he said, "Of course you are – I mean the one who is like my daughter."'

Greta blushed. 'Can I go and see him tomorrow then? When you've finished, maybe? I don't want to tire him out.'

'Course you can, love. He's asked you to, hasn't he?'

She went in the next day on her way back from work, with a big bunch of daffodils for him. The

334

hospital felt big and bewildering and Greta didn't like the idea of Anatoli being in here. He belonged in his house with his comfortable armchair, his clutter of music scores and violins, his colourful pictures, his big cup of tea. When she saw him, halfway along the ward, he looked smaller too, and defenceless.

'Ahh!' he cried, his face lighting up. 'Hello, my dear! I was hoping you were going to come and had not deserted me!'

'I brought you these daffs—' Shyly, she held them out. 'Oh – I've got something to put them in.' She had taken with her a big jam jar from home so that she could arrange them for him and not have to ask anyone. She was glad she had because the ward was busy with visitors and the nurses looked forbidding.

'How lovely – a bunch of sunshine,' Anatoli said. Turning to the man in the next bed he said, 'This is one of my daughters . . .'

The man called a chirpy hello to her. 'Lovely wench, that,' he said.

Once again the warmth of Anatoli's affection spread through Greta. She filled the jam jar from the sink nearby and put it on the bedside cabinet to arrange the flowers. She saw that propped against the water jug he had a little watercolour painting Edie had done for him of snowdrops and crocuses.

Anatoli watched her, smiling. 'Thank you, my dear. Now do come and sit down and tell me everything – how is our lovely little Francesca? I can't offer you tea or anything in the way of hospitality, but you may be lucky if they come round – you never know. I expect you have come straight from work haven't you?'

'Yes, but I'm all right, I don't need a drink,' she said. 'How're you feeling?'

'A little stronger,' he said, slowly, thinking about it. 'I am weak, I know that. Even the thought of walking along the ward to the bathroom feels like climbing Mount Everest. But I do feel a bit better each day.'

He told her he had kept himself occupied reading the paper and he read snippets out to her. He was very interested in what was going on in Czechoslovakia, the movement known as the Prague Spring, where the Communist Party had lost overall control.

'Imagine living in a country where there is no freedom, where everything is ruled by the state,' he said. 'Now all that will change. It is a great liberation, an upsurge of the will of the people!'

Greta loved to hear him talking about so many things she felt ignorant about. And as well as the news he gobbled up his usual detective stories. He talked cheerfully about the routines of the ward and one of the nurses who had been especially kind to him. Greta could see that he would charm them and make them want to be kind.

'But I am longing to be home,' he told Greta. His deep brown eyes looked deeply at her, and he reached out and took her hand in his, cradling it close to him for a moment.

In two weeks he was allowed home. They were so excited that it was like having royalty coming. Edie and Greta cleaned the entire house and made everything especially comfortable and attractive for him, with fresh flowers and books to look at. Peter, who was talented like his mother, had also done a painting for his Daddy, of himself, by looking in the mirror. He had cleverly captured something of his pale, dark-eyed face and mop of curls, and Edie had stuck the painting carefully on to a piece of card so that it would stand up against a vase.

Edie told Greta it was one of the first things Anatoli noticed that afternoon when he walked slowly into the room, looking thin, fragile, but overjoyed to be home. By the time Greta got home from work Anatoli was in his comfortable chair.

'Is that our girl I hear?' he called out as she came through the door. His voice sounded thinner, but it made her so happy to hear it.

'Hello!' She put her head round the living-room door and there was everyone, just as they should be, Francesca half toddling, half crawling over to meet her, squeaking with excitement, Edie and Peter there and Anatoli with his cup and saucer, and things felt right again.

Chapter Forty-Six

That spring and summer, Greta's life revolved round her work at Cadbury's and at home, around Francesca and Anatoli. She took very little notice of anything else, and it was only because of sitting with Anatoli after he had read the morning papers that she knew that a black American preacher called Martin Luther King had been shot, that there were anti-Vietnam War demonstrations in London and student riots in Paris.

Anatoli seemed to gather strength after the operation and things felt hopeful. For a few weeks he rested, only occasionally calling into his business. Then he went back to working in the mornings. He slept for a while after lunch then enjoyed the company of whoever was at home. Greta often sat with him, sometimes outside on warm days, in the pretty square of garden. Sometimes she did the weeding for him while he gave instructions. Or she read to him.

'It's not that I need you to read to me really,' he said with a twinkle. 'I just like the company and the sound of your voice.'

One afternoon, while Francesca was having her nap upstairs, they sat outside, a rug wrapped round Anatoli's legs even though it was warm.

'Now I've become such a thin old stick I feel the cold,' he joked.

He had asked Greta to read him a chapter from Georges Simenon's *Maigret and the Idle Burglar*. At first when she had read to Anatoli she had felt self-conscious and stumbled over the words, afraid that her reading wasn't good enough, and she said so.

'But you read perfectly well!' he protested. 'Why are you always so critical of yourself?'

After a while she had learned just to relax and read, and she enjoyed the Maigret stories herself.

'D'you want me to go on?' she asked, at the end of the chapter. They were quite near the start of the book so they hadn't got to the really exciting bits yet.

'No – that's enough,' Anatoli said, sipping from a glass of water. 'I want to ask you something.'

He put his head on one side and looked at her closely. 'How old are you now, my dear?'

'Twenty-three,' Greta said.

'And you are soon to be divorced from young Trevor?'

Greta nodded.

'Your marriage was not a success for either of you, obviously,' he said straightforwardly. 'Otherwise you would not be divorcing. And you are sure this is the right thing?'

'Oh yes,' Greta said, wondering how Anatoli could have any doubt. 'Anyway, even if I wanted to be with Trevor, which I don't, he's got a family of his own now – with Marleen. And they want to get married sooner or later.'

'Quite so,' Anatoli said. 'Don't imagine that I am criticizing. I am thinking of you, here as a young, beautiful woman . . .'

A blush spread up Greta's cheeks and she looked

down at the table, the tatty copy of the book they were reading in front of her.

'Here you are, with two much older people – like living with your parents again, and your little baby, who is a jewel. But you have no young life for yourself, no lover . . .'

'But I love it here!' Greta looked up at him passionately. 'I love living with you and Edie, and I've got Francesca. I don't need anyone else in my life – I like it just as it is!'

'But you are a lovely girl – do you not have men queuing up to ask you to go out with them?'

'A few,' Greta admitted. 'But I keep this on, you see—' She still wore the brass wedding ring which Trevor had given her. 'That puts them off. I really don't want anyone else.'

Anatoli looked troubled. 'I wonder if your experience has put you off the thought of marrying?'

'Well – not really,' Greta said slowly. 'I like it here, that's all.'

'That's very gratifying,' Anatoli said. 'But things cannot stay the same for ever here, you know. I don't know how long I . . .' He stumbled over the words. 'And I would like to think of you being here with Edith. But we must not be selfish. It is possible, you know, to marry again and for it to be better. You must never lose sight of that.'

'But you and Edie are different – you're special!'

'No,' Anatoli said sharply. 'Not special – no we're not. We love each other, truly we do – but we are also more aware.' He sighed. 'My first wife was a wonderful woman, but I know I was not a very good husband, or at least not until it was almost too late. When I was young I was too preoccupied, too busy trying to build

340

up a business and with my music. I suppose I assumed she was there to supply me with everything I needed while I earned the money.' He smiled sadly. 'Sometimes I was harsh, rude and selfish. You may wonder why my own children have not rushed to my side in these weeks. But that is why. They did not grow up to admire me – there is a distance between us and I do not know whether we shall be able to overcome it before it is too late.'

He paused, shaking his head.

'After Margot died, they said things to me, harsh, angry things. I did not want to hear them and I was angry towards them. All I know is that when I met Edith, and was suddenly in love again without ever expecting this to happen, I was utterly determined to be different, to learn . . . And she had been alone for a long time – very like you, bringing up David. We were older and we knew we had mistakes to learn from – that you cannot take the other for granted so easily. But it is worth it, Greta. I hope you believe me?'

'I believe you,' she said lightly. 'But I can't magic up the man of my dreams, can I?'

'No – I'm just begging you not to close the door, just because you have a child, You are still a young woman . . .'

A little cry came through the open window upstairs.

'Ah – she's waking up!' Greta cried, getting to her feet thankfully.

'Bless her little heart,' Anatoli said.

Greta went up to fetch a half awake Francesca, feeling stirred up. What was Anatoli going on about? She was happy here in this little cocoon she had made for herself, with Francesca to lavish all her love on and not needing anything else. Raw feelings of longing lurked inside her but she pushed them away. Who needed men or marriage? She was quite happy as she was, thank you very much!

The summer passed, intensely precious. Anatoli's health held up, and for those months it seemed he was all right, that the operation had given him a new chance of life. Even his times of depression seemed to have vanished, as if they had been removed with the tumours.

When not at work, Greta spent time with him, or had happy times at the Cadbury's lido at Rowheath. She and Pat and some other friends would go and spend the afternoon. Francesca loved being in the water, and Greta had bought a little rubber ring for her to float about in. The little girl's face was always a picture of delight as she kicked vigorously and beat her hands against the water. Greta would tow her round the shallow end, loving being in the water herself and laughing at Francesca's enthusiasm.

'She'll be an early swimmer that one,' Pat said, breast-stroking alongside them, one of the first times they went. 'She's in her element isn't she?' Francesca had been in the pool last summer but had been very young then. Now she was coming into her own. As the summer went by she gained almost too much confidence.

'Oh – there she goes again!' Greta would cry, having to get up from her circle of friends on the grass in their colourful swimming costumes and tear after Francesca's toddling figure as she made her way determinedly towards the water. She would scream with fury at being brought back.

They spent lovely lazy afternoons there in August,

minding each other's children so that each of them could have a proper swim and sitting picnicking and chatting on the grass. Edie came occasionally, though she didn't like to leave Anatoli for too long. Greta found the time passing in a kind of dream. Anatoli read to her, in great dismay, news of Soviet tanks moving into Prague to crush the spring uprising. Ruby – she heard through the grapevine rather than from her mother directly – had been seen going about with a new man. This news made Greta shrug. So what was new? Another in a long line of disasters.

And in the middle of the month Marleen was rushed into hospital, where she had another baby, this time a girl who she called Sandra. Greta thought about going to see her. She decided not to bother. Marleen and Trevor felt like another world now. They were nothing to do with her. Her divorce would soon come through and she and Marleen had never lost much love between them as sisters. So what? she thought.

It was evening when the telephone call came: September and a whiff of autumn in the misty mornings. Greta hardly ever answered the telephone, which stood on a table in the front hall, but Anatoli was sitting down and Edie was bathing the children.

'You take it!' Anatoli called as it clanged away.

'Hello, hello?' The voice on the other end was female, high-pitched, and at first Greta could make no sense of anything she was saying.

'Hello?' she said encouragingly.

'Hello – Edith?' And there was a confusion of language at the other end. Greta knew it was someone foreign but had no idea what she was saying.

343

'Can you wait a moment, please,' Greta said. The woman at the other end sounded so frantic that she wasn't making sense in any language.

'Who is it?' Anatoli came out into the hall.

Greta held the receiver out to him, shrugging. 'I don't know – someone foreign.'

He put the receiver to his ear. 'Hello?'

In the quiet of the hall Greta could hear a torrent of speech at the other end. Anatoli's face seemed to set hard as granite. Greta could see it was something dreadful. She felt her innards tighten. When he finally said a few words they were in German. He seemed to be consoling, reassuring. At last he put the phone down and kept his hand on it, closing his eyes.

'Oh God in heaven . . .'

Upstairs the bathroom door opened and Peter appeared, beaming, at the top of the stairs with his pyjamas on.

'Peter – is Mummy there?' Anatoli said. 'Please tell her to come down.'

Edie came carrying Francesca, tousle-haired and wrapped in a big white towel.

'There's a lovely warm, clean girl – you can go to your Mummy now,' she said, handing the happy bundle over to Greta. 'Who was on the telephone?'

'My darling,' Anatoli said solemnly. 'Please come and sit down.'

'What is it?' Edie faltered, hearing the sombre tone of his voice. As she went to sit in the front room her mind rushed into explanations. 'Was it the hospital? Are you all right? Not bad news – tests or something?'

'No, nothing like that—' Anatoli knelt by her chair. Greta stood in the doorway holding Francesca. She could hear Peter still rollicking about upstairs.

'My darling, there is some terrible news.' Anatoli paused, as if he could not say it.

'What is it?' Edie clutched at his hand, a wild expression on her face. 'What is it? Who was that? David – what's happened? The army – is he fighting, has something happened?' This was the worry that haunted her always. She had barely recovered from the war last year.

'No – David is fine. But that was Annaliese.' Anatoli swallowed. 'Today there were bomb explosions in Tel Aviv. Gila was there with Shimon.' Edie's hands went to her lips, her eyes opening wide in horror.

'They were very close to it . . .' Anatoli was struggling for words. 'Gila was wounded – quite badly. She's in hospital. But Shimon . . .' The words hung unspoken between them. Anatoli shook his head and Edie started to shake hers as well.

'No! Not . . . Dead? Little Shimon?'

Anatoli did not have to answer. His face said everything.

Chapter Forty-Seven

Afterwards David scarcely remembered driving to Tel Aviv.

A secretary from the medical school lent him the car. 'Of course – in the circumstances . . . Keep it for as long as you need . . .'

All memory of the journey, the baked, dusty roads, was lost to him. All he could remember later was the sense of his body, hard as steel all the way, anger locking his hands to the wheel, the throb of his head . . . *My son, my son* . . . As the sun went down he found himself driving through Tel Aviv's block-ish suburbs. Twice he asked directions to the hospital.

Aunt Miriam had telephoned the medical school with the news, the message reaching him during a lecture on orthopaedics. The secretary who tiptoed in to find him, the shock plain in her face, had been motherly, offered him money, food, the telephone to contact Miriam in Tel Aviv, where Gila had been staying. Finally she lent him the car.

'Does she know about Shim?' he had asked Miriam.

'She knows, of course.' Miriam struggled to speak, as if every word was made of broken glass. 'She was with him. She saw. Yes – she knows.'

He is dead. My Shimon is dead.

She told him of cuts, broken bones. Gila and Shimon had been hurled aside by the blast. The hospital was full of the injured, too many to be sure of numbers. There had been three bombs in the city that day, she said.

His mind was spinning, full of pictures of his son, his wife: his family. *The baby* . . . Miriam had not said anything about the baby. He imagined Gila, injured, disfigured even, surrounded by the whiteness of walls and sheets. With all his being he ached to give comfort.

He drove into the grounds of the hospital.

They have killed my son . . .

Casualties of the bombings were still coming in and the hospital corridors were in turmoil. Finding himself here in another hospital, he wanted to behave like a doctor, to be in command, detached. Instead he felt bewildered, barely able to function or think who to speak to. It was some time before anyone could tell him where he would find Gila. When he reached her ward, she was not lying swathed in whiteness as he had imagined: she was not there at all. A complication had developed, a nurse told him. He was handed to a doctor, a middle-aged man with soulful brown eyes.

'She will be all right,' he assured David, gently. 'But I'm sorry to say – you knew she was pregnant? She was thrown some distance by the blast. The impact and shock have made her miscarry. There are complications . . .' He wiped a hand wearily over his face. 'They have her in theatre now. You should come back tomorrow.'

'Where is my son?' David asked. All the energy his anger had given him had left him and he felt like weeping.

'Your son?'

'A little boy. They said he was killed . . .'

The doctor's face tightened a little. 'I'm so sorry.

347

At the moment I don't know. You should ask in the morning.'

'I must see my son,' David insisted.

'Please, young man—' The doctor touched his arm for a moment. His face seemed to crumple in sympathy. 'I cannot help you just now. Wait a little while.'

'Doodi?'

David jolted awake, hearing her voice. He was in the chair beside her bed. For the remainder of the night he had lain crushed up on the back seat of the car, woken often by discomfort and noises from outside. In his distress and lack of sleep nothing seemed real, as if he was swimming through a dream.

When it grew light they had let him come in and sit by her now she was back from the recovery room. Her head was bandaged, her left arm and leg were each in a plaster cast and there were other dressings on her face, next to her left eye and down her left cheek. She seemed to be in a deep, drugged sleep. Again he dozed, dragged queasily to the surface again every few moments by the routines of the ward.

But now she was waking, her weak voice reaching him. He leaned towards her.

'Doodi . . . Doodi . . .' It seemed to be all she could say.

'I'm here . . .' He reached under the sheet for her hand and found more bandages along her right arm. Her hand seemed to be unhurt and he held it, longing to climb into the bed beside her, for them to be at home so that they could hold each other.

She managed to turn her head and he sat close so that he could look into her eyes. There were cuts on her face, and grazes. He had a primitive urge to nuzzle and lick them, as if he could give healing. She was looking urgently at him.

'The baby ... It's not ...' Her distress was mounting. 'It's not there any more. They had to take it ...'

'It's OK.' He stroked her hand. At this moment he could feel nothing.

'Shimon!' Her eyes jerked open as if she had just remembered and she started trying to get up. 'Oh my God – Shimon, my little Shimon, where is he?'

'Don't move!' David stood up to restrain her. 'You mustn't get up, my love!'

'But I must find him! My little boy, he is missing!'

She was struggling with him, her voice becoming hysterical, and a nurse came running, seeing immediately what was wrong.

'My boy!' Gila sobbed. 'I want my boy!'

She knew, surely? David thought wildly in those seconds. Miriam had said that she saw Shimon dead. It was as if she had forgotten. And then he saw that perhaps it wasn't true – it was all a mistake. Anything could be true. Nothing was normal or real.

'We shall have to sedate her,' the nurse said. 'It will give her some relief. It is best.'

Within a few moments they had given Gila an injection. David watched as her dark-lashed eyes closed, her face with its grazes and dressings relaxed and she was gone from him again, leaving him alone, still clasping her hand.

I wish they would sedate me too, he thought.

He sat with her for a time, then walked out, dazed, from the ward. Things seemed quiet now and more under control. He stood in the corridor for a few moments, at a loss. His mind would not work. He did not realize the extent of his shock.

Shimon . . .

At last he found someone who could help. A nurse showed him to the mortuary, where inside he was met by a man with a thin, sensitive face.

'I need to see my son,' David said. 'Last night they could not tell me . . . Perhaps it is a mistake . . . Perhaps he is not here?'

'Come this way,' the man said, with deep gentleness.

Within moments he was looking at the figure of a small boy lying cold and very still, under the harsh mortuary lights, still in tattered clothing, although he was wearing no shoes. The boy had thick, dark curls which were greyed with dust, a pale face, almost half obscured by bruising which spread in a creeping stain from the wound on the left side of his head. A thick pad of gauze was still taped to his head, though the bleeding had stopped.

Recognition was instant. David knew the second he saw him that it was Shimon, despite the awful changes to his face. Every line of him, the angle at which his soft, bare feet lay splayed apart, his hands, the set of his body, was Shimon, whose tiny form he had known so intensely for the past eight years, and could not be any other being but Shimon.

He fell to his knees beside the low trolley. He saw the attendant react for a second, as if to stop him, but then he stood back. Neither of them spoke. Very gently, David took his son's body in his arms, pressing his dust-covered, bloodied form close to him. He heard himself groaning, sounds which came without his bidding at the feel of the tender, lifeless body in his arms.

'Daddy's here,' he said, over and over again, rocking Shimon in his arms. 'Don't be afraid, your Daddy's here, my little one.'

After a time, he had no idea how long, the attendant came and touched him on the shoulder. Dazed, David stood up, letting go his hold on the boy.

'I shall need to take him to Jerusalem,' he said.

Soberly the young man nodded.

Afterwards he walked out of the hospital, shivering though it was already warm. There was a light breeze blowing litter across the parking lot. David had no idea what to do next. He wandered along the perimeter with no aim in mind, until he came to the end, where he was met by a wall. He stopped and stared at it as if he could not make sense of why he was there. Then he turned and sank down with his back to it. Dry, yellowed grasses and sprigs of fennel had struggled up through cracks in the asphalt. There was a stench of urine. David squatted against the wall, watching a parched fragment of newspaper rise in an arc on the breeze, then flutter again to the ground. He turned his face up to the sun, feeling its warmth stroking his cheeks as if caressing him.

Only then did he begin to sob.

Chapter Forty-Eight

There were frantic telephone calls for days between Annaliese, Aunt Miriam and the two mothers, Rachel Weissman and Edie, as the scattered family tried to take in the news. The truth they all dreaded to hear, that each one of them willed with all their being to be proved a mistake, gradually began to sink in. Shimon, their beautiful eight-year-old nephew or grandson, who had written them letters in his childish Hebrew and English, of whom each of them had smiling photographs on their tables and mantelpieces, was dead, his life taken by a bomb.

Gila, it appeared, was not seriously wounded. She had a broken arm, leg and ribs, and many cuts, but she was healing. The other distressing news was that she had lost the baby. She had been four months pregnant when she went to Tel Aviv at the beginning of September.

Greta heard Edie's distraught voice when she finally managed to speak to David.

'Oh love – oh my poor love,' she kept saying, trying not to weep, to be strong for him. 'Should I come over – I can come at once?'

She was frantic with need to be with him and do something. Yet at the same time she didn't want to leave Anatoli, and David advised her not to come. Anatoli needed her more, he assured her: he and Gila had plenty of help. After a few days Gila had been discharged from the hospital and was recuperating in Miriam's apartment. David was staying there some of the time, but he was planning to shuttle between Tel Aviv and Jerusalem to continue his studies. He advised Edie to stay where she was for the moment. There was very little space, Gila's mother was coming down and none of them, including Edie, got on particularly well with Miriam.

'He says he and Gila will try to come and see us when she's better, maybe at Christmas,' Edie told Anatoli, seeming slightly comforted. 'It'll do Gila good to have a break – a holiday somewhere else, once she's recovered. Oh the poor girl, and poor David . . . He says he'll feel better if he can get back to work . . .' She broke down, now she was off the telephone. 'I wish I could do more for them, I really do!'

Greta's heart ached for all of them. As if Edie hadn't had troubles enough already! She was determined to be as helpful as she possibly could. She thought about David, his handsome face smiling down from family pictures of him with Shimon and Gila. Though she remembered him well from when they were children, he was like a foreigner now, removed by distance and all that he had experienced. He had already seemed rather distant and godlike by the time he was eighteen, with all his thinking and studying. And she had always thought Gila sounded intimidating as well. But this tragedy brought them closer and she could feel it with them. They had lost their child and she hugged Francesca tightly. How precious her little life was!

Janet came round as soon as she heard the news and was kind and comforting. Greta went to tell Ruby. When she went round to the house she found a man she had never met before, a stocky fellow, his bald head rimmed with a neat circle of dark hair, and leathery features which creased up into a friendly smile.

'Mac – this is my other daughter, Greta,' Ruby said. 'And this is my little granddaughter, Francesca.'

The man shook Greta's hand. His sleeves were rolled to the elbow and he had strong, hairy forearms.

'Hello there!' He nodded towards Francesca. 'Very nice,' he said. He had a broad Scots accent and spoke awkwardly, as if he was not used to it, but he seemed friendly enough.

'What brings you here?' Ruby asked, hardly disguising her sarcasm. Then she took in the expression on Greta's face. 'Oh my God – what is it?'

'Edie's had some terrible news, Mom. It's David's boy, Shimon – he's been killed by a bomb.'

'A *bomb*?'

'There were bombs planted in Tel Aviv. Gila was there with him.'

She saw Ruby's face change, turning first very grave, and then full of pity.

'Dear God – poor Edie,' she said.

'Go and see her, Mom?'

'Course . . .' This was something which cut right through all her grudges, her envy of Edie. They'd been pals since they were fourteen. 'Course I will.'

On Saturday when they usually went to the shops in Selly Oak, Edie said she'd like to go up to Bournville instead.

'It's a nice day,' she said bravely. 'Let's make a bit of a morning of it.'

354

It was still warm, a mellow day, the sky blue with big puffy clouds sitting lazily above. Greta put Francesca in the pushchair and they set off up the hill with the shopping baskets hanging from the handle, Peter holding Edie's hand.

The Green in Bournville was like a warm, green haven and they did their shopping there, in the timber-framed buildings which ran along one side of the grassy space.

'I don't know why we don't come up here more often,' Edie said as they came out of the bakery with a loaf and Anatoli's favourite, jam doughnuts. She was doing her utmost to be cheerful. 'Now, Peter, you've been a really good boy so you can have an ice lolly.'

Edie smiled, looking at Francesca, who was beginning to strain against the straps of the pushchair. She was a picture, her head a mass of golden curls. 'I suppose her majesty could manage one as well. Tell you what – let's all have one, shall we?'

Peter chose a Rocket ice lolly and Francesca a Funny Face with chocolate nose and eyes. Edie and Greta had strawberry Mivvies. They went and sat on the benches outside the Rest House in the middle of the Green, facing the Day Continuation School, where each of them had spent a day a week having lessons from when they joined Cadbury's until they were eighteen.

'Ah – happy days,' Edie said, looking fondly over at it. She seemed to find it soothing being here surrounded by lovely buildings, the old timbered Selly Manor, the Friends' Meeting House, where she went every Sunday, and the Ruskin School, which had given her so much pleasure in developing her painting. But she added more thoughtfully, 'Well, happy in some ways anyway.'

'School days are supposed to be the happiest of your life, that's what they say, isn't it?' Greta said.

'Well that's blooming nonsense for a start,' Edie declared. 'I couldn't wait to get out of school. Oh no – these have been the happiest. With Anatoli . . .' Her eyes filled suddenly. 'Even now, with all this . . . Oh sorry, here I go again.'

'It's all right,' Greta said, moved. 'I think you're very brave.'

'No—' Edie shook her head. 'I'm not at all.'

As she spoke, the bells of the carillon above the junior school began to ring out one of their chiming tunes and Edie smiled, wiping her eyes.

'I remember when David was little he was absolutely fascinated by that. He used to keep on and on about how many bells there were and how did it work and of course I could never remember. I don't have a good head for facts like that. In the end I took him to see the man playing it. Have you ever seen it?'

'No,' Greta said.

'It's played by a keyboard called a Clavier which is wired up to the bells. David was allowed to have a little go and the man told him all about it. That was David – always having to know about everything and how it worked. I must take you to see it, mustn't I, Peter? And you too, Franny!'

They sat until the pretty, chiming tune had finished ringing across the Green. Greta noticed that Francesca's hands and legs were thoroughly smeared with vanilla ice cream and she got up to clear her up.

'Can we go to the park?' Peter said.

'I tell you what, why don't we do that?' Edie said. 'Anatoli won't be home until two.' He was still struggling in for short periods when he could. 'We can give the ducks the crust of this loaf.'

They walked down the hill, following the stream until they reached the little boating lake where a couple of older boys were floating sailboats and other children were feeding the ducks and geese or being pushed slowly round by their chatting mothers.

Edie handed Peter some bread and he went off to throw it for the ducks.

They strolled round slowly in the warm sunshine, following Peter, but Greta began to notice that the buoyant mood Edie had managed to keep up so far was slipping and she became silent and sad. They stopped to watch Peter throw in the last of his bread, overarm, and the ducks rushed to reach it. Once more Edie's eyes filled with tears.

'David used to do that. I always dreamed of seeing the two of them here together – Peter and Shimon . . .'

She shook her head. There was no need to say any more.

Chapter Forty-Nine

Within a day of Gila moving from the hospital to Miriam's apartment in Tel Aviv, David felt that he could stand it no longer.

Her mother was also staying, and as the apartment had only two bedrooms, David was sleeping on a mattress in Gila's room and Rachel Weissman slept on a couch in the living room. Night-time was the only chance he and Gila had to be alone without her mother or aunt fussing over her.

Miriam already tried David's patience. Her softer side had shown itself with Shimon, who had adored her, and David had never doubted her care for him, but in general she was a tough, bossy woman who had never married and was used to living alone and having her own way in everything. Her relationship with her nervy elder sister was quarrelsome and full of resentments of an intensity that David could never fathom. Gila had never been able to explain it either. Whatever Rachel said, Miriam had to contradict, had to be in charge of everything, and there seemed to be a power struggle going around Gila's head all the time. It had enraged David before. Here they were, fortunate enough to be sisters, to have proper relatives when he had so few, and they couldn't even manage to be civil to each other over the smallest of details! Now, after what had happened to his family, he found their self-absorbed quarrelling cruel and absurd.

'Why don't we just go home?' he begged Gila one evening. He was sitting on the edge of her bed, the sound of angry female voices coming from the kitchen, Miriam's powerful, like a foghorn, Rachel's high and plaintive. A squabble seemed to have broken out over yoghurt, with no point to it that David could discern. It just made him loathe Israel more, with its loud, emotional people. Though he could see that the roots of their conflict and Rachel's neuroses dated back further than anything he could possibly know about, at this time he didn't care what they were or feel any sympathy. He was in too much pain himself, an anguish which enveloped him and Gila totally and separately, only isolating them more from each other.

Gila had become someone he scarcely recognized. She lay there day after day, with no energy, hardly speaking, locked in shock and grief. He couldn't get through to her at all. And surely all these hysterics around her were not helping, he thought.

'We can go back to our own place and you won't have to put up with this all the time. We'll sleep in our own bed together. You can rest until you're better, with no pressure . . .'

Gila's face remained blank. 'No. I must stay here.'

'But why? I'll look after you. We can be together.'

He ached to have her at home. He had been back and forth twice now, trying to concentrate on his studies, to keep going. Facing the silent apartment had been terrible. There were Shimon's toys, his swimming trunks wrapped in a towel, little winter boots still behind the door in the hallway, his bed with its blue and orange quilt, just as it had been before. He wondered whether he should just get rid of everything, bundle his son's few possessions into a sack and dispose of them. But then he decided that he could not bear the apartment to look as if Shimon had never been, to be bereft of him. He was not ready for that to happen. And he knew Gila must come here first and see, and somehow say goodbye.

More than once he woke in the night, convinced he had heard his son cry out, as if Shimon was there, sleeping in the next room. One night, still befuddled with sleep, he got up to check on him. He found the bed empty, and climbed into it, curling up, needing to capture the smell and feel of his small son, needing to be held himself. He fell asleep, tears wet on his face.

If only Gila could come home, he thought, then slowly, slowly they could begin ... They could try to find an idea of normal, if things could ever be normal again. They could have another child. As it was, everything seemed frozen, as if time had stopped when Shimon died.

Each time he went back to Tel Aviv, hoping. But she would not come, would not speak to him about their lost children, or weep with him. Each time he came into the room he would find her lying much as he had left her, on her back, her dark brows two slender arcs across her pale forehead, her dark eyes looking up to the ceiling, a slight frown on her face. If he spoke to her about something ordinary – did she want some soup? was she warm enough or comfortable? – she would answer him in a detached way as if he was a stranger. It was the same with Miriam and Rachel. None of them could get through to her.

'I tell you, she should see another doctor,' Miriam

decreed as they ate dinner one evening while Gila stayed in her room and picked at a little food they took to her. 'My friend Therese knows a very distinguished psychiatrist . . .'

This provoked the most hysterical outburst that David had yet heard from Rachel Weissman towards her sister, and later she ambushed David in the tiny hallway, whispering urgently.

'I do not want her to see a psychiatrist,' she implored, weeping again. 'Don't make her, please . . . It will finish her . . .' She leaned forward and touched David's hand for a second. Instead of feeling comforted he found himself deeply irritated. He couldn't stand these histrionic women with their tears and quarrels. But he also knew that the state he was in meant no one could do anything right for him.

Except Annaliese. When he spoke with her on the telephone, heard her gentle, kindly voice, he felt eased a little. With his mother, with Edie, it was less so, but he was still grateful to talk to her. He did not tell either of them the truth though.

'Gila is getting stronger every day,' he would say. 'Yes – we are very sad, heartbroken. But we shall be all right. Don't worry about us. We have had a terrible shock, but we are together and we will be all right.'

This was what he wanted to believe.

Sometimes when he could not stand any more of the atmosphere in the dark apartment he went out into the glare of Tel Aviv's white buildings, walking towards the sea to stare at the endless blue choppiness of the waves. He felt lost. His son had been his direction, the one person in this world who pulled him into the future. Sometimes he sat on the sea wall staring out with tears running down his cheeks. It was as if he had been travelling a road and had come upon a high wall built right across it. He could not see who he was or where he was going any more.

Chapter Fifty

At the end of September, Greta's divorce from Trevor came through. She stared at the papers without emotion. So she was no longer married to Trevor by law. She shrugged. Was she ever really married to Trevor? Not the way Edie and Anatoli were married, close and loving, with a real understanding between them.

She put the papers away in a drawer in the bedroom with a great sense of freedom, then looked at herself in the mirror over the chest of drawers, at her rounded, pretty face, the waves of blonde hair round her brow.

'So – I'm Greta Sorenson again,' she whispered. The little picture of her Dad, Wally, was propped up against a box of talcum powder. 'Free as a bird.' Here she was, in a lovely place, with a beautiful daughter. She wasn't going to be like her Mom, chasing after everything in trousers. If she chose, she could keep away from men and marriage for the rest of her life!

She told Pat the next day, when they managed to coincide for a tea break at work. Pat looked stricken. Divorce to Pat meant disgrace.

'You must be upset, aren't you?'

Greta shook her head. 'I s'pose it's not very nice being divorced. No one sets out wanting to get divorced, do they? But it had to come and I'm relieved it's over now. I mean, Trevor takes not the blindest bit of notice of Francesca now he's got his own family. He was rude enough about her name, said it was too posh. I'm best off without him.'

'I wish my Mom could say the same.' Pat came out with this forthright remark so suddenly that she seemed to take herself by surprise and she went red. 'Gosh – I didn't know I was going to say that! But it's true!' she added defiantly.

Greta, who had privately thought Stanley Floyd was a nasty piece of work for years, looked at her sympathetically.

'If I thought I'd ever marry a man like my father,' Pat went on hotly, 'I think I'd lie down on the railway track and end it all, I really do!'

'Well, you won't though, will you?' Greta said. 'And anyway, you live like a nun, so I don't think that's likely to happen is it?'

'You're a fine one to talk!' Both of them laughed, ruefully. 'We're just as blooming bad as each other!'

Greta was so caught up in what was happening in the Gruschovs' household that she didn't see much of her own family. Though Edie struggled to be brave, Greta knew she was full of aching grief over Shimon and anguish for David, and that this only added to her worries about Anatoli's health.

Though looking thinner and more tired than he had been before, for the time being Anatoli's illness seemed to be stabilized, and the crisis of his operation faded into the background compared with the news from Israel.

As the summer truly died and they swished their way home through drifts of rusty leaves into autumn, the news from there began to improve. After several weeks at her aunt's apartment in Tel Aviv, Gila was ready to go home to Jerusalem – but home would be another new apartment that David had rented.

'Bless her,' Edie said. 'Oh, it's going to be so hard for her when she walks in for the first time and there's no Shimon, even if it is a different place! It breaks my heart to think about it.'

A brief letter came from David, saying that they had at last been able to have a proper funeral for Shimon, that there was a grave for him in a Jerusalem cemetery not too far away from home. He said that he had laid some flowers there on Edie's behalf. Gila had had her plaster removed and was almost ready to take up her job back at her dental practice. He was studying hard and they were trying to look to the future. Edie had repeated her invitation for them to come to England, saying that she and Anatoli would pay for them. Everyone commented on how brave they were, how strong. They would have another child, people predicted, and try to keep moving ahead. Everyone's grief for Shimon continued, mostly under the surface.

And then, overnight, the shadow which had faded over the summer gathered once more and grew darker. Anatoli was taken ill again. One day he was going along as before, the next he woke in pain and being sick, and could not leave his bed. He quickly grew weak, and Edie stayed away from work and called the doctor.

It was not Martin Ferris this time. From the kitchen door, Greta saw the man come into the house at dawn and go solemn-faced up to Anatoli. She was gripped by fear. For some time she could hear nothing except the faintest murmur from upstairs, and she carried on giving Francesca her morning milk, all the time straining to hear any movement in the house.

At last she heard footsteps down the stairs and the front door closing. Then Edie came into the kitchen. Greta could see everything by her face, the way she looked as if she had received a blow, the tears she was struggling to quell.

'He says Anatoli will have to go up to the hospital for more tests, when he's feeling a bit better . . .' She couldn't hold back her emotion any more as she choked out the words. 'But he says it's come back. And there isn't any cure!'

'Now, my dear, I think I have the strength to drink my tea, if you wouldn't mind giving me a hand.'

It was a month later and Greta, home from work, was with Anatoli. On better days, like today, he came downstairs, where they made him comfortable on a couch in the living room.

'If I stay all day every day in my bed I shall become a cabbage within a fortnight,' he predicted wryly. 'I must see you all and have some life around me. And these little children don't want to come into an old man's sickroom.'

He was recovering from a few days of acute sickness and was very weak, but Greta could see that he was happy to be downstairs, where the children could come and go and he could supervise Peter's violin practice. They were learning to treat him gently, and even Francesca, though only eighteen months old, seemed to sense that she must not roar around Anatoli in her usual energetic fashion.

Edie had gone out to collect Peter from school. The days when Anatoli was at his lowest, wretched with vomiting and very weak, were a torment for her and she looked thinner and tired. Greta was feeling the strain too. She found it unbearable that this man whom she loved was suffering so much. But now there was a lull, and he could come downstairs on her arm. She loved tucking him up under the red and black rugs on the couch and pampering him. It was heartbreaking seeing how thin and weak he was, how his magnificent crop of white hair was thinning, compared with the strong, handsome man Greta had seen photographs of when she was younger. As an older man he had still been very striking to look at. These days his cheeks were hollow and his limbs so thin they looked fit to snap, but now he was feeling a little better his lovely brown eyes still danced with life and his sense of humour had returned.

She leaned over and offered her arm to help him and he hoisted himself up with a groan.

'Oh!' He sat back, in relief. 'These days I am creaking like an old farmer's cart!'

'Can you manage anything to eat with your tea?' Greta asked, hoping he would say yes.

Anatoli considered, rubbing his hand over his abdomen, wincing. 'I shall have to be careful. Anything which brings back that sickness seems like poison to me. I feel as if a whole herd of cattle have trampled over me. But yes – I think I could manage a couple of those nice plain biscuits if we have any.'

Of course they had some! Edie went straight out and bought anything that they thought he might have a ghost of a chance of eating. Greta went gladly to the kitchen and arranged some biscuits on a plate for him. When she came back she was happy to see that he was sipping the sugary tea.

'Where is that little one?' Anatoli asked.

'Still asleep – she's having a long one today.'

They sat contentedly in silence together, drinking their tea. Greta's chair was positioned close to the couch and she took Anatoli's cup when he had finished.

'Any more?' she asked, hopefully.

'No – I think I shall stop there. But that was ... You know what the advertisement says, "Aaah – nectar!"'

Greta laughed. 'No – just Tetley!'

'Well it tasted like the food of gods to me.'

He let himself lie back and relax, glancing over to the piano.

'You know, it's weeks since I've played.'

'I know.' It was something she had missed, the sound of his music. It was a horrible reminder of how the house would be without him, none of the beautiful sound of his piano and violin playing, and only Peter's beginner's exercises to take their place. 'Would you like some music?'

Sometimes she would put his favourite records on the old gramophone, beautiful haunting pieces of music which touched her deeply, though she dreaded it when they did this because often Anatoli wept and it was awful seeing it. Last time they had put on Mendelssohn's Violin Concerto and it had almost been too much for both of them.

'I think I'll just lie here in the quiet today, thank you,' he said. 'Unless you would feel like reading to me a little? Do we have another Maigret adventure somewhere?'

Greta jumped up. She had been to the library in Selly Oak, looking for picture books for Francesca and new Maigret titles for Anatoli.

'We have *Maigret in Montmartre* and *Maigret and the Headless Corpse*.'

Anatoli chuckled. Greta heard how thin his voice and laugh had become. 'Well, what a splendid choice – a tour of Paris or a gory murder . . .'

'Oh I expect there'll be a murder whichever one you choose!' She held them up so that he could see the covers.

'Let's begin with *Maigret in Montmartre*. A headless corpse might demand more strength than I have today!'

Greta sat beside him and began to read, and they were just getting involved when they heard Edie, and Peter's head came round the door.

'Is that my boy I hear?' Anatoli said.

Peter ran to him and Anatoli ruffled his hair. Edie appeared, smiling.

'Oh, you managed to get down – that's lovely! And you've had tea. Well, I could do with one. I'll put the kettle on again. Can you manage another cup, love?'

Releasing Peter, Anatoli twinkled up at her. 'You know, I think I probably could.'

The two women caught each other's eye and smiled with delight. This was a good day, a day to cherish. They both knew that such days were going to run out.

Those weeks of Anatoli's illness were ones that Greta came to treasure. They were autumn days of mists, the poignant smell of decaying leaves along the pavements and the smell of smoke as fires were lit once again. The nights were drawing in, the air becoming cold and raw. And, Greta found, she experienced everything more sharply because it was set against the prospect of death and loss. Sometimes she looked at Francesca's fresh round face, her blue eyes and soft tumble of blonde hair, and felt she would overflow with love for her. Although she went to work still, her life centred on the Gruschovs' house.

'It's hard to explain,' she said to Pat one day, when they were eating their lunch together. 'Some days it feels as if the house is just full of love. You can feel it.' As she spoke she found tears welling up. 'Sorry—' She wiped her eyes. 'Don't know what's come over me. I'm turning into a soppy old thing.'

'No you're not,' Pat said kindly. 'Anatoli's a lovely man. It must be terrible seeing him so poorly.'

'It is.' Greta looked down, feeling more tears fill her eyes. 'And there's poor little Peter – he's only eight ... And Edie – I've never known a couple as close as they are ...'

Edie had given up work to devote her time to her husband. Anatoli's business was being run by his manager, a good, reliable man who was also very fond of Anatoli, so they did not have money worries. Edie spent all the time she possibly could with her husband. Greta knew that often she just slid into bed beside him and they held each other for the comfort of it, no matter what the time of day.

Amid all the kind enquiries and offers of help from Quaker friends, Janet came round more often. Sometimes she brought Ruth and Naomi, who were nine now and would play with Peter, and at others she came during the school day and spent time listening to all Edie's worries. Greta had always been a bit intimidated by Janet, but all she could see now was her kindness, her real sadness on Edie's behalf. And Ruby came too, her good-heartedness overcoming any hard feelings, and she sat and kept Edie company.

One thing that was really worrying Edie was the question of Anatoli's children. One afternoon when she and Greta were sitting talking in the kitchen as they often did, she said,

'Well, I've taken the risk. I've written a proper letter to Caroline telling her exactly what's happening and asking her to visit. Richard has always kept in touch anyway, though goodness knows if he can come over from Canada. But Caroline seems to have taken so much against her father ... Neither of them came to our wedding.'

'He never went to see her either though, did he?' Greta asked.

'He did try, but she gave him the cold shoulder and she seemed to be living a very busy life. She's a musician as well ...' Edie sighed. 'I don't really understand it all. Anatoli has so many regrets about the past, and since I wasn't there it's hard for me to know what has happened. But I really think they should both at least have a chance to see their father before ...'

She left the sentence unfinished.

Chapter Fifty-One

'Mom!' Peter came running through to the kitchen. 'Look – letters!'

They had heard the clatter of the letterbox. All of them were still in their nightclothes.

'Ooh look – one from David!' Edie glowed with happiness as Peter handed over the blue aerogramme. She tucked it into her dressing-gown pocket. She already looked pink and cheerful as Anatoli had had a good night. 'I must get this tray upstairs before I settle down and read it. And you need to get going, Peter – you should be dressed by now. Get moving or you'll be late!'

Just as Greta was leaving for work, Edie came down, her curvaceous little figure dressed in black slacks and a royal blue polo-neck jumper, hair fastened up in her usual pleat at the back. She was full of excitement.

'They're coming. They're really going to come over! David's booked for them to fly on December the tenth, so they'll be here for Christmas. Oh, the poor things – they've been through such a terrible time. I want to spoil them rotten!'

Greta said how pleased she was, but the truth was that the news gave her very mixed feelings. It was on her mind all day at the factory. She was used to having Anatoli and Edie all to herself, and she loved their cosy household, where she felt special. The thought of David coming over was difficult enough. After all, he was Edie's son, or near enough. Edie thought the world of him and would want to give him all her attention, especially after the tragic time he and Gila had had. Greta felt very guilty for her resentment of them coming when she thought about this. They've lost their little boy for heaven's sake, she told herself. What on earth are you making a fuss about? But it wasn't just that she dreaded feeling pushed out. She was in awe of David, or her memory of what he was like. He was clever and serious and she had no idea what they could say to one another. As for Gila, she seemed like a person from another planet altogether. Edie had described her as tough, 'a real Israeli sabra'. The combination of her toughness, grief and inability to speak much English seemed terrifying. She could never say it to Edie, but secretly she felt really miserable at the prospect of them coming.

Perhaps Ruby had been right, Greta thought. She really would be in their way now. And David and Gila had lost their son how would they feel about living in a house with two young children running about? With a heavy heart she decided she had better offer to move out. She could put up with living with her Mom for a bit, surely? And it would give Francesca time to get to know her granny better. By the time she went home she had persuaded herself that it was a good idea.

Edie and Anatoli were both downstairs: Anatoli was having one of his good days and they had a record playing, soft piano music. Edie was knitting: she had decided that David and Gila would need extra woollies when they came over. Francesca was with them, sitting happily on the floor amid a pile of wooden bricks. She shrieked with joy as Greta appeared and ran to be picked up.

'Ah, the mother returns,' Anatoli said. 'Come in and sit with us. There is tea – and Edith has made some very good cake.'

Greta sat down, as Francesca toddled back to her toys. She took some tea, but said no thank you to the cake. She felt tearful before she'd even begun speaking.

'I just wanted a word with you both . . .' The tears started to well in her eyes and she struggled to speak because of the lump in her throat. 'I've been thinking: while your David's here, I think I ought to move out. It'll give you all more space – you don't want me hanging about. And they've lost their little boy and everything. It wouldn't be very nice for them having Francesca running about as a reminder . . .'

Edie and Anatoli were exchanging glances and protesting before she had finished speaking.

'But you can't leave us!' Anatoli cried.

'Well, where on earth were you thinking of going?' Edie asked.

'To Mom's. She's always on at me to go back and live with her. She wants to see more of Franny.' She could feel her face colouring up. A tear overflowed from her left eye and trickled down her cheek.

There was a pause, as Edie and Anatoli were obviously searching for the right thing to say.

'Well,' Edie said tactfully. 'You don't need to go because of David and Gila. This is your home, love, and there's plenty of space for them in the big room at the back. As for Francesca – they know perfectly well she's here living with us. I tell them all about her, and she's no more of a reminder than Peter, and he'll be here. But if that's what you really want to do, then of course you must. Would you like to go and live with your Mom for a while?'

Greta looked down into her lap, blushing even harder. More tears fell. 'Not really. Not if it's OK for me to stay,' she admitted. 'I just thought I ought to offer to get out of the way.'

'OK for you to stay!' Anatoli said. 'If you left we should be bereft, shouldn't we, Edith? You and that little monkey down there!' He nodded at Francesca. 'If you want to make an old man very unhappy then you will go and leave us!'

'I don't know where I'd be without you,' Edie said, tears in her eyes as well now. 'I mean I don't want to keep you from Ruby – that wouldn't be right. But you're one of the family, love. Don't ever feel that we don't want you here, will you?'

Greta looked up tearfully at these two people whom she'd come to love so much.

'I'd much rather stay, if that's really all right . . .'

'Of course it's all right,' Edie said, wiping her face. 'Don't ever think differently.'

'So – is this piece of nonsense all settled?' Anatoli looked back and forth between the two women, who each had tears streaming down their faces, and began to laugh. 'Good God, it's like a scene from a Victorian melodrama in here! For goodness sake, let's have more tea and some of that lovely cake and be cheerful!'

A few days later, Edie read out from the newspaper that there had been another bombing in Israel, this time in Jerusalem.

'Mahaneh Yehuda market in Jerusalem,' she announced. 'Oh God, I wonder where that is, if David or Gila ever go there? It says there were twelve killed and fifty-two injured.' She shook her head in distress. 'There always seems to be something – all that fighting over the Suez Canal and trouble on the borders. I don't think it's ever going to be safe there.' She put the paper down with a sigh. 'At least they're coming here for a while. But I do wish really that David had never gone to live there.'

Chapter Fifty-Two

The first thing Greta noticed about Gila was how terribly thin she was. It would have been impossible not to notice, even with layers of jumpers she and David were wearing against the English winter.

They arrived on a bright, cold December day. Greta knew they would be there when she got home from work. Once inside, she heard voices coming from the back, and wavered nervously at the bottom of the stairs, tempted just to go up and stay in her bedroom out of everyone's way, but she knew this would disappoint Edie. She pulled her shoulders back, stood tall and went to the kitchen.

'Oh, hello, love!' Edie greeted, looking radiant. To Greta's surprise though, only Edie and David were sitting at the kitchen table. 'Come and join us – David, you remember our Greta, don't you?'

The 'our' Greta warmed her heart. After all, a little voice said in her head, when it came down to it, David was no more related to Edie than she was!

A tall man was standing up to greet her, wearing the enormous Aran sweater that Edie had knitted. It looked lovely against his tanned skin. He had wavy brown hair, a strong face dominated by a large nose, and a direct, interested gaze which she remembered in him and which made her like him again, at once.

'Hello Greta.' He held out his hand, smiling. 'It's been a long time.'

'Hello,' she said, a little overwhelmed by the height of him. Her hand was taken into his big sinewy one. 'Nice to meet you.' She blushed. 'Not meet you – I mean, see you – again.'

'Have a seat—' Edie pulled a chair out and brought another cup to the table. 'You must be ready for a cuppa. Shift all right?'

'Yes – much as ever,' Greta said.

She realized that David had not changed as much as she had expected. His face was thinner, the cheekbones more pronounced, he was more tanned and simply older looking. And the strain of the past weeks showed in the exhausted look in his eyes. She had seen pictures of him, of course. But when he spoke there was the same slightly lopsided smile, the way his mouth moved, the gentle, well-spoken voice.

He was evidently not thinking the same. As Edie sat down with a fresh pot of tea, he turned to Greta and said frankly, 'I don't think I would have recognized you, to tell you the truth. You have changed a lot since I was last here.'

'Well it was nearly twelve years ago,' Edie pointed out. Though she and Anatoli had visited Israel regularly, David had not been home in all that time. 'She was still in short socks when you left, weren't you, Gret?'

He had been scarcely aware of her existence then, she knew, and she had always felt far more than five years his junior.

'Yes, I suppose so,' David said. He looked perturbed for a moment, then laughed, looking down at his tea-cup, shyly, it seemed. 'Somehow you forget things change when you're not there. I can't get over the size of Peter these days!'

'Where's your wife?' Greta asked, trying to be friendly.

'She and Anatoli and Francesca are all fast asleep,' Edie said. 'So David and I thought we'd come in here and have a natter.'

'Gila is still very tired,' David said. 'And the journey has taken it out of her.'

'Poor thing,' Greta said. 'She must feel terrible.' Then to her embarrassment she realized that she had alluded to Shimon's death without meaning to, but had also not included David in the grief of it. 'I mean both of you,' she said stumblingly, her cheeks reddening. 'I'm ever so sorry – about what's happened.'

She was overcome by her own clumsiness. She hadn't meant to bring it all up and throw it in his face like that.

But David gave a wan smile. 'Thanks,' was all he said. 'Yes, it's been a very bad time.'

'Well at least you're here now for a bit,' Edie's eyes were wide with sorrow for him. 'Perhaps a change of scene will perk Gila up a bit.'

'Oh, I expect so,' David said lightly, obviously not wanting to discuss it further.

There was a moment's pause, then he sat up straighter in his chair. 'So – what news of everyone? How about Dr Ferris and his family?'

Greta still felt very young in relation to David, as if he was infinitely older and more mature. There was he, far away in Israel living his difficult and dangerous life of medical school, family, the army, while she was here

379

in the safe nest of his family with her quiet little life. He must find her so uninteresting, she thought! She had done nothing, been nowhere except America, and that was dictated by her mother. She felt very awkward after meeting him, though he was perfectly friendly and polite.

But with Gila it was far worse.

She did not appear until it was nearly time for tea. Peter and Francesca had already had their food and were at their most boisterous. Peter had a pile of cushions on the floor in the hall and was hurling himself on to them from higher and higher up the stairs while Francesca giggled ecstatically and tried to copy him from lower down. Greta was keeping an eye on them both.

'No, Peter – don't jump when Francesca's below you!' she called to him. 'She's going to have her jump – wheeeee! There!' Francesca landed in a gurgling heap on the cushions. 'Come on, babby, out the way and let Peter have his go.'

But as she looked up, Gila appeared on the stairs behind Peter. She was also dressed in one of Edie's knitted presents, a soft pink sweater with a loose roll neck which looked very pretty set against her black hair and fine features. But she still seemed to be freezing cold and was standing with her arms folded. Greta's heart went out to her. She didn't think she had ever seen anyone look so lost and miserable. 'Peter, wait! Gila's behind you – she needs to come down.'

She could tell by the way Peter stood back, pressing against the banister to let Gila pass, that he found her rather forbidding.

'Thank you,' she said to him, with a thin smile

which did not reach her eyes. When she reached the bottom of the stairs, Greta was holding Francesca in her arms, a smile on her lips, ready to give her a friendly greeting. But Gila, arms still folded, walked straight past her, staring down at her feet as if there was no one else there. Greta watched her thin back disappearing into the front room. She could feel the extent of the misery contained in that thin frame, with her bony shoulders and numb, expressionless face. Gila seemed locked right away somewhere that no one could reach and that she didn't want anyone to reach. Greta could not imagine how any of them were going to try and talk to her.

Of course the best person was Anatoli.

Though he was not feeling at his best that day, he was determined to come and eat with them all. Greta offered to help him get ready and found him sitting on the stool in front of Edie's dressing table as if gathering his strength for the journey downstairs. Near his elbow were Edie's bottles of moisturizer and perfume, Nivea cream and a little wooden jewellery box.

'I'm afraid I have been sleeping the afternoon away – which is not very polite or hospitable, is it?'

'Don't be silly,' Greta said. He allowed her to comb his hair. Even raising his arms was exhausting for him. 'Anyway, Gila has been asleep as well.'

'How is the poor girl?' Anatoli asked. He had already gone up for his nap when they arrived.

'I don't know,' Greta said carefully. 'I've barely seen her.'

Anatoli gave her a quizzical look which said, *You're not speaking your mind.*

Greta smiled in surrender. She was behind Anatoli, looking at him in the long oval mirror.

'She seemed . . . cold. I mean huddled up in a jumper, but not just that. As if she was cold all the way through. To be honest she walked straight past me without saying a word.'

'Poor child,' Anatoli said, his eyes full of sadness. 'Rachel weeping for her children, she will not be comforted, for they are no more . . .'

Greta frowned. 'What's that?'

'The Holy Bible. Jeremiah, I think. Now – we had better see if I can get myself down the stairs.'

Once they had achieved the slow descent to the back room, to Greta's surprise David and Gila were already at the table with Francesca in her high chair. She had already had her tea but was allowed to sit with them. Gila was sitting beside Peter, her head bent towards him and, in her broken English, she seemed to be talking to him, smiling a little. Greta was encouraged. How would she feel if she lost Francesca? Life would be unbearable without her little girl's chatter, her plump, clinging arms. It would be terrible to be near someone else's little girl, but comforting as well to be able to hold and cuddle her when your whole being ached for that. Maybe Gila found Peter a comfort.

They both got up to greet Anatoli and Gila managed a smile. Greta could see she was fond of him – how could anyone not be? She seemed to thaw a little.

'It's very good to see you,' David said as they hugged. If David was shocked by Anatoli's thinness he did a good job of disguising it. But then he was a doctor, she thought.

Immediately Anatoli was there, the atmosphere seemed easier and he asked David and Gila questions about their journey and how they were. It was David who did all the talking, but Gila did not go off into her own world, the way she had seemed to before. She was obviously listening and managed to smile a little at times.

'Ah – you're all here,' Edie said, carrying in a big pot of stew with lots of carrots shining in the gravy. Greta went out and carried in a dish of potatoes.

'Goodness, it's a long time since I've had a meal like this,' David said enthusiastically.

'Your mother's a fine cook,' Anatoli agreed. 'And some of us look as if we could do with feeding up.'

He smiled at Gila with rueful fellow feeling.

'Yes, she's all skin and bone, poor love,' Edie said, touching her shoulder.

Gila looked a bit bewildered, and Greta realized she had not really understood what was being said. She nodded politely as Edie served her a plate of food. Anatoli managed to draw her out a little, asking her about her dental training, her work, about the apartment they had moved to in Jerusalem, and Gila answered as best she could. She was certainly more responsive with Anatoli than with anyone else.

Later though, after they'd eaten and were moving into the front room, Greta was taking Francesca up to bed and in the hall she heard Gila say to Edie, 'I think I go to bed now.' Once again she had her cold, distant look, her arms tightly folded.

'Already?' Edie looked concerned. 'Are you sure? It's only half past eight. Wouldn't you like to come and sit with us for a while?'

Gila shook her head. 'I like to sleep.'

'Well, all right, love, if you're sure. I'm sure David will be up soon. Is there anything you want?'

Gila shook her head and followed Greta up the stairs. Greta saw her disappear into their room and shut the door silently behind her.

Chapter Fifty-Three

'I don't know how I'm going to stand it,' Greta confessed to Pat after a few days.

All the time she was at home she felt twisted inside by all the emotion around her, as well as not being very comfortable with the visitors. David was by far the easier of the two. He was sad and preoccupied with his problems, but he was friendly towards her. She found him easy to get on with and they usually had a chat when they met each other in the house. He was always very sweet with Francesca and she knew Edie loved him being there. Even she had begun to enjoy hearing his gentle voice around the place. But the terrible sadness in him weighed on her almost as if it was her own. She found herself thinking about him when she was at work, worrying about how he was. As for Gila, the combination of her bad English, her foreignness and her stony, unreachable grief meant that she could never seem to find a way of getting along with her.

'I feel so sorry for her. I can't think of anything worse. But it's ever so awkward at home with them there. You never know what mood Gila's going to be in and she just won't make an effort to talk to anyone. I just don't know where to put myself when she's there. And poor David – he's the one doing everything and making all the effort when he must be heartbroken as well. It's ever so hard.'

'Well come and see me more then,' Pat said. 'You know you're always welcome.'

'I know,' Greta said guiltily. Pat was forever on at her to come round and for them to do things together, but Greta tended to find excuses. By the time she had got Francesca down she was usually ready for a quiet evening, and the truth was, up until now she had loved being at home with Edie and Anatoli. She knew she had neglected her friend.

'All right, I will,' she said. 'That'd be nice.'

Suddenly going out seemed much more attractive. Maybe Anatoli was right – she had buried herself away too much. After all, she wasn't short of offers. There was a young man called John Foreman at the factory who had asked her several times to go out. He was a friendly bloke, and in a band, but she'd turned him down. David and Gila weren't sure how long they were staying apparently. Edie thought it would be almost a month because then it would be time for David to go back to medical school. But however long it was, Greta knew she had to get out of the house.

So, once or twice a week now, she started arranging to see Pat and sometimes one or two of her other friends later on in the evening. With Christmas coming up there was a festive feel to work. She and a group of her friends went carol-singing in town again, in the square outside the cathedral, and some of them went in to Selly Oak hospital to sing for the patients and add a bit of cheer to the place. They went out to see *Bonnie and Clyde* and *The Jungle Book*. And at other times they just sat by the gas fire in Pat's little sitting room and drank tea and cocoa and chatted the evening away.

And when Ruby said, 'I hope I'm going to see a bit

more of my granddaughter at Christmas this year,'
Greta agreed to spend Christmas Day, or at least some
of it, at her Mom's. Before she had popped in for a
little while, when Trevor and Marleen were round at
the Biddles, then scooted back to the Bristol Road as
soon as she could.

I ought to see my family, she realized. Try and make
it up with Marleen. She knew that as well as the arrival
of David and Gila, she was having to prepare herself
too for when Anatoli was no longer there. The cosy
nest she had been taking refuge in all this time was
never going to be the same. She couldn't hide there for
ever.

When Greta came home from work now she was so
affected by Gila's intense, withdrawn presence that she
would take Francesca off and play with her upstairs,
sometimes taking her in to see Anatoli if he had not
come down. Week by week he seemed more poorly
and it wrung her heart to watch it. She wanted to
spend all the time she could with him while he was
still with them, yet she didn't like the way she felt as
if she was spending her time hiding at home now.

But one afternoon just before Christmas she got
home and found the house quiet. Edie was sitting near
the fire with her knitting, with Francesca and her toys.

'Oh!' Greta said, as she put her head round the
door. 'On your own?'

'Yes—' Edie smiled, but Greta could sense the
worry behind her cheerfulness. 'They've gone into
town for a bit. David went to see Dr Ferris this
morning...'

Greta was startled by how hard her heart started to

thud, by her rush of tender concern for him. What on earth had got into her? She perched on the chair opposite. 'There's nothing wrong is there?'

'Oh, no! Not – I mean he's not ill. He just ... Oh bother it, look – I've dropped two stitches...' Distractedly she put her knitting down.

'I'm happy really – very ...' Edie's eyes filled with tears and she wiped them away, smiling at the same time. Greta waited. What on earth? Maybe Gila was expecting another baby. Perhaps that was why there had been a visit to the doctor.

'It's what I've wanted, all this time, but it still feels a bit of a shock ... Especially with Gila being as she is, poor lamb ... Things aren't easy between them.'

'Aren't they?' Greta asked. She hadn't been sure with David and Gila. She knew they were grieving over their son's death, that things did not seem warm between them, but as they spoke to each other in Hebrew she never understood their conversations.

'But I think it will be for the best,' Edie said, her face glowing. 'Dr Ferris – Martin – says it will be possible for David to finish his medical training at the university here. So he's decided to stay. They're not going to live in Israel any more – they're going to make their home here! And maybe if she's here away from all the memories, we can help Gila get out of the state she's in. I hope to goodness we can. The only thing is—' Edie looked troubled. 'He's made the decision, but he hasn't told Gila yet. You won't say anything, will you?'

'No of course not – it's not my business,' Greta managed to say, as the news sank into her like a horrible hard stone. She wanted to be pleased for Edie, but what she really felt was a turmoil of dread and a shameful fear that, if they stayed, things could never be the same again. It felt like the day that Marleen came home, only much worse.

'That's really nice for you,' she said, forcing out the words. 'You'll all be together as a family.'

Chapter Fifty-Four

David had put off going to see Joe Leishmann. He knew he owed the Leishmanns a visit, but was deeply reluctant and didn't like to ask himself why.

Joe Leishmann owned a well-respected tailoring business near Five Ways. It was Joe and his wife Esther who had befriended David in those early, confused months when he began to learn about his real family and his Jewish identity.

Joe and Esther had known David's mother at Singers Hill Synagogue, after she had come to England to escape Nazi Germany, and they remembered David as a baby. They had helped him to piece his family together and find his father Hermann and Aunt Annaliese, and it was they who had encouraged him to go to Israel to work on a kibbutz. At that time the Leishmanns had meant the world to him and he had felt as if he was their protégé, although he had gone against their wishes, and gone to a secular instead of a religious kibbutz.

At first, once he was in Israel, he had written to them regularly to let them know how he was getting on. But as his life there had become busier and more permanent, he had written less and less, and he felt guilty.

'You must come and meet them,' he said to Gila. 'They are people who have been very important in my life.'

'All right.' She nodded.

They were sitting up in bed drinking tea. David had made it and brought it up, trying to keep things pleasant between them and establish some sort of homely routine. It felt like trying to hold back the tide.

'They are good people – kind people.'

'All right. I said all right.'

She spoke with no tone, no emotion of wanting or not wanting, as she spoke of almost anything these days.

A tight, explosive feeling built inside David. *My wife! Where has my wife gone, the wife I loved? I have lost my children and my wife!* But he pushed the feelings aside. To look at them was too terrible. He must keep his head down, his feelings down, and keep trying to hold things together for all their sakes. He could not allow himself to need comfort.

But he glanced at her, her stick-thin wrist holding the cup close to her lips, her eyes staring ahead of her but not focused on anything, her expression blank. It was as if she was not there. Yet it was also as if she hated him.

He only found courage to say something when they were on the doorstep of the Leishmanns' gracious house in Edgbaston. It was a freezing day, like the ones David remembered when he first came here to visit, their breath steaming on the air. The house looked just the same, though he noticed that the white paint on the window frames was cracked and beginning to flake off.

Gila was bundled up in layers of clothing, topped by the soft pink jumper Edie had knitted for her and a navy blue coat of Edie's. Below it, her black-stockinged legs looked painfully thin. She had her hands in the coat pockets and was hunched up, her chin tucked in behind the roll neck of the jumper. David saw that it was wrong, her being here at all in this cold, grey country. He could only think of her in a place of blue sky, bright light, of colour. Here she seemed even more diminished and faded.

'You will try and speak with them, won't you? Be polite?'

In his nervousness he sounded like a bossy uncle, and he cursed himself. But was it too much to ask? He had lost his son too, lost their other child. All he was asking was for her to try.

'Of course,' she said, without looking at him. She never looked at him now. 'What do you think?'

'Aaah!' Joe Leishmann cried on opening the door. He looked them up and down for a second, eyes twinkling with pleasure. 'The wanderer returns at last! Come in, come in! And this is the lovely Gila! Welcome, welcome! Esther and I have been waiting for you.'

Joe had scarcely changed, it seemed to David. Still the same round face, same black-rimmed spectacles and crumpled, amiable features. His hair was a little whiter, he was a fraction more stooped than when they had first met, that was all. The hall, too, seemed unchanged, and David found this reassuring.

Joe steered Gila towards the living room, in his fatherly way, his arm round her shoulders. 'My dear, you have been through such tragedy. A calamity – such a calamity! We have been weeping for you, for your little Shimon.'

Edie must have told them everything, David

realized. He had not thought to write, not after it all happened.

He saw that Gila was struggling with tears and it tore at his heart. She had shown no emotion, it all seemed to be locked inside her, but Joe Leishmann's all-embracing kindness had got through to her. David wanted to go to her, to put his arms round her, say, *'Yes, my love, cry and weep, please. Let yourself feel, let us feel all our sorrow and be one together as we never are, not any more . . . Come back to me my wife, my love . . .'*

But they were met by Esther Leishmann. Gila composed herself with obvious effort and dragged a smile to her lips in a way that normally she only managed for Anatoli or Peter.

'Esther – at last, we have a chance to see these young pioneers!' Joe said, gently steering Gila towards his wife.

Esther Leishmann was getting slowly to her feet, and David was shocked by the change in her. Unlike her husband, who was ageing gradually and mercifully, Esther was much changed. The darting, bossy woman who David had first met over a decade ago looked faded and shrunken. He should have been prepared. Edie had warned him that Esther had suffered a stroke last year. She was recovering and seemed mobile, not disabled in any way, but he could see what a toll her illness had taken.

'Welcome my dears,' Esther said.

She reached out and embraced Gila, holding her close like a child, stroking her back in unspoken sorrow and sympathy. David wondered if this would make Gila cry again, but when she stood back she said, 'It is very nice to meet you,' in her careful English, and she seemed grateful for Esther's embrace. It was not something her own neurotic mother ever managed, David realized.

'Now.' Esther Leishmann stood before David. 'Let me look at you.' She reached up and stroked his cheek. 'You have grown up into such a man. And you are still so very beautiful!' She spoke to him with arch fondness. 'You look like a true sabra. It is good to see you again, David. Sit, please, all of you. We shall take tea.'

It was Joe Leishmann who brought the tea in: one tray with the silver teapot and cups, another with pastries and cake, plates and dainty knives.

'I'm afraid these are from a shop,' Esther said, shamefacedly, slicing into the sponge cake. 'I have not been very well, and Joe is not the baker of the household. I shall be better, but in the meantime we are eating from the bakery down the street. It is not so bad, but not up to Drucker's standards!'

André Drucker had set up his Viennese patisserie in Birmingham in the early 1960s, to give people a taste of the cakes and coffee he remembered from his Austrian childhood, and Esther was a fan.

David sat beside Gila on the settee in the elegantly furnished room. Joe and Esther each took a chair either side of the marble fireplace. Again, nothing seemed to have changed much, so far as David could remember. On the one hand he felt a little as if he had come home, yet he knew also how he had changed since he was last here! It was like stepping back into another life.

Except of course that his wife was beside him and he could undo nothing: not the happy times, nor the frozen state they had reached now. But they could pretend, he thought. They would sit and pretend, for

Joe and Esther, that despite their personal tragedy they were proud and thriving Israelis.

But first he asked Joe about the business.

'How is Leishmann's Bespoke Tailors?' he asked as Joe handed round the cups of tea and Esther watched him like a hawk and bossed him, 'Careful now, you'll spill it . . .' or 'Don't overdo the sugar, Joe!'

'Oh yes – it's going along well. I have not retired since no one is going to force me – even though in two years' time Esther and I will be seventy. Can you believe it?'

'No!' David said, though in Esther's case that was less true.

'And is Nadia still there?' One of his fond memories of meeting Joe Leishmann was of his stormy Italian assistant, Nadia, and their amazing capacity for falling out with each other over almost every stitch that went into every garment. But Nadia had been a pretty, curvaceous, motherly woman who had been kind to David, and he thought how nice it would be to see her again.

'Ah, no, Nadia has been gone some time. She and her husband moved away – to the west somewhere.'

'Swansea,' Esther corrected him. 'She had relatives there and they went to live near the sea.'

'Ah yes.' Joe was leaning forward, looking like a cuddly bear and scratching his head. 'Now we have two girls – Madge and Doreen. They are good girls if they would only stop gossiping and get on with the job. God in Heaven—' He rolled his eyes. 'Never have I known two women who can talk so much. On and on . . .'

'Madge is a good seamstress,' Esther remarked.

'She is,' Joe had to agree. 'Very fine. But dear God, the endless verbal torrent . . .'

David sensed Gila trying to keep up with the conversation.

'Now,' Esther said. 'Tell us your plans. You go back . . . When?'

There was a pause. David tensed even further. He could not tell them, not now.

'Esther is asking us when we are going home,' he told Gila. If there were things she did not understand he said them quietly in Hebrew so she could keep up. She was nibbling at a piece of the sponge Joe Leishmann had cut for her. He let her answer, as it was not a complicated question and so that he did not have to lie.

'I think we go – January,' Gila said haltingly. 'David has to go to . . . to school again . . .'

'Back to your studies,' Esther nodded approvingly. 'Very good, very good.'

The Leishmanns bombarded them with questions now, about Jerusalem, about the war, the army, the country in general. After Joe's sympathy when they arrived, they did not mention Shimon, the explosion, the bomb which had torn their lives apart. They talked about everyday life, about their new apartment.

'We have moved to a different place,' Gila said. When there was a question that was easy to answer David looked at her. They had an understanding during that visit. As if both knew they had to be united in front of the Leishmanns because they were such good people, they liked them and felt they owed them a version of life which was hopeful. So they pretended together without having agreed to do so. They talked about life in Jerusalem and how they would go back and start again in a new place, continue the struggle to maintain the state of Israel, because that was what they knew the Leishmanns wanted to hear. They were so sure of its rightness, of Israel's duty to survive at all costs. David would never mention to them his feelings after the Six Day War, the confusion and moral doubt that had assailed him even in victory.

And he could not explain all the other things that died on the day he saw his son's body in a hospital mortuary.

So he knew that he had already lied with his answer to their first question, and that with every following question he answered there was an untruth built into it. He was not going back to Israel in January. Somewhere deep inside him, at first like chips of rock beginning to fall down a mountainside, the decision had begun to be made. When the bombs went off in the Mahaneh Yehuda market in Jerusalem in November, with every border skirmish which meant that he, an Israeli, was forever the occupier in someone else's land, that he and his loved ones would never be safe from threat and violence while this was the case, the rocks had grown bigger and gained momentum. And when he saw again the green calm of England, when he sat in the peace of the Meeting House in Bournville and heard the chimes ringing across the Green, which spoke to parts of him long buried, he knew he had come home.

But he had scarcely put these deep instincts into words even for himself. And at this moment, for Gila, for the Leishmanns, he must pretend that his future was as an Israeli, that he and his wife would return bravely to that parched, precarious land and start again.

He was hanging in the balance between two lives.

Chapter Fifty-Five

As Christmas drew near it was becoming impossible for David and Gila to pretend any more. Gila's state of mind, instead of improving, was getting worse and none of them knew what to do.

Edie was so worried that she confided in Greta, and she didn't hide her concerns from Anatoli, although he was ill.

'She's just not right,' Edie said one afternoon when she and Greta were making little Christmas buns with Peter and Francesca. 'I mean she's up there now, all on her own. She doesn't do anything – just sits there. I know she's pining. I can hardly stand to think how she must feel, losing her little boy and the baby. But it's more than that.' She whispered above Peter's head. 'Anatoli thinks she's having a complete breakdown.'

'Oh, Mom!' Peter cried indignantly. 'Franny's gone and messed it all up!'

Francesca was puddling her hands in the cake mix as if she was making mud pies. Peter, who was rather a neat child, was not impressed.

'Come on, Franny-Panny,' Edie said, lifting her over to the sink to wash her hands. 'I think you've done your share. Let Peter finish them off now.'

Francesca, who was just as happy to play in a bowl of bubbly water in the sink, splashed about contentedly.

'I spoke to Martin about her,' Edie said. 'He's been ever so kind over the years ... He said he thought Gila ought to go to one of those mental doctors. I said to him, it's almost as if she's shell-shocked, and he said yes, that was how it was. She's had too many shocks all at once for her system to stand it, what with the bombs and losing her children – and on top of that she's in a strange country where she barely speaks the language ...'

'Oh,' Greta said doubtfully. It wasn't something she knew anything about, but she could see Gila was in a desperate state. She hardly left her room now, and when she did she was so withdrawn it was as if she had closed down completely, despite David's attempts to reach her, which it wrung Greta's heart to watch. 'Well maybe she should then.'

Edie gave a long sigh. 'Anatoli says he thinks Martin's right. But when I spoke to David about it he said Gila's mother is frightened of doctors – especially that sort. She's made Gila frightened too and she won't go near them.'

Greta thought the idea seemed frightening too.

'I thought they were for people who were really mad,' she said. 'You know – frothing at the mouth and that ...'

Edie turned, her eyes troubled. 'That's what I used to think. But Martin says that sometimes now they just let you talk. Or there are treatments they can have ...'

'D'you think she'd agree to go?' Greta said, wrapping a towel round Francesca's waist.

'Well that's the trouble. David doesn't think she will.' Edie gave a sigh. 'Oh I do wish he'd talk to me properly, poor lamb. He's shutting me out, trying to make out that they're managing when it's obvious they're not. I think we'll have to get Christmas out of the way and then see how things are.'

Just before Christmas, a card arrived from Anatoli's daughter Caroline. Greta and Edie had just helped Anatoli downstairs when it arrived and he opened it by the fire in the living room. Greta glimpsed lines of ornate handwriting inside the card. At first Anatoli's face was tense when he began to read, but she saw his expression soften and relax.

'Well, it seems she still has some use for her father after all,' he said.

'What does she say?' Edie asked gently.

Anatoli read, 'I am so sorry that we have got so out of touch and now to hear that you are unwell. I shall do my best to come up and see you as soon as the Christmas period is over. I'm afraid I can't bring any grandchildren to meet you. It seems Michael and I are not going to be lucky in that department, so I have resigned myself to the fact. My music teaching takes a good deal of my time and energy these days.'

He looked up. 'She sings and plays the piano. She always had a lovely voice . . .' Then he continued, 'We hear from Richard from time to time and all seems to be well. Wishing you a peaceful Christmas with your new family. Love to you, Caroline. Her married name is Brewer . . .'

Edie and Greta exchanged glances. Anatoli had not been invited to Caroline's wedding.

'Well, that's nice,' Edie said carefully.

'Yes.' He closed the card and looked thoughtful. 'I suppose you wrote to her?'

'Yes, I did.' Edie blushed. 'After all, she wouldn't have known anything – how you were.'

'No. And Richard – did you write to him?'

'Yes, love.' Edie took his hand. 'I thought they should know.'

'Yes – I suppose so. I should have had the courage to do it myself.'

He didn't seem either angry or pleased, just very thoughtful.

Francesca was a bit too young to know what was going on at Christmas, but she still woke early on Christmas Day and Greta took her downstairs to get some milk. She sat Francesca at the table with her cup and put the kettle on for a cup of tea, standing by the stove to keep warm as she waited for it to boil, watching Francesca's bulging cheeks as she downed the milk.

After a moment the kitchen door squeaked open, and to her discomfort David came in. The fact that he was already fully dressed and she was in her dressing gown and slippers made her feel awkward. She had also begun to admit to herself how strongly he affected her, his lovely face, the wistful smiles he gave. She still looked up to him as she had when they were little, but something about him also moved her, more and more with each week that passed.

'Oh, hello!' He seemed surprised to find anyone up. It was still only six o'clock. 'Hello little 'un.' He rumpled Francesca's hair as he passed and she let out a gurgle of pleasure. 'I didn't know anyone else was awake. I couldn't sleep.'

'I was making tea,' Greta said. 'D'you want some?'

'Thanks, I'd love one.'

She saw him watching Francesca, his dark eyes tender and slightly amused, and she felt a deep twist of sorrow for him. For a moment she felt like going and putting her arms around him.

'She likes her food, doesn't she?'

'Oh yes – always has. Better that way. It's not very nice when you can't get them to eat.'

Still looking at the little girl, David said, 'Shimon was like that. I remember being amazed by how much a two-year-old could pack away at times!'

It was new, his talking about Shimon so naturally. At first he had not been mentioned. But she realized he liked talking about him.

'How old was he, exactly?' she asked gently.

'He would have been nine – next March.'

'Of course – about the same as Peter.'

David nodded, a slight smile on his lips.

'She won't be two until the summer,' Greta said.

'She's lovely – looks very like you.'

'Yes, she's a good girl.' Greta was unsure what else to say. Usually they talked about day-to-day matters, but today deeper things seemed nearer the surface, things they never normally talked about: *your son, your wife* ... Fortunately the kettle boiled and she busied herself. David straightened up and looked out of the window over the garden, in silence. Greta wondered what he was thinking.

'Here—' She handed him his tea, struck once again by the size and strength of his hands as they curved round the mug.

'Oh—' He came to himself as if his thoughts had been miles away, and smiled. 'Thanks. Shall we sit down?' He pulled out a chair for her at the table.

Greta had been wondering whether to escape upstairs with her tea, but she also desperately didn't want to go. And he had asked her to stay! A tingling aliveness came over her as she sat with him, perched on the edge of the chair. David seemed more relaxed and sat back with his tea. He was wearing the big Aran jumper again and the neck came up high round his chin. There was a silence. They sipped their tea, then both went to speak at the same time and stopped, laughing.

'No – you first.'

'I was only going to say happy Christmas,' Greta said, feeling foolish. 'It's Christmas Day.'

'Of course.' David held up his mug as if it was a pint glass. 'Happy Christmas to you!'

Francesca saw what he was doing and copied with her little blue cup and they both laughed.

'Must be very strange for you being back here,' Greta said.

'Yes.' David rubbed a hand over his face. 'Much more than I expected. It's like . . . Hard to explain . . . Like stepping back into another life, but feeling . . .' He stopped, as if he couldn't find words. He looked at her. 'And you've been here all the time.'

'Except for when Mom took us to America.'

'Of course. I'd forgotten. You went to see . . .'

'My grandparents. My father's Mom and Dad. We were looking for my Dad, sort of, I suppose. I mean we knew he was dead, but it was a way of seeing where he came from. We'd still be there if it hadn't been for . . .' Her voice had grown bitter and it was her turn to trail into silence.

'For what?'

'Oh . . .' She was ashamed to admit what had actually

403

happened. Perhaps David knew anyway, but she didn't want to talk about Carl Christie, or Marleen. 'I s'pose we didn't all see eye to eye in the end.'

David looked at her, deeply. 'And did you feel as if you fitted in there? Belonged, sort of thing?' he asked, as if he needed to know. *What a lovely voice*, she thought again.

'I don't know. I was only young. I was very fond of my grandparents and one day I'll go and see them again. They were ever so kind.'

'I see.' David was looking at her as if with new eyes. 'This all passed me by I'm afraid. I'd already gone by then.'

'Yes. Long gone. It seems ages ago now. But since we came back, yes, I've been here, at Cadbury's, like Mom and Edie. Been married, been divorced.' She shrugged, giving him a wry look. There was no point in hiding that.

'Not easy,' was all David said, with no hint of judgement. He drank down his tea in silence, and Greta started to feel uncomfortable. Perhaps he had had enough of talking and wanted her to go?

But he looked up at her and said, 'I thought I'd go for a walk. It's nice out and the others are asleep. Fancy coming – you and this one?' Again he stroked Francesca's hair.

She leapt inside. He wanted her company – hers! She blushed, feeling flustered.

'I'm not dressed though . . .' She realized just how much she wanted to go with him, and because of that, was perversely glad of a reason not to be able to. 'I'd best stay here. I expect Peter will wake up soon and they'll want to have their presents.'

'Of course – how silly. I keep forgetting it's

404

Christmas.' David was suddenly remote again, as if he had gone off into his own world. He stood up. 'Well, I'll just pop out for a bit – I shan't go far. Thanks for the tea.'

Greta watched him go down the path, his coat thrown on, tall and yet slightly hunched as if all the cares of the world were laid upon him. She remembered again, with shock, that he was only five years older than her. It seemed a lot more.

She closed the door and stood lost in thought for a moment.

Chapter Fifty-Six

Greta had promised Ruby that she would go over to Charlotte Road after dinner on Christmas Day and stay the afternoon.

'I want to see some of my granddaughter at Christmas,' Ruby said rather huffily. 'And it's high time you lot could all be in the same room together without world war three breaking out.'

'All right,' Greta said. 'I don't mind.' She felt she could face Trevor and Marleen now without much in the way of hard feelings.

What had also changed was that she was quite glad to go out. Anatoli was having a very bad day, sick and weak, and had had to stay in his room without eating, which upset Edie. As the six of them sat round the table without him there, Greta could feel her thinking, *This is what it's going to be like soon ...* For they could all see that Anatoli would not last long into the next year.

And Gila sat at the table like a shadow, unable to hide her depression any more. She only ate the bare minimum and went upstairs after dinner, saying she needed to sleep. Greta quietly thanked heaven for the children at the table as Peter and Francesca enjoyed the decorations and the candles, and pulling the crackers which Edie had bought. Peter had had a new bicycle for Christmas and he spent much of the morning riding it in the front drive. He was hell-bent on going to the park with it and David had promised he would take him.

'Would you like to come, with Fran?' he asked Greta.

It was kind of him, as she was on her own with Francesca, and there was nothing she would have liked more, but she'd promised.

'Sorry—' She was already putting on Francesca's coat. 'I've got to go to Mom's.' She smiled. 'But thanks, anyway.'

When she got there they were still finishing dinner, on to the Christmas pudding: Trevor, Marleen and their kids were squeezed round the table with Ruby and her new man, Mac. The little house was very hot and full of cooking smells. There were glasses of ale on the table and everyone was pink-cheeked and merry, except for Marleen's son George, two months younger than Francesca, who was bawling loudly about something.

'All right, Gret?' Trevor greeted her, airlifting George away from the rest of the meal.

'All right, Trevor.' She could see Francesca was fascinated by the sight of a new crowd of people.

'Come in, bab – pull up another chair!' Ruby greeted her. She was full of cheer. 'We've only just got our pudding. D'you want some?'

'No ta, I'm full up already.'

'Hello there – a happy Christmas to you,' Mac smiled, and Greta responded, thinking what a nice, friendly face he had. Maybe, just for once, Mom was with someone who was all right.

''Llo sis . . .' Marleen called, adding importantly, 'Can't get up!' She was at the end of the table, bottle-feeding the latest baby Sandra. Marleen didn't hold with breast-feeding, which she said was 'dirty'.

Once they had cleared away the dinner everyone sat around and the younger kids played with the new Christmas toys, fought over them and made up, except for Mary Lou, who was now a sulky looking eight-year-old and sat squeezed into a corner with her nose stuck in a comic most of the afternoon. Francesca was used to having Peter to compete against, so she could hold her own, and Greta was gratified to see Trevor smiling at the sight of her giving George and Elvis as good as she got.

'She's a strong 'un,' Trevor said, laughing, and Greta was surprised how emotional she felt at his warm response. One day soon, Francesca would have to know who her real father was.

'I reckon this little 'un's going to be tough,' Marleen said immediately, looking down at the baby in her lap. Greta saw that she didn't like Trevor paying Francesca any attention.

But she was amazed by the change in her sister. Marleen had never been exactly pretty, her features always a bit too narrow-eyed and foxy for that. Now, after four children, she looked pinched and thin, her cheekbones very prominent. She had plucked her eye-brows to thin lines and her hair was scraped back in a ponytail. She had aged immensely. But at the same time she was Queen Bee in her household, and Greta could see she loved it. Having children had been the making of her and Trevor. Maybe now she's happy we can get along better, she thought.

'Want a game of cribbage, Mac?' Ruby asked, settled in an armchair next to his. She had recently bought a new suite for the front room in a lilac-patterned Dralon, and a new fluffy cream hearthrug, so the room was looking very smart.

'Right you are, love,' Mac said.

Ruby got out the cards and score board. 'Anyone else want to play?' she invited.

'Your Mom and Dad all right?' Greta asked Trevor, as the cards were dealt.

'Yeah, fine,' Trevor said. 'April's getting wed next year.'

'Blimey,' Greta said. 'I can't believe it. I'll pop in and say hello later on.'

'Mary Lou's going to be her bridesmaid,' Marleen said. 'Aren't you, Mary Lou?'

There was no reply.

'She loves reading,' Marleen purred. 'Forever got her nose stuck in a book – bit like you. She's ever so clever, Mary Lou is.'

While the others played cribbage, Marleen talked about her children, a subject she never tired of. Greta heard all about their ailments, their achievements, their diet, their school, and her mind wandered. How were things at home? How was David . . . ? Her mind leapt to him so often, dwelling on things he had said to her, on the look in his eyes . . . She was so . . . involved with him. More and more she couldn't seem to stop thinking about him: he moved back and forth through her thoughts and dreams, his face, things he had said to her, his imploring expression when he had asked her out for a walk . . . She dragged her attention back to her sister.

'Well, I s'pose you'll call it a halt there won't you, Marl?' she asked, when she could get a word in edgeways. 'Stop at four kids, I mean?'

'Ooh, I don't know,' Marleen said. 'The doctor said I'm *remarkably fertile*. Just made to have children. So you never know. And . . .' She leaned forward over Sandra's head and whispered. 'And Trevor's got a lot of lead in his pencil. He just needed a fertile wife to bring out the best in him.'

She sat back again and looked at Greta. 'Anyway – when're you going to stop rotting away with all those old people and find yourself a bloke? It's high time your little 'un had a brother or sister, isn't it?'

Greta flushed in irritation. 'I like living with Edie and Anatoli, thanks very much!' she retorted. 'They've been ever so kind to me!'

'How is Anatoli?' Ruby called across.

'He's very poorly today,' Greta said, tears filling her eyes.

'Oh dear.' Ruby said. 'Poor thing. He's a lovely man, Anatoli,' she told Mac, then whispered, '*Got cancer*, I'm afraid.'

'Oh dear, oh dear, 'Mac said. 'Poor fellow.'

He said it with such feeling that Greta looked at him. He really is nice, she thought, surprised.

'Would you like a cuppa?' Ruby said. 'Gret'll put the kettle on, won't you, bab?'

Greta went into the kitchen, smarting from Marleen's nosy remarks. She had been living in a safe little cocoon since Francesca was born, but she couldn't stay there for ever. And seeing her sister and Trevor together she saw that she was missing something. That having someone to share her life, her children, could be a good thing and not just a burden.

It's time I started making a life for myself, she thought. Maybe I'd better say yes and go out with John. She knew he was interested in her and she liked what she knew of him well enough. I'll make a point of speaking to him after Christmas. Then swiftly, her mind wandered to David again, to their conversation in the kitchen that morning.

Marleen appeared in the kitchen then with the baby, who was just waking.

'What're you smiling at?' she asked.

Greta found herself staying on late at her Mom's, playing cards, watching *Christmas Crackerjack* and entertaining the children. The room was a fuggy mess of dolls and bits of Lego, of sweet wrappers, half-eaten mince pies and cans of ale. Trevor and Marleen left early, as Elvis and George were getting really fractious and Marleen decreed that it was time they went to bed.

'They'll be impossible in the morning else,' she said. 'Trev – you get their coats on.'

Francesca was looking sleepy once the other children had left, and Greta realized that her Mom and Mac, who were warm and comfy on the sofa, really fancied being left on their own.

'I'll be off now, Mom,' she said, come nine o'clock. 'And thanks – it's been nice.' And she meant it.

Greta pushed a sleeping Francesca home through the cold darkness. The streets were very quiet, everyone behind closed doors and the pubs shut. The place felt like a ghost town, no trains or cars moving. She felt as if she was the only person left in the world, in this strange, peaceful night, and for those moments she felt mellow and hopeful.

411

But as soon as she opened the front door, all sense of calm was lost like a slap. Edie was sitting on the third step of the stairs and Greta could see something was dreadfully wrong.

'What's the matter?' She parked the pushchair and rushed to Edie's side, feeling terrible now for being out so late. 'Is it Anatoli?'

'No . . .' Edie began to sob, her shoulders shaking, as if Greta's arrival had released her feelings. 'He's not been well all day, but he's asleep . . . It's the others. Listen!'

Raised voices came from upstairs, David shouting, distraught, shrieking and sobbing from Gila, then moments of silence between as if the raw pain of each outburst was forced out, jagged, not flowing.

'Oh God,' Greta said.

'It's been awful,' Edie wept. 'I don't know how we got through the day. Gila barely said a word, she was so down and closed in on herself, and I could see David was getting more and more upset and not knowing what to do. He's so hurt and she's in terrible pain . . . I just don't know how to help them . . . And my poor Anatoli's been so sick and wretched . . .'

'I'm sorry I went out,' Greta said miserably. 'I've been no help.'

'No – you've got to see your family. I'm glad you went.' Edie rallied herself. There were more sounds from upstairs. 'Look, let's go in the kitchen and make a cuppa. I can't interfere. They need to do this on their own.'

Chapter Fifty-Seven

They made tea and sat drinking it at the kitchen table. About twenty minutes passed. Edie asked Greta about her day, but all the time they were tensed, listening for sounds from upstairs.

'Won't they wake Anatoli?' Greta said.

'No, I don't think so.' Edie, all nerves, kept chewing at the ends of her fingers. 'He's weak – I could scarcely rouse him to get him to have a drink. I'll go and see in a minute.'

A moment later she said, 'I don't know if I'm doing the wrong thing. Maybe I should go up there and see if I can help ... I don't want to interfere – I mean it's high time they had it out, but Gila seems so ... Well, I don't think she's very well. But she won't hear of having a doctor.'

Greta stared at the pale blue top of the table. She thought she heard a door open and close upstairs and things seemed to have quietened.

Then they heard someone coming downstairs, and a moment later David appeared. He looked exhausted, and distraught. Edie got to her feet immediately.

'Oh love, how is she? Are you all right?'

David sank down at the table. He seemed stunned and his face was pale, dark rings round his eyes. The sight of him moved Greta desperately, but she wondered if they would rather talk in private.

'Look, I'll go, shall I? See to Francesca?'

'No, stay – please.' David spoke with such conviction that she sank back down, glowing with gladness at his including her, even in such a sad situation.

'She says she's going to sleep.' David wiped his hands over his face. 'She's getting ready for bed.'

'Here, love—' Edie poured tea for him, stirred in sugar. 'Get that down you.'

Greta watched David's expression as he took the mug of tea and cupped his hands round it as if longing for comfort. He looked so hurt and bewildered and boyish all at once, and her heart seemed to melt at the sight of him.

'I just don't know what to do,' he said, staring ahead of him. 'What to do, what to say, how to be with her. I can't handle it. I've no idea who she is any more.'

'She's in a terrible state, love,' Edie said gently. 'I really don't think you should be trying to manage it all on your own any more. Why don't you let me call a doctor – not just anyone. We could ask Martin to come and see her . . .'

David was shaking his head. 'She won't. I've begged and begged her.'

'But why?'

'Her mother. She's got an obsession, a phobia about doctors of any kind, but especially anyone in the psychiatric line. She's got a history – she's not an easy woman at all – well, you remember.' Edie had met Rachel Weissman several times when she and Anatoli had visited Israel.

'Yes – she always struck me as nervy,' Edie admitted. She had told Greta that she found Gila's mother quite strange and abrasive.

'She had some kind of depressive illness in her

youth, before they left Germany. I gather she was put in an asylum there for a time. I don't know what happened but she's been terrified of anything like that ever since.'

'Poor thing,' Greta said.

'She hasn't had an easy life altogether.'

'There can't be many people in Israel who have,' Edie said.

'She wants to go home.' David brought out the words in a hard, flat voice.

'What – straight away?' Edie did not manage to hide her relief completely. 'Have you told her – that you want to stay?'

'That's what set it all off.' He put his head in his hands for a second, then looked up at them again. 'I can't go back there, I'm certain of that now. Not after all this. But she won't hear of staying.' There was an angry edge to his voice as he said, 'She wants to go home, and she says she doesn't care if I go with her or not.'

'But if she went,' Edie probed him gently, 'you'd have to go with her, surely?'

David leaned back and gave a long, sad sigh.

'Not necessarily.'

There was little noise from Francesca in the pushchair, and Greta went out to take her up to bed.

'Shall I look in on Anatoli?' she asked Edie.

'Yes love, if you would.'

All seemed quiet at the back of the house where David and Gila's room was. She imagined Gila in bed, her hair startlingly black against the pillow and her sad face.

Anatoli was in a deep sleep, on his back. Greta straightened the sheet, caressing it over Anatoli's chest. He looked so old now, especially in sleep, his cheeks sunken, hair thinner, and his left arm, outside the bedclothes, pitifully bony. He had had a sick, draining day. She wanted to stroke his head, his arm, she loved him so much, but she didn't want to disturb him.

'Don't die, you lovely man,' she whispered, tears filling her eyes. 'Don't leave us!'

In a turmoil of feeling she knelt by his bed and let the tears run down her face. She didn't know who she was crying for most, for Anatoli, for David and Gila's pain and grief, for herself, knowing that this man who had been like a loving father to her was slowly dying.

Wiping her eyes, she got up and went downstairs again. David and Edie were still at the table.

'Everything all right?' Edie asked anxiously, seeing her tear-stained face.

'Yes – he's still fast asleep.' She went to the sink. 'I'll just wash up the cups before I go up.'

'I'd better turn in,' David said. 'Thanks – both of you.' When Greta turned to say goodnight, he was looking across at her with a slight smile.

'Goodnight,' she said softly, and watched him leave the room, feeling as if he was taking her heart with him.

As Greta rinsed the cups, Edie sat in silence, pulling her hairpins out until her long hair untwisted down her back. Slowly she began to tie it in a loose plait. She had just begun saying something when the kitchen door burst open and David appeared again. He looked frantic.

'She's not there – in bed. I don't know where she is – she's gone!'

The first thing that came to them was to run out of the house after her.

'Where would she go?' Edie panted as she and Greta hurried along together, following David towards town. The road was deadly quiet and ice crystals could be seen forming on the pavement in the light from the street lamps. Greta felt the cold air stinging her nostrils. After a few moments she and Edie slowed to a walk.

'I s'pose there's no point in us all running after her in the same direction,' Edie said. 'If anyone can catch her up it's David. Unless she's gone a different way. What can she be thinking of? There are no trains running or anything.'

'I don't s'pose she's thinking straight at all,' Greta said.

'Perhaps we should have gone another way?' Edie stopped. 'I mean where on earth would you go? She could have gone in any direction. She doesn't really know the way because she's hardly been out since she's been here ... Honestly, the state she's in, I knew we should have phoned Martin ...'

They decided to walk back and check whether Gila had already returned home, or was wandering nearby in distress. After they had walked some way along the deserted streets of Selly Oak, they went back to the house. Edie ran up to the bedroom, but came down shaking her head.

'No sign of her. I'm going to call the police. And I think we'd best wait here in case she comes back.'

Edie telephoned the police station, and together she and Greta relit the fire in the living room. Edie went to look in on Anatoli, and then they sat up to wait.

'It's awful, this sitting, isn't it?' Greta said as they sat staring into the flames. All she could think of was David, her mind following his frantic quest through the streets. 'She could be anywhere by now.'

The clock on the mantelpiece ticked deafeningly. The hour from eleven to midnight seemed to take three. As the hand moved round to half past midnight, Edie said,

'Look, love, you go to bed and I'll wait up. There's no point in us all being exhausted is there?'

Greta shook her head. 'I'm not leaving you with all this! I couldn't sleep if I tried!'

As they waited the silence took on the echoey strangeness of the small hours of night, when tiny noises sound exaggerated and you can start to imagine things, so that at first, when they heard footsteps on the fine gravel outside the house they both thought for a moment they were imagining things.

'Hark—' Edie held her hand up. 'What's that?'

They both rushed to the front door. David and Gila came in out of the cold. As they came through the door he automatically put his hand on her shoulder to guide her and Greta saw her shake him off violently. Gila had clearly been weeping and seemed completely overwrought. Not saying a word to anyone, of either explanation or apology, she tore up the stairs.

'Right,' Edie said. 'That's quite enough of all this. I'm telephoning Martin Ferris – now.'

418

Chapter Fifty-Eight

It was comforting to hear Dr Ferris's car braking in front of the house. His tall, lean figure gave off such a sense of calm and reliability.

'She's going to be so angry,' David was saying agitatedly as he led Martin Ferris into the living room. He was beside himself with worry. 'She doesn't trust anyone, even if I say it's a friend.'

'Well, it's got past anything we can deal with, love,' Edie said.

Martin Ferris took off his hat and coat and laid them on the arm of the sofa. 'You think she's awake?'

'We've heard her moving about,' Edie said. 'This is ever so good of you, Martin. I'm so sorry – Christmas and everything.'

'Not at all. You say she ran off?'

'She went to the station at Selly Oak,' David explained. 'For some reason she thought it would make sense to follow the railway line into town. Luckily it's quiet, of course. She got as far as the university and she was scared, I think, and came up on to the road again, so I caught up with her eventually.'

'Good Lord. I'd better go up and take a look. Will you warn her I'm here?'

'I'll come up,' Edie said.

Greta found herself alone with David.

'Oh God,' he said wretchedly, turning to face the

fire. 'She'll never forgive me for this.' He stood leaning on the mantelshelf, looking down into the glowing coals. After a silence, he said, 'How can you be so close to someone, love them so much, then be so utterly far away as if they're a stranger?'

'I don't know,' Greta said helplessly. 'I've never had much luck with any of it really.'

David turned to her, managing a faint smile for a moment. 'Well, that's honest, anyway.' Distractedly he looked up at the ceiling. 'Dr Ferris is such a good man. I hope she can see that.'

Edie came back looking solemn. 'Well, he's in with her. She didn't want to see him, but as he was standing there she didn't have a lot of choice. I told her he's a family doctor, nothing else.'

There was nothing for it but more waiting. The clock gave a faint chime on the quarter hour, half past two, a quarter to three. After half an hour, Martin Ferris came down. David sprang to his feet.

'It's all right,' Martin held his hand up. 'I've sedated her, with her permission, of course. She'll sleep now. I know it's ridiculously late, but can we talk for a few moments?'

'I'll make more tea,' Edie said, and Greta made as if to help.

'It's all right, you stay there, love.'

There didn't seem to be any question of anyone going to bed. They were all far too keyed up. Greta sat quietly as the men talked.

'I just want to get a few things straight in my mind.' Martin Ferris sat down on the other side of the fireplace, facing David. Greta was always struck by the length of his limbs, the boniness of his face, which was fascinating rather than handsome.

'My first thought when I saw her was that she could do with a spell in hospital: somewhere like Holly-moor . . .'

David started to shake his head, looking aghast.

'I know she has a horror of anywhere psychiatric. But you do realize she's in rather a bad way, don't you? I mean I should expect both of you to be, after all that's happened.'

Martin gave David a long, penetrating look. Greta remembered Janet and Edie's conversations about their men, the nightmares, all they had seen in wartime haunting them. Martin knew exactly what he was talking about.

'Tell me—' He leaned back the chair. 'It would help to know a bit more about your wife's background: mother, father, past events. The family moved to Israel – from where?'

'Germany,' David said. 'Düsseldorf.'

'Ah,' Martin Ferris said meaningfully. 'Does that mean . . . ?'

'Oh, no!' David corrected him. 'They came before the war. No – they hadn't been through any of the camps or anything. They made *aliyah* in 1933, went to live in Tel Aviv when her mother was about seven-teen. The father was an architect, Bauhaus trained. They could see what was beginning to happen under Hitler and they had thought of emigrating anyway. Gila's mother got married – to an engineer – just as the war broke out, and had Gila within the year. Her husband was killed two years later, working on a site in Haifa. A building collapsed. Gila's mother was left alone with her, of course. She decided she'd like to be part of kib-butz life so she went to Hamesh – the kibbutz where we met – just after it started in 1950. Gila grew up there.

421

Her mother is not the easiest of women. She has bouts of depression, paranoia at times, but I think her troubles had already started before.' He told Martin about the depression, the spell in the asylum in Düsseldorf.

Martin nodded. 'So there's an unstable mother . . . Any signs before this, would you say?'

David hesitated. He thought of the night he had come home from Sinai, of other times when her emotions had to him seemed overwrought. He had put his reactions down to his Englishness, his maleness. Gila had always had a fiery temperament. 'I'm not sure. Maybe.'

'And then this double blow – the bombs, your son . . .'

'She was pregnant at the time. We lost that child as well.'

David spoke abruptly and pain flickered in his face. The conversation put Martin Ferris in the role of a father confessor, and it was stirring up David's emotions, as if he would have liked to let go and weep.

'Yes, I know,' Martin said gently. He sat quietly for a moment, obviously thinking.

'She seems very clear that she wants to go home.'

'She hates it here. I thought it would give us a chance to get away from it all, to see things afresh . . .'

'But instead it has been just one more shock, another disorientating change?'

As he spoke Edie came in with a tray of tea and started to hand the cups round.

'Yes,' David said. 'I can see now that it's been too much for her. Now it feels as if she is like an animal in a trap, trying to escape.'

'And you?' Martin stirred his tea. 'How has it been for you?'

David looked down and Greta could see him fighting his emotion again.

'Important,' he said. 'Yes.' He looked up suddenly, almost defiantly. 'I can't go back there.' He gave a small shudder. 'No – it's tainted now – all of it.'

Martin gave him a long sad look.

'You know you'll have to let her go?' he said. 'I don't think it's psychiatric treatment she needs. She needs lots of time to grieve in a place where she feels at home. And Israel is her home . . .'

The words 'even if it can't be yours', and all that implied, were left unspoken.

Chapter Fifty-Nine

No one tried to talk Gila out of going home. It was obvious that there was no point, and the fact that Martin, a doctor, said she ought to go convinced all of them that it was the right thing for her health.

It was only David who really knew that the marriage was over, yet he even tried at first to convince himself that things could get better.

'You'll see,' Edie said. 'When she's gone back and had more time to recover, you can go and join her again, love, perhaps start again – have another baby . . .'

Once she knew she was going back to Israel, Gila was a little calmer, and they saw glimpses of the sweet-natured woman she could be when well and happy. But she was very distant from them and showed no signs of affection to David or sense that he was her husband and part of her future – or even of her past. It was as if she had cut the past off completely, could not bear anything to do with it, and all she could think of was getting on the next plane to Tel Aviv.

The day she left, when David was to travel to London with her, Greta saw Gila for the last time, in the hall as Greta was putting on her coat and scarf to go to work.

'I hope you have a good journey,' she said, speaking slowly and clearly. She had never got to know Gila at all, and could not think of anything else to say, except, 'It has been very nice to meet you.'

Gila reached out a bony hand and said mechanically, 'Thank you. It was nice to meet you also.'

And she walked off towards the kitchen. Greta watched the heartbroken, scrawny woman moving away from her and felt such pity for her, but she felt so sad for David as well. The picture of them when they were first married, which Edie kept propped on the mantelpiece, showed them looking so happy and hopeful together.

They were on her mind all day at work, the sadness of it weighing her down. She imagined David waving goodbye to Gila at Heathrow airport, how awful it must be. Her mind was with him every step of the way, as if she wanted to hold his hand and give comfort.

'Wakey, wakey – I'm talking to you!' a voice said close to her ear, and she jumped. One of the other women was standing beside her, grinning. 'That's the third time I've said it. Must be love!'

'Oh no – it isn't that,' Greta snapped. 'Don't be stupid.'

But the woman's words burned in her. How stupid *she* was! Was that it, the way David brought her alive every time they were in the room together, the way her mind flew to him constantly and she lay awake thinking of him, longing for him, the way he had become the most important person in her life apart from Francesca, even more important, she realized with a shock, than Anatoli? Was this how it was: the way her heart reached out for him, the feeling that she would do anything for him to make him happier? Could that be it – she was in love with David?

David, who would never look at her because she was not good enough for him, David, who was married, and confused and heartbroken?

The hopelessness of her feelings made her angry and wretched all day. How could she have been so stupid as to fall in love with David of all people? Who did she think she was, a factory hand having stupid dreams about him when he was a doctor?

When she left that day, walking out towards the men's grounds, she met John Foreman. She had a feeling he had been waiting for her but she wasn't sure. But John was not one to pretend.

'Hello!' he said enthusiastically. 'I was hoping I'd meet you. Came this way specially.'

He was a tall lad, about her age, she guessed, with thick, wavy blond hair and blue eyes.

'Oh, hello, John,' she said. Seeing him did cheer her up a fraction, and she liked his straightforward friend-liness towards her.

'You off home?' he said, walking beside her.

'Yes – done for the day.'

'Only I was wondering if you'd come out one night – for a drink or to the flicks or summat. Or you could come and hear us play if you like.' John was in a band called the Banana Boys, one of the many hopefuls playing in pubs all over Birmingham.

Greta hesitated for a second. She didn't really want to go at all. She should be at home with Francesca and Anatoli, with ... No, not with David. A surge of determination passed through her. She managed to smile at John.

'Thanks. That'd be nice. When were you thinking of?'

John's face broke into a delighted grin. 'You serious? I thought you'd turn me down! Well how about tomorrow? We're playing over at the Greyhound.'

They arranged a place to meet and John said, 'That's great – I'll look forward to it! See ya tomorrow, Greta!'

He almost skipped away and his enthusiasm made her smile for a moment. Above all though she felt she'd done something right, and she felt lighter for it. She had to get David out of her mind and this seemed a way to do it. John seemed a nice enough bloke, a bit of a laugh. And these days a laugh was certainly something she could do with.

She walked into the house smiling and heard Francesca call 'Mamma!' as she opened the door and saw her come toddling out to greet her.

Edie followed her, smiling bravely, but Greta could see the tension in her.

'Did they get off all right?' she asked, scooping Francesca into her arms.

'Yes. She should be on the plane by now. I expect David'll be making his way back.'

Greta didn't hear David arrive home because she was with Anatoli. The days when he got up were becoming fewer now. They were keeping the pain at bay with morphine. She tried to spend time with him every day, reading to him or talking as he lay propped on his pillows. He was always pleased to see her and she treasured every moment as he grew thinner and more sick.

'Hello, my dear,' he greeted her. 'You're looking very cheerful today.'

She could see that this pleased him. There had been a lot of sadness in the house.

'Ah well.' She put down the tray of tea she had made and settled on the chair by his bed. 'I got asked out on a date!'

'Aha!' Anatoli said, with great interest. 'And who is the young prince who has dared to request such a thing?'

Greta laughed. 'His name's John – he works in the Chocolate Block. Seems nice enough – I don't know him yet, really. He plays the guitar in a band.'

'Hmm – *nice enough*?' He teased. 'I'm not sure that's good enough for you my dear. Whoever goes out with you needs to be very special.'

'Well, we'll see, won't we? P'raps he will be special. Now here's your tea – and would you like another chapter?'

'Ah yes – we had reached the crucial moment, hadn't we? I have been trying to puzzle it out, but he has defeated me, as ever.'

She set off reading another chapter of their latest Maigret mystery. Greta was enjoying the story herself and Anatoli usually listened with great attention, trying to guess what would happen next. At the end she put the bookmark back in, closed the book and looked up at him, smiling.

But instead of looking back at her with his usual twinkling expression, Anatoli's head was lolling to one side on the pillow and his eyes were closed. Greta froze. She stopped breathing in those seconds. He looked . . . Surely he couldn't be . . . ? His face was so sunken and lacking expression! Heart pounding, she got to her feet, groping for his pulse. Then she heard him breathing, and her own breath flowed again. He had fallen asleep, that was all!

She watched him for a moment, with sad tenderness. He had never once fallen asleep before while she was reading. Though she kept trying to deny that he was getting worse, she knew this was a sign. She drank in the sight of him. Here he was, still alive! How many more days would she see him for? Tears pricked her eyes as she left the room.

Downstairs she wanted to find Edie for comfort. She would not tell her what had happened. She just wanted to be with her and do ordinary things like making the dinner in the nice bright kitchen.

But she came upon another sad sight. Edie and David were sitting at the kitchen table, her arm round his shoulders, David had his face in his hands and both of them were crying. Edie looked up at her, tears running down her cheeks.

'Oh, sorry,' Greta said, blushing.

She went to leave but Edie said, 'No, it's all right love, come in. David's just got in. You don't mind, do you, Davey?'

David took his hands from his face, which was also wet, and he seemed rather stunned, but not embarrassed or angry that she had come in and found them like that.

'No, come in, it's OK,' he said, wiping his face. 'I've just got back from London. It's been a hell of a difficult day.'

'I bet it has,' Greta said. She stood feeling helpless for a moment, so frantic at the sight of his distress that all her determination earlier in the day was completely lost. 'Look – have you both had some tea? I made Anatoli some, but no one else was about.'

'No, we'd love some, wouldn't we?' Edie said.

Greta took refuge in making tea but she was full of emotion.

'It was a bit delayed,' he was saying. 'I felt I should wait with her but I think both of us were desperate to get the goodbyes over with. In the end she just said, "Look, Doodi..." His voice broke again when he used her nickname for him. '"Please, you just go. Let me be alone." So we just sort of held one another and said goodbye as if this was almost normal and I would be home in a few days, like when I was in the army. And she turned and went.' He was crying as he talked. 'I just watched her walk down the corridor until I couldn't see her any more. And all I could think about was the first time I ever saw her at Hamesh, out in the fields, and how she was – fierce and girlish at the same time...' He stopped, unable to speak for a moment. 'That's what kills me – that we are estranged is bad enough, but the real thing is, what has happened to her. What this has all done to her.... So sad, and thin and far away, when she was so alive before ... And I wonder how much of it is me, what I have done to her...'

Greta spooned tea into the warmed pot, hardly able to see for her own tears as she listened to him pouring out his grief.

'Oh, love, of course it's not you!' Edie said. 'It was the explosions, the shock, losing Shimon and the baby. And there's instability in the family – you've always known that. How can any of that be your fault?'

'But it wasn't just that – it was before. Things were

wrong, as if everything was slipping away from me and we were becoming strangers — and I couldn't seem to stop it. What happened just made it worse. It finished us off . . .'

Greta took the tea to the table and sat down.

'Thanks, love,' Edie said. 'You're a gem, you are.'

David thanked her too, and took in the fact that she was crying as well. She saw the surprise on his face, and then for a second, through his tears, he smiled.

Chapter Sixty

'Well, it's time I went in,' Greta said, as they reached the gate of the Gruschovs' house. 'Thanks, John – I've had a really nice time.'

It was her third date with John in the past two weeks. Twice she'd stood in smoky pubs tapping her feet to songs by the Banana Boys and admiring John's guitar playing. He looked good on stage with his thick blond hair and he moved well. And tonight they'd been dancing in town, leaping about to the Hippy Hippy Shakes, the Beach Boys, the Beatles ... Greta had not had so much fun in a long time, not young people's sort of fun! She and John had grinned with pleasure at each other on and off all evening. She was still tingling all over and could feel her cheeks glowing in the cold air. John was an easygoing companion and they'd chatted on the way home in a relaxed way about work and their families. But now things felt awkward.

Greta wanted to get inside. She liked John, he was good company and up until now he had behaved like a gentleman, but she could see he was rapidly becoming besotted with her.

'I hope we can do this again soon,' John said, moving closer. They were in the shadows of the tall bushes by the gate.

'Yes, I'm sure we can. Thanks,' Greta said, trying to step away. Things were moving more quickly than she wanted. She remembered the way she had thrown herself at boys before, the humiliating disaster with Dennis Franklin, and she didn't want a repeat of that. She didn't feel anything special for John. He was just nice, that was all, and not at all full of himself like Joe, the lead singer in the band. Maybe something could develop . . . But he was in more of a hurry.

'You're so lovely, Greta.' His voice turned low and seductive and he put his arms round her. The light from the street lamp lit up the top of John's blond hair, while the rest of his face was in shadow. 'I don't think I can stand it if I go home without kissing you.'

Greta found herself up against the gatepost, John pressed against her, his tongue pushing into her mouth. She was full of confused feelings. It was nice to be kissed again and feel desirable after all this time! She felt herself begin to respond, but thoughts came into her mind like a cold shower. This didn't feel right. It almost felt as if she was being unfaithful, which was ridiculous – unfaithful to who? But she wasn't going to throw herself at him, or lead him on – she was determined!

Managing to free her arms she pushed against the wooden gatepost so that John let go, startled.

'What's up?' he asked huffily. 'I thought you liked me.'

'I do,' she said, straightening her clothes. 'But let's not go too fast, eh? We hardly know each other, and I've got a kid, remember? I can't just muck about. It's been a nice evening, John, and I've really enjoyed myself – thanks.'

She thought for a moment he might turn nasty as she had rejected him, but he was too nice a bloke for that.

'All right,' he said dismally. 'Sorry – I was pushing it. I just like you – a lot. It doesn't bother me that you've got a little girl.' He turned away as if he was going to walk off, then looked back at her. 'So d'you want to come out again?'

'Yes,' Greta said, relieved. 'That'd be nice. Somewhere quiet maybe, where we could have a chat. Shall we just go for a coffee or something?'

John shrugged. 'All right. Tomorrow?'

'Can't tomorrow. Day after? And John—' She went a bit closer. She wanted to like him, she wanted to fall in love. She just couldn't force it to happen. 'Don't get the hump will you? I just want to do things right.'

John looked appeased. He leaned over and kissed her cheek. 'All right then. See ya.'

'Why don't you come out with us – both of you?' she asked Pat the next day on the way to work, their breath white on the bitterly cold air. Pat had finally admitted that a young man from her church was paying her attention.

'Oh, I don't know . . .'

'You can't just stay in for ever,' Greta encouraged her.

'Yes I can – I think being an old maid will suit me,' Pat said ruefully. She hammed it up, pushing her hands further into her coat pockets and walking with a stoop. 'I'll just stay on the shelf, thank you very much!'

'You don't mean that. Come on – you don't have to *marry* him, do you? Just come out and have some fun. You could come and hear John's band – they're a bit like the Beatles really.'

Greta was keen to be out as many evenings as possible at the moment. She had to get over her crush on David, and stop kidding herself. David had taken Dr Ferris's advice and gone off walking for a few days on his own. He came back saying he had taken the train to Aberystwyth, where he had been on holiday as a teenager, and walked along the coast, beside a rough winter sea. Edie told her that David also said he was thinking about going to finish his medical training somewhere else. New York, he thought, or Boston. When she heard this, Greta felt a massive stab of pain, and then a surge of relief. She was nothing to him and she could close the door on this painful, confusing time and stop thinking about him all the time. She told herself it was only because she felt sorry for him that she felt so much. There wasn't anything else. She could see that Edie wanted to argue, to beg David to stay because she needed him, but she managed to be selfless and kind, and listened to all he had to say.

So that was that, Greta knew. He would soon be gone. She spent as much time as she could with Anatoli, but tried to keep out of Edie's and David's way. There was so much pain in the house that sometimes it was easier to go out and get away from it.

Pat's date turned out to be an earnest young man called Andrew.

'I put my foot in it straight away by suggesting we go to the pub,' Greta told Edie later over a late-night cup of cocoa. 'Course he doesn't drink, so we went into town to a coffee bar instead. I mean, he's nice enough, but I think Pat needs someone with a bit more life in him.'

'And what about John?' Edie asked with a smile. 'You seem to be seeing quite a bit of him.'

'Oh yeah – he's nice, John is,' she replied, carefully.

'I know it's selfish of me,' Edie said, looking up at her rather shamefaced, 'but I hope in a way he's not *too* nice. If he is, he'll take you away from us, won't he?' Her eyes filled with tears suddenly. 'Oh, I'm sorry. What with David – and Anatoli, it feels as if everyone's going. And poor Peter! He knows his Dad's poorly and he asked me yesterday if he's going to die. He's never said that before.'

'Oh dear,' Greta said, feeling a lump come into her own throat. She tried not to keep thinking about how sick Anatoli was, and the reality of it hit her afresh and was almost unbearable.

Very soon it got worse. One night, when she had been out with John, Pat and Andrew, she let herself into the house after John had walked her home and insisted on kissing her goodnight. These days she felt she had to let him. She couldn't just keep stringing him along. She crept in, trying not to disturb anyone, but as soon as she was in the hall she realized things were not quiet in the house. A door opened and closed upstairs, letting out the sound of men's voices.

While she was changing into her nightclothes in her room, she heard someone leave the house. There was a tap on her door.

'Gret? Sorry to bother you,' Edie said. She was trying to speak normally but Greta could tell there was something terribly wrong.

Edie came and sank down on the edge of her bed.

Greta didn't need to ask what had happened. Edie started to shake, and the tears came.

'He's been in such pain. It just came on really bad, all of a sudden. He couldn't speak with it, he was just moaning – it was terrible. I had to call Martin – he's so good, he said to call any time – and he's given him a higher dose . . .'

Greta sat beside Edie, an arm round her shoulders while she cried in shock and grief, her loose hair falling forward.

'Martin said he may have to go into hospital. He said he knew we'll do our best to look after him at home but that at the . . .' She caught her breath, weeping again. 'At the end, it'll be too much for us. He'll need drugs and proper nurses and everything . . . Oh God, it was awful. He was in agony. I've never seen him like that . . .'

A tight ball of pain formed inside Greta. Anatoli had hung on so long, so much without complaint, that sometimes it had been easy to forget just how ill he was, what a short time he might have left.

'Oh—' Edie remembered. She sat up, pushing her hair back. 'And today there was a call – from his daughter Caroline. She's coming to see him on Saturday.' She added bitterly, 'It's a good job she didn't leave it any longer.'

Greta answered the door to Anatoli's daughter when she arrived at midday on Saturday, having travelled up from Brighton.

'I don't know if I want to see her,' Edie said. 'The way I feel at the moment I'm just as likely to speak out of turn.'

'What's she done?' Greta asked, puzzled.

Edie sighed. 'Ignored him for years on end. Seems to have some grudge against him about her mother.'

All Greta knew about Anatoli's daughter, Caroline Brewer, was that she was thirty years old, married and a music teacher. But she had built her up in her mind into an imperious little madam who would put on airs with them all. How could anyone reject someone as lovely as Anatoli? she wondered. Feeling fiercely protective of him, she was prepared thoroughly to dislike his daughter.

When she opened the door she found herself looking at a slender young woman with her dark brown hair taken back in a ponytail and a thin face with a serious expression. She was wearing a brown tweed coat with the collar turned up against the cold, and she looked nervous.

'Hello—' Her voice was posh and clipped. 'Have I come to the right house? I'm Caroline Brewer. I believe my father lives here.'

'Yes,' Greta said. 'This is it. Come in.'

She stood back for Caroline to pass.

'And you are?' she enquired.

'Greta Sorenson – I lodge with Edie and Anatoli.'

Just then Edie appeared from upstairs. Greta saw her force a smile on to her face as she came and shook hands, not hiding away after all.

'You must be Caroline. I'm Edie. It's good to meet you at last. Would you like a cup of tea or coffee?'

Caroline looked very uncomfortable in this new situation. 'I think I'd better just go and see my father, if you don't mind. Perhaps we could have some coffee . . .'

'Yes, of course,' Edie said. 'Let's take your coat and I'll show you up to him.'

'You take the tray up,' Edie said to Greta when she'd come down again. 'I don't think I can stand it.'

Greta carried up a tray with coffee and biscuits on it and tapped on the door of Anatoli's room. His daughter opened it, then retired to her chair by the bed.

'Ah, come in, my dear,' Anatoli said. His voice was so weak and reedy that it wrung Greta's heart to hear it. 'Greta, have you met my daughter Caroline? Caroline, Greta is part of our household here – very much one of the family.'

'Yes, we've met,' Caroline said. Greta nodded in agreement as she put the tray down.

'Is there anything else you need?' she asked.

'No I don't think so. But I expect Caroline will stay and have some lunch with us, won't you?' Anatoli saw her hesitate. 'Perhaps we could have it up here?'

'All right,' Greta said. 'We'll bring you up some.'

The two of them were shut away together for two and a half hours, had coffee and lunch, while Edie and Greta got on with the day-to-day routine, both quietly in an agony to know what was passing between Anatoli and his long-lost daughter. Just after half past two they heard the door open and Caroline Brewer's voice as she came down, reclaiming her coat from the end of the banisters.

'I shall need to be on my way now,' she said. 'It's a long journey.'

'Yes, of course,' Edie said.

The young woman softened for a moment, and gave a brief smile. She was attractive, very intelligent-looking, Greta saw. 'Thank you for letting me come. I can't keep visiting, but I shall telephone him.'

'You're ever so welcome,' Edie said, rather gushingly, obviously relieved that things seemed to have gone well. 'Do come again . . .'

'No – I don't think I shall do that. But thank you.'

There was an awkward silence.

'Goodbye then.'

And they showed her out and went to the living-room window to watch her walk to the gate. Her hair was caught inside her upturned collar, her head down and she seemed lost in thought. She didn't look back.

Chapter Sixty-One

David had gone to Aberystwyth to try to clear his head.

'Give yourself a change of scene,' Martin had suggested. 'Get out in the countryside, climb some hills. That always helps.'

David had the utmost respect for Martin. He was a fellow medic and he had known the horrors of war. He was also prepared to help David in any way he could.

'I'm sure we could arrange for you to finish your training here in Birmingham if that's what you'd like. But give yourself some time to think. There's no need for a snap decision.'

David loved the calming effect of the sea, the way it offered a bigger perspective on things. He chose Aberystwyth because he had been there before in his teens with Edie and Frances Hatton at another time of deep confusion. He travelled there by train and booked himself into a guest house on the front, not far from where the three of them had stayed before. It had been summer that time, busy with swimmers and ice-cream sellers, the sky and sea meeting in a mauve haze as the sun sank in a late afternoon. Now the colours were all steel and ink, wet brown sand, mouse grey of the dryer rocks, plants forcing up through their crevices to be whipped by the wind.

He didn't take much notice of the boarding house. Anything would have done and it was simple and adequate. He ate, slept, went out. Above all, he walked, for hours and hours. For those five days he barely spoke to anyone. He welcomed the physical exhaustion of being on the move all day, feeling the muscles in his legs pull and strain, falling exhausted into bed at night. It reminded him of the army, except that here there were no orders, no drills, no burning heat – and this time he was entirely alone.

The physical tiredness was a relief because his mind was so fragmented. Concentration on any one thing for long was impossible. It was shock, Martin Ferris had told him. Shock upon shock. It would get better, with time.

'You may not be ready to study again yet,' Martin advised.

David had dismissed this at first. Of course he should study! It was his refuge, all he had left! But now he saw what Dr Ferris meant. When he tried to think about things his mind threw up a series of jagged, jumping images and he could not always fit them together. Past and present were a jumble.

Israel seemed far away, like a dream. Sometimes he stopped and sat hunched up in his raincoat at some vantage point looking over the wind-roughed sea, moist air beating at his face, and tried to remember Jerusalem on a July morning, the sounds and smells. He could bring it to mind of course, very easily. It was only weeks since he had left. But already it felt impossible that he had lived there for so long. It seemed astonishing that he spoke Hebrew fluently, that he had had a son, a family . . .

At first he would not think about Gila and Shimon.

Each time his thoughts led him to them he forced them away again, locking them into a strong-box in his mind that he would not visit. Instead, he thought about the army, the war, the hospital where he had worked. Sometimes he thought about Annaliese. He knew he must write to her. She would be so distressed to know what had happened and that he was not coming back. And these thoughts led him back to his wife, his son, and once more he shied away.

His mind was like a drunken butterfly, flitting and looping round to places where he didn't want it to rest.

He kept finding himself thinking about Greta Sorenson, the young woman sharing the Gruschovs' house. Why did his mind keep turning to her? She was so kindly, and they had known one another as children. She was as different from Gila as it would be possible to be. There was the colouring of course, her blonde, pink-cheeked looks when Gila was dark, exotic, volatile. But there was also that measured calm about Greta, her rounded, curving form moving round the house, her sweet yet inscrutable face and wide blue eyes. There was something about her which was both wholesome and powerfully, mysteriously, feminine. He found himself just watching her sometimes as she moved round the kitchen. She soothed him somehow by the quiet, inevitable way she got on with things. And by the way she listened to him and took him seriously. Sometimes he found himself longing for her to be here, sitting beside him. He was shocked by the thought. But then all his thoughts jolted him like shocks.

For those days in Aberystwyth he got up very early and walked before breakfast on the silent, colourless beach. In the evenings he went back to the guest house

443

after dark, ate his meal and fell into bed early, hoping to lose himself in sleep. But his dreams were less controllable than his waking mind, and each night that passed he dreamed more and more vividly. The night before he was due to go home, his son came to him very clearly, alive and whole, playing in the old apartment in Jerusalem. He was sitting on the floor of the living room, his curly head bent over his favourite toy, a car that Edie had sent to him. 'Broom, broom!' he was saying. He saw David and stood up, dressed in his shorts and little leather sandals.

'Abba, why have you taken so long?' Shimon asked impatiently. 'It's time for us to go!'

Full of beans, he came running towards David. In the dream the room was very long, not like the real one at all. Shimon ran and ran towards him, his arms outstretched. Just before he reached David there was a bang and Shimon disappeared. Nothing was left but a thin column of smoke rising from the rug on the floor.

David woke to the sound of his own groans and sobs. He could not shake the dream off. He was distraught, in an agony of loss and guilt. He could have stopped it, all of it. Surely he could if he had tried hard enough? He was racked by sobs.

A sharp tapping at the door brought him to himself. 'Are you all right in there? What's going on?'

'Nothing. I'm all right,' David managed to say.

He squeezed his eyes closed, mortified. For comfort he held the lumpy pillow in his arms and cried, more quietly, in the shadowy dawn.

All that day the dream tormented him and he could no longer shut down his thoughts. As he walked in the cold and rain his whole body was full of pain. His arms ached to hold his son. Should he go to Israel, he asked himself over and over again, find Gila, beg her to start again with him? But he knew it was no good. Her heart was closed to him. It had begun already in small ways, but the moment that bomb went off, killing their boy, destroying their unborn child, it had stripped them of a future. The way forward was closed, and David knew it was as true for him now as for her. He simply could not bear it. Never in his life would he set foot in Israel again. He must make a new life elsewhere.

That afternoon he sat on a bench at the end of the prom staring out at the sea. He had not eaten that day, had not thought about it, and the rain had come down and down. David had barely noticed, he was so taken up in the pain of his thoughts.

'You all right, son?'

An elderly man was standing in front of him under a black umbrella. His face was pink from the wind and he had kindly eyes. He had a dog, a terrier of some sort, on a lead.

'I'm sorry, what did you say?' David asked him.

'I said are you all right? You're soaked to the skin!'

'So I am.' David stood up, looking down at himself. He tried to speak sensibly to the man. He was being kind after all. 'Yes, I am rather wet. I've been walking but I'm going back to change now.'

'I should think so,' the man said. 'Catch your death . . .'

He felt it his duty to go and see the Leishmanns again when he got back. Sooner or later he would have to face them, and they had not heard what had happened. This time there was going to be no pretending.

Once more he was invited up to their sitting room and tea was served, this time by Esther Leishmann, who seemed more recovered than on his last visit. Some of her former vigour had returned. There were pastries and a chocolate gateau, which they ate with little silver forks.

David still regarded the Leishmanns as having a parental sway over him, even though he had not always followed their ideas for him to the letter nor had he always been in close contact with them. But he still came to them in the spirit of a son seeking consolation.

His news silenced them. Even the click of forks against bone china grew silent. Eventually Esther Leishmann said,

'So, she has gone back to Israel? Of course she is upset, she is prostrate with grief. And you are her husband. You are not going after her?'

'She doesn't want me to. She says it is over: the marriage is finished.'

'But no, how can that be?' Esther cried. 'She is mourning her son, she is overtaken by her suffering. But why end her marriage? You could see she was not well, the poor girl, so thin and shrunken like a little twig on a tree. But why leave her to grieve alone? You should be with her, Rudi! At her side as her husband!'

David was silent. He looked down at his plate, feeling a surge of anger against Esther Leishmann, who always thought she knew best how other people should be living their lives.

'What is your thinking, boy?' Joe Leishmann asked, more gently.

David looked up into his kindly face.

'Our son is dead. Our marriage is dead. I cannot go there again.'

'Not to Israel?' Joe's face wrinkled in pained confusion. 'But you have made your life there, surely?'

David had begun to shake his head but Esther Leishmann's voice cut in shrilly.

'Rudi, you must go back to Israel! You have made your *aliyah* – Israel is your home. You have trained as a doctor there and it is your job to stay, to build up the state. You are a Jew! It is your duty! What are you even thinking of, saying that you will not go back there? You simply must!'

David felt the rage break over him like a wave. He put his plate down and stood up.

Why must I? The words screamed in his mind. *Why must I go to Israel? Why should I stay there? It is your dream that I go, not mine! If you think Israel is so important then why don't you go there yourselves instead of sitting here in safety and telling everyone else what to do while their husbands and wives and sons and daughters are killed defending the state of Israel? You are Jews as well, so why is it me who has to fulfil your dreams – why don't you go instead of expecting me to do it for you?*

'I must be leaving,' he said quietly.

'David . . .' Joe tried to stop him. He could sense the trembling emotion in the young man beside him.

'You must rethink,' Esther was instructing him even as he was going through the front door.

'Goodbye,' David said abruptly.

And he left, storming away along the sedate Edgbaston street.

Why, he raged in his head, *do I have to spend my whole life worrying about whether I am living the right way as a Jew? Why can't I just live my life?*

He stopped suddenly, outside the Edgbaston Friends' Meeting House. Across the street stood an impressive dwelling which had belonged to George Cadbury, so there was a strong Quaker influence in the area. The Meeting House was a well-proportioned brick building. David felt its quiet peacefulness beckon him. He wished he could go inside and just sit, but it wasn't open. And seeing it somehow increased his sense of conflict.

He walked on, more slowly, sadly.

I am always going to be neither one thing nor the other, he thought. Maybe I have to move on from here. Go somewhere where there are more Jews, but which is not Israel.

It was then that he decided he would go to America. Surely he could fit in there? The New World felt like the answer to his old problems.

Chapter Sixty-Two

Anatoli was dying. There was no doubt about it now.

Even though the normal routines of life had to go on, everything was dominated by what was happening upstairs in the Gruschovs' house. Greta was glad to go to work, for the friendly faces on the line at Cadbury's and the cheerful normality of it all. But even when she was there a part of her mind was always with Anatoli, wondering how he was, whether he would still be there when she got home.

'I'm going to have to stay in nights at the moment,' she told John.

He tried to be understanding but was obviously put out.

'He's your landlord, isn't he?' he asked, puzzled.

'Yes, he is, but . . .' How could she explain how much more Anatoli had become for her? 'I want to help look after him.'

John's disappointment was nothing to her, not compared with doing everything she could for Anatoli.

He needed round-the-clock nursing now and they took turns to be with him, all desperate to keep him at home for as long as possible. But he was declining fast.

'It's almost as if he was waiting for Caroline to come before he could let go,' Edie said a few days after the young woman's visit. She and Greta were in the kitchen while David kept watch upstairs. She yawned, exhausted, sitting at the kitchen table. 'He never said much, but it must have meant the world to him.'

'They made their peace then?' Greta asked. She had not felt she could ask Anatoli what had happened. It was such a private thing about his past.

Edie sighed. 'Yes, they did. Anatoli's always said that the best part of his marriage was the last two or three years, after Margot became ill. He said he wasn't a very good husband before – not at home enough, too busy trying to make a success of his business, involved in too many other things ... Course, that's what the children remembered – that he wasn't there, that their mother was unhappy and lonely, and they blamed him.' She smiled gently. 'I think when he was younger he was much more uppity. Traditional man of the house, his word is law, that sort of thing. When things changed at the end I think they fell in love again, and it made him gentler. That's what he said. But Richard and Caroline had left by then and were getting on with their own lives. They just thought he didn't care about any of them.'

'I can't imagine him being like that,' Greta said.

'No, I know. But he was able to explain to Caroline. Richard's kept in better touch anyway. He seemed to think she had forgiven him – he was happier afterwards.'

Greta thought about Anatoli's 'wolf moods', as he called them, his depressed times. She had always thought they were because of the war and all that he had seen, but she wondered if it was to do with his family as well.

'I think he's made his peace,' Edie said.

*

The main prolem was keeping Anatoli's pain under control. Martin Ferris and another doctor called in regularly. Each time, they suggested moving him to hospital.

'He'd be cared for very well, you know,' Martin assured them on his latest visit.

'I suppose so,' Edie said, barely able to hold back her tears. 'But give us a little bit longer – please.'

At first Anatoli was awake for some of the time.

'Come and sit with me, my lovely girl,' he would say to Greta. She always called in as soon as she was home from work, and a happy, loved feeling would pass through her when he spoke to her.

One afternoon she popped in, gently pushing the door open to check whether he was awake. She had Francesca by the hand and the two of them crept to the bed. Francesca seemed to sense the solemnity of the room and was always quiet and still when they visited.

'Hello . . .' Anatoli's voice was very weak, but she could hear the affection in it. She felt her chest tighten, her grief dammed up inside at what had become of him. This was the most important thing now. She had put her feelings for David back in their place, she thought, even though the sound of his voice in the house seemed to vibrate through her each time she heard it.

Anatoli raised his head a fraction. 'Come here.'

'How're you feeling?' She sat by the bed, taking Francesca on her lap and holding Anatoli's thin dry hand. A slice of sunlight fell across one side of his face. His mop of hair was quite white now, and so sparse. Francesca watched him with wide eyes.

'Oh, not so bad,' he said, as he always did. 'You have been to work?'

'Yes – I've been back for a little while. It's nearly four o'clock.'

'Good girl.'

His speech was short now, as if distilled. He hadn't the breath for more. And he did not seem to want to take in much more from outside himself. It had been some time since she had read him any of his detective stories. He was moving beyond day-to-day interests. Life had shrunk to the feel of sheets, the view from his bed, chair, window, the pale blue of the walls, to the effort of bodily functions – yet a deep final journey was taking place inside him.

Greta felt a faint pressure on her hand and looked into his eyes, still bright in his face, which was now so thin that the cheekbones protruded like blades.

'You are quite grown up now,' he half whispered. 'You have changed. You're so beautiful ... Both of you.'

Greta's eyes filled with tears. 'So are you,' she said. She wanted to pour everything out, say, *You've given me everything, given me love and a sense of myself*, but the words wouldn't come.

Often she spent part of the night up beside his bed, in turn with the others, ready to answer any need.

The nights were mostly quiet, now that Martin was getting Anatoli's doses of morphine adjusted and he slept, well sedated. Whoever was with him sat in the chair close by and Greta found she often caught snatches of sleep and did not feel too bad the next day. At some point in the night Edie or David would come and take over. Janet, kind as ever, had also offered to come and help keep watch, but so far they were managing without her.

Greta had watched David turn back into a doctor as Anatoli grew sicker. She could see it was a relief for him to be able to work again in this way. He had lost so much, but at least he could still be a doctor. He would bend over Anatoli, his expression serious and absorbed, examining him with skilled eyes and hands. The sight always moved her, seeing his gentleness and seriousness.

If Anatoli was awake, he often looked up at David and said, 'You're a good boy. A good doctor.'

This would make David smile bashfully and say, 'Oh, I'm not so sure about that!'

That night, the three of them took turns as usual to keep guard by Anatoli's bed. David had taken over from Edie at one o'clock after snatching a few hours of sleep and Greta promised to get up in the small hours to relieve him. She had set an alarm, and unlike some nights when to wake was like struggling up from a well, she was alert the instant it went off. Wrapping up warmly with socks and slippers and an extra jumper under her dressing gown, she went along the landing to Anatoli's room. Now that he was so sick, Edie was sleeping in the little box room next door.

As usual there was a dim light burning on the table in the far corner of the room and David was sleeping in the armchair placed in front of it, his face deep in shadow. Although she made next to no sound, he stirred the moment she came in.

'Ah,' he whispered, stretching his long body, then

sitting up straight. He rubbed his eyes, seeming slightly bewildered, then smiled. 'I thought I was back on nights at the hospital for a moment! Is it that time already?'

'Nearly half past four.'

David looked across at Anatoli. Greta couldn't hear his breathing and she felt compelled to go and check that he was all right.

David gently read her thoughts. 'It's all right. He's been peaceful. He's still here.'

The night time and darkness seemed to take away her shyness, as if it made them equals. She realized that although she was still a bit in awe of David she no longer felt inferior the way she used to. He treated her as an equal, which made all the difference, and they were united in their affection for Anatoli. She stood looking down at the ravaged face of the man she loved so much, the sight of whom always made her want to weep now. Tears in her eyes, she whispered, 'He's been so brave, bless him.'

'Yes—' David came to stand at her side and they watched Anatoli together for a moment. His breathing was very shallow and he lay still, calmed by the morphine. Greta wiped her eyes, seeing David watching her, a tender expression in his eyes.

'You're good at nursing him. Very devoted.'

'He's been so good to me,' she said simply.

'He adores you.'

Greta covered her confusion at this compliment by saying, 'You should get some sleep.'

'I suppose I should. I feel wide awake though now, as if I've slept for hours!' He hesitated. 'Mind if I stay on for a bit?'

Her pulse quickened. Of course she didn't mind!

She couldn't think of anything she'd like more! Once more there was that feeling of being truly alive when he was near.

'Course. If you want.'

'You could go back to bed if you like,' he offered.

'No – I'm wide awake now too.'

David insisted that she have the chair and Greta, feeling very conscious that she was in her nightclothes, sat down, tucking her feet up as well. Of course they passed in the night sometimes in their night things, but this was different. Now she was sitting with David in this intimate way, he perched on a stool next to her. She saw that he had not got changed and was still dressed. He sat forwards, arms resting on his knees.

Greta could not think of anything to say. Day-to-day chatter seemed silly in the circumstances, and sitting there in silence didn't feel tense or wrong. She loved him being beside her, drank in the look of him, his strong, lean body and curling hair, in the lamplight.

He turned, and as he often did, just plunged in with a direct question.

'You've become so important to my moth— ... to Edie and Anatoli – it's obvious. How did you come to live here?'

Greta blushed with surprise. Surely Edie had explained to him by now? But then Edie didn't gossip, she let other people give whatever information they wanted to about themselves.

'Well, I was expecting Francesca, and Trevor, my husband, threw me out because he wanted to be with Marleen instead. So I had nowhere to go. Least, I could have gone to Mom's, but I didn't want to ... I came here one evening and they let me in and were so kind, and I've been here ever since.'

455

David took this in quietly.

'I've been too taken up with my own problems,' he said.

'Why shouldn't you be?' Greta leaned forward, passionately. 'You had the worst things possible happen to you. Your little boy and Gila and everything . . . I can't imagine how you must feel!'

David said nothing for a moment, just shook his head. 'It's all terribly confusing. Trying to make sense of any of it.'

The understatement of this tore at Greta's heart.

'I don't know who I am, half the time,' David said. 'When I left here for Israel I thought I had answered the question, am I David Weale, an English Quaker, or am I Rudi Mayer, an Israeli Jew? For a time it was clear, it was blended, even. Gila used to call me Doodi, you know? It all made sense. England was behind me – I'd found a new way to marry the two things together. I had things to fight for with others, building the state, all that idealism. But now . . .'

Greta frowned. 'D'you have to be one or the other? Can't you just be both?'

David gave a self-mocking laugh, putting his hands over his face. 'You're wonderful.'

'I just meant . . .'

'No – you're right. All this confusion – perhaps I'm just making an issue of something that doesn't need to be so complicated.'

Greta thought of Dennis, of how she had never known how to be with him, how to behave or who she really was.

'I do sort of know what you mean,' she said hesitantly.

After a pause, David said, 'D'you remember those

456

Christmases we had as children – always at Frances's, then New Year with Martin and Janet?'

'Course I do. They were always so kind to us. Especially Frances.'

'Always a lovely meal, and the games she got us playing, and a log fire and her enormous Christmas cakes!'

Greta smiled. 'Frances was the nicest lady I've ever met. Edie always says she owes everything to her – and she's been kind to me the way Frances was to her.'

'Yes – and to me. I owe Edie everything really.'

In the silence Greta sat up straighter, tucking her soft, furry dressing gown round her knees. David turned to look at her.

'You warm enough?'

'Yes thanks.' She was touched by the tender concern in his voice. Even the sound of his voice moved her, so deep and well spoken.

'Edie said you're thinking of going to America.' She tried to sound calm and detached, when she wanted to beg, *Don't go – please don't leave me!*

David looked away, down at the floor. 'Yes. I think it's the best thing. I've asked Martin to look into it for me. It seems like a good place to make a fresh start.'

'It will be very hard for her.'

'For Mum – Edie?' He sighed. 'Yes, I know. But at least she's used to visiting me in far-flung places. I'll most likely end up in New York. I feel I've got to put everything behind me – my marriage, Shimon . . .' His voice trembled a little as he named his son. 'And Israel – and England . . . God,' he shrugged, almost comically. 'I don't know.'

'I can't really imagine living anywhere else,' she said.

'No, but that's what's so nice about you. You know

457

where you are and where you come from. That's far more of a gift than you can imagine to a wandering Jew like me! You're like a tree that's been planted in the right place and knows how to grow . . .'

David had turned and was looking into her eyes. He reached for her hand. Greta almost held her breath. She was overcome by him talking like this to her, his seeing something in her. *I love him.* She thought. *God help me, I love him so much.*

'You're so sweet,' he said, and there was such longing in his voice.

'Am I?' she said stupidly.

For a few seconds they looked intently at one another. Greta slid her feet to the floor and moved forwards and she and David took each other in their arms. He held her tightly, but preciously, stroking her head, her back. She felt him let out a long, sobbing sigh.

'God, you're lovely. And you've no idea, have you?'

His lips searched for hers, kissing her passionately, and she returned his kisses, swept away by him, hardly believing it was happening.

'Oh God, sorry—' He pulled back, quickly moving back to the stool. 'I'm so sorry. I'm in such a muddle. I don't want to mess you about . . .'

'But you're not,' she protested. 'I . . .' She wanted to pour out how she felt, how much she loved him, how the very sight of him made her feel weak and full of tenderness, but now he had pulled away she couldn't, she was afraid. She ached for him to turn round and take her in his arms again.

'I must go away. I've done enough damage already,' he was saying.

But as he spoke there came a little sound from

458

across the room, a sort of gasping sigh. Both of them rushed across to Anatoli and Greta immediately saw David transform into a doctor again, casting a hurried professional eye over his patient.

'Something's changed . . .' His voice was tense. 'I could do with a bit more light . . .'

Greta hurried to switch on the overhead light. David bent over Anatoli, feeling his pulse, listening to his breathing.

'Right,' he said after a short time. 'This is it, I think. He really should be in hospital. I'm going to telephone Martin – and an ambulance.'

Chapter Sixty-Three

'Look after him. Oh please be careful with him!'

Edie's cry as the doors of the ambulance closed echoed in David's head. Never had he been so glad that he was a doctor as that night. He might not be able to work, not for a little while yet, but that was who he was: a doctor. In all his confusion he could retreat into his professional life where he could make some difference to events. There were procedures, drugs, scientific answers: not like the rest of life, which was a whirl of emotional confusion.

And yet as he watched the ambulance drive away with Anatoli inside, accompanied by Martin Ferris, the thought that kept coming was, *I kissed her, I love her, God in heaven, what have I done?*

Greta was the one to take Edie's arm and lead her back inside. Edie needed to dress before going to see her husband later. David watched the two women from behind, the small, yet somehow indomitable figure of his adoptive mother, supported by the pretty, self-effacing woman whom he could not keep from his thoughts, day after day.

Anatoli was taken to Selly Oak Hospital and never regained consciousness. Edie sat with him all day, holding his hand, talking to him, even though he could not answer, and just after eight o'clock that night, he slipped away.

'He left us very quietly,' Edie told them, once she was home. 'One moment he was breathing, and then he was gone.'

Over those days before the funeral all their care and attention was directed towards Edie, and also to Peter, who had lost his father so young. Francesca kept asking for ''Toli' as well, and David heard Greta explaining gently that Anatoli was not coming back.

He came upon her one afternoon in the sitting room, holding the little girl on her lap, her other arm round Peter's shoulders. The sight of them on the sofa in the pale afternoon light, this lovely woman with the children gathered to her, filled him with such longing that he said, 'Oh, sorry to interrupt,' and walked out of the room again.

He saw the hurt, confused look on her face when he treated her like a stranger, but he didn't know how else to behave. He was in a storm of confusion and he was disgusted at himself for not being in better control. Why had he kissed Greta the other night? How could he let himself behave in such a way when he was still married to Gila, who had only been gone a few weeks, and when he too was about to go away across the Atlantic? Was this love? Surely he could not love again so quickly! All this turmoil made him panic and he tried to keep his distance from Greta. He was polite, but avoided being alone with her. During those days after Anatoli's death that was not too difficult, as they were all looking after Edie. But once or twice he caught her looking at him with a sad, puzzled expression.

When he saw it he looked away. He did not know what else to do.

There was a service for Anatoli at St Francis's Church, on the Green in Bournville. The funeral was on a crisp March day, clouds flitting across the sun and the daffodils' stalks round the Green swaying in a stiff breeze.

David was impressed at how many people came, how many lives Anatoli had touched in his kind way – employees from the pharmacy, neighbours and well-wishers, as well as close friends like Janet and Martin. He looked around as people came in, aware of the stiff, unfamiliar collar of the shirt he had bought for the occasion. He found himself observing, weighing up his responses, his place in it all. Edie was beside him, with Greta the other side of her. She had insisted that Greta was like a daughter to her, and should be included as family. Edie was dressed not in black but in a pale blue suit, which looked lovely on her.

'Anatoli hated people wearing black at funerals,' she'd told them. 'He said someone's life ought to be celebrated, not have everyone there looking miserable.'

At the moment she was composed, aware of being on view, but David knew the depth of her loss and grief and was glad to be able to be beside her and support her.

She turned to him as the organ was playing softly, and whispered, 'The first time I set eyes on you, the night you were given to me – that was in a church!'

David nodded and gave a faint smile. He knew this, but hearing it still felt shocking. He had been handed to Edie one night during the Blitz when she was

462

working in a church sheltering those who were bombed out. Handed over, his young life, like a parcel.

Martin Ferris nodded at him as he came in, and Janet smiled sadly and came over to have a word with Edie. David was so grateful to Martin Ferris, and full of respect for him. As they went to sit down, David glanced back and saw Ruby, Greta's Mom, coming in with Mac beside her. Mac, stocky and strong-looking, was very spruce. Ruby, who was quite wide in the girth these days, was dolled up in a tight black outfit with an almost indecently high hem and was tiptoeing along the aisle, the way people seemed to feel they had to in churches. She wore a black hat with net over the brim, which gave her a rather rakish look, and was leaning on Mac's arm. David felt his mouth twitch with amusement. Talk about mutton dressed as lamb! There was something about Ruby that he liked, but never quite trusted. She had a big heart but seemed to him unruly in some way. The sight of her filled him with admiration for Greta. How different she was from her mother!

He faced the front again. He wanted to lean round and look at Greta. There was barely a second when he wasn't aware of her sitting there the other side of Edie. She was so upset at Anatoli's death, and he longed to comfort her but didn't know how without making a mess of it and hurting her even more.

At last the ceremony began and he was grateful to stand and struggle through a hymn, 'Lead Us Heavenly Father Lead Us', which he barely knew. As the service progressed, Edie and Greta were both weeping beside him and he fought the need to break down himself. What he most wanted was to be alone with Greta, to be in her arms, to hold her and be held himself.

After the simple funeral they left the church, he and

Greta supporting Edie each side, and everyone milled around outside in the cool, sunny morning. David felt a tap on his arm and broke away to speak to Martin Ferris.

'All right, old chap?' Martin asked.

'Not bad,' David said. 'He's such a loss though.'

'He is,' Martin agreed, looking up at the basilica-style church. Martin wasn't a man to discuss emotions. 'Fine church this.'

'Yes – very simple,' David said. 'I like it. It's not gloomy and cluttered like so many.'

Martin frowned. 'I thought old Anatoli was Ortho-dox – or a Quaker or something.'

'No, he gave up the Orthodox Church years ago,' David said. 'I think he went to the Friends to be with Edie – he was very open like that. But so far as I gather he went into the Church of England when he was young – tried to embrace all things English.'

'Except motor cars,' Martin chuckled. 'He was still driving that American box of tricks! It was one of the last things he said to me, with that little twinkle of his: "I never did get an English car. I think I might have left it a bit late in the day!"'

David laughed, fondly. He was just about to say, 'I must tell Greta that – she'll like it . . .' But he kept his mouth shut.

'You getting anywhere with your decisions about your training?' Martin asked. 'You know they'll have you here, at the medical school, soon as you like.'

David looked down for a moment, at his formal black shoes which made him look like a respectable English man.

'Yes—' He felt stronger saying it. 'I've decided. I'm going to go to New York.'

Chapter Sixty-Four

He had gone now, really gone.

After all the weeks of waiting for and dreading Anatoli's death, when it came it was more desolating even than Greta expected. Each night she lay curled up in bed, at last able to weep and weep, knowing that never again would she come home to Anatoli's presence in the house and the lovely sound of his voice saying, 'Come here, my dear. Come sit and read to me!'

What made everything infinitely worse was that David had announced soon after the funeral that he was going to leave for the USA. Edie was more prepared for this than Greta, and although she was grieved about it, knew that she had to let David go his own way. She had lived with him settled abroad before after all, and she would have to cope with it again.

But for Greta the fact that he was really going was devastating. After that night when she and David kissed she had stopped pretending to herself. Here was the man she had waited for all her life, whom she loved as no one before and whom she had thought loved her – he too was to be snatched away. The sound of his voice around the house, that lovely, deep, well-modulated tone which before had made her heart skip with happiness, was a cause of pain now. She was terribly hurt by him. Surely she had seen the force of love and passion in his eyes – she had not been mistaken?

And now he was snatching that away from her. It was far more cruel than if he had never said anything in the first place!

'Why does everyone I love get taken away?' she sobbed, night after night. It all brought back the wound of not ever knowing her father, Wally Sorenson, of death claiming him before he could ever meet his child. And death had taken her beloved Anatoli too young, too fast ... But it was not death which was claiming David. What made it agonizingly worse was that David was choosing to leave her behind.

Pat could see how unhappy she was, but Greta didn't feel she could say anything and let Pat believe that she was simply mourning Anatoli. She could not talk about David. It brought out all her insecurities: she felt rejected, ashamed. How could she have ever thought she would be good enough for someone like that? She had only a basic education, while he was a doctor. He had travelled and experienced so much and here was she, what had she ever done? And here was David, having so recently been bereaved after losing his little son, by his wife's breakdown and her leaving him. How dare she expect anything of him when he was so hurt and confused? No wonder he wanted to fly halfway across the world to get away!

At times when she was feeling stronger she stopped feeling sorry for herself and tried to understand. And then she saw his grief and confusion and tried to stop expecting anything from him. All she could do to save her own feelings, she saw, was to keep away from him. She had to make a life of her own that did not include David, however much she loved him.

*

She did not really want to see John Foreman again, but he was persistent. As soon as the funeral was over, he asked her out, repeatedly, and after a while she agreed. She had to do something, after all. And John was a nice man. Most of the dates she had with him were quite enjoyable and she liked the Banana Boys and being included with him and his friends. She had also discovered how much she liked dancing, and it was fun to go out to hops in various halls, put on some trendy clothes, like her miniskirt, all the rage now, and leap about to the Rolling Stones and Marvin Gaye, to Neil Diamond and the Beatles. And sometimes they went to the cinema. It was all right most of the time, just having fun, until the slow numbers came up on the dance floor, or they were going home, and these were the times she dreaded. That was when John wanted more than just a nice friendly time. He wanted kisses, wanted her to declare far more about what she felt for him than she ever could.

'I'm sorry, John,' she said one night when she had failed to respond to his overtures again. 'It's not you – you're a lovely fella. I s'pose I'm just feeling a bit sore and bereaved at the moment. I'm not really myself.'

John, who was basically a decent bloke, tried to understand and Greta felt she owed it to him to explain about Anatoli, what he had meant to her, especially as she had never had anyone else to call a Dad. About David, the other cause of her heartache, of course she said nothing. And in a way she felt badly about stringing John along. She just hoped she could spend time with him, get used to him, and that in the end it would all come right.

*

But all the time, David was now preparing to leave, full speed, as if he could not get away fast enough.

With Martin Ferris's help, he had secured a place to continue his training at a Jewish hospital in New York, and flights were being booked and dates talked about for his departure. The flight was arranged for the fifteenth of April.

'It's so soon,' Edie said, reeling from all the changes. 'But I know I've got to let him go.'

'I think now he might be best finishing and getting qualified,' Greta heard Martin saying to her. 'He's been through a hell of a time. You never know, it might not be for long in the end. Once he's qualified, who knows? Being over there might help him get things in perspective.'

Greta, heartbrokenly, realized she was one of the 'things' that needed getting into perspective, and she suffered in silence. Even Edie had no idea of her feelings. What made the situation even more poignant for Greta was that Anatoli had left David some money for his future, which had enabled him to finance his journey and his fresh start in America. Anatoli could never have guessed the pain he was causing her by giving David the means to go!

She came to wish that he would go straight away. His presence was an agony to her, while all the time she was trying to behave as if there was nothing wrong. She avoided him as he avoided her, pretending that anything she might have felt was over and done with. She went about with a brisk, cheerful air while her heart was as heavy as lead. And David was very busy making arrangements, having to buy clothes and organize accommodation for his new life.

'Oh, I'm going to miss him so much,' Edie said. 'But I suppose I'll have to let go of him again. The poor boy has had such an awful time – but selfishly, I so much wished he'd settle down and stay here!'

The day of his departure sped closer. Greta was both dreading it and longing for it to be over at the same time. And then one evening she heard a tap at her bedroom door. Somehow knowing it would be him, she went to answer. She opened the door with a closed, cautious expression on her face.

David seemed lost for words for a moment, then managed to say, 'Look – this is really difficult. The thing is, you probably know, I've only got a couple of days left here. I don't want us to part as strangers when I go. Could we ... I wondered ... Might I take you out for a meal?'

Greta was still recovering from the words *you probably know*! Probably know! As if she could think about anything else!

'Well,' she said lightly, 'that's a nice thought, David. I'm not sure why you'd want to do that though.'

She was sure she saw him blush, but he remained in command.

'I've been in a bit of a state and I don't think I behaved very well towards you sometimes. But we ... Well, we go back a long way and we could be friends. Would you like to come – tonight? Or do you have something else to do?'

'No,' she said truthfully. Her heart was beating like a drum. Did she trust herself to go out with David and 'just be friends'? But the idea of going anywhere with him at all was more than she could resist.

'That'd be nice,' she said. 'Thanks, David.'

'D'you like curry?' he asked as they set off. 'There's a place I know on the Alcester Road which is good, I think.'

'I think I do,' Greta said. 'I haven't had a lot of it.'

But she agreed that she would like to give it a try, thinking, this would have been what life with David was like, new experiences, learning things from him, the sort of things she longed for and which Trevor had found so baffling. But it was not to be.

The restaurant was dark inside, and rather scruffy. She wasn't in the mood to take in her surroundings as she was too affected by being with David, but she had the impression of dark walls and little tables, the air full of the scents of spice and a sweet smell which David told her was incense.

'Have you not seen joss sticks?' he asked. 'Sort of tapers – you light them with a match and they burn with a lovely smell?'

No, she had not seen joss sticks. She had had a sheltered life, she thought, shutting herself away while everyone was talking about the 'Swinging Sixties'.

David helped her order from a bafflingly detailed menu, something with chicken, and rice and vegetables. The waiter was a small man who seemed to be doing his best to remain invisible. Between them on the Fablon-covered table were thick tumblers of water, a brass ashtray and a little plastic flower in a brass pot.

'You would like *lassi*?' the waiter asked in a rare moment of obtrusiveness.

'It's a drink made of yoghurt,' David said. How did he know everything? He picked everything up quickly.

They agreed that no, they did not want *lassi*.

And then they were alone, and after the bus ride, the discussion of food, there was nothing else to hide behind.

Greta knew she could not stand a heavy silence falling so she said, 'So – is everything arranged? Have you got somewhere to live?'

She already knew he had, Edie had told her, but it was somewhere to start.

'Yes, the hospital will put me up to begin with,' he said, taking a sip of water. 'They've been ever so helpful. They say Americans are very hospitable and I must say it's been a good example of that so far. It feels as if they can't do enough for me.'

'Oh,' Greta said, 'that's good.' She couldn't think what else to say and felt foolish, but David started talking then, about where he was going and what he had to do to complete his training. He talked and talked as if he was afraid to stop, but it was a relief just to let him. She found herself half listening, the other part of her mind drinking in the sight of his face, the sound of him, allowing herself to pretend they had a future together, that she might sit opposite him and hear this beautiful voice for years to come.

The food came, steaming and aromatic, and there was a pause while spoons were arranged and rice and chicken laid on her plate. She liked the smell which came from it and knew she would enjoy the meal.

'I'd like to go to India,' David said, once the waiter had gone. 'Actually these people are from Pakistan, I think.'

Another thing he just seemed to know.

471

They began eating and she forced herself to say, 'Have you heard from Gila? Do you know how she is?'

David put his fork down, shaking his head. 'Not a word. I haven't contacted her either – she seemed to need to be away from me completely. Whatever happens, if there is ever contact between us, it's going to take a very long time.'

There was a second then, a silence in which a choice was made about whether the conversation could be allowed to run deep, to touch on feelings about past and present, and both of them pulled back from it. Instead they talked about Edie, about good memories they shared of childhood, of films they had seen and about New York. They finished the meal with warm, sweet tea and walked out into the dark evening to the bus stop with an air of being casual friends. Between them, they carried the weight of things unsaid. Words sat in Greta's chest like stones which grew heavier and more unbearable as the evening passed.

They sat on the bus side by side and things felt truly awkward then. They could not think of anything more to say and sat staring ahead of them. Greta was very glad of the other people on the bus and the lurching and squeaking of brakes which kept dragging her mind back from any desperate thoughts. She was acutely conscious of David beside her, of his brown jacket, the upper part of his arm pressing against hers. He was here, now, beside her and soon he would be gone for ever, that was all she could think.

When they got off the bus on Oak Tree Lane she was close to tears, after holding back her feelings all evening.

'Would you like to get the other bus, or walk down?' David asked.

Greta shrugged, not trusting herself to speak. Then she forced out the words, 'We might as well walk. It's not far.'

The silence went on and on as they went down the Bristol Road, as if both of them had lost the will to keep talking brightly and making light conversation. When they were almost home, it had become so unbearable that Greta could stand it no more.

'Why did you invite me out tonight, David?'

The words burst out of her, and David looked round, startled.

'I suppose ... I wanted to make things right. To ... like I said, to make sure we were friends.'

'Well, why would you want to be friends?' Suddenly all her hurt streamed out, raw and angry. 'What's the point in being friends with someone who's not on your level, who you're never going to see in your brand new life and who you obviously don't care about anyway?'

He stopped abruptly, saying furiously, 'What on earth are you talking about? Not on my level? Don't care about? What on earth are you talking about?'

'Well, it's true isn't it? You're a doctor and I work in a factory! And you just ... just ...' To her huge annoyance she started to cry and could only speak in sputtering outbursts. 'You just played with me ... You don't realize, do you? ... Just because I'm not educated like you and I don't know things ... It doesn't mean I don't feel anything. And now you're going away after taking my heart away and I can't bear it because I love you so much ...'

The last came out in a rush and she put her hands over her face and sobbed, all the pent-up feelings finding release.

'Oh God,' she heard David say, and she assumed it was scorn or impatience in his voice, and that lack of sympathy stemmed the flow of her tears. Angrily she wiped her eyes, wondering if she had mascara all down her cheeks just to make things worse. She looked up at him defiantly.

'That's it – I'm stupid aren't I? A silly little factory girl falling for a doctor and thinking she has a chance!'

'For God's sake, will you stop it!' David roared at her so loudly that people turned to look, and he lowered his voice again and took her arm, forcing her to walk. In a moment they reached the Gruschovs' drive and stepped inside. 'What's all this rubbish – factory girl, doctor? It's nothing to do with that!' He seemed on the point of exploding himself. 'Don't you understand that the reason I've got to go away is that I'm afraid of myself? I'm no good to anyone! For God's sake, you're a lovely girl. Don't waste your feelings on me. You're too good for me, Greta, and I mean that. I may be a doctor and everyone thinks that's such a good thing and makes you a noble person, but I'm not good or noble. I'm a mess! I just go about doing damage. I've just got to get away from here to be able to see clearly. And then, who knows?'

Here he seemed to run out of steam. For a moment he took her by the shoulders and looked down at her with such tenderness that tears sprang into her eyes again. David shook his head. Almost as a groan, he said, 'God you're lovely.'

And then he released her and walked determinedly to the front door.

'I'll be gone in a few days. Please – live your life. And . . .' He turned, speaking softly, 'Look after my mother. You are so important to her.'

He held the door open for her, and she passed him, unable to look at him. Going upstairs she checked that Francesca was asleep, looking down tenderly at her. Suddenly she felt very calm, after her storm of released emotion.

'Well, that's that,' she said softly, feeling herself shut down. She knew she could expect nothing from him now.

Chapter Sixty-Five

And David was gone too.

He left for America while Greta was at work. Of course she knew the precise time Edie would go with him to New Street Station to see him off on the first leg of the journey to London, knew the time of the flight. But she said nothing to him the night before, and got up for work the next morning and left without seeing him. She didn't trust herself. All she wanted now was for him to be gone, so that she could begin to try and forget him, even though she was living in a house where photographs of him were proudly displayed on the shelves, the piano. She tried not to look at them.

That day at work she tried to be as cheerful and chatty as she could manage, and on the way out Pat said, 'You're in good form, aren't you? That John seems to be doing you good.'

Greta winked at her. 'Maybe that's what it is!' Quickly she switched the conversation away from herself. 'What about you and Andrew? How's lover boy?'

'Oh, he's all right,' Pat said matter-of-factly.

'You don't sound too swept off your feet!'

'I'm not the sweeping off your feet type,' Pat said, pursing her lips. 'Not any more, anyway.'

Greta stayed in with Edie that night. The arrangements had gone smoothly so far as she knew, Edie said. Greta could see her trying to be brave, despite her tearstained face.

'He'll drop me a line when he gets there, he promised,' she said. 'Things'll soon settle down again and we'll get used to it.'

The next night Greta had promised to go out with John, who was full of excitement because he was about to buy a second-hand car with the help of his Dad.

They went out together to have a coffee and Greta heard an awful lot about the car, but she was content just to let John talk, while she sat and wondered if David had landed yet, whether he had caught his first views of New York. And had he, at any time in the day, thought about her? A lump rose in her throat. This was her life now, she told herself with bitter realism. She would live with Edie and bring up her beloved Francesca, work at Cadbury's and make do with men who bored her silly.

But as she undressed that night after John had walked her home, still enthusing about his blessed car, she sat on her stool in front of the mirror in her bedroom. In the soft light she saw her round, pretty face, blonde hair which she had let loose in waves. The mirror showed her a young woman of almost twenty-five, soft and pretty-looking, but who regarded her with wide, sad eyes. She knew she had loved David, loved him with a passion she had never felt for another man, a love which had opened her and made her raw and vulnerable. In the face of his rejection she had closed up – that was how it felt – unwilling ever to be hurt again.

He's the only one I'm ever going to feel like that

about, she thought. So what am I playing about at with John? What's the point?

The next time she saw John she told him she wanted to call it off.

'I'm sorry,' she said, in the face of his hurt reaction. 'You're a good bloke, John, but I'm just not your type. And I'm still recovering from . . . Well, from someone else. So it's not fair on you.'

John protested, but she was firm about it, and eventually he had to accept her wishes. She went home with a sense of relief, feeling free.

The spring was well advanced now, the days warm. Gradually Edie and Greta fell into a routine, looking after Peter and Francesca between them. People were kind, work was fun and Greta started to join in with things again. Edie went back to work at Cadbury's as well and waited to hear from David. He had arrived, and begun work at the hospital. People had been good to him and he was working very hard and finding Manhattan very stimulating. Of his feelings and personal life, he said nothing. Nor did he write very often. It was as if he needed to cut his ties and strike out alone.

Greta tried to keep on the right side of her mother and took Francesca round to see her almost every weekend. Ruby was pleased to see Francesca in short doses, and showered her with sweets and other treats. She had bought her a Cindy doll with a tiny wasp waist and a selection of outfits to squeeze her slim, rubbery limbs into, and Francesca was delighted and spent hours dressing and undressing her.

As often as not, when Greta went round, she found Ruby's boyfriend, Mac MacPherson, there as well. She never expected much of her Mom's men, but over the weeks, seeing more of Mac, she had come to respect and like him. She found him a solid, kind character, who had lost his first wife in a brutal way when she died of a brain haemorrhage. He was also obviously very fond of Ruby and was good with Francesca.

That afternoon, a sunny, serene one in May, Greta pushed Francesca around in the pushchair. Expecting to find the usual Saturday afternoon scene of Ruby and Mac sitting drowsily in the front room after a good dinner, she was surprised to find the front door open.

'Hello-o!' She had unstrapped Fran from the pushchair and they went up the steps. Francesca was clutching her Cindy doll as usual. 'Mom? You there?'

To her surprise her mother was not sitting drowsing but came through briskly from the back room dressed in a flowery frock. She also seemed to be alone and full of beans, a big smile on her face.

'Come in, bab – that's it, park the pushchair.' She swooped down on Francesca and gave her a big cuddle and kiss. 'Hello, there's my babby! You got your dolly with yer? I've got the kettle on – come on in.'

Greta was taken aback at this welcome. In the kitchen she found a chocolate cake on the table and cups already set out. 'Goodness, is it someone's birthday?' she laughed.

'No, but I am celebrating,' Ruby said, looking as if she was going to burst. She couldn't hold back the news any longer. 'I'm dying to tell you – it's Mac. He's asked me to marry him!'

'Oh!' Greta said warmly. 'That's lovely Mom – I'm pleased for you.' But she couldn't resist teasing. 'You mean you're *really* going to marry this one?'

'Oi – that's enough from you!' But Ruby wasn't really offended.

'You deserve some happiness, Mom – and he's a nice feller.'

'We're getting married in July, so it'll be all go now – lots to arrange!' Ruby was girlish and excited. She talked about her plans as she made tea and cut up the cake, handing a sliver to Fran on a plate.

'I thought she could be my bridesmaid – her and Marleen's little 'uns, keep it fair,' Ruby said. 'I'll get her summat really pretty to wear.'

'You going to stay living here?' Greta asked when she could get a word in edgeways.

'Oh, I expect so – to begin with,' Ruby said, going on grandly, 'But then maybe we'll rent somewhere bigger. Who knows what the future will bring?'

She talked on about Mac and the wedding while they drank their tea, and then changing tack she started on Greta.

'You want to get yourself sorted out, my girl,' she said, ominously. 'Living the way you do – your young life's trickling away. You want to get yourself a man and get married – not be so flaming fussy. You'll end up an old maid else.'

'Mom, how can I be an old maid when I've already been married and divorced?' Greta asked wearily.

'It amounts to the same thing,' Ruby sniffed, cutting another slice of the cake. 'You're still on the shelf when you're on your own, either way. You want to stop hiding behind Edie, and get yourself a man!'

Greta leaned over to wipe Francesca's face to hide

her angry expression. If only her Mom knew how she felt, how much she was struggling to recover from a broken heart and carry on, when she had had a vivid glimpse of how love might be. Go out and get a man, Ruby said, as if it was like shopping for shoes. If only it were that easy!

Chapter Sixty-Six

Pat's face was white as a sheet.

She had been absent from work that day and Greta thought she was ill. But she was waiting for Greta outside the factory after her shift. It was unheard-of for Pat to miss work.

'What's up?' Greta took her arm immediately.

'It's Josie . . .' Pat was beginning to shake, clearly in shock. 'She . . . She . . . Our Mom came to find me this morning, first thing. Josie had a turn in the night and Mom had to call an ambulance. And . . . Oh Gret – she's . . . She's passed on! They say she had a heart attack and she didn't even make it into the hospital!'

'Oh, Pat – no!' Greta was utterly shocked.

'Mom heard her in the night. She wasn't feeling too well, obviously, but being Josie she couldn't explain what was happening to her.' Pat poured out her story as they walked along. 'She was thrashing about and very uncomfy, Mom said, but there was nothing she could really put her finger on. But Mom said it was getting worse and she asked my Dad to call an ambulance. He wouldn't – he said she'd be all right, that Mom was making too much of a fuss over her and it was a waste of the phone bill.' Pat's eyes widened with rage as she related her father's part in the whole sad situation.

'Dad just went back to sleep of course, and Mom

sneaked down and called an ambulance herself. Josie was unconscious by the time they got to the house and she just faded away. Mom could hardly believe it when they told her . . .' Pat shook her head, distraught. 'I've been with Mom all day and the neighbours have been very good, but I just had to come out and tell someone else.'

'Oh you poor love!' Greta had her arm round her friend's shoulders, but she pulled her into a proper embrace and Pat broke down and cried then as the fact of losing her sister began to sink in.

'It was never easy looking after her,' she said, wiping her eyes. 'I even used to wish sometimes that she could be taken away somewhere else to let my Mom have a break. I know it was bad of me. And she was sweet really – gentle, and such a character. And she was my sister . . .'

'Of course she was,' Greta said, with a pang at how little fellow feeling there had always been between her and Marleen.

'I came to ask you,' Pat said. 'Will you come to her funeral? You were always good to her and I'd like you to be there.'

The service was in a little brick church on the edge of Harborne.

'Her Dad's an elder there or whatever they call it,' Greta told Edie.

'Poor man,' Edie said, 'having to do that for his own daughter.'

Greta bit back the sharp comment she was about to make about Pat's father. She almost wished Edie would come with her, as she didn't like the idea of walking into this strange church on her own, but Edie didn't offer. She was exhausted, and had had enough death and sadness for the moment. There was very little news from David either. Greta was relieved about this. It gave her some peace, some time to try and get over him, but Edie worried of course, and Greta knew she was secretly hurt by his going, however generous she tried to be about it. She wrote to him regularly telling him all the news.

Greta walked nervously into the plain little church, which was more like a hall. Inside were rows of chairs facing a table at one end which had a wooden cross on it and a flower arrangement. Otherwise the walls were bare and white. As she came in, Pat turned and smiled encouragingly at her from her place at the front beside her mother. Greta saw a few other people examining her from under their sober hats and was glad to sink down on to a chair in the middle, out of sight. She did catch a glimpse of Andrew, the young man who was sweet on Pat, positioned a couple of rows in front of her.

Well, he's not exactly exciting, Greta thought, but at least he seems steady and kind. Maybe exciting's not everything, she thought, calling David to mind with a pang of bitterness.

At the front of the church there were two chairs facing the congregation, and she saw Mr Floyd seated on one and another man beside him. Both looked self-conscious, with the air of people who felt very important while trying to appear humble. Mr Floyd failed miserably in the humble department, Greta thought. She watched him rubbing his narrow chin as if weighing up the mighty words he was about to utter.

The first hymn took her straight back to Anatoli's

funeral and the thought of David, and she was so busy fighting back her tears that she didn't hear the reading and prayers which came after it. But she paid attention when Mr Floyd took the floor to pay tribute to his daughter. By the time he had finished, Greta was almost choking with rage.

'My daughter, Josephine, was an angel,' he began ponderously. He went on and on about how her life was a blessing, what a gift she had been to their family, what tender memories, in a sober, sanctimonious way which had Greta clenching her fists.

You mealy-mouthed, mean old hypocrite! she wanted to scream at him.

Here was the father who could not accept that his daughter was different, was handicapped, who left all the care of her to his wife while he was out sitting on church committees to make everyone think what a great and worthy man he was. Here was the man who rejected his other daughter when she didn't fit his religious ideals, who had not an ounce of kindness to show to her in her time of trouble! She watched him, finding herself actually trembling with loathing, knowing all that Pat and her Mom had been through at the hands of this cruel, self-righteous man.

Afterwards, a few people went back to the house. Mrs Floyd had wept during the service but she was calm afterwards.

'It's good of you to come,' she said to Greta. 'You were always so good with Josie.'

'I liked her,' Greta said simply. 'She was a nice person.'

Mrs Floyd smiled, tears filling her eyes for a moment. 'Yes, she was. Only not everyone could see that.'

Andrew was at Pat's elbow all the time they were there, and Greta could see that despite Pat's worldly-wise attitude to men, she liked him and was grateful.

Greta tried to avoid Stanley Floyd since she could not think of anything polite to say to him, and it was not difficult when he showed no interest in talking to her. He had always looked down on her, she thought. Just as he looked down on Pat for working in a factory.

She left their house and went out into the lovely summer afternoon. Loath to go straight home on the bus, she walked back down to the Green. The air was full of the smell of blossom and she enjoyed the feel of the sun on her face. For a while she sat down on the seat round the circular Rest House and stared back across the gleaming grass. There were people going in and out of the shops, but she had the green space and the seats to herself.

In those moments she allowed herself to feel. Now that her rage against Stanley Floyd had abated, the beauty of the day brought out her own sadness.

'Oh, David,' she whispered, seeing his handsome, tormented face in her mind. 'Why did you have to give me any hope? I love you, *damn* you . . .' A surge of grief came over her and she sat and wept, hands over her face, not caring if anyone saw her. Here she was, alone again, the one man she had ever really loved far away across the world, having turned his back on her.

She cried until no more tears would come, then got up and walked slowly back towards Selly Oak. All she could do was just go on.

Within a month of Josie's death, Pat announced – though only to Greta: she kept quiet to anyone else –

that her mother had moved out and refused to live with her husband ever again.

'Now Josie's gone, she says she's had more than enough!' Pat said, looking awed and excited at her mother doing what for years had been unthinkable. 'I never ever thought she'd do it!'

'Blimey!' Greta laughed. She found it hard to believe too, of dutiful, respectable Mrs Floyd, but she was delighted. Once again though she bit back any comment about Stanley Floyd. He was still Pat's Dad after all.

'What's she going to do?'

'Well, she's moving in with me to start with,' Pat said, dimpling. 'And she's going to get a job and we'll find somewhere bigger to live. Another flat or something. Oh, Gret – I'm so pleased for her, even though it's awful really, isn't it? I can't imagine what people in the church will say.'

Greta grinned wickedly. 'No – nor can I.'

Chapter Sixty-Seven

New York, June 1969

The water was a calm blue, broken by tiny, foam-edged waves.

David sat on a bench, looking out from Battery Park at the tip of Manhattan, drinking in the sensation of the sun's rays on his face. In the hazy distance two of the harbour's islands rose up in the water, Lady Liberty's verdigris figure holding high her torch. And he could make out the ghostly, skulking buildings of Ellis Island, once the entry point for countless desperate immigrants fresh off the boats, but now closed down and left to rot.

He thought of all the Jews arriving with their meagre bundles of belongings from the shtetls of middle Europe. And how he had arrived, so smoothly in comparison, with money behind him, to find himself a home, just as they had. Here he was, also trying to be an American, clad here in a new pair of denim Levis and casual tie-dye shirt. New world: new life.

For a moment he closed his eyes, breathing in the billowing air which offered whiffs of cigarette smoke, of fried onions from the hot dog vendor a distance along the path, and a whiff of the brackish water. He was living in a city of discovery, its youth swathed in flamboyant ethnic clothing and swinging with novel trends, with political activism, with poets and songsters, artists and drug-burned visionaries . . . And he was still young. Yet why, instead of feeling at one with them, did he feel so in tune with the older people, many living with the residue of traumatic experiences deep within their nervous systems? He knew that it was because of his father and because of Israel. Because of Gila.

He himself felt weary to the core, like an old man.

The medical school had welcomed him warmly and his studies were going well. Another year, he thought, and he would at last be qualified. What was a year of study when he had no other responsibility than to achieve that? Yet it loomed higher than the Rockies, seeming impassable. He had lost his energy. All that New York offered, the excitement, friendships, a carefree life and his medical qualification, simply enervated him.

As he looked up, a couple strolled past with their small daughter in a pushchair. They were eating ice cream, and looked serene and happy. The woman had long black hair and her husband's arm rested loosely round her waist. They looked Jewish, he thought. A couple from Tel Aviv or Jerusalem. A couple just such as he had once made up half of, strolling in the sunshine with their child . . . They glanced at him, still smiling, but not at him. Their smiles passed over him since he was part of the view, then moved on.

I came here too soon, he thought. Seeing the couple was like a punch in the guts. It was all that he tried not to think about or long for. *Shimon . . . Shimon . . .* Martin was right, I should have waited much longer.

He had not heard from Gila, nor contacted her. He could not bear to.

Nor could he bear to feel, to allow himself longing. Numbness was what he welcomed and tried to hold on to.

Looking out over the water he thought of the different seas he had fixed his gaze on – the sapphire Mediterranean, the metallic Irish Sea and now the gentle Hudson River, all in search of peace and direction.

'Tell me,' he whispered to the shifting water, as if he might sit at its knee looking up for guidance. 'Tell me . . .'

Chapter Sixty-Eight

'And so, on behalf of our Holy Mother the Church, I pronounce you man and wife!'

The priest of St Edward's Church beamed at Ruby and Mac as they stood before him. He had had to speak up to be heard over the restless chatter of Marleen's two youngest, George and Sandra. George had broken free of Trevor's grasp and run up and down the aisle in the middle of the marriage service, but the priest was a cheerful Irishman who seemed well disposed towards children.

Ruby and Mac turned to process back down the aisle. Mac looked very spruce in his suit and was boyish with pride, while Ruby was pink-cheeked under her mauve hat, and all smiles, a bouquet of pink rosebuds in her hand.

She looks so happy, Greta thought gladly. Today she felt generous and happy towards her mother. She'd not had it easy, Greta knew. She deserved to be happy.

That morning she had helped Ruby get ready for the wedding.

'I've told Marleen to get her lot ready at home,' she confided in Greta. 'I can't be doing with all that around me on my wedding day.'

So, for one of the few times in her life, Greta found herself helping her mother dress in her finery. ('I'm far too long in the tooth for white and all that.') And just for once there was a friendly, confiding atmosphere between mother and daughter.

'You look nice, Mom,' Greta told her once Ruby was safely wrapped in the mauve satin dress she had chosen. And it did fit her well, snuggling tightly over her ample curves.

Ruby laughed gladly, turning this way and that to see herself in the long mirror.

'Is it all right, bab? Really?'

'It's lovely. You look a million dollars!'

She deliberately said something American, and her sincerity seemed to touch Ruby because she turned, her expression suddenly solemn.

'I loved your Dad – you know that, don't you?'

Greta nodded, her eyes filling. She couldn't speak.

'Wally was the love of my life and there's been no one else to touch him . . . Oh Lord, I've set myself off now, look at me!' She wiped her mascaraed eyes carefully and the two of them laughed. 'But Mac's a lovely man – good to me . . .'

'I know,' Greta said. 'I can see.'

'I do love him, you know – it's not just loneliness, though God knows there was that too.'

She looked appealingly at Greta, seeming to need her approval, and again Greta was touched. Sometimes she felt her Mom was still a child.

'I know, Mom,' she said. 'I'm sure you'll be very happy.'

And now she looked as happy as a bride ever was. To everyone's amazement she had also said that to marry Mac she would become a Roman Catholic, as he had been brought up in staunchly Catholic Glasgow and it mattered to him. Since they were a widow and widower, there was no obstacle in the eyes of the Church to them marrying.

'I might as well,' Ruby said. 'Won't do me no harm, will it? The Catholics aren't killjoys like some, anyway. They'll have a drink with you. And it might do me some good, you never know! I've never had much guidance about anything from anyone.'

Her two bridesmaids were Mary Lou and Francesca. Mary Lou, now eight, thin and narrow-eyed like Marleen, took her responsibilities very seriously and shepherded Francesca around, holding her hand as Ruby and Mac made their vows. Greta watched Francesca, melting with pride. She was wearing a sweet little lilac dress with smocking and flowers embroidered on it, her blonde hair was a haze of curls and she was wide-eyed and serious, solemnly following her big cousin Mary Lou.

'You're a peach!' Greta said, scooping her up afterwards as all the guests showered Ruby and Mac with confetti in the afternoon sunshine. There was a sea of glad faces: Edie with Peter, Janet and Martin with Ruth and Naomi, Marleen, who was already evidently expecting baby number five, was holding Sandra while Trevor tried to keep the boys in check. They were married now too, quietly, in the registry office. Trevor's family, the Biddles, had come along to wish Ruby well, as well as other neighbours and a clan of Cadbury girls, some of whom Ruby had worked with for years. Then there were Mac's sons and their families, his sisters all the way from Glasgow and a gaggle of his friends, all spruced up to the nines.

'Glad you've found someone to keep you out of trouble, Mac!' one of them shouted as the scraps of confetti whirled round them on the breeze and everyone was laughing and cheering.

Mac grinned and punched the air. 'Oh yes – the missus'll keep me in line all right!'

'That remains to be seen!' someone else shouted.

'You going to throw us your bouquet Ruby?' a voice called.

'Oh yes!' Ruby said. 'And I'm not leaving it to chance – I know who this one's for.'

Her eyes met Greta's. Fortunately she had already put Francesca down, as the pink flowers came flying towards her. Instinctively she reached up and caught them, laughing with surprise. The flowers were lovely and matched her pink, sleeveless dress.

'Thanks, Mom – but you'll have a bit of a wait!'

The marriage was to be celebrated with a ceilidh in a nearby hall. Greta had never heard of a ceilidh before.

'It just means a good old dance and jig,' Ruby told her. 'I went to that one with Mac when his nephew got married. It's much nicer than just standing around with a sausage roll in your hand. And the kids'll enjoy it.'

Mac's family had taken charge of the hall and there were streamers across the ceiling and trestle tables along one side laden with food, with small vases of flowers at regular intervals. In the middle, in a larger vase, was one large bouquet.

As they all trickled in, the band was already playing, and Greta found herself longing to dance to the accordion and fiddle. Everyone immediately looked happy and started tapping their feet.

'Oh my goodness . . .' Ruby breathed as she saw the

decorated hall. Greta realized she was almost in tears of surprise and thankfulness. 'It's *lovely*, Mac!'

'Only the best for my wee gal,' Mac said, putting an arm tenderly round her shoulders.

Greta felt a deep pang of longing. Her mother had found something good, she could see. Something real and solid and loving, you couldn't mistake it.

The dancing was irresistible and began almost straight away, with one of the band shouting instructions for the steps of the dance. Greta found the steps easy to learn and everyone, old and young, could join in. There was a bit of a shortage of men there, although quite a few of the Cadbury women were married and had brought their husbands, and there were Mac's strapping sons, but in some cases women were dancing opposite women, children dancing with anyone who came along and everyone having a very good time.

Greta held Francesca's hand to begin with, but the little girl was soon taken into the dance and looked after by whoever was nearest, and she saw Peter and Elvis and George, Mary Lou, Ruth and Naomi being looked after in just the same way.

The dancing made everyone look flushed and happy and Greta found herself with a huge smile on her face as they jigged the evening away to the lively fiddle music, sitting a dance out every so often on the chairs at the edge of the long room to get their breath back. She sat for a time with Francesca on her lap, feeding some pop and a sandwich to her wriggling little girl, who was mad keen to get up for the next dance.

'Just rest for a bit and have a drink,' Greta cautioned her. 'Or you'll be worn out!'

Cuddling Francesca, she enjoyed watching Martin

Ferris, tall and very long-limbed, as he danced the lively Scots and Irish dances, and Janet, who was usually so sedate, joining in and laughing unreservedly at the sight of her husband. Edie was chatting with some of the other Cadbury workers and seemed to be enjoying herself. Greta grinned at the sight of Alf Biddle, pink-nosed and staggering slightly as he made his way along the row apologizing for trampling on people's feet. She sat sipping a glass of lemonade and the dance came to a triumphant, clapping end.

'Very sensible, having a rest!' Martin Ferris came up to the table beside her in search of a drink.

'Oh, I expect I'll dance the next one,' she said, smiling up at him. 'I was just thinking how much Anatoli would have enjoyed this.'

'Yes indeed,' Martin said, soberly. Then he smiled. 'A great man.'

Greta nodded gently. 'No one like him.'

Then a voice behind her said, 'Fancy a dance?'

To her surprise she saw Trevor, a cautious expression on his face.

'Marleen's not up to much this evening, what with the babby and that,' he said.

'Oh, so you're going for second choice are you?' But she didn't say it sharply – was able to tease – and she jumped up. 'Come on then. I'm ready to go!'

They stood opposite each other as the dance lined up and off everyone went. She wondered at how much less gawky Trevor was these days, as if he had grown into himself.

'Your Mom's looking good!' he shouted over the music. Ruby was leading the dance with Mac, and they could hear her laughter from the other end of the room.

'Yeah!' Greta agreed. 'She's all right!'

They were split up then as the partners shook hands and switched round, and she didn't meet up with Trevor until the end. He bowed to her and she said, 'Thanks, Trev.'

'Gret—' He looked at her solemnly in the middle of the crowd. 'I hope you find someone else soon.'

'Oh, I'm all right,' she said lightly. She could see Marleen watching them with Sandra asleep on her lap. 'Go on – go to your wife.'

The evening passed in a very jolly fashion and everyone ate and drank, burning it all off on the dancing. The musicians seemed to be tireless. As the sun went down and the pace picked up they barely stopped and the party became well lubricated and faster and louder.

Greta danced a lot of the dances and sat others out, amazed at Francesca's energy – she still showed no sign of flagging and was full of excitement. Sometimes she made her come and rest a little, and Greta was pleased to spare her burning feet and sit and chat instead, glad that she hadn't worn heels that were any higher. But each time, Fran soon wriggled and wanted to get down.

'Dance, Mom – want to dance!'

'You'll be the death of me!' she said, after what seemed the umpteenth dance. It was getting quite late now and her feet were very sore. The Scottish revellers seemed set to go on all night. 'All right – but this really is the last one – then I'm taking you home.'

Francesca ran off into the crowd of merrymakers and Greta had just straightened up, smiling after her. She saw Edie in front of her in her pretty green frock and was about to go to her and have a word when she saw the expression on Edie's face. She looked shocked, disbelieving, and was staring down at the back of the hall.

'Edie?'

She wasn't listening. No one else seemed to have seen anything and were all drinking and dancing as before. Greta moved closer to her and turned, trying to see what the trouble was.

And she stopped, frozen to the spot.

'David?' Edie said, as if she couldn't believe her own eyes.

Greta caught sight of his face, seeing him with the swimmy strangeness of a dream. He was heading straight towards them, so unerringly that suddenly he was standing right in front of her. All she could think was that he was wearing a dark blue denim jacket, and that she had never seen it before.

He went to Edie and kissed her, keeping a hand on her arm for a moment as if to stay her questions. But his eyes were fixed on Greta.

'I'm sorry,' he said at last. 'I'm so, so sorry.'

She stared back at him, a sense of melting inside her, of warmth and hope being reborn.

'Will you come outside for a minute?'

'David!' Edie called, utterly bewildered. 'What's going on? What's happened?'

But he was already moving away and Greta followed, seeming to float through the crowd, and they went out and round to the patch of grass at the side of the hall. It was dark now and the grass was newly cut and smelt sweet.

David stopped and turned to her.

'I'm a mess and a fool,' he said.

'No—' she went to protest. She understood what he had been through and was humbled by it.

'I didn't trust myself – what I feel for you.' He looked down for a second. 'New York has been a lesson. I can't find someone else to be there. I'm a stranger, I have no one. It doesn't solve anything. Everything I am is here. And you – I've not stopped thinking of you all the time I was there. I've been so stupid . . .'

She stopped him. 'You didn't mean to be.'

He stepped up to her. 'Here's where I belong. With you – if you'll have me. May I have another chance?'

Edie was waiting as they came back in, and the look of astonishment on her face as Greta and David came back into the hall holding hands made both of them laugh.

'Is this your good-looking lad back again?' one of her Cadbury friends asked.

Edie nodded, quite overcome.

'I think I need to sit down,' she said, breathlessly.

'Oh no you don't!' Greta cried. 'You're coming with us!'

She and David each took one of Edie's hands and the two of them whirled her away, laughingly, into the dance.

Chapter Sixty-Nine

Birmingham, 1971

Greta woke from a light new mother's sleep, hearing the snuffling breathing of the tiny baby in the carrycot beside her. Leaning up on her elbow she looked anxiously down at him, her breasts tightening and filling with milk in anticipation of his morning cries. But he was still sleeping peacefully after his night feed.

She lay down again and snuggled up to David's naked body. He didn't like sleeping with anything on, after the long habit of living in a hot country, and she laid her cheek against the strong muscles of his back.

'Hello,' he said softly.

'I thought you were asleep. Did I wake you?'

He turned and they cuddled up together. 'No – I was half there already. I take it his majesty's still sleeping?'

'Like a baby,' she said.

Their little son was only ten days old and she was basking in the happiness of a safe birth and of being home from the hospital, in her own bed with her husband of a year, since their quiet Quaker wedding in Bournville. Her strong body was recovering well from the birth.

They lay under the high ceiling in the big back room

of Edie's house, their permanent home since their marriage, the summer dawn filtering through the pale floral curtains.

It had hardly taken any discussion for them to decide to call him Anatoli after the man who had acted as a father to each of them, and whom both of them had loved. Greta cried after he was born, remembering the last time, when she'd had Francesca far away in a London hospital and he was the person who had stayed faithfully with her and come to see her. She ached for him to be there and see her and David's little son.

There had been no question either that they would live anywhere else than with Edie, in the big family home with its pretty flower garden at the back. And they knew their son would have a loving crowd of adults round him: Ruby and Mac and Janet and Martin, and David even hoped that Annaliese and her new husband Pierre would be able to visit later in the year. Annaliese's letter from Haifa, full of loving greetings to them, was balanced on the mantelpiece downstairs, with the other cards of congratulation.

'I understand why you do not wish to come to Israel, at least for the time being,' Annaliese wrote. 'That this is now such a place of sadness for you. I know you do not hear from Gila, but I do have news of her. She is working very successfully as a dentist in Jerusalem and is doing well in the practice. I gather that she has not remarried but I do not know, of course, what else she has going on in her life. I am told she is well enough though, to continue with life.'

There were cards from the Ferrises, from Pat and her mother and from all the Cadbury crew. There were others from the Queen Elizabeth Hospital, where

David had just completed his training. He had qualified as a doctor shortly before little Anatoli was born.

Pat had come to visit Greta in hospital as soon as she heard that the baby was safely born, and had been quite emotional at the sight of him.

'Sorry, Pat,' Greta said, feeling badly for her. 'It must be hard for you.'

'No,' Pat said, wiping her eyes and smiling sweetly. 'It's just lovely. He's a beautiful babby, Gret. Well done you!'

Greta kept to herself the obvious remark that perhaps Pat could have a baby of her own if she'd get on and marry Andrew, who had asked her several times already. But Pat seemed intent on having the longest engagement in history and was not to be hurried.

'I expect I'll get round to it one day,' she sometimes said. 'I'm all right as I am for now though.'

As Greta and David lay snug in the warm, there was a tap at the door.

'I couldn't keep her away any longer!' Edie said, as Francesca launched herself enthusiastically into the room to kiss her baby brother. She took her role as big sister very seriously. 'Would you two like a cup of tea?'

'Oh yes, please!' Greta said fervently. Breast-feeding certainly gave her a thirst.

Edie returned a little later with a tray, just as little Anatoli was waking.

'Stay and drink it with us won't you?' David said, smiling as he handed the baby, screaming in hungry outrage, to Greta for his feed.

Edie settled on the chair, watching the baby and smiling. Francesca watched, awed by the volume of the screaming.

'He's got a big voice,' she remarked.

'You wait,' Greta told her. 'He'll be bigger than you one day!'

She took the little boy to her breast and the room went quiet again. David laid his hand on her thigh under the bedclothes, as if for comfort, and she looked round at Edie, her hair loose, girlish though she was a grandmother, at her little daughter and her husband, and thought that whatever else life might bring, today, here in this room, she had everything she ever wanted.